Ladykiller

About the author

Tony Phibbs died suddenly in the late summer of 2002, aged 50, shortly after completing this novel. He kept his literary skills largely under wraps, thus it was a revelation to the family when his work came to light. It is undeniable that the thorough research and attention to detail makes this a most readable and accomplished thriller, definitely worthy of recognition.

Ladykiller

Tony Phibbs

BROWN
DOG
BOOKS

Published under licence by Brown Dog Books and

The Self Publishing Partnership

7 Green Park Station, Bath BA1 1JB

www.selfpublishingpartnership.co.uk

ISBN printed book: 978-1-903056-82-0

ISBN e-book: 978-1-903056-83-7

Cover design by Kevin Rylands

Printed and bound by CPI Group (UK) Ltd, Croydon CR0 4YY

Chapter 1

To the untrained eye there was nothing to set him apart from the hundreds of other pedestrians that on a daily basis made their way across the walkway connecting the short term departures car park to the airport. The man was in his mid-twenties, six foot one, medium build, short blond hair, dressed in the smart-casual attire of the affluent young professional, black leather briefcase at his side. Walking through the concourse he glanced at the Tag Huer on his wrist, and, noting that there were still ten minutes to go, joined the other shoppers browsing in the large, open plan newsagent situated on the right-hand side of the cavernous hall, a bureau de change to its right, a fashion boutique to the left. The airport was teeming with people as was normal in the mid-afternoon, which was one of the reasons why he chose this time. There was always the danger of bumping into someone he knew, but he figured he could cover himself without arousing suspicion: "Meeting a business colleague flying up from London on the shuttle. Little bit early so I thought I'd take a look around. The airport changes so quickly these days."

There was an element of truth in the statement for the airport was in a constant state of flux as the marketing men and realities of modern day economics dictated policy, forcing the owners to utilize every available square foot, cramming more and more retail outlets into the limited space available, determined to relieve the traveller of as much of his cash as possible before sending him on his way. Black out the large glass plate windows at the far end of the concourse that provide a panoramic view of the business end of the operation, planes of varying make and size sporting the colours of their carrier tethered to the piers that jut out into the concrete apron, and the first-time visitor would find it difficult to differentiate between the internals of the airport and the small shopping malls that litter the country. The names were the same, the signs were the same, the layouts were the same, the goods for sale were the same; homogenous offerings in a sanitized world.

Browsing through the paperbacks on one of the many shelves that lined the walls he kept one eye on the milling crowd through the open front of the shop but, as expected, he saw nothing to arouse his suspicions. The business man in the dark suit, briefcase held to his side, striding purposefully across the concourse towards the door marked British Airways Executive Club, full of self-importance; the middle class family heading for the winter sun, father already changed into knee-length khaki shorts and designer polo top, mother shepherding her excited brood towards the departures lounge; the fat man in his tracksuit trousers and Nike trainers, washed-out t-shirt advertising a long forgotten Grateful Dead concert, bulging arms displaying an impressive display of artwork, dragging his partner towards the Bricklayers Arms, the holiday mood upon him, determined to start as he meant to continue. He took all this in. He remembered once reading somewhere that you are what you eat. Forget it, pal. You are what you wear.

It would be time to get out soon; nothing lasts forever and sooner or later somebody was going to make a mistake. He had made plenty of cash and so a few more trips and he'd pull the plug. It wouldn't be easy, he couldn't see them taking kindly to his decision. It wasn't like working for the gas board. You couldn't just arrive at the office one day and inform your colleagues that you had decided to take early retirement. He intended to disappear. No announcements, no preparation, no little clues, just fucking vanish. Hare today, gone tomorrow, he thought, smiling to himself, the slight alteration to the punch line to a joke he couldn't quite remember. Some people could tell jokes and some people couldn't, now there was one life's great truths, he thought. Him? No, he couldn't tell a joke, couldn't hold the audience. Probably why he never remembered them. He glanced at the watch, five more minutes.

He didn't know how big they were and that was part of the problem. But not that big. Not big enough to seek him out, exact punishment. No, they'd swear and curse a bit, call him a few names, do a bit of digging around, but after a few weeks it would all blow over. They'd forget about him, find a replacement, get on with their lives, too busy making money to give a monkeys. He saw himself on the Mediterranean coast, Porto Banus area; secluded villa, swimming pool, Jacuzzi, nothing too ostentatious. Maybe a yacht in the harbour, elegant clothes, sophisticated friends, the bohemian lifestyle. Accompanied or alone? The relationship was good but with a wad in your pocket you could take your pick. There were only two ways of gaining entrance to the more exclusive clubs and bars of the southern Mediterranean, and probably every other up-market joint in the world: you were either stinking rich or you were young, nubile of body, with film star good looks and a willingness to come across. The vision flooded his brain. The sun reflecting off the blue waters of the swimming pool, reclining chairs tastefully covered in lemon yellow cushions, palms providing a dappled shade, the bright purple of the bougainvillea against the white wall of the villa, the young body bent over the patio table, him behind, feeling, exploring, awaiting the moment. He quickly shifted the briefcase in his right hand to cover his embarrassment, glancing again at the watch, waiting a minute for the erection to subside.

As the minute hand approached three minutes to four he left the shop, retraced his steps to the entrance to the concourse, took the lift down to the lower level, and made his way down the short corridor that led to international arrivals, past the lost luggage office, airline enquiry desks and bureau de change, and out into the reception hall. He barely noticed the rows of metal tubular framed seats, the overhanging monitors or the newspaper vendor. The gents' toilets were off to the left at the end of a short passageway.

The location was well chosen. Nobody could follow him down the corridor without him being aware of it. Precisely on the stroke of four he pushed through the inner door of the toilets, saw that there was only one other person in the small room. He placed the briefcase on the floor and braced his back against the inner door to temporarily block the entrance for anybody who may have been following. The other man nodded to him in recognition, pulled back the zip on the large blue holdall, extracted an identical briefcase, replaced it with the one he had placed on the floor, zipped up the bag, swung it over his shoulder and headed for the door. The exchange had taken less than ten seconds.

As the courier exited from the toilets the man entered one of the stalls, lowered his trousers, and settled down for the statutory five minutes before leaving himself. Back in the car he tumbled the combination locks on the black leather Antler briefcase and opened it a couple of inches, just sufficient to glimpse the contents. The used twenty pound notes were neatly stacked in bundles of one thousand, an elastic band around each bundle. Seeing the cash always made him feel good. He would count it when he was safely ensconced in his flat. It would all be there of course, it always was. There was no point in anybody trying anything on. After all, it was what the business theorists called the perfect deal; one where both sides made money, and plenty of it.

The woman walked down the street in the dark cold February morning, the Jack Russell bouncing along beside her still tethered by his lead but excited by the prospect of what was to come, conditioned by the daily ritual to a knowledge of freedom soon to be his. She looked at the dog and smiled to herself. There was a time, years ago, when she herself would have been similarly excited by the prospect of an outing, anticipating the possibilities that the as yet unrevealed future might offer. What happened to that girl? Responsibility, she thought, responsibility and life. Her mind drifted back to a time long ago. I wonder what happened to Chuck, where he is now? Dead, probably, she thought glumly. Her life would have been so different with Chuck. She had been a gay young thing then, bit of a reputation round the village, bit too flirty with the boys, he the most handsome man in the world, the debonair pilot, the sophisticated self-confident traveller. In reality he was rear gunner on a B52, a tall, gangly twenty-year-old with a thick mop of unruly dark hair, a crooked grin and a ready supply of cigarettes and chewing gum whose only experience of life prior to arriving in England was the butchers shop in Chicago and ten weeks at training camp in a field five miles outside Cincinnati.

But she had fallen in love, really in love. Sweet seventeen and completely head-over-heels in love. She had lost her virginity that summer, her virginity and her innocence. It would hardly make headline news today but in those days it was different. She remembered the look of horror when, unable to contain herself any longer, desperate to share her secret, she'd confided in her best friend, Maisy.

"And you did it? All the way? My God!" She didn't regret it. She had the memory, which was more than the rest of them had, and that was all that counted when you reached her age. Chuck was transferred back to the states in the autumn of 1945, full of plans for the future, promises of a better life. Three months later the letters stopped coming and she spent the next four months locked in her bedroom, imagining the terrible circumstances that must be preventing him from writing to her, inventing stories in which she arrived at the final hour, breathless but determined, ready to save him from the terrible fate, the two lovers finally united to live in blissful harmony. She slowly emerged from her purdah, youthful exuberance overpowering teenage dramatics, the pull of the Saturday night dance too great to resist.

That was all behind her, of course; the daily grind of old age was now her lot and she accepted it with grace. She'd had her day and she couldn't complain. Not that she was the complaining type.

Two years later she met Arthur at one of the regular Saturday night dances and eighteen months after that they were married. It wasn't the same, would never be the same again. But they had been happy, had brought up the kids as best they could, and the family was more than compensation for the lost passion. They'd lived in the pre-war semi on George Street for over 40 years – she still thought in terms of 'we' even though her husband had been dead for nine years now. The dog had been his idea.

"Give me some company now that I'm retired. Something to get me out of the house." After forty-three years' service with the gas board, retirement for Arthur lasted precisely eighteen months before the coronary stopped him in his tracks. Didn't seem fair really, but best not to dwell on these things. The park was just five minutes walk from the house which was one of the reasons why they chose it. When the children were young it had been ideal: pick up the football (or hula hoop or whatever the latest fad was), walk down the street, across the road and there you were. Now it was just her and Sammy. The kids were still there for her, of course, but Janet, her daughter, and husband Charles and the grandchildren lived in London and Steve had joined the Navy so she didn't see much of them. They had their own lives to leave, she understood that.

The entrance gates to the park were about fifty yards along a drive that branched off from the junction where the town's two main streets met. A towering beech and assorted shrubbery flanked the drive, obscuring the view of the imposing gatehouse from the road. The woman walked straight past the entrance and on down the lane that flanked the southern side of the park, the boundary wall to her right and a modern housing development, lights in some of the windows testament to the early risers preparing for the day ahead, to her left. It was only 6.45 in the morning, still dark, and she knew that the gates to the park would not yet be unlocked. One hundred yards further down the road she turned right into the entrance to the golf club that was formerly a part of the park, strode across the car park, her feet scrunching on the gravel underfoot, and turned left up the small track leading to the first tee. She'd been taking this route for nearly two years now. The dog gave her the idea. One day he had run into the car park chasing some imaginary quarry and, though wary about crossing the threshold protected by the members only sign, after ten fruitless minutes calling after him she had been forced to follow. She knew that the course bounded the park at this point; she had often seen the golfers beyond the fence while walking in the park, their brightly coloured clothes contrasting with the verdant background, trolleys dutifully pulled along behind them. Following the dog's distant barks she had crossed the car park and walked down the small path leading to the first tee. Standing on the tee, the fairway stretching out before her, the early morning frost turning the entire scene a surreal white, she noticed the stile in the fence to her right that marked the boundary between course and park. It was about sixty yards from the tee, presumably built to afford errant golfers the opportunity of retrieving their sliced drives from the out-of-bounds beyond the fence.

The stile presented the alluring opportunity of an illegal stroll in the early morning half light. The first few times, creeping through the car park before hurrying down the path, she had actually felt a certain youthful fission, the excitement of doing something slightly illegal, but now it was just routine. She was sure they knew, the golfers that is. Whenever there was a hoarfrost she left an unmissable trail of footprints leading straight to the stile. But if they were aware of her pre-dawn trespasses they showed no concern.

Safely in the park she released Sammy from his lead. Her choice was either to turn left down the dirt track that led eventually to the hall or backtrack to the right to join the main tarmacadam driveway. In the summer she would have taken the dirt track but at this time of the year the rain turned it into a quagmire in parts so she opted for the cleaner route. It didn't really make any difference, the two ran pretty much parallel to each other, the drive being fifty yards to the right of the dirt track. The walk was the same every morning and she knew from experience that she would be back at the main gates shortly after 8.00. Reaching the main driveway she turned left and started to walk towards the hall, her eyes becoming accustomed to the darkness, able to identify the darker shadows of bushes and trees dotted among the rolling parkland to either side of the driveway. Her friends often told her she was mad, walking in the dark as she did, but it didn't worry her; maybe she had always been a bit mad. Sammy was his usual self, she could hear and sometimes see him as he scurried from one side of the drive to the other, searching out the early morning smells and chasing long gone rabbits.

She was about a mile down the path, the light starting to appear on the horizon, the vast expanse of water to her right, and the birds excitedly announcing the start of a new day, when the dog started playing up. There was a small copse twenty yards to her right, halfway between the path and the Mere, and she could hear the dog barking and growling in among the trees. Continuing on her way she called the dog to her, knowing that as she disappeared into the distance he would eventually give up the chase and search her out. But he ignored her shouts and continued barking. She retraced her steps and walked back towards the copse. In the half-light she could see the dog prancing around, barking, and she could make out the outline of something lying on the ground. At first she was unsure. A dead or wounded sheep, a bundle of clothes? No. It was clearly a man lying on the ground. She could see the back of the head, the dark overcoat and the lower legs and shoes protruding from the bottom of the coat. The lack of movement initially quelled her fear. Her first thoughts had been a tramp, an alcho, and she was frightened at the thought of the reaction the early morning wakening might induce. She moved around, still about six feet from the man, to try to get hold of the dog. As she did so she saw the man's clothing was open at the front, exposing the bare flesh of the stomach and chest. The shock of the wounds was almost too much and she gagged as the vomit rose in her throat, the sweat glistening on her forehead. Without looking again she reached over and grabbed the dog and hurried back to the driveway. Her heart pounding she reached inside the shopping bag she always carried with her and found the mobile phone the kids had given her for Christmas. At the time the present had been a disappointment, she couldn't see that she'd have much use for a mobile phone. Now she punched in 999 and waited for an answer.

Chapter 2

The ringing finally brought Mike to life and, fumbling for the phone on the bedside table, he noted the green luminous figures on the clock radio showing 7.05. Lifting the receiver he was aware of the fuzzy, 'not quite with the world, almost a headache' feeling that a combination of one too many lagers, that damned cigar and the early morning call had induced.

"Hello?"

"DCI Judd?" questioned the voice.

"Yes."

"It's PC Bradley, Sir. Afraid we've found a body."

"What's the SP?"

"Lady out walking her dog in Tatton Park has just phoned us on her mobile. Sounds pretty messy. She was very upset and not making too much sense so until the patrol gets there we don't have much information. But from what she said it sounds like you need to take a look. One dead body, blood and guts everywhere, was the gist of it."

"Have scene-of-crime officers been informed?"

"We're still trying to contact them, it's a bit early in the day for those boys."

Mike's brain was slowly coming to life. He'd been seconded on a couple of violent deaths as a DI but this was his first one as a Chief Inspector. The fact was, despite the impression given by the television such situations were rare. To be landed with one just two weeks after his promotion was a bit of a bugger. Or an opportunity? If I cock this up it could be a very quick end to the fast-track career path, thought Mike as he tried to gather his senses.

"Get hold of the patrol. Tell them to seal the site but not to touch anything. Also, get SOCO down there as quick as you can. I'm on my way." As an afterthought, he added, "Better get the pathologist out as well."

"Will do, Sir."

"And where the hell is Tatton Park?"

Forrest Gump looked expectantly up from the settee, face raised, the doleful brown eyes almost hidden by the thick black fur, mouth open, pink tongue hanging out, ready for the start of another day.

"Forrest, what have I told you about sleeping on the sofa? Get off there," he said in an exasperated voice as he gave the dog a playful whack on the backside. For the thousandth time he wondered what on earth he could have been thinking about. Sure he was down at the time – Suzie had kicked him into touch for the third and final time – and yes he liked dogs and they probably were a lot more reliable than women when it came right down to it, and it was true that the little puppy had been ever so cute. But a Pyrenean Mountain dog, I ask you? Forrest had two missions in life, eating and growing. Mike made his way through to the kitchen – the dog barging against his legs, pushing him out the way – emptied the last half of the tin into Forrest's bowl, shook some of the biscuits on top and filled the water bowl from the tap.

"That should keep you going for a while, partner."

He grabbed a cup of tea and a quick shower, threw on the chinos, casual shirt and fleece jacket, the standard uniform among the plain-clothed brigade, and jumped into his police issue Ford. Forrest sat next to him on the passenger seat, upright, front legs braced, staring out of the windscreen invariably causing a stir among other road users as they realized the 'passenger' was in fact a large black hairy beast. Mike had moved up from Birmingham two weeks ago on the back of a promotion and had temporarily moved into a police flat in Sale. The flat was functional and served his needs for the time being although he'd have to sort out a place with a garden soon.

"We're going to the park," he said by way of explanation to Forrest.

The house in Edgbaston was on the market and he'd decided to wait until he had a firm offer on that before starting to look for somewhere on his new patch. Enquiries at the local gym had put him in touch with a lad that ran a five-a-side team, nothing heavy, a friendly game against like minded souls on a Wednesday night. Last night had been his first outing and all things considered he'd not performed too badly, scored a couple of goals; with any luck they'd invite him back. The so-called quick drink afterwards was responsible for the slightly hung over feeling this morning. That and the cigar. He'd sworn to give up the fags once and for all when he left Birmingham and could just about hack it except when he was in the pub downing a lager. He compensated with a small cigar from behind the bar. Trouble was that one cigar made you feel ten times worse the next morning than the half dozen fags he would normally have smoked. Sorting out a social life was in many ways the hardest part about moving to the new area. The job followed the same routines but finding new friends, particularly now he was a DCI and not just one of the boys anymore, was proving more difficult.

Pushing through the gears he drove down the Washway road, a major artery into Manchester, moving against the main flow of traffic, the two lanes opposite already choked with the beginnings of the morning rush hour as the commuters made their way into town for the start of another day of toil. Leaving Altrincham the drive became easier; the road a dual carriageway now with less traffic to hinder his progress and the urban sprawl on either side replaced by green fields. Crossing over the M56 he was temporarily delayed by the traffic lights at the roundabout before continuing his journey and reaching, four miles further on, the set of traffic lights with the Swan Hotel on the left. Following the instructions he'd received over the phone he turned left at the Swan, the road becoming narrower as it twisted through the Cheshire countryside, the large, individually designed house appearing on his right-hand side as he made his way through the millionaires' retreat known as Mere. Mike looked in awe as mansion after mansion passed by on the right-hand side, catching occasional glimpses of the stretch of water beyond the grand houses that gave the area its name.

Five minutes later he found the drive leading up to the park and turning in he rounded the bend to find two patrol cars and an old Volkswagen Golf parked in front of the large Victorian wrought iron gates. The gates were fully twelve feet across and nearly fifteen feet high, housed within an impressive gatehouse built of sandstone blocks with smaller pedestrian gates on either side.

As he opened the door and stepped out of the car the uniform standing by the gates walked over to him.

"What's happening?" asked Mike.

"Nothing to concern you, Sir. If you could just get back into your car and move on please, Sir." Mike fumbled in his inside pocket and extracted the leather wallet that held his warrant card.

"DCI Judd. What's going on?"

"Srry, Sir. Didn't recognize you. PC O'Neil, Sir. The gates are locked. They aren't opened until 8.00 and we can't find the key holder." Mike glanced at his watch, 7.25.

"So how do we get in?"

"The pedestrian gate on the right-hand side is open, Sir. It's just that we can't get the vehicles in."

"So the side gate isn't locked?"

"It wasn't when I arrived, Sir, so I suppose not."

"How far to the body?"

"It's about three quarters of a mile down the road and then about twenty yards off to the right."

"Who's there now?"

"PC Roberts and PC Walker plus a lady from SOCO. She arrived about 10 minutes ago so she'll just about be there now. We thought I'd better wait up here and deal with any of the public who show up."

"What about the woman who found the body?"

"She's sitting in the patrol car. That's her dog tied to the railing over there. She's badly shaken."

"OK. Keep her here for now. I'm going to walk down and take a look at the crime scene then I'll come back up and have a talk with her. Make sure nobody gets in until I say so. Try to get hold of the bloody keys. And radio the station and tell them to get DC Daniels down here ASAP."

During his induction week at the station Mike had interviewed the five DCs under his command. The opening with DC Jack Daniels was too obvious to miss.

"Your parents certainly had a sense of humour."

"Not really, Sir. I was christened John. In those days I don't think the majority of people in England would have the faintest idea of what a Jack Daniels was. My family calls me John. It was only when I went to college that some bright spark came up with the Jack bit. I guess I'm stuck with the handle now."

Daniels was forty-seven years old, some twelve years older than himself. He had an excellent record and seemed to accept the command of the younger man without any of the rancour and back biting he thought he detected in some of his other DCs.

He retrieved Forrest from the car, attached the lead, and headed for the gate. "Giving the dog some exercise", he muttered to the constable as he passed him, feeling slightly ridiculous, realizing that this wasn't helping his image any, the huge dog straining at the lead pulling him along. Mike suddenly stopped, leaning backwards against Forrest's eager pull.

"Has anybody touched the main gates?"

"Sir?"

"The padlock, the gates. Has anybody touched them?"

"Not as far as I know, Sir, although the other patrol was here before I was so they may have tried to undo them to get in."

"Right, well make sure nobody else does until SOCO have had a good look. The bugger must have got in here somehow."

Once inside the park he set the dog free, watching the huge bulk rampage around, still a frisky puppy at heart. That was a close one, thought Mike. A cardinal sin. Failing to secure a potential source of evidence. Any slipups like that and he'd get bloody crucified at the debrief. Still, now he had the chance to collect his thoughts as he walked down the driveway that dissected the park. First, the weather was on their side. It was a cold crisp February morning with a clear blue sky and no sign of rain. He remembered that from the training courses. With outdoor murders the biggest problem is bloody rain. Everything gets covered in mud, people squelch round and pretty soon the whole scene of crime becomes a quagmire, plus morale drops through the floor after a couple of hours of standing around in the wet and cold. Second, he was dying for a fag. He'd given up two weeks ago apart from the odd cigar in the pub. He'd managed so far but knew he was going to really feel it today. As every nicotine addict knows, you think that bit more clearly and calmly in a crisis after a fag. Third. Well, there wasn't a third at this point.

The light was improving by the minute and Mike spotted the small group off to the right of the path while still some distance away. Red and white tape was secured between convenient tree trunks marking a rough rectangle around a patch of brown earth in the middle of which he could see the bundle of clothing lying on the ground. The two uniformed officers were standing at one corner of the rectangle outside the tape, the woman from SOCO on her hands and knees to the right of the bundle intently examining the ground. He called Forrest to him and put him back on the lead.

Seeing Mike approaching, the uniformed officers stood up rigidly and he guessed that the PC at the gate had radioed ahead that he was on his way. He walked over to the uniforms.

"Who was first on the scene?"

"We were, Sir," replied the one on the right. "The woman phoned in just after 7.00. We were out on patrol. Arrived here about ten past."

"Was the side gate open when you arrived?"

"Yes, Sir That's how we got into the park."

"Hold on to this for a minute, will you?" With a sheepish look he handed one of the constables the lead.

Approaching the tape he called across to the woman examining the ground.

"Alright to enter the crime scene?"

The woman looked up from the ground and gave him a not very welcoming look.

"Depends who the hell you are."

"DCI Judd," replied Mike in a tone of voice that he hoped conveyed an air of authority. She seemed unimpressed.

"Right, enter by that tree over there, walk straight to the body and leave the same way. Oh, and it's pretty gruesome so don't go throwing up all over the evidence. You're going to need more bodies down here pronto. Could do with at least half a dozen scene-of-crime to have a good poke around. It's not like a house; there you have natural boundaries. Here we don't know how far to go to secure the scene. Maybe the whole bloody park."

While the woman was talking Mike had followed the instructions and walked carefully towards the body that was lying with its back to him. Moving round to the front he saw the large reddish-brown stain of dried blood. The front of the victim's body was naked. The coat, suit jacket and shirt had been pulled open and the chest and abdomen hacked to pieces. Christ, what a bloody mess. Mike could feel the vomit rising in his throat. He moved back towards the tree. Throwing up was one thing, throwing up inside a cordoned-off crime scene, as the woman had made clear, quite another. He gagged a couple of times but then felt his head clearing as the nausea receded. It was usually like that. Even the really experienced officers he'd spoken to had told him that in the first few seconds after you have seen the wounds and the flesh torn apart, the nausea always rises. It's a human reaction. After that you're alright.

Recovering his senses he mentally noted the initial impression: male Caucasian; late forties, early fifties; slightly balding; overweight; dressed in a grey suit and dark overcoat. Mike called to the woman who was studiously ignoring his presence, still on all fours intently examining the ground.

"Found anything interesting yet?" he enquired.

"Not sure. Plenty of footprints but so far that's about it," replied the woman.

"How come you're here on your own?"

"They rang me at home this morning. I live locally so I came straight here. Thought I might get a head start before the cavalry arrives and messes up the scene."

Mike chose to ignore the criticism.

Despite what the annual review would no doubt label an 'attitude problem' he figured that at least she'd got herself down here, seemed to have done all the right things in terms of securing the site, and was getting on with the job. He wasn't that much impressed by all the political correctness bit that seemed to be more important than doing the job nowadays but he wasn't so stupid as to not realize that if he was going to get on in his career, and he intended to get on, you had to toe the line when speaking to senior officers. But every so often you came across one like this. Couldn't give a damn and tell it as they see it. Probably decided she'd gone as far as she's going on the career ladder so what the hell. Still, he reckoned he'd try his man management skills to get her on his side. Better to have her working with him than against.

"Look, I'm going back up to the gate. I can't do anything here until the pathologist arrives and I need to talk to the woman who found the body. How about coming along with me? As you said we need to get a full team out down here and I need someone to have a look at the padlock and gate before we open it up."

The woman stood up, walked out of the taped area and pulled the hood back on the white polyester all-in-one suit she wore to keep any loose fibres or hair from contaminating the scene.

"Why not? It beats crawling around on the ground for a living."

Now that she had removed her hood Mike guessed she was in her late thirties with quite an attractive face, medium length dark brown hair and about five foot nine. Her figure was still hidden beneath the all-encompassing suit that gave away nothing of the shape within.

With a last instruction to the two uniforms he retrieved Forrest and they headed back towards the gates.

"Sorry, I don't know who you are."

"WPC Owen, Sir."

"Right."

"Who's this?" she asked, patting the dog.

"Forrest," he said as he bent down to undo the lead. "Forrest Gump." Forrest was off and away.

"Nice dog."

The morning silence was abruptly broken by a loud splash, quickly followed by the squawking of the mallards as they flew low across the water, looking for a safe haven.

"Forrest!" Mike shouted, jogging over to the water. "What do you think you're playing at? Get out of there! Oh Christ, look at you." The dog was happily paddling round in the shallows, tail wagging, the thick coat saturated.

"Come on, out, now," he barked. He remembered just in time and ran for cover as the dog emerged from the lake before shaking itself vigor-ously, sending showers of muddy water in all directions.

"Sorry about that, he's a bit out of control," he apologized to the policewoman.

"He'll dry himself off," she answered grinning, feeling sorry for him as he stood with a forlorn expression on his face, looking at the huge wet mass that was once again bounding round the park, but unable to suppress the laughter.

The estate had seen better days; many of the flats were empty, the windows were boarded up, the walls of the communal hallway were covered in graffiti, the lifts were knackered and the whole place stank of stale piss. The door of the third floor apartment was solid steel, secured by an eight lever mortise and four sliding bolts, with a small opening about six inches square covered by a removable flap at eye level. The door surround was also metal, a quarter inch plate attached to the wall by steel pins driven deep into the brickwork. The only window in the flat looking out onto the exposed walkway that ran the length of the building was covered on the outside by wire mesh through which could be seen the iron grill attached to the inner wall.

The man climbed the stairs, the briefcase in his right hand, his accomplice two steps behind. It was a rough area, not one where strangers would be advised to walk unaccompanied for fear of losing their valuables to a knife-wielding fourteen-year-old with time on his hands and a habit to sustain. One look at the men told you this would not be a good idea. They looked the same, they dressed the same. Both were about five foot eleven, squat but not fat with thick, powerful bodies, the type of build associated with rugby union prop forwards. Both had their hair shaved to a quarter of an inch and the type of face that caused you to look away in the pub, fearful that you might catch their eye, that they might take offence, come over and beat the shit out of you. Both wore black shoes, dark trousers, black crew neck tops and black leather bomber jackets.

The man holding the briefcase knocked on the door, his partner standing with his back to him, feet planted two feet apart, chest out, arms folded, facing the parapet. The flap was removed, a black face looked at him.

"Tell Benjie Tommy's here." The voice was like gravel. It wasn't a request it was an order.

A minute later the bolts were slid back, the mortise unlocked and the door opened. Tommy entered, the door closed and bolted behind him. His partner remained on guard.

"How ya bein, man?" The thick Jamaican accent was difficult to decipher.

Apart from the fact that Benjie was black and Tommy was white, the contrast between the two men was startling. Benjie towered over Tommy, being nearly six foot four, his head topped with a wild mass of dreadlocks, but weighed considerably less, his body thin and lean. He was dressed in a bright multi-coloured shirt and a pair of red cotton trousers, the ensemble set off by green trainers. Tommy wore a single band on his wedding finger, Benjie wore enough gold to stock a small jewellry shop; several earrings hung from each ear, a diamond stud pierced his left nostril, three or four gold chains of different weights and sizes hung around his neck, gold bracelets adorned each wrist and the fingers of both hands were covered in rings.

They shook hands. Benjie attempted the Rastafarian shake, lifting the hand and reversing the grip. Tommy's hand didn't budge a centimetre, he retained a firm grip on Benjie's hand, with his eyes boring deep and his face impassive, unmoved. It was important to let them know: he might be on their turf but nobody messed with Tommy Barnton. He'd seen it happen before. They got greedy, thought they could bypass the middleman, go direct to the source. Better to put the fear in them now, stifle the idea at birth than have to sort it out later. Could he take them now? He wasn't sure. Ten years ago, no trouble. But the iron fist and the baseball bat were no longer the ultimate deterrent. These bastards thought nothing of blowing some poor fucker away with an Uzi over some minor squabble. Get the politicians down here, he'd show them a fucking arms race. Releasing the hand he gave Benjie a half smile. Point made.

"Cool man, no sweat," said Benjie, relieved to be out of Tommy's grip. "Ya got da merchandise?"

Tommy placed the briefcase on the table and flipped it open. Benjie went to work testing a small sample from each packet. Completing the last packet and satisfied with the quality, he laid out a line with the spatula, took the cardboard tube from the breast pocket of his shirt, and snorted deep into each nostril. By way of keeping matters friendly he offered Tommy a line, knowing in advance that he would refuse, as he always did.

"Sixty sousan?" asked Benjie. Tommy nodded.

Benjie disappeared into the back room for two minutes before returning with the money, laying the thousand pound bundles in the briefcase. He didn't bother counting. It was another subtle signal to Benjie: We don't care that much, we'll count it later; it had better be right or you're fucking dead.

"See you in two weeks," said Tommy as he left the flat.

Benjie couldn't work Tommy out. The merchandise was good, there was no questioning that. But who was his source and who else was he supplying in Manchester? And how big was his organization? He acted tough but Benjie had met the type before, being hard didn't count for much when the lead was flying.

Chapter 3

The remainder of the walk was completed in silence, the two of them watching Forrest as he cavorted around the park. Approaching the gate Mike glanced at his watch and noticed that it was just after 8.00. Two motorcycles had joined the uniform at the gate and he could see Daniels' car parked next to his own. Returning through the pedestrian gate he tied the dog to the railings and called over to the uniform.

"Where's Daniels?"

"Interviewing the lady with the dog, Sir."

"What about the pathologist?"

"Due in five to ten minutes."

"Any sign of the keys?"

" No, Sir. The station has just called in. They've managed to find the lady at the council who controls them. She said there's a spare set at the council offices but by the time she's been and fetched them and driven back down here it would take forty minutes. The park keeper, a chap called Tom Groves, normally opens up. He should be here by now."

"Well let's hope he hasn't decided to have a lie in," remarked Mike caustically.

Mike turned to the two motorcycle police. "How well do you know this area?"

The larger of the two answered. "Lived here all my life, Sir. Know it like the back of my hand."

"Good. So how many entrances are there in and out of the park?"

"For cars, Sir, just this one and the Rostherne gate at the other end of the park open to the public. There are another couple of lodge houses but those gates are only opened for special occasions. And then of course there's the farm entrance. The Rostherne gate is about three miles from here. For pedestrians there are any number of ways in. There are probably a dozen gates and stiles, plus it's easy enough to just jump over the wall or push through the hedge."

"Has anybody secured the other gate?"

"Sir?"

"To your knowledge, do we have a police presence at the other gate?" Mike's tone conveyed his agitation.

"Don't know, Sir." The motorcyclist was defensive now. Play it by the book, give him only the minimum.

Jesus, this is what they warned them about in training, thought Mike, don't expect any initiative from your average bobby. What may seem blindingly obvious to you will not happen unless you bloody well issue instructions for it to happen. Another mistake and it was only 8.00 in the morning

"Get up there now, secure the gate and don't let anybody, and I mean anybody, touch it until our crime people have had a look at it." He turned to the other motorcyclist. "Stay here and await further instructions."

As the motorbike roared off Mike noticed an old fawn Metro ambling down the road. The car pulled in at the entrance and the occupant stared quizzically out of the open driver's window. Mike walked over.

"You the park keeper?" Mike enquired.

"Yes, what's going on?" replied the man.

"Afraid we've found a body in your park."

"What sort of body?"

"A murdered body. We're going to have to keep the park closed for a while but we need the keys to open the gates."

"Park's already open." He was a man of few words, used to working on his own, seeing no need for superfluous explanation. If it was conversation that you wanted, well, his wife was the one for that.

"What do you mean it's already open?" Mike was confused, he could see the locked gates behind him.

"I opened the Rostherne gate 10 minutes ago."

"Shit!" The keeper ignored the expletive. Mike glanced across to where Owen was still dusting down the padlock area on the gates. He walked over to the second motorcyclist. "The keeper's already opened the other gate. Get on over there and join your mate, round up anybody that's already in the park and get them out."

Three more cars arrived as the motorbike sped away. The pathologist, a Doctor Seymour, arrived seconds before two more Mondeos containing six scene-of-crime officers. People were milling round everywhere and the scene was beginning to resemble a jamboree.

Doctor Seymour stepped out of his Volvo estate, surveyed the scene in front of him and boomed out in a loud voice, "Who's in charge of this circus?"

Mike called back, "I am, Sir." Bollocks! Why had he called him 'sir'? The man had natural authority and Mike could feel his slipping away at a rate of knots. He'd better sort this shambles out before he totally lost it. He turned to the crowd by the gate.

"OK. You scene-of-crime people stay by your cars, shut up and wait for orders. Owen, we need to get the gates open. How are you getting along with the dusting?"

"Give me the keys and I'll open them. So long as nobody touches the rest of them we're OK," she replied.

Mike turned to the park keeper who was still sitting in the car next to him. "Keys, please."

This was more like it. He felt he was gaining some measure of control. He looked over to where Dr Seymour stood. The man presented an imposing figure. About six foot two, late fifties with neatly trimmed grey hair and beard, dressed in a dark overcoat and suit, he exuded the confidence of one who had dealt with similar situations on many occasions in the past.

"I take it you're the pathologist," said Mike, approaching Seymour. A slight nod. "DCI Judd. I'm in charge." Mike emphasized the 'I'. "We'll have the gates open in two ticks. The body's about three quarters of a mile up the track on the right. WPC Owen here will go with you. She's marked out the crime scene so she'll show you the entrance point."

Turning to the scene-of-crime people he continued, "Four of you follow the pathologist down to the scene. I want a complete sweep of the whole area. Owen's already been down there so take your instructions from her. One of you stay up here and see if you can find anything on the gates or surroundings. One of you drive up to the other gates and do the same up there. Any questions?" Silence.

"Right, get on with it."

As the cars moved off Mike turned his attention to Daniels who was now standing next to the police car with the woman in it. He beckoned him over.

"What have we got?"

"Not a lot. She's a Mrs Jean Miles, widowed. Lives half a mile down the road. Takes the dog out every morning for a walk at 6.30 on the dot." Daniels trotted out the information without any reference to his notes.

"You mean she voluntarily gets up at 6.30 every morning?" interrupted Mike.

"It's old people. My mum's the same. Says you don't need the sleep as you get older. Fact is she also goes to bed at about 10.00 so perhaps they just live in a different time zone. She enters the park via the golf club, takes her usual route. The dog is attracted to something in among the trees, won't let it go. She goes over to see what's wrong, sees the body, and phones us on the mobile. That's about all there is."

"The golf club?" asked Mike. Daniels explained.

"So, both the main gates and the side gates are normally padlocked," surmised Mike.

"That's what she's saying."

"The mobile, that's a bit unusual for a lady of her age, isn't it?" Mike asked, searching for a flaw in the story.

"Kids bought it her for Christmas. Says she never uses it but always carries it round with her. That's it. I don't think there's much more she's going to be able to tell us."

"Got her address?"

"Of course."

"Right, let her go home. Tell her we might want to call round for a further chat. Once you've done that drive up to the main gates and make sure there's some semblance of order up there. I want to take a look at the golf club and then I'll return to the body, see how the pathologist is getting on. Once you've checked the other gate join me down there. Hopefully we'll get some form of ID off the body so we can start checking out who the hell he is and how he ended up here. And check out the keys for the gates: where are they and who has access?"

"Right, Guv."

He liked that. They'd not called him 'guv' before. A mark of respect. 'Sir' just meant they were following etiquette as demanded by the rules. 'Guv' meant a lot more. That was bonding. That was saying 'We're a team and you're in charge'. He walked down the gravel drive, turned right and found the entrance to the golf club. The car park was in front of him, the clubhouse to the right and a small wooden sign to his left signaled the path to the first tee. Taking the path he emerged twenty yards further on at the tee, the lady's footprints leading to the stile still clearly visible on the frosted fairway. Jumping over the stile and into the park he made his way back to the gates.

Forrest was still dripping water and Mike decided he was best left where he was. Returning to the murder scene he thought things looked reasonably well ordered. The pathologist was examining the body, Owen and one of the other officers were on their hands and knees conducting a finger search inside the tape and the other officers were looking around the wider area for any signs of evidence. This was good; he felt he'd regained control of the situation. He stepped out of the car, leant back against the bonnet and waited for Dr Seymour to complete his task.

Five minutes later Dr Seymour rose from his hunched position beside the body, picked up his black bag and walked slowly back towards his car. Mike stepped out to meet him.

"So what can you tell me?"

"Well he's definitely dead. I wouldn't have thought it was suicide, not unless he has Japanese ancestors and an amazing ability to hide a long sharp object shortly after disembowelling himself."

Mike gave the pathologist a look that he hoped said 'Cut out the crap and get on with it'.

"Basically I would say he died between six and ten hours ago – I'll give you a more accurate time after the post mortem. He's been stabbed twenty or thirty times in the stomach. Probably with a long-bladed knife judging by the depth of some of the incisions. Again, I'll be able to tell you more after the PM. Oh. And somebody's carved a cross on his chest."

"A cross?"

"Yes. Quite separate from the frenzied attack in the lower abdomen area there's a cross carved into the chest. Marks about 1 inch deep. Anyway, you can move the body now so I'll head back to the morgue and await the arrival of our Mr X. I take it we don't have a name yet?"

"No, not yet. We'll just finish off the photographs and then I'll get him back to you. By the way, was he killed here?"

"Judging by the amount of blood on the ground I would say almost definitely yes."

Mike walked over to the taped off area. "You people finished with the photographs? I want to search the pockets, see if there's any ID."

"Yea, we're finished. Help yourself."

Mike gingerly put his hand under the man's open suit jacket and pushed towards the inside pocket. The shirt and inner jacket were soaked in congealed blood and he could feel the bile rising in his throat. Bingo. His hand felt the top of the wallet and he gently pulled it out and away from the jacket. Ignoring the blood he quickly looked inside the wallet and saw what he was hoping to see; credit cards, money and a blessed driving licence. He noticed Daniels approaching from the corner of his eye and turned and waved the wallet in his direction.

"Looks like we've hit pay dirt. Stay outside the cordon. No point in messing things up any further than we have to. I'll be out in a minute." He quickly patted down the other pockets and turned up some loose change, a handkerchief and a set of keys. "According to this our man is Keith White of 23 Acacia Drive, Altrincham. Aged 49. And his business card says he's a sales executive for Garnet and Johnson Insurance Brokers. So Keith, the question is, what were you doing here in the middle of the night, how the hell did you get here, and what happened to you? Have we checked the roads around the edge of the park?" Mike asked Daniels.

"Not yet, Guv."

"Right, get onto it. We've found a set of keys including a car key, but no car. I'll have a word with the station and see what they can dig up on the electoral register. See whether I'm going to have to break the news to his missus or not."

Five minutes later the station radioed back to inform Mike that the electoral register showed just one person registered at the address, a Mr Keith White.

Back at the gate there was no sign of Forrest Gump.

"Where's the dog?" he asked the uniform.

"WPC Owen took him. She said she'd be back in ten minutes, gone to dry him off, Sir."

He's obviously a big hit with the ladies, thought Mike as he waited in the car.

Benjie spent the rest of the day cutting the coke. Half the packets he placed to one side, the other half he took to the table. Emptying the contents of the first packet on the table he picked up the little black book where he kept a note of his regular orders and went to work with the scales. A couple of times he was interrupted by his mobile.

"No trouble, my man, can do. Deliver tomorrow?" He made a further note in the book.

He used all of the first package and half the second fulfilling the orders of his more discerning customers. The rest of the coke he split fifty fifty with baking powder and made up into one ounce packages. These were for the street trade, the hookers doing tricks and the kids in the clubs who wouldn't know the difference. Roel answered the occasional knocks on the door, removing the flap, taking the order, collecting the money and fetching the drugs from the back bedroom before returning to the flap. It was quiet today; he didn't encourage passing trade and all his major pushers knew to stay away until tomorrow when he would have the packages ready for them. The work was complete by 7.00 and he went out the back for a shower. He emerged half an hour later dressed in a grey suit, white shirt and floral tie, dreadlocks gone, hair slicked back, most of the jewellry removed. The nearest he'd ever been to Jamaica was the Isle of Dogs but the less people like Tommy Barnton knew about him the better. He packed the remaining five bags in the briefcase, reached his hand through the flap quickly checking in the small vanity mirror he held that the passageway was clear and unbolted the door.

"You don't open that fucking door to no one, you hear, shit head?" Roel nodded, shaking with fear as he closed and bolted the door behind him. He knew what Benjie was capable of and he didn't want any part of it.

The black BMW was a work of art. Suspension lowered, wide alloys, body kit. He drove across town and on into Bury, making a call on the mobile as he approached the town centre. The bulk stuff wasn't as profitable as the small packets but it was quick turnover. They kept to their own turf and it saved him a hell of a lot of graft. They met in a deserted car park behind the row of shops, Benjie handing over the two packages in exchange for fifteen grand. From Bury he made his way to Burnley, then Blackburn and finally Preston. It was just after 11.00 when he turned on to the M61, the evening's work complete, nine big ones to the good, thirty-six grand sitting on the back seat of the beamer.

He was feeling randy; he always did after a profitable day's work. He punched the number into the mobile.

"My place in one hour Tracey, honey."

The house was a large detached in Cheatham Hill. The interior design would not be to everyone's taste being extremely ornate and quite out of character with the house itself. The bedroom was hung with red damask wallpaper, the windows covered by black velvet curtains, a large gilt-framed mirror hung on the wall and a pair of Louis XV chairs were positioned either side of a small half-oval table, the onyx top holding a large gold coloured lamp in the shape of a naked lady, her arms stretched above her head as if holding the pink lamp shade.

Tracey was lying face down, her hands tied to the head rail of the brass bed, rump in the air, knees apart on the black silk sheets, tears streaming down her face. Her blonde hair was spread around her on the pillow, ugly red weals vivid against the lily white skin of her raised cheeks where the leather strap had left its mark. He was kneeling behind her now, the strap around her neck, forcing her head back, one end in each hand, riding her like a horse.

"Tell me who the main man is, Tracey," he asked as he thrust deep inside her.

"You are, Benjie."

"Who's the biggest cock in all of Manchester, Tracey?" he asked, once again pushing into her.

"You are, Benjie," she whimpered, vowing once again that this would be the last time, that even three hundred pounds and all the coke she could snort didn't compensate for the pain.

Chapter 4

He smiled at her, she smiled back. It hadn't always been like that. Six weeks ago the face that looked back at him had been a grotesque parody, something from a cheap vaudeville act. Those first few days he had almost given up, abandoned the whole project, told them to think again, but the weeks of painstaking trial and error had paid off. He remembered his embarrassment during those early days. Walking into the chemist, trying to look casual as he strolled over to the pay desk with his basket of shampoo, toothpaste and eyeliner, convinced that the girl at the checkout would make a connection, understand why he was there, realize that the other goods were no more than camouflage for the real purpose of the visit. The first couple of trips he'd been in a cold sweat as he approached the counter but the bored indifference of the girls behind the pay desk had gradually put his mind at ease. They weren't interested, didn't make any connection. No "Hey, here's a guy buying women's cosmetics, bet he's some sort of weirdo."

He used a variety of shops to buy the items he needed and hid the purchases among a shopping list of other goods. He didn't want anybody remembering if questions were asked later. "Yes, I recognize him. Came in regular, always buying cosmetics." He could have used mail order, but that was traceable. No, always pay by cash, wait until the shop was busy, always three or four other innocent items. Sure, he had enough tooth-paste and shampoo to last half a lifetime but that wasn't important, in the grand scheme of things that wasn't important at all.

In the early days he'd concentrated solely on the cosmetics, if he couldn't get that right then the rest would be pointless. His gut instinct told him that the key lay in the face. Everything else could be fashioned, padded and shaped, but not the face, that was on view. If he couldn't pass the face test then none of this was going to work. He knew he was lucky in some respects being naturally thin, the face androgynous, fair skinned with regular features, the beard light. The teenage girls' magazines with instructional articles under headlines suggesting that the correct application of make-up would secure a dead cert date with the hunk of the sixth form for the Saturday night disco were purchased along with his regular copy of the Guardian. From these he'd discovered what to buy and the basic concepts of how to apply the various powders and pastes. He studied the techniques, experimented with the suggestions and from there on in it was just a case of trial and error. The early results of his work had been awful and, as he surveyed the results of his efforts, he couldn't help wondering how many young teenage girls were sitting in their own bedrooms with blacked-out eyes, smeared red lips and cheeks looking like they'd suffered an altercation with an apprentice plasterer. But slowly he'd learnt. Sitting in the bedroom of the small terraced house he'd toned down the colours, learnt how to gently apply and grade the powders until finally he felt comfortable with the results.

The next requirement had been the wig. This was more difficult. It was a major purchase, required fittings. Somebody was going to remember him. After thinking the problem through he decided he'd go to London for the day and purchase one there. He figured a) If there was any checking later finding anything in London would be like looking for a needle in a haystack and, b) His cover story would be that he was an actor who was playing a woman's part. Whether they believed him or not was unimportant. The capital was full of strange people with bizarre life styles; one more potential transvestite would hardly raise an eyebrow.

In fact, as with everything else he had done so far, purchasing the wig proved remarkably easy and the woman who served him, pedantic in her work, carefully checking the fit, returning from the stockroom with yet another box, had shown not the slightest interest in why a twenty-five year old male should require a mid-length, brown coloured lady's hairpiece. The one hundred and fifty pound price tag was more than he had expected but the result was well worth it. Emboldened by his success, and with time to kill before the journey home, he'd started to put together the rest of his ensemble. The part he knew he'd find most difficult, the one that was going to cause the most embarrassment, was buying the underwear. On the other hand, he reasoned men regularly bought sexy underwear as presents for their wives and girlfriends and the shop assistants were probably used to being confronted by abashed males handing over their baskets containing an assortment of flimsy garments in garish colours. He found a Knickerbox shop in Kensington and casually walked in. Damn! Not another male in the place. He was committed now, wanting to get the ordeal over with and he quickly picked up a few items, making rough guesses as to the appropriate size, before sidling over to the pay desk. The sixteen-year-old girl behind the counter gave him what he thought was a you-dirty-old-bastard look before packing the items into a carrier bag.

"£46.49. How will Sir pay?"

Opening his wallet he found he didn't have enough cash left. In his state of embarrassment he hadn't bothered checking the prices, hadn't realized how expensive women's underwear could be. Momentarily flustered, the colour rising to his cheeks, he extracted the Visa card and handed it to the girl. The shopping trip had exhausted him and after a quick fuel stop at the McDonalds on Kensington High Street he made his way back across London to Euston to await the train home.

Back at the rented terraced house he shaved closely, went through the rigmarole of applying the make-up, and carefully pulled on the wig. The difference was amazing. He had never been in anyway theatrical and certainly not a transvestite, yet as he looked at the reflection in the mirror he was sure that what he was seeing was indeed a woman, a creation quite distinct and separate from his own identity. Over the next couple of weeks he made several sorties to the department stores of central Manchester, purchasing the garments that would complete the disguise. The transformation was complete.

Whenever possible he wore the low-heeled black shoes as he wandered around the house, checking the walk in the half a dozen cheap full-length mirrors that he had purchased and placed at strategic positions. He needed to perfect the walk, the mannerisms.

Finally, he knew he had to test the creation. The calm that he'd felt over the last few weeks disappeared and once again he experienced the rising fear, the sweaty palms and heartbeat pounding in his ears, as he opened the front door of the house, peering up and down the road, searching the darkness. Nobody in sight. Inhaling deeply, filling his lungs with oxygen like a diver about to plummet from the high board, he took one last look at the street and then, leaving behind the sanctuary of the house, closed the door behind him, walked the ten feet to the front gate and out on to the pavement. The carpet in the house had deadened the sound of his footsteps but out on the pavement the loud clack the low-heeled shoes made each time the heel impacted upon the concrete slabs reverberated around the empty street, each step signaling his progress to the prying eyes he felt sure must be watching from behind the net curtains. Bought up in the era of trainers and thick rubber soled shoes, he was acutely self-conscious of the din the leather-soled shoes were creating and all the careful preparation deserted him as he careered down the road. Slow down, slow down, he told himself, forcing himself against all his instincts to lessen the pace. Nobody had appeared at their front door to find out who was making the infernal racket, no curtains were twitching. The car was parked about four hundred yards away on the next street, part of the precautions. He didn't want any nosy neighbours making connections. Rounding the corner at the end of the street he saw two teenage lads ambling down the street towards him but with all escape routes behind him he had no option but to carry on towards them, sure that they would rumble him, that he would be speared by some acidic comment. The lads walked past him, swapping teenage banalities, with barely a sideways glance at the well-dressed lady who passed them. Approaching the car, heart pounding, he reached inside his trouser pocket. Panic. He couldn't find them. He remembered. The keys were in the large casual bag swaying from his left arm.

Once inside the car he started to relax. Fear gave way to exhilaration, a sense of achievement. He sat for five minutes, allowing the adrenalin to subside, before driving to the Tesco on the other side of town. Walking across the car park he was once again aware of the knot in his stomach, could feel the sweat on his forehead as he approached the large glass doors.

The supermarket was quiet; the occasional late night shopper cruising the aisles; the majority of the checkouts closed; the overhead green light turned off for the night; the stackers replenishing the stocks for the next day's trading. Pushing the trolley from shelf to shelf, exposed to the full glow of the harsh phosphorescent lighting, his antennae finely tuned, he looked for a reaction from the few people he encountered. The sideways glance, the barely concealed look of horror in the eyes, but there had been none. Handing over the ten pound note he smiled at the woman on the checkout. She handed him his change, said goodbye. He nodded a reply, not yet ready to risk the voice. That was another hurdle for another day. Five minutes later he was back in the car, the carrier bag containing assorted groceries beside him, mission accomplished.

Parking in the adjoining street he retraced the route to his front door, turned the key in the Yale and was finally home and dry. He kicked off the shoes, removed the wig and sank back into the armchair with a large scotch. Job well done.

Over the next few weeks his outings grew bolder and longer. He didn't think the voice would be too much of a problem but, as with everything else, it was the first step that was the most difficult. The fear of discovery, the shame of being outed. His own voice was fairly neutral in tone, and he was naturally quite softly spoken. By softening it just a touch more and raising the pitch slightly he thought he'd get away with it. Again he used the supermarket as the test, engaging the women on the till in small talk as she scanned the groceries. It worked. The woman showed no signs of being in any way aware of anything out of the ordinary as she joined the conversation.

His confidence increased with each outing. No sweating, no pounding heart. He knew he was good. There wasn't even a hint of suspicion, he'd have known if there was. It was time to begin.

Captain Nicholia Andreus was a regular in the bar, if you could call it a bar – 'dive' would be a better description. Situated on the ground floor of a small hostelry that purported to call itself a hotel, the bar was reached via a grimy passageway off the Rue Castille, one of three roads linking the dockside area to the town centre. It was Nicholia's type of place. The barman sported two days' growth, his collarless shirt in need of a wash. Dog ends and egg shell littered the floor beneath the bar stools, the once cream paintwork was stained orange by nicotine and a bright blue neon sign shone brightly inside the only window, proudly proclaiming that the Ritz was open for business to any unsuspecting strangers that should happen by. But the food was passable, the beer cheap and nobody complained if you made a little too much noise later on when the brandy had taken hold, nobody suggested that it was perhaps time to move on if you slurred your words and tripped over the step on the way to the bar, nobody tut-tutted as you slipped off your chair and under the table.

He remembered the young Arab from his last visit. That in itself told him something. Nicholia knew from experience that he could rarely recall anything after the eighth beer and brandy chaser, the alcohol wiping the memory clean, exorcising the spirits, drowning the ghosts of a wasted life. That was the whole point of the exercise, to wipe the memory clean. You could either choose to remember or you could choose to forget. Nicholia chose to forget.

"Captain Andreus, how nice to see you again. How are you?" asked Rashid walking over and proffering his hand.

"Hello again. Fine, thank you, and yourself?" Nicholia replied, rising from his seat, taking the hand, searching his memory in vain for the young man's name.

"Very well, thank you. Will you take a drink with me?" he asked.

The strict Arab formalities were observed even in a dump such as the Ritz where the lowest members of society hung out and the captain knew that to refuse would be an insult, that the man had offered him friendship and respect, metaphorically invited Nicholia to join his family, share his bread, enjoy his hospitality. Rashid was in his early thirties with handsome Arab features, clean shaven, smooth olive skin, smart tan suit, white shirt, green silk tie and an expensive watch on his wrist. Not at all typical of the regular clientele yet the man seemed at home here, unphased by his surroundings, fitting in easily despite the contrast of his own appearance with the rest of the customers. Rashid returned from the bar, placing the beer and brandy chaser in front of the captain, taking the seat opposite at the small circular table, lightly holding the tall glass of orange. Nicholia was impressed. He had expected a beer, that was sufficient to comply with the code of etiquette; the brandy was above and beyond what was necessary. Nicholia looked at the man's drink. He hoped the orange was laced with something exotic, something that would repay the favour when it was his turn to buy the drinks. A double gin perhaps, a large vodka. For Nicholia may have many faults but failing to hold his corner in a bar was not one of them. They toasted each other across the table.

"Rashid," said the young man by way of introduction, being reasonably sure that, given the state he was in when they had last parted company, the captain would remember little of him. "How long are you staying with us on this visit, Captain?"

"A couple of days, Rashid," replied Nicholia. "We leave on Thursday morning."

It was unusual. Normally the tramp steamer was in port for no more than two or three hours, the occasional overnight stop when they arrived on the evening tide. But the cargo had been delayed, the compensation for the disruption to the schedule agreed with the Northern Star's owners, and Nicholia was looking forward to the luxury of a day of imposed idleness. The conversation continued on into the evening. It struck Nicholia as strange that such a personable young man, and one who appeared, judging from his dress, to normally mix in better company than he was keeping tonight, should chose to spend his evenings sharing a table with an old salt like himself. But as the evening wore on and the drinks continued to flow the incongruity of the situation no longer seemed important and he put the matter from his mind.

The woman arrived as they were finishing their fifth drink and Nicholia was once again telling the attentive Rashid the story of how in his youth, caught in a gale force nine five miles off the coast of Brazil, he was nearly washed overboard, saved only by the fortuitous positioning of a davit. She wasn't young, probably mid-forties, and a little on the plump side but it had been a long time since Nicholia had enjoyed any female company apart from that which he paid for, and that rarely involved any conversation. He couldn't place the nationality. Not pure Arab, of that he was sure. Possibly southern European, maybe mixed race. Rashid made the introductions as Anita joined them at the table. Had he been a little more sober Nicholia might have been suspicious that a wholesome woman, past her prime admittedly but still with plenty to offer, should find such pleasure in the company of an alcoholic old man, the balding pate covered in brown sun spots, long strands of badly cut greasy grey hair meeting at the nape of the neck, round face with veined cheeks dominated by a red bulbous nose, beer gut spilling over the waist band of the stained woollen trousers, the creases in which had long since disappeared, wearing an unironed shirt open at the neck and a blue donkey jacket that doubled as his captain's uniform.

When she put her hand lightly on his arm, her face laughing at the anecdote he had repeated a thousand times in a hundred bars without any such response, he knew that she was his type of woman.

He awoke the next morning in a strange bed with little memory of the previous evening. The room was modern, the plastered walls painted in a tinted green emulsion, the window looking out onto the blue sky, the metal frame indicating the recent construction, the furniture pine, the bed large and comfortable, the dresser top covered with the perfume bottles and other paraphernalia that indicated the presence of a woman. It came back to him just as she opened the door, the short silk dressing gown tied at the waist, a mug of steaming coffee in each hand.

"Thought you might need this, tiger," she said, sitting on the side of the bed and handing him one of the mugs.

"Thank you," he muttered, taking the coffee, unsure as to whether he had or he hadn't, not remembering. Surely he would remember that. He thought back to the time three years ago when he had woken up in the hospital in Naples, two molars knocked out, three broken ribs, his face and body bruised and battered. The barman told him later it had been a brute of a fight, the Yugoslavian deck hand built like an ox, upset when Nicholia had described the inhabitants of the Baltic states as little better than Neanderthals, but he could remember nothing of the incident. It had frightened him at the time. He'd even taken it easy for a while, cut back on the booze. He was unsure how to take the conversation forward.

"Thank you for your hospitality." It sounded wrong even as he said it.

"It should be me who's thanking you," she rejoined, giving him a wink. "I'll leave you to get dressed."

He climbed out of bed, the obese body naked, and retrieved his clothes from the chair in the corner, cringing with embarrassment as he noted the state of the dirty white vest and underpants. Looking out of the window he realized he was in one of the modern tower blocks to the south of the city, could see the upper part of the superstructure of the Olympic Voyager two miles away, her spars white against the blue horizon. The Northern Star was berthed to the right of her as he looked, about one hundred yards further down the quayside. But she wasn't big enough to show above the grey breezeblock wall of the warehouse.

He was mildly surprised to find that this disappointed him, that he still retained affection for the old girl, could still muster enthusiasm for the sight of her.

Later they went for coffee in the old town, taking a table on the pavement, enjoying the spring sunshine. Rashid joined them, dressed more casually than the previous night in a pair of pale green cotton slacks, brown loafers and a primrose yellow Ralph Lauren polo shirt. Nicholia felt miserable, the contrast between Rashid's appearance and his own a clear indication of just how far he had let things go. He looked like an old tramp in his shabby clothes, grey stubble covering his unshaven chin. Anita excused herself, shopping called, and surprised him with a kiss on the cheek as she rose, arranging to meet later for drinks and a bite to eat, leaving the two men to their conversation. Rashid watched her as she sashayed down the street.

"She is a beautiful woman, no?" he asked.

"A very beautiful woman, I don't know what she sees in me," replied Nicholia, feeling sorry for himself.

"She has the hots for you, you're a lucky man."

"She could do a lot better."

Rashid looked him up and down. "She likes a man of the world, a man with some experience of life. But maybe you should smarten yourself up a bit, put on some nice clothes, a decent haircut, eh?" He said this not in an insulting tone but as one man talking to another.

"You're right, but..." Nicholia gestured helplessly. How could he explain to his young friend that he couldn't afford the clothes even if he wanted to, that the company paid him a pittance, that what little he earned went straight down his throat. Rashid was ready for him.

"I understand, the company reward you poorly. They don't appreciate your value. I have travelled this route, my friend. Three years ago I couldn't afford the price of a coffee. Look at me now. I was fortunate, that is all. What do they pay you?" Rashid guessed at a figure. It was more than double his salary. Nicholia shrugged, noncommittal.

"Come with me my friend, let us see what we can do."

Nicholia tried to object, but Rashid would hear none of it, leading him along the pavement and into the labyrinth of passages that crossed the old town, laughing, joking, dismissing Nicholia's protests. Rashid ushered him through the beads that hung from the doorway and into the small shop, little more than a narrow passageway, both sides lined from floor to ceiling with row upon row of hangers holding suits, trousers, jackets, and casual tops in every conceivable colour and size. He did not see the shopkeeper gesturing to Rashid, holding his nose between the finger and thumb, or Rashid glare at the man, making it plain that the impertinence would not be tolerated, that he had better watch his step. The next stop was the barber's shop where the man expertly trimmed the hair, applying the oil to make it shine, the cut-throat razor cold against his skin.

Chapter 5

"OK, Daniels. I'm going over to the house. You get back to the station and commandeer an incident room. Get the SOCO people finished up and tell them to set up a separate database on the system. Once you've done that go over to the insurance brokers and find out what they know. I'll meet you back at the station in a couple of hours," instructed Mike as they prepared to leave the park.

At 7.00 he'd been happily, if subconsciously, anticipating another hour of sleep and now here he was not two hours later on his way to examine the house of a man whose disembowelled body had been discovered in a local park. C'est la vie. He was also starving and desperate for a fag. Reflecting upon the events of the morning Mike reckoned that he had earned a bacon sandwich and a cup of tea, that half an hour one way or the other wasn't going to make much difference to the outcome of the enquiry. He noticed the greasy spoon in a small arcade of shops on the left and pulled in, calling at the adjacent newsagent to purchase a paper, gazing longingly at the cigarettes behind the counter but managing to resist the temptation, before settling down for the much needed sarnie and mug of tea.

The street was about two hundred yards long, the houses at first glance well kept, nondescript, a typical road of suburban semis. He rang the doorbell and, just to be on the safe side, waited. Satisfied that no one was at home he tried the key in the lock. Worked like a dream. The house was a mid-wars three bed semi; small hall with stairs to the right, two rooms to the left, and kitchen to the rear. The first impression was of ordinariness. Everything neat and tidy, nothing unusual: sofa; chairs;

coffee table; TV; video. Just like thousands of other homes, but soulless. One or two cheap ornaments scattered around but no family snapshots, no framed photographs, nothing to indicate any attachment.

Moving methodically through the house he quickly searched each room, looking for any clues as to the identity of the occupant or indication of his lifestyle. He found opened mail in the kitchen addressed to a Mr K White – a gas bill, a bank statement. Upstairs, one bedroom was turned into an office, a computer on the desk, files and books neatly stacked on the adjoining table. He'd get the experts to check out the computer. On one of the shelves he found a stack of photographs in their processing sleeves which he quickly thumbed through, mentally trying to place the locations. Spain, Greece, hard to say. Among the holiday snaps he found the odd family shot, the same people appearing in several sets. Definitely the same people but on different occasions. This lot Christmas, this a barbeque, this a cricket match. A woman, a man, and two children. The ex-wife? The girlfriend? The sister? Mike selected a couple of the photos and moved on.

Coming back downstairs he noticed a briefcase behind the front door. He hadn't seen it before because the opened front door had hidden it from his view. Inside the briefcase he found the usual paraphernalia and a Filofax. Pocketing the Filofax and the photographs he stepped outside and closed the door behind him. One last check before he left. Walking round the side of the house and down the short drive he peered through the window and found, as he expected, that the garage was empty. At least empty in the sense of there being no car in it. Like just about every other garage he'd ever seen it was full of junk, but no car.

Heading back to the station Mike started to piece together what he now thought he knew about the murder victim: Keith White; forty nine years old; insurance salesman. It hadn't been confirmed yet but that was just a matter of time, of that he was sure. Motive? Not robbery. The wallet containing money and credit cards had been found on the body and besides you didn't hack people to pieces in the middle of a park at midnight just to relieve them of their credit cards. No, there was something more sinister about this case. Fact. The car was missing. Fact. The body was found in the middle of a park but no car. Suspicion. Our man has gone out for the night, met a second party, voluntarily walked for some reason to the middle of a park and was then ritually slaughtered. Did he know the person he met? Was he homosexual? We'll find out soon enough, thought Mike. This would look good on the record. The way things were going he could probably wrap it up in a week.

Daniels had already returned from Garnet and Johnson with a make, model and registration number for the company car. They were also able to confirm that Keith had visited a Mrs Johnston at 4.00 yesterday to discuss her business insurance. He left the appointment at 4.35 and as of this moment that was the last time he was seen alive, although he had checked in with the office on his mobile at about 5.15. Keith had worked for the company for five years, was a good employee, conscientious, did his job, but kept himself to himself. Their records showed that Keith was divorced, had been for some time as far as they could tell, had no children, and lived alone. One of the girls in the office was sure that he had a sister who lives with her husband locally, although she didn't know her address.

"We need to find this sister. We've got to have positive ID before we can release any information, plus we need to start building background," said Mike.

"It's got to be him, everything points to it."

"I'm 99% certain you're right, Daniels. But have you seen 'Day of the Jackal'? One cock up like that and I can kiss goodbye to my career. No, I definitely want a positive ID before we go any further. Wait a minute. Does Keith have a company pension? Check it out. If he does then he'll almost certainly have life insurance cover. That means he would have had to name a next of kin on the form."

A quick phone call and they had the name and address. No answer from the sister so she's either out shopping or out at work all day. Not to worry, Mike felt sure he'd have a positive ID by the end of the day. Next stop was the pathologist's office; Seymour had left a message to say he'd completed his preliminary examination. Forget the TV programmes where the detectives stand watching while the pathologist carves up the corpse with the electric saw, Mike had no intention of getting anywhere near the sharp end as far as pathology was concerned.

Dr Seymour's office was reached by a connecting door that led off from the general office and they found the doctor seated in a large leather executive chair in front of an equally imposing desk. Mike and Jack sat on the other side of the desk in what Mike felt were rather tatty, and considerably smaller, plastic leather chairs. He'd studied office psychology as part of his coursework and the symbolism was not lost on him. Perhaps it stopped people asking too many awkward questions.

"So, what can you tell us?" asked Mike.

"Have you an ID for the victim yet?" countered Seymour.

"Yes, 99% sure. We're still waiting final confirmation but we should have that by the end of today."

"Good. The victim was five foot eleven, Fourteen stone five pounds, and I would think between the age of 47 and 52. He died between 11:30 and 12:30 on the night of Wednesday 23 February. Cause of death was multiple stab wounds to the lower abdomen. It's difficult to say which one actually finished him off as there are several deep wounds severing major arteries and causing extensive damage to kidneys and liver. The weapon was a knife with at least an eight-inch blade, three quarters of an inch wide at its widest point, and with one heavily serrated edge. I would guess at a kitchen knife of the type readily available from many high street retail outlets. After death a cross was carved on the victim's chest using a smaller knife with a smooth edged blade, possibly a Stanley knife. The victim last ate at approximately 7.00 last night when he consumed a meal of sausages, mashed potatoes and peas."

Dr Seymour looked to the ceiling in a way that readily conveyed his distaste for such a lack of culture in one's eating habits. Mike guessed that the doctor would be equally unimpressed with his own previous evening's meal of take away Rogan Josh.

"Would the victim have made much noise during the attack?" Mike enquired.

"I should certainly have thought so. Of course, there would have been huge trauma after the first couple of wounds, but nevertheless I would expect the victim to have been screaming at the top of his lungs for the first few seconds."

"Anything else you can tell us?"

"Such as?"

"Any strange marks on the body, any signs of the victim being moved, any signs of sexual activity?"

"There was nothing at all out of the usual on the body. No signs of struggle. There was blood under the fingernails and on the hands but everything I've found so far belongs to the victim. Clutching at his stomach as the knife went in. If the victim had been dragged or moved the marks would show on the clothing rather than the body – your own people will have to check for that. Looking at the scene of crime I stick to my original prognosis that the victim was killed where we found him. There are no signs of recent sexual activity and no signs of any homosexual activity which is, I suspect, what you were really wanting to ask."

"And would that show, if he was, you know, engaging in gay sex? Would you be able to tell?"

"Oh, yes."

"So, you can categorically state that our man has never had gay penetrative sex."

Seymour glared at him. "No, obviously I can't say that. But I can say that it is highly unlikely that he had gay sex within the last six months. If he had it would normally be possible to detect."

Mike wondered why he felt the urge to needle the doctor. Partly because of the man's attitude but also because he'd just given him an answer he didn't want to hear. All his instincts and all his training told him that the crime was tied in to some sort of sexual misadventure.

"How much strength would be required to inflict those wounds?"

"Quite a bit. Again, I think what you're really asking is could a woman have done it. Yes, it's possible. Statistically highly unlikely, but possible. She'd have to be quite strong but then, with all these women working out in the gym and what have you nowadays, who can tell?"

"One final question, Doctor. To the layman's eye the attack looked out of control, frenzied, as if somebody had just gone ape shit and totally lost it. Is that how it was?"

Seymour visibly winced. Mike had known that the crude phraseology would upset him and again wondered why he was deliberately trying to provoke the man.

"Far from your somewhat lurid description of an out-of-control attack, I suspect that the perpetrator was actually very much in control. Firstly, the area of attack is highly concentrated. The murderer isn't lashing out in a frenzy; they're quite deliberately aiming at one point of attack. Secondly, what appear to be the first three or four wounds are very deep and very severe and the murderer appears to have deliberately twisted the knife and pulled out in order to disembowel the victim. Finally, there wasn't a great deal of movement at the crime scene. All the action appears to have taken place within a very confined area. The murderer had control of the situation. I think you're looking for a madman, or madwoman of course, but I don't think you're looking for a lunatic, if you take my meaning."

"Well, thank you for giving us the benefit of your expertise, Doctor. When can you have a written report available?"

"The typed report will be available at 10:30 tomorrow morning."

"Oh, one last thing. When we get hold of the sister I'll need to bring her up here for an ID. Is he in a fit state to view?"

"I shall make sure that he is. As long as she doesn't need to look at his stomach to identify him."

Pompous git, thought Mike, as he left the doctor's office.

Returning to the car Daniels turned on the mobile and collected his text messages.

"Still no sign of the car," said Daniels, reading the first message.

"Right," replied Mike, noncommittally.

"Still no joy with the sister," as the second message appeared.

"Terrific," said Mike, sarcastically.

"The Super wants to see you." The third and final message.

"Damn, better head back to the station," Mike replied, belligerently.

"Any chance of grabbing something to eat? I've managed two cups of tea since 7.00 this morning."

The digital clock on the dashboard was showing 4:10. Mike guiltily remembered the bacon sandwich.

"Do we go past a McDonalds on the way back?"

"We do if I turn right at the traffic lights up ahead, Guv."

"Fine, let's go for it. The Super's not going to be any the wiser and with any luck either the sister or the car will turn up in the next half hour."

But it wasn't proving to be his lucky day.

At 4:50 Mike knocked on Superintendent Anderson's Office.

"Come."

The Super was sitting behind his desk resplendent in an immaculately pressed uniform and starched white shirt, Mike cringing with embarrassment as he became aware of his own scruffy appearance. This wasn't going to help his cause. The Super eyed him over the top of a pair of half-moon reading glasses and indicated for him to sit down.

"Right, this murder enquiry. What have we got and where are we up to?"

Mike filled him in on the details.

"So what do you think we're looking for?"

"Don't really know at the moment, Sir. It doesn't look like your run of the mill murder. More of a ritual killing."

The Super cut in sharply, "I don't want to hear anybody mentioning words like 'ritual killing' in reference to this case. If the press gets hold of that they'll have a field day. As far as the public are concerned we are conducting a murder enquiry with regards to an, as yet, unnamed man who was brutally stabbed to death. Do I make myself clear?"

"Yes, Sir." Mike felt about two feet tall. He battled on.

"We need to find the car. That should tell us where he was last night and then we can start asking questions. I'd like to put it out on the media. Somebody will spot it soon enough."

"We've already briefed the press. For the moment it's strictly unidentified man murdered. We can't release details until we've found the sister and have a positive ID. Make that your priority. Find the sister."

"We are doing, Sir. I'm sure she'll turn up tonight. Probably out at work. We're watching the house. As soon as she turns up I'll know about it."

"And you are intending to go and see her yourself?"

"Yes, Sir. There are questions I need to ask."

"Good. Well for God's sake before you do get yourself a shave and a change of clothes. It's bad enough that we have to inform her of her brother's tragic death without having her think that all policemen spend their working day disguised as tramps. OK, get on with it."

Interview over. He knew the Super had a reputation, now he knew why.

The wine bar was crowded, the usual Thursday night crowd in, and Dan hardly noticed the girl at the end of the bar as he took her order. He added the ice and slice of lemon to the Bacardi and coke before placing it on the counter, taking her money with a cursory nod, his eyes looking beyond her, surveying the scene, checking to see who was in tonight. Only the stunners registered, and you got more than your fair share of those in the

Green Room. It was one of the reasons why he worked there. He quickly moved on to the next customers, flashing a smile at the two girls trying to decide, if push came to shove, whether he'd choose the gorgeous blonde or the equally lovely brunette.

"What can I do for you two lovely ladies tonight?"

She moved to the back of the bar where it was quieter, leaning against a wooden pillar, sipping from the drink, watching the small groups as they formed and reformed, some staying for one drink and then moving on, others evidently there for the night. She saw the flitters, the good looking young girls who moved from crowd to crowd confident in their loveliness, welcomed by everyone: the boys genuine, hopeful, the girls through false smiles, jealous, bitchy. She watched the tryers, the good and not so good looking lads, homing in on the girls-only groups, dropping the line, turning on the charm, sometimes rebuffed, sometimes staying. She must have stood there for half an hour, people watching, calm now, almost forgetting.

"Haven't seen you in here before," he said.

Marginal improvement on 'Do you come here often', she thought, in the split second before the nerves took over. She turned to look at him. A nonentity was about the best she could come up with. He was thirty-two going on fifty-five, one of those men who thought shopping at C&A was a fashion statement, who still went to a back street barber called Fred because 'you can get a damn good hair cut for £3.50 so why pay £15.00 at one these modern places', and whose idea of a good night out was visiting some godforsaken pub in the back end of nowhere that hadn't had a lick of paint in thirty years but served 'real ale' to obese men with hirsute faces. He was wearing a green and brown checked sports jacket, a pair of cheap looking brown slacks, and a drab green polyester shirt worn open at the neck.

"No, I haven't been here before," she said, deciding that maybe he was just what she was looking for.

"I come here quite often, it's local for me," he said.

"That's nice. Where do you live then?" she responded, encouraging the banal conversation, figuring that this was probably as far as he had ever got in his life, that he'd normally been sent on his way with a dismissive comment by now.

"On the other side of town, it's only a ten minute walk. What about you?"

"Didsbury," she blustered, caught out by the question, realizing that this was just what she wanted, to find the loopholes, test the theory.

"You must have driven here then?" he asked.

"That's right," she replied, wondering where the conversation was headed.

"What do you drive?"

"A Mondeo," she answered, not latching on.

"I drive a Porsche," he said, springing the trap. "Not a new one of course. The 944 coupé with the two and a half litre four cylinder overhead cam block. '94 model but in good condition.

"Very nice," she replied, trying to look impressed. "You must have a good job if you can afford to run a Porsche."

"Contract programmer. Cheshire County Council. The rates are pretty good and I don't have a lot of overheads. Not married or anything like that," he said, letting out a stupid little laugh. "The Porsche is quite cheap to run actually. It's a common misconception that they're going to cost you an arm and a leg because they're expensive to buy new but as long as the bodywork's in reasonable condition and she's got a decent service history you can run them quite cheaply."

Over the next hour he explained to her in minute detail the set-up of the Porsche's suspension, the workings of the internal combustion engine, the advantage of Pirelli tyres over Dunlop and the pros and cons of a turbo charger. At least I bummed a couple of drinks out of him, she thought, deciding to call it a night.

"Nice to meet you, afraid I must be going," she interrupted as he launched into a diatribe about the relative merits of the 944 versus the 928.

"Oh, right. Nice to meet you. Perhaps I'll see you in here again some-time?" he asked, as she started to leave.

Not if I see you first sunshine, he thought. Back at the car he kicked off the low heels, donned his trainers, and pulled the wig off. Easy, he thought.

Chapter 6

The phone box was situated on a rough patch of what had once been grass at the entrance to the council estate. He dialled the number and waited. A man answered with a grunted 'Hello?"

"Ten minutes, 01365 743453," he said before ringing off and returning to his car to wait.

Ten minutes later the phone rang.

"Hello?" The man again.

"Wednesday, 3pm, twenty bags. Five thou a bag. OK?"

"OK."

The call was over. He insisted on the security arrangements. He guessed that the police probably knew about his friend, that they were possibly watching him, maybe had a tap on his phone. Hence the precautions. Making stupid mistakes did for most of them and he had no intention of letting that happen to him. The original meetings had been purely social; they were on the same party lists. One night they'd been chatting, early in the morning, long after most of the guests had departed, holding on to the evening, finishing off the last few cans of lager. The idea evolved, as such ideas do in such circumstances, as no more than a mind game, the imaginings of an alcohol befuddled brain to be forgotten about in the morning, one more madcap scheme that would never see the light of day. But his friend hadn't forgotten. At first it had been small time, a kilo of dope once a fortnight. And the pay was good, no doubt about that. He could earn more from one trip than he normally pulled in a month. As things progressed it became more sophisticated and about two years ago it suddenly struck him that this was no back of a fag packet operation, that his friend was far more than just a small time pusher. It was then that he introduced the security. They would never meet again, all communications would be phone box to phone box, the drops and exchanges carefully orchestrated, all but invisible to any prying eyes. His friend had readily agreed; he was making too much money out of this to put it at risk.

At 5.40 the phone went at the flat.

"The sister's just arrived home, Sir. Do you want the officers outside the house to talk to her?" the desk sergeant enquired.

"No, not unless she tries to leave the house. Otherwise, wait for me. I'll be about twenty minutes. And phone the morgue. Tell them we'll be coming down for a viewing at 7.00," replied Mike.

"They won't like that. Sir. They finish at 6.00."

"Tough." After the day he'd had Mike wasn't about to take any crap from a jobsworth.

He'd taken the Super's advice and had even gone so far as to put a tie on. Show a bit of respect. Did bad news come better from a plod in a tie? Who knows? He wasn't about to argue the toss now. This was the worst part of the job, really did your brain in. He was desperate for a cigarette. Just one Marlborough Light, what harm could that do? He reached over to the glove compartment for the half empty packet that he'd hidden in there. It was locked. He'd have to pull over to remove the ignition key to get at the packet. Hold on, take your time, breathe deeply, have an Amplex. You don't need a fag. Crisis over.

He arrived at the house and walked over to the patrol car parked up the street. "Who's in the house?"

"Mother arrived home with two children at 5.30. Dad got in about twenty minutes ago."

"Right. You come with me, you wait in the car."

The WPC stepped out of the car and together they walked up the driveway. The woman answered the door.

"Mrs Bentley? Mrs Joyce Bentley?"

"Yes?" The woman was immediately on edge, the uniform a harbinger of something seriously amiss.

Mike waved his warrant card.

"I'm Detective Chief Inspector Judd. This is WPC Wright. May we come in for a minute? We need to talk to you."

The woman looked terrified as she ushered them into the sitting room of the modern detached house. All eyes turned on them as they entered the room. The husband was sitting in an armchair watching the television, the two children he had seen in the photographs, although older now, sprawled on the settee. Mike judged that the girl was about fourteen and the boy about twelve.

He addressed the husband, "We need to talk to your wife, Sir. It may be better if the children weren't present. Is there somewhere they could go for five minutes?"

The tension was palpable. This never happened on the TV either, thought Mike. You didn't have concerned husbands and frightened kids to deal with.

"Go upstairs and play with the computer until I call you." It came out sounding harsh. Mike could tell it wasn't meant that way; it was the tension getting to him. The kids sloped out the room, doleful eyes watching him, feeling the tension, wondering what this stranger was doing in their midst.

Oh well, thought Mike, straight in at the deep end. It's the only way. The longer you hold back the worse it gets.

"Mrs Bentley, I understand you have a brother by the name of Keith White who lives at 23 Acacia Drive, Altrincham."

"Keith? Yes. Why? What's happened?"

"Do you have a recent picture of Keith?"

"Somewhere, yes. There's been an accident. What's happened to him?" She was crying now, losing control.

He couldn't say anything, not until he knew for sure. "Do you have a picture, please?"

The husband moved over and opened a drawer in the wall cabinet that adorned one wall. Without saying a word he pulled out a batch of photos and began leafing through them. Finding the right one he passed it over to Mike, keeping his eyes on his wife he sat next to her on the sofa. Mike found final confirmation of what he had known for some time now.

"I'm afraid your brother was murdered last night. His body was found in Tatton Park this morning. You may have seen the item on the evening news."

From then on in it was all downhill. The woman was hysterical, shoulders heaving, tears streaming down her face, the husband trying to comfort her. Mike felt guilty as hell, as if he owed the woman an explanation, as if he was in some way responsible. We're the police, we try to solve the mystery, catch the culprit. But explain? How the hell can you ever explain?

The husband made a discreet phone call and five minutes later a next-door neighbour arrived to offer comfort and tea. His wife regained some composure.

"I'm afraid we're going to need somebody to identify the body."

He felt like a right shit but it had to be done. The husband volunteered for the gruesome task.

"You stay here with Cathy, I won't be long."

Mike was actually quite pleased by the arrangement. He wasn't going to get anything out of the sister tonight and the journey would give him the chance to ask Mr Bentley a few questions.

"How well did you know Keith?" asked Mike as the car pulled away from the kerb.

"Pretty well. He popped in quite often for a visit. Always keen to see the kids. And then there were all the special occasions, Christmas, birthdays, that sort of thing. I always got on alright with him."

"What about his private life. Girlfriends?"

"Never really discussed it. I don't recall him mentioning anyone since his divorce."

And that was about the gist of it. He knew him as the brother who visited, but nothing at all about his life outside of the doting uncle role.

They arrived at the morgue at 7.20. If it's shut I'll brain that bastard doctor, thought Mike. He needn't have worried. Dr Seymour was efficiency and politeness itself, helping the man through the difficult situation with solicitude and encouragement. At the end of it all Mike had to admit a grudging respect for the doctor. He also had a positive ID confirmed just 13 hours after finding the body. Keith White was their man. Not bad.

He dropped the husband back at the house at around 8.00 and was immediately on the phone to the station. The Super was raised at home and agreed to Mike's request for a press release for the morning paper seeking help in finding the car. The PR department would take care of it. Whatever next, thought Mike, a police station with a PR department. Welcome to modern policing.

That was enough for one day. He phoned Daniels in the operations room. "We've gone as far as we can today. Tomorrow we start the hard slog. Send the team home. Briefing tomorrow morning, 8.00 sharp."

Which takeaway should I have tonight, he wondered. Life was full of difficult decisions.

The next morning the ops room was bedlam. The lucky ones were seated on chairs, the rest perched on the edge of desks, clutching polystyrene cups of coffee and talking animatedly to each other as Mike walked in.

"Quieten down."

Mike surveyed the room. It was about half the size they needed which accounted for the jumble of bodies in front of him. There simply wasn't enough room for everybody to fit in. A whiteboard hung on the wall adjacent to where he was standing and a flipchart on an easel nearby. All together there were now twenty other people in the room. He knew he could call in as much resource as he needed, this was a murder investigation after all, but at present they simply didn't have the information to know where to start looking.

"Right, first things first. We now have confirmation that our victim is a Mr Keith White." He handed the photograph borrowed from the sister to one of the DCs present. "Get this blown up and copied. Other than that we know very little at the moment. I'm going out to talk to his sister again this morning; she was too upset last night to provide much information. From what we can tell he seems to be a bit of a loner, so that's going to make our job more difficult. I want a house-to-house team up at Acacia Drive to see what we can find out. I want another team to cover the area around the park, see if anybody's seen or heard anything. I want a team to go through his house. There's a computer so take one of the IT people with you. Find out what he did with the computer. Find out if he used the Internet. If so, was he talking to anybody in chat rooms? Was he arranging to meet anybody? The pathologist report is coming this morning but Daniels can give you the bare facts when I'm finished." He nodded towards Daniels.

"Anything from scene-of-crime?"

An older man in the middle of the half dozen officers to the right stood up.

"We've found nothing on the gates. Didn't think we would on that surface. But, unless they had the padlock keys they didn't open the gates anyway. My guess is they walked through the pedestrian entrance. By the body we've found a good few footprints. Most of them could be anybody out walking in the park, that's quite a busy area. The most interesting one we've found is close to the body and has blood underneath the print. That means it was made after the blood was spilt. We haven't finished the analysis yet but I'd say from experience it's a woman's low-heeled shoe, quite big, probably about size eight."

There was an intake of breath as those in the room looked at each other in mild astonishment. They'd all either seen or heard about the injuries and had presumed the perpetrator was going to be a man.

Mike looked up. "Anything else?"

"Nothing further at the scene. We're still looking around the edge of the park but without knowing where to look or what we're looking for it's proving difficult."

"OK. We need to find the murder weapon. Start with that. We're looking for a long-bladed knife with a serrated edge."

"It's going to take us weeks to comb that park, there are acres of undergrowth. It could be anywhere."

"Start from the body and work outwards. Get some metal detectors," barked Mike. "Any joy from your end, Daniels?"

"Not much, Sir. We checked out the keys for the park gates. There are three sets. The council keeps one at the offices in Macclesfield, the park manager keeps a set in his office in the hall and the park keeper has the third set. All three sets are where they should be. But somebody opened the pedestrian gate. The park keeper is absolutely certain the padlock was there on Wednesday night when he locked up. The problem is they have quite a few functions in the park – corporate entertainment, that sort of thing – and the park keeper quite often loans the contractors the keys when they're setting up if they're expecting late deliveries. I'm getting them to draw up a list of all the companies who've used the park over the last two years but I can't see it helping much. It isn't a formal arrangement so there's no record of who had possession of the keys. The lady who found the body checks out. I don't think there's any doubt that she is exactly who she says she is. That's all we have for the moment."

An hour later, Mike was back at the sister's house. She was calmer now but the eyes were red and puffy. He could tell she'd taken it badly.

"I need to know about your brother. Where he went. Who he met. I know it's difficult but we have to build up a picture."

"I don't know what I can tell you. He was a very private sort of person. Came round here once a fortnight or so to visit and see the kids. He didn't talk much about his private life."

"Do you know if he had a girlfriend?"

"He never mentioned anybody. Didn't seem that interested."

"There's something I've got to ask. It's not easy." Mike inwardly cringed as he faced the woman on the sofa. "Do you know if he had any homosexual tendencies?"

The woman gave him a defiant stare.

"No. Definitely not. I think after the divorce he gave up on that side of life. It had all become too painful for him. I think he just sort of decided it wasn't worth the effort."

"When did he get divorced?"

"Eight years ago."

"Do you know where his ex-wife is now? I'll need to speak to her."

"No. I think she moved to London. Remarried. I've no idea where or even what her married name is now."

"Don't worry. We'll find her. Didn't he ever mention any other socializing? Playing sport, going to the pub, that sort of thing?"

"He mentioned the George a few times. That's the pub on the high street near his house. You might try in there. I think he used to play squash with some of the people where he worked. But other than that I really don't know."

"That's OK. You've been most helpful."

Next port of call was Garnet and Johnson. Daniels had already spoken to them but he wanted to get the feel of this man. At the moment he wasn't getting anything, certainly nothing that would lead to a hideous death in the middle of a park on a cold winter's evening. No more joy than Daniels. He'd worked there for five years, was a good employee, but socially nobody knew much about him. He'd been a regular squash player at first but had stopped playing about two years ago. No particular reason. Nobody had seen him socially out of work since then other than at the firm's Christmas dinner.

Maybe he'd fare better at the George. The pub was a typical town pub, brick frontage set among the small row of shops that constituted the high street. Yes, the landlord knew him. Came in regular on a Saturday night. Didn't seem to belong to any particular crowd. Just stood at the bar, had a few pints, and then went home. Never caused any trouble, occasionally in conversation with other loners at the bar but he'd never seen him leave with anybody.

Mike was beginning to get an uneasy feeling about the case. Johnny No Life turns up ritually murdered on a cold winter's night in the middle of a park. No apparent motive, no friends, nothing.

Five more leg presses and that would do it. She could feel the muscles in the thigh starting to quiver, pushed to the limit, fighting the weights attached to the pulleys on either side, the gym a torture chamber of high-tech machinery, stretching the sinews, forcing the body to the limits. She undid the foot straps and climbed out of the chair, taking a minute for the legs to recover, rubbing herself down with the fluffy white towel, taking a large gulp from the isotonic drink, preparing herself for the next ordeal. She could hear Jake ushering the other members from the gym, wishing them goodnight – See you next week, keep up the good work, Mrs Morgan – turning on the charm, keeping the customers happy. And God knows he needs to keep them happy, thought Sheila, aware of how much the young Australian was in debt, how much it had cost him to set the venture up. He was losing money hand over fist. She'd already lent him £10,000. If Dennis found out it would take a bit of explaining. But nothing much seemed to worry Jake. He sailed through it all with a big grin on his face as if he didn't have a care in the world. "Something will turn up" said in his broad Australian accent, was his answer to everything.

She looked at herself in the mirrored wall of the gym. Not bad, she thought, not bad at all. Eight months ago she'd been a flabby thirty-four year old with the effects of childbirth, a sedentary life style and an unhealthy diet leaving her body sagging in all the wrong places and her feeling depressed, unhappy with herself, unwilling to accept that youth could be over so quickly. For the first time in as long as she could remember she felt unattractive and unwanted. From the first awareness of herself she had known she was pretty, the long blonde locks flowing over an angelic face. The teenage years brought true beauty as the body developed in all the right places and the boys came flocking, boosting her confidence, dispelling any nagging doubts, final confirmation of what she had always known. And she loved it, flaunted it recklessly. Not promiscuous, she was never that. Not like some of the plainer girls. Plenty of flirting, the quick snog at a party, the hands going just so far, but she was smart enough to know they'd always come back for more, that the attraction of what they had never had was far greater than the attraction of that they'd already sampled. Some of them called her a tease but it didn't worry her; they still came back for more. She married nine years ago and, for a while, everything was wonderful. She was in love. He was a handsome man with a good job and could afford to buy her the things she craved: the cottage in Thames Ditton; the Peugeot convertible; meals at the best restaurants; the holidays in the Bahamas.

Then the kids had arrived dictating a change in lifestyle and a change in her priorities. For the first few years she had given them everything, staying at home to look after them while her husband toured the country, his job demanding more and more of him, their time together confined to snatched hours at the weekend, exhaustion damping the ardour. None of this bothered her, she was as happy as she'd ever been. But then came the rumours, the pitying looks from women she hardly knew at parties, his eyes straying just a little too obviously at dinner parties. And he hardly showed any interest nowadays, she couldn't remember the last time they'd made love. That's what prompted her to join the gym. She'd taken a good look at herself in the mirror and it wasn't a pretty sight. No wonder he didn't fancy her anymore; she needed to make an effort.

The purple leotard stretched tight over the athletic torso, the thighs lithe and firm, the muscles of the shoulders well-defined, the blonde hair, big and bouffant, tumbling down either side of the Barbie doll face.

She turned around, forcing the knees back, stretching the ham strings, tensing the buttocks, giving them a slap to confirm the firmness. Not bad, not bad at all. She walked over to the chest press, convincing herself that this was purely coincidence, next on the list, the next stage in the work out. Sitting in the chair she raised her hands to shoulder height and placed her palms behind the leather pads, the back of the seat pushing her chest out, and her breasts forward and unprotected. Forcing the pads away she brought them together in front of her face, fighting the weights, feeling the pectorals working. Relaxing a little, her hands still behind the pads, she let the machine pull them back to the resting position and counted to five, pulling in deep breaths, pushing the oxygen deep into her lungs. Anticipation flowed through her body. She knew it was coming but the thrill of not knowing quite when was what excited her.

She completed the sixth press, the sweat now rolling from her face and shoulders, gathering in her cleavage. The hands came from behind her, one clutching each breast, a firm grip, holding them as if they were separate entities, not part of her.

"My Sheila's got great tits," he whispered in her right ear, his one and only joke.

Big dumb Aussie, she thought, although her mind was already straying to other things as he continued to fondle her breasts through the thin material of the leotard. She could feel his breath upon her ear, his head behind her, the tongue gently licking the lobe, the hands expertly massaging her breasts, the nipples hard against the leotard, her not attempting to move, the hands still on the pads, the back of the seat bending the spine, forcing her body out to meet him.

"I'm going to make you come, baby," he whispered. She groaned, the sexual senses awakened, the beautiful tingling feeling in her groin. He continued to fondle her, squeezing the hardened nipples between thumb and forefinger, pushing slowly against the breasts with the palms of his hands. The feeling grew stronger in her groin, a feeling she never wanted to end.

"I'm going to make you come and come and come, honey." The breath hot, the words exciting her even more. She knew he was right.

He reached up and gently pulled her left wrist down, pulling the thin strap of the leotard off her shoulder and over the wrist before replacing the hand on the pad. Repeating the manoeuvre with her right arm he freed the straps and slowly pulled down the front of the leotard, exposing her breasts. His hands went back to work on the naked flesh, more vigorously now, kneading the nipples with his knuckles, sending her wild with the feel of it.

He knew he had to be good tonight; the equipment suppliers were getting heavy, threatening to repossess the machines, unwilling to wait any longer. He'd wheedled five grand out of that stupid Carter bitch but he needed more. He reached behind him and selected two pieces of ice from the polyester cup. He rubbed them slowly round the nipples, inscribing small circles before gently dragging them over the hard tips.

"I'm going to make you come like you never came before, honey", he whispered in her ear.

No man had ever done this to her before; she'd never had an orgasm just from her breasts. She was a tart, a scrubber, sitting there letting him do this to her. But he could do it every time. She felt the heat rising, her body writhing in the chair as the cold ice tweaked the nipple. He watched, seeing the face change, the flush on the upper chest, and the wet patch on the leotard between her legs. He was pinching the nipples firmly now, almost hurting her, willing her on.

"Come on honey, come for Jake. Let me see you come."

The sensation flooded through her, an explosion that reached every nerve end, sent stars shooting through her brain, her body coming out of the chair, supported only by the shoulders, reaching up to him. He continued for a minute, watching the storm raging through her and then, judging the moment, moved round to the front, reaching round her, pulling her to him, her arms round his neck, the body still shaking, her holding on as if her life depended on it.

"Oh my beautiful Sheila," he said, soothing her, stroking her hair, letting the storm subside.

"You fancy doing a line?" he asked, the coke laid out neatly on the polished counter top. When he'd first suggested steroids she'd refused point blank. She had done a bit of grass in her youth but that was as far as she went. It's up to you, he had told her, but the shape you're in it will take three years of hard work to get any definition back. With the steroids you can cut that to three months. She'd been reticent at first, imagining bulging muscles on an overdeveloped body, like the bodybuilders she'd seen on TV. But after two months of sweat and tears and with very little to show for it she'd allowed herself to be persuaded, convinced that taken in moderation the drugs would do no more than firm up the flabby muscles, redefine the shape. Next stop was the uppers. Give you a bit of a lift and besides it is nothing more than your kids will be doing in ten years. The coke had been a small, final step. And the rush was fantastic, made her want him more and more.

She was lying on the inclined board where they did the pull ups, holding on to the foot strap to stop herself from slipping down, legs spread wide, watching his firm young body in the mirror, the taut butt, the definition of the thigh muscles, like a Greek god kneeling in front of her, his tongue working her to a frenzy once again. The coke was still buzzing in her head, the combination of the drug and his tongue bringing her once more to a peak. He timed the moment carefully, surreptitiously dropping the last few dregs of the white powder on to his tongue and then working it round her love bud. Jesus, she thought she was going to explode; never in her entire life had she experienced anything like it. The intensity of it frightened her.

Later, sitting on the stools at the counter, they were chatting.

"I'm in deep shit, honey. If I don't find ten grand by next week they'll close me down. And it's all cash flow. I'll be able to pay you back in a month or so, soon as the subs start rolling in."

"I don't know, Jake, it's difficult for me to lay my hands on that much cash."

"See what you can do, honey, otherwise I'll have to sell up and head on back to Aus."

Later they'd made love again at Jake's flat. Quieter, more conventional.

Chapter 7

Dennis Watson, Master of the Universe, top dog. Thirty-eight years old, Sales Director for Interactive Systems, loving husband and doting father and life couldn't be better. As he closed the front door of the four bedroomed detached on the small exclusive estate just outside Esher and hit the remote alarm for the BMW 5 series, he knew he wouldn't be seeing home again until Friday evening. Went with the territory. The job took him all over the country and that was part of the attraction, although of course that wasn't the impression he conveyed to the family. The fat salary cheque and even larger commission bonuses that were posted to his account at the end of each month helped to quell the occasional moan about the time he spent away from home. He had always known he was good, better than all the rest, as the song goes, but the move to Interactive five years ago had been a stroke of genius. At the time he was working as a salesman with Hewlett Packard, earning a more than reasonable salary and picking up some pretty tasty stock options, but he always kept in touch with a couple of the recruitment boys he knew from his early years. You could never tell what was round the corner in this game and it paid to keep your finger on the pulse. Luke had mentioned the job to him one day over lunch at the wine bar.

"They're into network systems and that market's growing like crazy. Started off with two of them last year, now there are about a dozen of them and they're taking on new people all the time. Trouble is, they're all techies. What they're looking for is somebody to take on the sales and marketing function. Of course, it's going to be very much hands on at first, bound to be with a small company like that, but I reckon whoever gets their feet under the table, as long as they don't make a complete botch of it, could be in for a very nice little earner."

He decided it was worth an evening of his time to at least meet with Craig and Silvia, the joint founders and major shareholders, and hear what they had to say. As he discovered later they were also sleeping partners, but not in the business sense. The picture they painted really fired him up. Apart from anything else at HP he was a small cog in a very large machine, a very well paid cog but nevertheless a cog. At Interactive he would be in among the decision makers with a chance to really make a difference and they were prepared to offer a handsome package to bring him on board. Convincing his wife had not been easy; it was a risky move, and she was not one of nature's gamblers. The rest, as they say, is history. The company floated on the AIM last year, the alternative market for small cap companies, and apart from the monthly cheques he was currently holding stock options worth nearly two million at yesterday's close. Not bad for a lad from a council flat in the East End of London.

The traffic on the M25 was bumper to bumper as he crawled past Heathrow but he finally made the M40 and headed out towards Oxford. The meeting in Preston would take most of the day and then it was back down to Birmingham on Wednesday, two meetings in Manchester on Thursday and finally Glasgow and Aberdeen on Friday before heading back to London on Friday night. Meeting the sales targets was surprisingly easy; being in the right market at the right time was the secret. When, two years ago, Craig and Silvia had announced at the board meeting their intention to concentrate the company's resources on web-enabling technology he hadn't been totally convinced. Sure, the press was starting to pick up on the Internet but he still thought it was basically a toy for the college kids and the propeller heads. Where was the commercial interest? He spent his days talking to directors and senior managers and no one was asking him about web servers and e-commerce. How wrong can you be? Within six months nobody wanted to talk about anything else. They were riding the crest of a wave, companies practically begging for their services, not enough resource to go round.

The meeting in Birmingham had been straightforward. Anne, one of his better sales people, had completed all the spadework and he was just there to cross the T's and dot the I's. There was always a bit of last minute negotiating on contract terms and price; directors flexing their corporate muscles, showing the managing director what they were made of. The deal was signed, sealed and delivered by 4.15 and he headed on up the M6 feeling particularly pleased with himself. He called Craig on the mobile to pass the time and give him the good news as he cruised up the motorway. Following a brief discussion on the contract requirements, Craig already knew the most of it and he was just updating him on the last minute changes, they lapsed into some banal football banter. Dennis actually had no interest whatsoever in football but Craig was originally from the North East, a fanatical Newcastle fan, and most of his social conversation revolved around the latest news from the Premiership so Dennis made a point of at least keeping a weather eye on the football news, and particularly that referring to the 'Hammers' and the 'Magpies', so that he could join in the chat. A few more calls and he soon found himself pulling off the M6 and heading down the Chester road towards Manchester. Four miles on he hit the M56 roundabout and travelled for ten minutes towards the airport before dropping down off Junction 5 and pulling into the car park of the Four Seasons. He'd found the place many years ago and, although it was thirty minutes from the centre of town, used it whenever he stayed in Manchester. Apart from being a very good hotel with an excellent restaurant the main attraction was the lively Irish bar that was appended to, and formed part of, the establishment. The place was always buzzing and could usually guarantee a few girls out on the town even on a dreary Wednesday evening in February.

His secretary had pre-booked the room and as he approached reception the attractive blonde behind the counter smiled in recognition.

"Nice to see you again, Mr Watson."

He was sure she was there for the taking with a little work and she certainly presented a most alluring possibility. But it would complicate matters. He used the hotel on a regular basis and could do without the agro of dealing with the aftermath of a night of passion. It was one of his rules, keep it simple. Ships that pass in the night, strangers that you had never seen before and would never see again. He wasn't interested in an affair, too complicated. Love them and leave them, that was his motto. He certainly didn't need the hassle of dealing with a heartbroken young receptionist. And heartbroken she would be when she discovered that he wasn't available, of that he was sure. No, very tempting, but best not to get involved.

After completing the formalities Dennis retired to his room to look over the files for tomorrow's meeting. At 8.30, showered and changed, he entered the restaurant anticipating a first class dinner and looking forward to a night on the town. An hour later he was leaning against one of the balustrades that formed part of the interior decor of the Irish bar, bottle of Sol in hand, surveying the scene, wearing a grey Armani suit with a black cotton crew neck top, a look he'd picked up from the sleeve of an Eric Clapton album. The bar was basically a large square room along one wall of which hung a phalanx of large video screens showing a combination of sporting action and cartoon features. The central bar was about twelve foot square and had a pretty bog standard theme pub decor – something old, something new, Irish pastiche. He'd been told it was a favourite haunt of the many United and City footballers that lived in the area but he wouldn't recognize most of them if they were standing right in front of him.

The place started to fill up towards 10.00 and by the time Dennis went to the bar for his third bottle he had to wait behind a group of four lads for his turn at the bar. The girl was sitting on the far side of the bar, face turned sideways to him, previously hidden from his view by the bar's central pillar. He could only see the top half as the bar concealed the rest. Late twenties, medium length brown hair, reasonable pair on her. Nothing to write home about, but he wasn't looking for Miss World.

He left the queue and sauntered round to the other side of the bar, empty bottle still in hand, leaning against the railings, keeping an eye out for two or three minutes, assessing the situation. Maybe the boyfriend's gone for a leak. The bar was busy enough for him to not appear conspicuous as he awaited his moment standing a couple of feet behind her, and as one of the bar staff approached he stepped forward, leaning across in front of her and thrust the empty bottle towards the bar with his left hand, the large Rolex prominent on his wrist.

"Another of these, please mate".

As he said it the bottom of the bottle caught the top of the cocktail glass on the bar and sent it spilling over into the central bar area.

"Oh, I'm sorry, was that your drink?" he asked, his face a picture of earnest apology.

"It doesn't matter, I was finished anyway," she replied.

The barman was both clearing up the mess behind the bar and waving away his offers to pay for the damage. He knew Dennis well, if not by name, and had seen him pull this stunt several times before. He also knew there'd be a fiver in it for him.

"I insist. I'm Dennis by the way."

He proffered his hand.

"Hello, Dennis. I'm Jane."

Half an hour later and they were chatting away like old mates. Dennis reckoned there were only two difficult moments in the one-night stand game; breaking the ice and suggesting bed. The first had been straightforward and from the signals he was picking up he couldn't see there was going to be much problem with the second. The bar staff were already calling for people's glasses.

"Let's move on," she suddenly suggested.

Dennis was taken aback. He glanced at his watch. 11:25.

"Move on where?" he asked.

"I'm sure we'll find somewhere."

The way she said it and the way she looked at him suggested to Dennis that there might be a bit more to this lady than he had thought.

"But, I can't drive now. I'm way over the limit."

"No problem. I'll drive."

"You sure?"

She gave him a backwards look as she walked towards the exit and Dennis quickly followed her out of the door and across the large car park to the dark blue Ford Mondeo parked at the far end.

Heading out towards Wilmslow she turned into a small lane after about half a mile, him completely lost as they sped through the Cheshire countryside, wondering where the hell they were heading, thinking that maybe the woman had a screw loose, that agreeing to her proposal had not been such a good idea. Eventually she pulled in to the open gate of a field entrance, driving in over the pastureland and behind the hedge so as to conceal the car from any passing motorist. Dennis decided that maybe the night wasn't going to be wasted after all.

"You northerners certainly have some quaint customs. It's years since I had a bonk in the back of a car!"

"We're not going to bonk in the back of a car."

He tried to give her his what-the-hell's-going-on look.

Climbing from the car she reached for the shopping basket from the back seat and stooped down to look at Dennis still sitting in the passenger seat. Her hand reached into the basket and pulled out the end of a woollen blanket for him to see.

"Come on," she said, giving him a smile. "Come and see what you've been missing."

It was totally unexpected. He barely caught sight of the glint of the blade in the half light as she withdrew the knife from the basket and thrust it deep into his abdomen, twisting and pulling before thrusting it once more, forcing it all the way to the hilt. He screamed as he had never screamed before, his hands clutching at the entrails hanging from the wound, the lifeblood already flowing from him, unable to respond to the murderous assault, the trauma too much for his system to take.

Benjie reckoned it was worth a few hours of his time. The way he figured it Tommy wouldn't want to hold on to a stash that big for any longer than was strictly necessary, he'd be looking at ten to fifteen if caught in possession, which meant he was probably making the collection on the Friday and distributing the same day. Parking the BMW he retrieved the three year old Escort from the lockup, one of four cars he kept on the go at any one time, bought through the small ads and changed on a regular basis, a necessary tool of his trade. He followed the Jaguar from the house in Wilmslow to the club in Manchester, Tommy's front, the legitimate part of the business, and waited until the early afternoon, completing the crossword, reading the paper from cover to cover. If he hadn't been so bored he probably would have missed him. To while away the time he invented a game; the traffic was sparse on the back street but for every passing car he had to remember ten facts and hold them as long as possible. Otherwise he wouldn't have paid much attention to the car that turned out of a side street further up the road. One, BMW 3 series; two, metallic silver; three, registration BRG 263 S; four, alloy wheels (was that cheating, he thought, do alloys count as a fact?); five, driver wearing – shit, driver is Tommy Barnton. Bugger must have left by the rear door, he thought, pulling the same stunts I do. He watched the BM turn right at the end of the road and, as it disappeared from view, quickly swung the Escort around and set off in pursuit.

When the BM turned into the car park Benjie decided he was too close to follow him in; one look in the rear view mirror and Tommy would suss him. He pulled into the arrivals drop zone adjacent to the multi-storey and leant on the car, catching a glimpse of the BM through the gaps in the concrete as it spiralled up the car park ramp. So you got somebody flying in with the goods, thought Benjie, watching the car climb higher and higher. The car stopped at what Benjie judged to be the seventh floor. So what the hell do I do now, he thought. He sidled over to the large automatic glass doors that gave entrance to the airport's interior and was standing on the pavement, pondering his next move, when the lift doors five feet on the other side of the doors opened and out stepped Tommy. Benjie swung round, facing his back to the doors, and quickly walked a few paces to the left, getting out of sight. He knew Tommy probably wouldn't recognize him unless he had a good look at the face – he'd only ever seen him in the Rastafarian outfit with the dreadlocks and all the gold – but he didn't fancy the consequences if he did make the connection.

He risked a peek round the edge of the doors and saw Tommy's back as he ambled across the large hall, blue bag slung over his shoulder. Benjie followed him in and headed to the left, keeping an eye on Tommy who was now standing in the middle of the hall, just one of many people here to greet friends and relations as they returned from their trips abroad. Benjie sauntered over to the coffee shop, ordered a coffee and sat at one of the tables. The fact was that a six foot four black man was conspicuous even in a place like this, and standing he felt like a beacon, calling Tommy's eyes to him.

Tommy hung around for ten minutes and Benjie was convinced he had the drill. Seemed a bit risky though, flying in that amount of coke, he thought, they must have devised a brilliant means of concealing it. Suddenly Tommy was on the move heading for the gents' toilets over to the left of the hall. My sphincter would be quivering a bit if I was picking up five kilos of coke, thought Benjie with a smile. Five minutes later Tommy reappeared and walked straight across the hall to the automatic ticket machine, paid the fee and made his way over to the lifts. What the hell, thought Benjie, waiting until the lift doors shut before walking back out to retrieve his car. He threw the £20 fixed penalty ticket onto the passenger seat and picked up the BM again as it exited the car park, following it back through Manchester to the club. It was 4.15, Benjie was due a call at 5.00.

He must have collected the gear somewhere, thought Benjie as he made his way over to the flat. You don't drive all that way just to go for a crap. He forced his mind back, going through the sequence of events. The man entering the toilets, that had to be it. He couldn't recall any of the details but he definitely remembered a man entering the toilets just before Tommy reappeared.

Chapter 8

It was now six days since the murder and things were decidedly flat. The car turned up on the Friday morning; one of the wardens who patrolled the car parks dishing out fines to errant motorists made the connection as she was writing out a second fixed-price penalty ticket for the silver Vauxhall Cavalier -yesterday's ticket was still under the windscreen. If the car was still there tomorrow she'd call the pound and have it towed in. She walked off and was busily checking the pay and display tickets two rows down when she suddenly remembered the item on the radio about the missing car. Something to do with that awful business over in Tatton. She often went to the park on Sundays with her kids. It was a bit of a trek from her home in Timperley but worth the effort; best park for miles around. She walked back across the car park, over the footbridge that crossed the railway, and into the town centre. Looking down the long pedestrian precinct she spotted Jim, one of the local bobbies, walking slowly towards her. She hurried to meet him.

"What are you doing here, Brenda? You won't find many parking offenders in a pedestrian precinct!"

Jim was always good for a laugh and they usually had a bit of banter when they met. Not like some of the beat bobbies who seemed to think they were a cut above.

"Shut up, you daft bugger. Look, you know that car they're looking for, the one in the murder? I think it's over in the car park behind the station."

"Jesus. Right, let's go take a look-see. Better make sure before we make right fools of ourselves."

Ten minutes later the area surrounding the car was cordoned off, at least as well as it could be given the close proximity of cars to either side, and the scene-of-crime people were giving it the once over. Jim and Brenda stood to one side, heads held high, revelling in their roles as heroes of the hour. Mike arrived and after a brief chat with the two of them quickly ascertained, as he'd suspected, that there was nothing they could add by way of detail. No wonderful little titbit. No "Oh yes, I remember seeing a man get out of it on Wednesday evening accompanied by a woman wearing a gold lame evening dress". That was too much to hope for but you had to cover every possibility, the training had taught him that. The number of cases where some vital piece of evidence had been missed because somebody had failed to ask the stupid question, had failed to follow up the mundane.

The car yielded next to nothing, the only extra pointer it gave them was the location. Keith had driven two and a half miles from his house and parked his car in the large car park at the rear of the station. Considering how little they'd managed to discover about Keith's private life the options were almost limitless. He might have parked the car, walked over the footbridge as the traffic warden had done and gone for a drink in one of Altrincham's many pubs. Mike was certain he could rule out the restaurants; the pathologist had identified his last meal and they'd found the wrapping paper and potato peelings for the sausages and mash in the kitchen bin of Keith's house. Or, he could have walked into the station and caught a train. Altrincham was the western terminus for the Manchester Metro in addition to its role as a railway station. On the one hand he could have walked into the station, bought a ticket at one of the automatic ticket machines and caught the Metro into Manchester or alighted at any one of the dozen stops along the way to Manchester. Alternatively, he could have bought a train ticket and gone the other way towards Chester. The fourth stop on this journey was Knutsford, the station less than a mile from the entrance to the park where they'd found his body. There again he could have bought a train ticket and headed off towards Stockport. Just to add to the possibilities, directly adjacent to the train station was the main bus station with the newly privatised buses shooting off at all times of the day and night to God only knows which destination. Oh, and just to finally finish things off at the far side of the bus station, less than one hundred yards from where Keith left his car, was a taxi rank. Of course if he was keeping a liaison with person or persons unknown he may just have stepped into another car in the car park and driven off into the night.

He found Daniels in the train station organizing the troops.

"What do you think?" Mike asked, more in desperation than in hope.

"It's a nightmare, from here there are about half a dozen different options he could have taken. We didn't find any tickets on the body, did we?"

"No."

"If he took the Metro he didn't even have to see or speak to anybody to buy the ticket, they are issued by the automatic dispenser. Quite frankly, he couldn't have picked a worse spot to leave his car if he'd been deliberately trying to make our job as difficult as possible. I'll put a team down here and start asking some questions. About six, if that's alright with you?"

Mike nodded. "Check out the Knutsford angle. Maybe he took the train over to Knutsford, met somebody there, walked into the park and met his untimely end. Check the pubs. See if anybody knows him."

"I'll start one team round here and send another over to Knutsford. We'll start pushing his picture in people's faces, see if we can stir any memories."

That had been four days ago. And what had they turned up? Diddly squat. The house-to-house had revealed nothing whatsoever; some of the neighbours knew him to say hello to, nothing more. Pleasant enough but not one to stand around and pass the time of day. The search of the inside of the house was equally unrewarding. The computer threw no further light on the character of the man, he seemed to use it mainly to enter details of his customer contacts, normal business notes, nothing out of the ordinary. Yes, he had an Internet connection and the history file showed that he spent most of his time looking at classic car sites. He'd also recently been looking at motels on the west coast of America. Planning a holiday perhaps? But nothing salacious, nothing to suggest a secret life, some dark corner that he kept separate from his mundane day-to-day existence. His finances were also white as white. Monthly pay straight into his account, normal outgoings.

The good burghers of Altrincham were unable to shed any further light on the life and times of Keith White. Same story in Knutsford. They'd talked to the British Rail staff, the bus drivers, the cab drivers, the publicans, the pub staff, the pub customers, people shopping, people waiting for trains, people on trains, people waiting for buses, people on buses, taxi drivers and just about anybody else they could think of. Not one of them had shown the slightest trace of recognition as they looked at the photo of Keith White.

No further luck at the park either. Apart from the one footprint they hadn't turned up a single shred of evidence. Never mind a murder weapon, right now Mike would settle for a single hair or fibre thread out of place.

He was due to brief the Super at 4.00 and he was dreading it. He genuinely didn't have a clue what else he could do. What a great message that was sending out. Mr Dynamic, Mr Proactive, I don't think so. Three weeks in the job, one unsolved murder and no idea what to do next. Bloody wonderful.

The Northern Star attracted little attention from the dockside as she chugged past the breakwater, smoke bellowing from the single funnel, paintwork peeling and blistered, the combination of Mediterranean sun, salt water and five years without a paint job leaving her looking old and tired as she slowly made her way into the dock. And that was exactly what she was, old and tired, coming to the end of her useful life, barely worth keeping afloat. The tramp steamer had spent the last fifteen years plying her trade in the Med, sedately making her way from her home port of Piraeus, where the small shipping company that owned her was based, along the northern Mediterranean coast calling at Palermo, Naples, Calgary, Marseilles, Barcelona, Valencia and Gibraltar before turning for home hugging the African coast with stops at Oran, Algiers and Tunis. The schedule was flexible as it depended on the cargo. If the price was right the ship diverted, the radio message from head office stressing the urgency, Captain Andreus smiling, knowing that even with a rocket up her backside the old girl would not be hurried, the engines incapable of pushing her beyond the twelve knots which was her standard cruising speed.

The ship berthed at the far end of the dock, the stevedores would unload the four crates in the morning and they would be underway again by 11.00. The captain no longer had a girl in every port; like the Northern Star he was coming to the latter stages of his working life, would probably retire with the ship in a couple of years' time, no longer plagued by the urges of his youth. That's what had caused the problem. The Masters ticket had been his gateway to the world; a couple of years as junior officer and he would have his own ship, the culmination of a dream, the ambition realized.

He remembered the evening well, it was not something he was likely to forget. The silver service laid out in the dining room, he in his immaculate white uniform, buttons polished, body young and lean, a Greek Adonis. His guests that night were the Texan oil millionaire and his wife and daughter, the Austrian professor and his wife, a German author and her chaperon, a retired British colonel and his wife and two elderly ladies from Switzerland. The Americans were seated to his right on the round table, the daughter next to him, the Germans beyond them, the Swiss opposite him and the British next to them with the Austrians to his left. Hosting the table was an element of the job he didn't particularly enjoy but it was part of the cruise ship experience, expected by those paying the inflated prices for first class cabins, and he turned on the charm, able to converse in passable English and German which covered most of the requirements for that particular gathering.

The Texan was living up to the stereotype, a loud and boorish man who was happy to proclaim his ignorance to the world in a loud Texan drawl, the rest of the table too polite to interrupt his ramblings.

He was in the middle of espousing some ridiculous theory about the origins of the pyramids when Nicholia felt the hand on the inside of his thigh. He nearly spilt the soup down the front of his uniform before regaining his composure. He looked to his left but quickly discounted the Austrian professor's wife if for no other reason than that both her hands were plainly in view. He looked to the right. The daughter's face was turned away from him, oblivious to his look, a dutiful child listening with wide-eyed innocence as her father continued to hold forth. He judged her to be about seventeen or eighteen, blonde, buxom, the puppy fat showing on her upper arms beneath the short sleeves of the summer dress she was wearing. Her left arm was hanging by her side, reaching down under the tablecloth, and her hand had now found his cock, massaging it through the lightweight cotton trousers, feeling him grow as she curled her fingers round his length, gently teasing it through the thin material with the palm of her hand. It was without doubt the most erotic experience of his young life and for a couple of minutes he was unable to do anything other than luxuriate in the experience, sitting back in his chair, the spoon lying untouched and forgotten in the watercress soup, lost in his own world. She had discovered his weakness. His own hand found its way under the tablecloth, unable to resist the temptation, finding the plump virgin flesh on the inside of her thigh above the stocking tops. She prepared, knowing, the dress pulled up, legs spread. She still ignored him, face turned away, showing no acknowledgement of the passions she was arousing, his hand brushing her bush, caressing the mound, fingers exploring the lips, feeling the warmth, her juices wetting the tips, no knickers to impede his progress. It was only when he realized that things were about to get seriously embarrassing that he withdrew from the secret tryst, came to his senses, lifted her hand from him, firmly pushing it back behind the overhanging cloth, fighting the urges that were wracking his body.

Later in her cabin she'd been a willing participant, practically ripping the uniform from him, pushing his mouth to the firm full breasts, grinding her crotch against his thigh, his tongue searching out the young nipples, her hand caressing his balls. He was thrusting deep into her, trousers and underpants round his ankles, she with her back to the bunk beds, balancing on one leg, the other wrapped around his waist when her father walked in.

It turned out she was fifteen. That was the end of the cruise ships and the beginning of the end of his career. He eventually found work on a Panamanian registered container ship plying the Buenos Aires-Amsterdam route and after that a succession of similar contracts before finally happening on the job with Hellenic Shipping. They needed a first mate but they couldn't afford to pay much, he was desperate for work. Four years later the captain left and they'd offered him the job. The ship was an old rust bucket, the pay lousy and the benefits non-existent, but he was his own boss in charge of his own ship.

Nicholia Andreus was a well-known figure in most of the seedy establishments that serviced the needs of the dockworkers and ships' crews who populated the dockside area in any one of a dozen ports. He'd known they were hitting on him that night, had worked it out as he stood on the small bridge of the Northern Star, easing her out of port between the dock walls. Don't have any savings worth talking about, they don't pay me enough for that, he thought. And they'll be kicking me out in a couple of years, putting the old girl to rest – maybe it's time to start looking after number one. On his next trip Rashid had been there to greet him, had suggested an option, a way to earn a little nest egg, something put by for his old age. And so it had begun.

He walked down the gangplank, dark trousers, blue woollen blazer, the canvas gunny sack slung casually over his shoulder, and proceeded along the dockside passing the two container ships at berth, the cranes hovering nearby ready for the morning's work silhouetted against the evening sky. Passing through the open gates with barely a nod to the two customs men sitting in the control booth he joined the throng of pedestrians out for an evening stroll, surveying the brightly lit bars and cafés that lined the waterfront. Turning off the main street he followed the route he now knew by heart, turning first left and then right as he made his way into the heart of the old quarter, the crowds left behind him, the narrow cobbled streets empty apart from the occasional local, the drab dress distinguishing them from the garishly clad tourists. The man was waiting for him at the entrance to the dimly lit alley, the exchange made, the bag relieved of its contents and with a quick shake of the hand, he turned on his heels and headed back to the waterfront, thirty thousand francs the richer.

Chapter 9

The house was located on one of the better residential roads on the outskirts of Bolton set in a half-acre of well-tended gardens, the large rhododendron bushes and mixed shrubbery partially shielding the view from the road offering a degree of privacy to the front of the house. A curved gravel driveway led from the wooden gates up to the front door of a Victorian detached built of polished red brick, the large sash windows and high ceilings giving the rooms a feeling of space beyond their actual dimensions. George and Mary bought the place in 1961 and despite the considerable wealth that would allow him to move into a far grander residence George had never felt the need or inclination to do so. Even after all these years the place reminded him of Mary; the few happy years God granted them had largely been spent at the house. In those days they had great plans and very little money. They married in 1960 and spent the first year in the small terrace George inherited from his maternal grandmother. The transport business George started with a second-hand lorry was doing reasonably well and they decided to buy somewhere larger that they could do up before starting the family. The house had stretched him to the limits financially but Mary decided that this was where they would bring up their family and once Mary had decided there was little point in arguing. Then disaster had struck. Mary was diagnosed with leukaemia in the spring of '63 and a year later she was dead.

After three months spent grieving and drinking George realized that life had to go on. He used work as an escape. Fifteen hours a day, seven days a week, no holidays, no rest. What was the point of holidays without somebody to share them with? He'd tried it once at his parents' insistence. In 1966 he'd booked a two week sightseeing tour to Egypt but after three days of abject misery he had taken a taxi to the airport and booked on the first plane home. Too much time to think, that was the problem. It had been ten years before he took another proper break. By then the hurt had healed and the business grown to the point where he was quite a wealthy man, his vacations expeditions to the historical and cultural centres of the world. His father had died from a heart condition in '88 and his mother had followed six years later.

The house was a treasure trove of trinkets that he had accumulated over the years. He could afford the best and that was what he bought. He'd also developed a keen interest in philately and possessed a fine stamp collection that took up much of his time. Socially, his outings were restricted to the odd dinner with the few close friends he had made over the years. It didn't worry him. He'd never had the time or the inclination for socializing since Mary's death and was quite content to spend his evenings listening to his classical record collection while searching through his extensive library of stamp catalogues.

The only immediate family left were his niece, Margaret, and her son, Craig. Craig's grandmother, Sally, was George's younger sister. She and her husband, Graham, were killed in a horrific car accident on the M6 when a lorry lost control and crossed over the central reservation. George had been deeply shocked at the time but was at least grateful that both his parents had died before the tragic accident robbed them of their only daughter. Craig had joined the company after three fruitless years studying design at the local polytechnic and was now a general manager responsible for overseeing the European long haul operation. His father had also worked in the business but had died three years ago following a serious stroke the previous year. George was never quite sure about Craig but he put that down to the generation gap and the fact that he had no children of his own. It's not just the fads and crazes that you lose touch with; it's also the change in attitude. To George's mind Craig was ungrateful and often irreverent in his attitude towards his elders, but whenever he raised the question with any of his friends they told him that was the way kids were today, better just accept it.

The doorbell rang and he heard the soft footfall as Mrs Jeffries walked through from the kitchen towards the front. Mrs Jeffries had been his housekeeper for the last twenty-seven years and her husband, Tom, looked after the garden. Funny that, thought George, I know Tom as Tom, but Mrs Jeffries is always Mrs Jeffries. She came in six days a week, often only for an hour or so, cleaned around the place and sometimes prepared something for his evening meal, although George was actually quite good around the kitchen himself and enjoyed cooking so it wasn't an issue. The relationship had grown informal over the years; Mrs Jeffries would just put her head round the door while she was going about her business and call over,

"Would you like me to make a steak and kidney pie for your tea tonight, Mr Lister, or are you going to cook something yourself?"

He knew how lucky he had been to find a Mrs Jeffries. She was a good, old-fashioned, honest and hard worker who enjoyed her job. He barely noticed the fine furniture, porcelain, pictures and other adorn-ments that were scattered throughout the house but to Mrs Jeffries they were treasured items to be cherished and respected. He knew this and it gave him pleasure to watch the look on her face as she carefully dusted a Capodimonte figurine or Wedgewood china bowl.

Craig entered the room.

"Hello, Uncle George. How you keeping?"

"I'm fine thank you, Craig. How about you?"

"Couldn't be better."

George was semi-retired and only went to the depot a couple of days a week. As Craig was often away on business they rarely met during the working week and to stay in touch Craig had taken to calling round every couple of weeks for an evening meal. Despite his misgivings about Craig George always enjoyed the visit. Margaret spent most of the year at her flat in Spain and the meal gave George a chance to catch up on the latest news.

"Drink?"

"Thank you."

The pattern had established itself over the years. George walked over to a side table where a Waterford decanter and four eight ounce tumblers sat on a silver tray next to which was an ice bucket with four bottles of something with an unpronounceable name that was apparently Czech lager. This was another of Mrs Jeffries's traits. After Craig had complained about the supermarket beer George had asked Mrs Jeffries to purchase as a precursor to his visits, she had found out what was required via some discreet enquiries as Craig was leaving one evening, and now the cooled lagers were always in the ice bucket on the evening of the visit. George helped himself to a scotch and water, opened one of the bottles and handed it to Craig. He might not be totally au fait with all the latest fads but he knew that a glass was definitely not required.

On a previous visit George had told Craig about finding the secret compartment welded to the underside of the chassis between the axles of one of the trucks. He'd noticed oil on the yard beneath the truck and, his early years getting the better of him, had been unable to resist getting under the flatbed to see what the problem was. The compartment was about two foot square and six inches deep with a hinged flap at one end. Craig had seemed unconcerned, probably smuggling a few extra cigarettes in, you know how much they cost nowadays, but promised to look into it.

"What did you find out about the secret compartment?" asked George.

"It was what I thought, Bill Fenwick's been using it to bring in a few extra fags. Do you know Bill?"

George tried to picture the face. There was a time when he'd known everybody in the firm by their first name, knew their families as well. But as the company grew and he became more removed from the day-to-day management it became harder and harder to keep up with all the new faces.

"I don't recall him."

"He joined us about three years ago. Good driver, very reliable but a bit of a Jack the Lad. I gave him a right bollocking, told him he'd be straight out the door if it he tried anything like that again. The trailer's in for an overhaul next week so I'll have the compartment removed then. Not a sackable offence is it? The man's got two youngsters and it's hardly a major crime."

George smiled as he thought back to some of the stunts he'd pulled in the early years to keep the business afloat: tax discs 'borrowed' from friends; cash delivery of loads on a no-questions-asked basis.

"Just as long as he's got the message. Any more trouble and he's out."

They made small talk until dinner was served in the dining room. George always insisted it was a waste to buy a joint for just one person but as far as Mrs Jeffries was concerned a man was in grave danger of fading away if he didn't tuck into roast beef, Yorkshire pudding and two veg on a regular basis. Craig's visit gave her the excuse to buy a nice piece of meat.

"Mrs Jeffries is a very good cook isn't she?" commented Craig.

"Yes, she is."

"This is a treat for me you know. I usually survive on baked beans and Indian takeaways."

"You should look after yourself, your mother would be upset if she thought you weren't eating properly."

"Don't worry, Uncle, I was laying it on a bit. I'm actually not a bad cook, not as good as this though. Does Mrs Jeffries cook for you every night?"

"No, it varies. Probably about three or four times a week."

"Must be difficult for her. I mean, being here 'til late all those evenings. You'd think her husband would get fed up."

"She doesn't stay normally. That's only when you're here so that she can serve the meal and we can sit and talk. If I'm on my own she just prepares everything ready for heating up and then she's gone by 3.30,

4.00 at the latest. We established the pattern years ago when her children were young. She had to be at the school to meet them by 4.00. Of course they're grown up now. June, the eldest has just finished teacher training college and Rose is at university in Sheffield. She's proud as punch, and rightly so. I don't think Tom would mind anyway. After a day at work he's probably glad of a bit of peace and quiet."

"I thought Tom was your gardener."

"He is, but it's not full-time. Just something to earn a few extra bob."

"But it's quite a big garden. When does he find time to do it all?"

"Well, this time of the year it doesn't need much. He just comes for a few hours at the weekend to tidy up. In the summer he comes a couple of evenings a week after work to do a few hours."

The conversation drifted on in a similar vein until Craig announced at about 10:15 that it was time he was getting on. "Work in the morning, you know."

"Keeping you busy are they?"

"Absolutely. See you down at the depot."

With that he was gone. Mrs Jeffries stuck her head round the door to say goodnight as she left.

Mike undid the lead and gave Forrest his head. The mad dog charged off around the park, bounding up and down in an ungainly motion, like an overly large, black spring lamb. He couldn't help smiling as he watched the dog; it was about the only thing in his life worth smiling about at the moment. The meeting with Anderson was not one of his better moments, the Super ripping into him about the lack of progress, suggesting that if he didn't feel he was up to the challenge then perhaps it was time to let somebody with more experience take a crack at it. Mike had lost his cool, felt the criticism was unjustified. He was doing all the right things, had teams covering all the bases, was asking all the right questions, but the facts were that nobody knew anything about Keith White and there was no apparent motive for his death. Maybe it was some sort of ritual killing, maybe there was no obvious connection.

He was lost in his thoughts when he saw Forrest making a beeline for an old gentleman walking along the path at the far side of the park.

"Forrest! Stop!" he yelled as he ran across the park. "Bad boy, come here."

The commands had no effect, Forrest wanted to be friends with everybody. He was still twenty yards away when he saw Forrest leap up, front paws on the man's chest, the man toppling over under the weight. He helped him to his feet.

"I am so sorry," Mike apologized. "He's still a puppy really, doesn't know his own strength."

Luckily the man was a dog lover. "No harm done", he said, patting Forrest on the back, "I shall have to watch out for you in future won't I, boy?"

Chapter 10

Mike was standing on the station platform when the call came through. After the bust up with the Super he was licking his wounds, looking for inspiration, once again pondering the possibilities of Keith White's final fateful journey. The team had been out in force the previous evening, questioning everybody in the immediate vicinity hoping to stumble upon the elusive witness, somebody who always used the car park on a Wednesday night or caught the Metro into town for the regular Wednesday evening outing with a friend. Somebody who had slipped through the net so far, somebody who would recognize Keith.

He answered the mobile.

"Report of another body, Sir. Sounds like the same MO." It was Daniels calling from the ops room where Mike had left him collating the results of the previous evening's work.

A sharp intake of breath.

"Give me the details."

"A 999 came through five minutes ago. Wilmslow Golf Club. Two of their members out for an early morning round walk up to the seventh green and find the body just lying there. From the brief description it sounds very similar to the Keith White murder. There's a patrol on its way, should be almost there by now, scene-of-crime are just leaving and I've asked the pathologist to get down there ASAP. Where are you now?"

"At the station. The train station. Altrincham."

"Right, do you want me to pick you up? The golf club isn't an easy place to find if you don't know the area."

"OK."

"See you in ten minutes."

Mike wandered back into the station, inserted fifty pence into the vending machine, received in exchange a plastic cup containing the murky brown liquid that passed for coffee and walked out into the bus station to await the arrival of Daniels. Two murders. What the hell was going on? What am I looking at? Is this a Sutcliffe, a Neilson, a Sams, at work? He'd studied all the classic cases on courses over the years. The lecturers always made the same points. Interesting cases, but the chances of ever having to deal with one were one in ten million; these crimes just didn't happen every day. Ninety-nine point nine percent of murders were straightforward with straightforward motives. Look for greed, look for revenge, look for anger, look for jealousy: that's how you'll solve the crime. He was disturbed from his reverie by the sound of tyres screeching on the tarmac as Daniels pulled into the bus station à la Starsky and Hutch. The bus station was a busy place with pedestrians and buses intermingled in what seemed to Mike to be a totally random fashion. He allowed himself a wry smile as he mentally pictured the headline. 'Police driver kills three in search for Cheshire ripper.' Dropping the nearly empty cup into the rubbish bin beside him he climbed into the car.

"Take it easy. We've enough dead bodies on our hands as it is without you adding to them."

"Sorry, Guv," said Daniels, chastised.

"So, what do we know?"

"Nothing more than I told you on the phone at this stage. We should be there in about fifteen minutes."

They forced their way through the build-up of traffic on the high street and out into the substantial commuter homes that lined either side of the road. Five minutes later these were left behind and they were speeding through the narrow twisting lanes that crisscross the Cheshire country-side. Rounding a bend they turned in between the gateposts and the sign warning off unwelcome guests – Wilmslow Golf Club, Members Only.

Well that should narrow the field down a bit, thought Mike, feeling somewhat lightheaded at the prospect of dealing with a multiple murder enquiry. Two police cars were already parked on the gravel in front of the imposing clubhouse and Mike noticed a uniformed officer talking to a man in a blue blazer and grey flannels. The man was clearly agitated and as he left the car Mike saw the PC pointing in his direction.

"I say, are you responsible for these people," the man asked, approaching.

Mike flashed his warrant card.

"Yes, Sir. I'm in charge, and might I ask who you are?"

"I'm secretary of the club, dammit, and one of your chaps has just driven straight down the course. Never seen anything like it. I'll have his guts for garters when I get hold of him."

Mike held up his hand to stop the flow and looked questioningly at the PC who had joined them by the car.

"The pathologist, Sir. Asked where the body was and then roared off round the side of the clubhouse and straight down the first fairway."

Mike suppressed a smile. "How far is it to the body?"

"About a mile and a half, Sir. It's at the far end of the course."

Mike turned back to the still agitated secretary. "Right, Sir. You're going to have to close the course until further notice. And I'm afraid we're going to have to take the vehicles down to the body."

The secretary tried to protest but Mike overrode him. He wasn't in the mood for playing games. "The constable here will stay on the gate." Turning to the constable he continued, "Don't let anyone in. Tell them the course is closed for the day. Don't give any details. Where are the golfers that found the body?"

"In the clubhouse, Sir."

"Keep them there for the moment, we'll talk to them later." He indicated to Daniels and climbed back into the car. "Right, let's go for it."

They pulled round the far side of the clubhouse and sped down the first fairway, easily following the tracks left earlier by Dr Seymour's car. Daniels possessed the demented grin of a ten-year-old let loose on a fairground dodgem as he headed out towards the furthest reaches of the course. They could see the doctor's car and the small huddle of people by the raised green as they rounded yet another small group of carefully positioned trees. Seymour walked over as they pulled up.

"What have we got?" asked Mike.

"A duplicate, by the looks of it. Male Caucasian, bit younger than the last one. About forty, I'd say. Multiple stab wounds to the lower abdomen plus the cross carved on the chest. Died between eight and twelve hours ago. You can move the body whenever you're ready. Get him back down to the lab and I'll have a proper look at him."

Mike glanced at his watch. 8.35. "Thanks, Doctor. I'll just take a quick look and then we'll get him shifted. By the way, the secretary's not too pleased about you treating his course as a race track."

"I don't think that will be a problem. I'm due to play with the captain on Friday afternoon, I'm sure he'll square things up," replied Seymour, the suggestion of an impish smile playing on his lips.

Mike walked towards the taped off area and made his way over to the body. The wounds were equally as gruesome as in the first murder but somehow the shock was nowhere near so profound. This suit didn't come cheap, he thought, as he sought the opening for each pocket, trying to disturb as little as possible. A handkerchief, a bill clip containing thirty-five pounds and some loose change in a trouser pocket. That was it. No wallet. No indication as to the identification of the man lying in front of him. The large brown patch staining the otherwise immaculate green suggested the man had been murdered where he lay. He was considering the implications of this thought when his attention was disturbed by the sound of a car approaching. Turning as the engine noise increased, he was just in time to catch a fleeting glimpse of blue paintwork as the car passed beyond the hedge not fifteen yards to the right of where he stood. He walked over to the hedge. Well, not really a hedge but a small grass covered mound topped by the occasional bit of coarse vegetation.

Every twenty yards or so a large tree grew from the mound and the whole thing was completed by a three foot high fence consisting of two strands of barbed wire strung between fence posts that had clearly seen better days. Looking over the hedge Mike could see into the lane that followed the side of the course at this point. He could also see that getting from the lane onto the course would be no problem whatsoever. Daniels had followed him over and also taken in the situation.

"I'll get some of our people out on the other side. See if we can find the point of entry. If they've had to climb over that fence they might well have left some evidence, snagged clothing or the like"

One thing was still bothering him and he walked back over to the green. The imprints left by Seymour's brown brogues were clearly visible on the green where he'd dropped on his haunches to examine the body. He noticed Owen among the officers searching the ground near the body and called her over.

"Have you found any footprints?" he asked.

"Only one set, and we're fairly certain they belong to the deceased."

"So, no lady's low-heeled shoe."

"No."

"But on that surface I would have thought anything that moved would leave an imprint."

"You're right. It's absolutely perfect from our point of view. Unless you're wearing a totally flat shoe you're going to leave some sort of mark."

Ten minutes later Mike was sitting in a deep leather armchair in the luxurious surroundings of the clubhouse. A quick chat with the two golfers had elicited no further information. A local solicitor and accountant out for an early round seemed as unlikely a pair of serial killers as ever there was and, after taking their details, Mike allowed them leave. He ordered a pot of tea and bacon sandwich from the steward who was busying himself behind the bar.

"What time did you arrive at the club this morning?" asked Mike.

"I live here, Sir, in the flat upstairs. It goes with the job," the steward replied.

"And did you hear or see anything out of the ordinary last night?"

"Not a thing. Very quiet night, Sir. We had a few members in the bar, last two left at about 10.30. After that I cleaned up and then went upstairs at about 11.15, watched TV for about an hour and went to bed just after 12.00. Went out like a light, didn't hear a thing until this morning."

"And what about this morning?"

"Up at 7.00. I was pottering around the flat when the two members came banging on the door downstairs. That would be just before 8.00. I don't normally open up until 8.00 during the week. I unlocked the bar and they came in and telephoned the police. They were in a bit of a state. From what they said it wasn't a pretty sight. I poured them a brandy, for their nerves, and made them coffee. After that we sat and waited for the police to arrive."

Daniels returned from the scene of crime ten minutes later.

"Looks like we might have a set of tyre prints in a field by the lane. Could be coincidence of course but somebody has parked a car in a field entrance ten yards up the lane from the scene fairly recently. We're tracking down the farmer now, see if he can shed any light on it. There's also a very nice footprint nearby. Trainer by the look of the pattern. That's about it so far."

"First thing we need to establish is who the hell he is. No means of identification on the body. No wallet, no credit cards, no driving licence. But robbery wasn't the motive. He still had a bill clip in his pocket with notes in it and a bloody expensive Rolex on his wrist. Our murderer didn't seem to worry about us identifying the first victim. Let's take a look at what we have here. Victim is expensively dressed, smart-casual, sort of thing you'd wear for a night out. Not many people put on their Armani suit for a night in front of the TV. Victim had money on him but didn't need his credit cards or car keys. Of course the car tracks we've found could belong to his car. The murderer could have killed him and then used his car to leave the scene. Fact is we don't know where to start looking. Until some-body comes forward and reports him missing we're snookered."

The two men sat quietly for several minutes as each pondered the implication of the second murder. The ring of Mike's mobile broke the silence.

"DCI Judd."

"From the early reports I understand that the modus operandi is very similar to the Tatton Park case," said the Super.

"Identical from the look of it," Mike replied.

"We need to be very careful what we say to the press. At this stage I don't want any linkage between the two crimes. I take it the press are at the club?"

Mike hadn't given the matter any thought. He had been too busy concentrating on the crime to worry about the PR implications. "I'm not sure, Sir. But word's bound to have leaked out by now so I would imagine there will be reporters at the clubhouse. We're just making our way back there from the scene of crime." He winked at Daniels. One of the advantages of mobiles was nobody ever knew quite where you really were.

"All you tell the press is that a body has been discovered and that it looks like murder. For any further information they should contact the station. Is that clear?"

"Yes, Sir."

"What's your next move? I need a briefing ASAP."

"We're just about finished here, Sir. Should be back at the station in about an hour at the most."

The press were indeed waiting in the car park. The news had spread quickly and half a dozen reporters and two photographers were waiting in the car park, kept in check by the uniform boys guarding the entrance. As Mike and Daniels emerged from the clubhouse the small group rushed forward, shouting questions as they approached. Mike put up his hands to quieten the group and issued his bland statement. The hounds could smell blood.

"Is it the same man as the Tatton Park murderer?"

"Is it a serial killer?"

"Who's the victim?"

Mike edged towards his car. "That is all I can tell you for the moment, gentlemen. Please contact the station for further information."

As they left the car park his face was set rigid. "A serial killer. What a bloody nightmare. Do you think it's possible, Daniels? Do we have an out and out nutter on our hands?"

"It's beginning to look that way, Guv. I've never seen anything like it in all my years on the force."

He was in the Super's office at 10.40.

"And you say it's definitely the same person that killed our man in Tatton Park," asked the Super.

"The pathologist will need to confirm it, Sir, but I don't think there's much doubt. The wounds were identical."

"What about identity? You say there's nothing to indicate who this chap might be."

"Nothing whatsoever, Sir. I think we need a television appeal. And sooner rather than later. Usual sort of thing. Unidentified man found murdered. Rough description. Police are appealing for information."

"Quite so. I don't think we have any choice. I shall arrange for an item to be included on this evening's news. However, until we have confirmation from the pathologist I still want to keep the fact that this is linked to the Tatton Park case quiet. You know what the press are like, once they get a sniff of this sort of thing, they will be all over us. Makes it a damned sight more difficult to do our job. So, what's your next move?"

"We'll keep working on the Tatton case but there's not a lot more we can do on this one until we get an ident. Nobody knows anything at the golf club. At the moment we don't know where to start looking."

bv"Right. I am due to brief the Chief Constable over lunch. This is not looking good, Judd. I want you to crosscheck with all the other forces and Interpol for a similar MO. Let's see if we're dealing with a known quantity here."

None of the neighbours paid any attention to the young man at number 12 as he busied himself in the small back yard of the terraced house. Having lined the bottom of the brazier, a cylindrical green metal mesh affair standing on short metal legs he'd purchased from the DIY super-store, with pages of scrunched up newspaper and added a dozen pieces of broken wood from the small pile outside the back door, he lit the paper at several points around the circumference. As the fire took hold he added a generous dose of paraffin from the metal can and watched the flames reach high into the air. Satisfied that the fire had taken hold he returned to the house and fetched the bundle of rags from the drainer in the kitchen, throwing them on top of the burning wood and adding a further dose of paraffin, making sure that every last scrap was reduced to grey ash.

Chapter 11

June began her shift on reception at 8.30. She'd worked at the motel for eight years now ever since dropping out of college at seventeen, a move which horrified her parents, but she enjoyed the friendly atmosphere and variety of duties. At 10.15 she received a call from Interactive trying to contact Mr Watson. He had been due at a meeting in Manchester at 10.00 and had failed to show. Furthermore, his mobile was switched off. Could they check his room, get him to call them? She sent one of the cleaners to check out the room. The occupant of room ten was nowhere to be seen but his overnight case, briefcase, laptop computer and assorted belongings were still in the room and, by the looks of the bed, the occupant had not spent the night in his room. June smiled quietly to herself. She was rather taken with Mr Watson and she'd noticed the expensive suits and the Rolex. He'd obviously picked up some company and spent the night playing away. Worth remembering, perhaps next time he stayed she'd make a bit of a play for him. Now he'd overslept. Probably waking up even now in some strange bedroom with a slightly groggy head, peering at his watch and realizing the error of his ways. She could just picture it: "Christ, why didn't you wake me you stupid woman. Look at the time." In the meantime she had to work out what to tell his office. She rang his secretary. "I'm afraid we can't locate Mr Watson at the moment. No, he hasn't checked out yet. Yes, I'll ask him to call you as soon as we locate him."

At 12.00 she contacted the duty manager. Mr Watson had only checked in for one night and according to the rules he should have vacated his room by 12.00 to allow the cleaners to prepare it for the next occupant. Stephan knew Dennis from his many visits and had, on several occasions, taken a drink with him at the bar. He sided with June's view of events; Dennis was always chasing skirt and probably become embroiled with one of the local girls and not yet made it back. That would no doubt take a bit of explaining to the office when he finally returned. Serve the arrogant bugger right. Stephan packed his few possessions and moved them into the manager's office where they would be safe until he returned.

By 4.00 they were beginning to worry. Oversleeping was one thing, disappearing for the whole day was something again. The office had been on the phone several times, becoming increasingly frantic as the day wore on. Stephan decided he had better inform the police and check with the local hospitals, just in case there had been an accident. The call came through to the station at 4.10. Daniels found Mike in his office.

"Looks like we might have something. Just had a call from the Four Seasons motel. One of their guests has gone missing. Fits the description."

Mike was already halfway out the door pulling on his jacket. "Let's go. Do we have a name?"

They arrived at the motel twenty minutes later. A brief chat with the duty manager and a look through the possessions pretty well confirmed Mike's view that this was their man and his conversation with the receptionist all but confirmed it. Just to make sure he arranged for fingerprints from the corpse to be checked against those on the BMW's steering wheel. By 5.15 they had a positive identification. He rang the Super.

"No need to put the request out on the news, Sir. We know who our victim is. Still need an official identification but there's no doubt about it. We can't release any details yet, not until we've informed the next of kin. Can you arrange for the PR people to release a suitable statement?"

"I'll take care of this end. What about the murderer? Any indication that we're making headway in that direction?"

"Not as yet but now we have something to go on. We'll start tracing the victim's movements last night, somebody must have seen who he met. This could be the breakthrough we've been looking for."

Mike turned to Daniels. "Get back to the station and contact Surrey police. They're going to have to inform his wife. And we need her up here as quickly as possible to perform an ID, tomorrow morning at the latest. I'm going to stay here and interview the staff. And get the scene-of-crime people down here – we need to go over his room."

He wandered back into reception to question the girl about Mr Watson's movements. "Were you on duty yesterday afternoon?"

"Yes, Sir."

He was surprised by the deference. It was unusual in this day and age, particularly among the young. It would be her job of course. She was trained to treat the customers with respect. She was simply applying the same criteria to him. Not bad looking either, he couldn't help noticing.

"So, did you check Mr Watson in?" asked Mike.

"That's right. It would have been about 6.00. Maybe a bit earlier," June replied.

"And did you notice anything unusual, anything out of the ordinary?"

"Nothing at all. Mr Watson checked in as usual, collected his key, and went to his room."

"What time were you on until last night?"

"6.30."

"Did you see Mr Watson again after he checked in?"

"No. He went to his room and that was the last I saw of him."

Mike went through the events of the day with her. Very attractive, well worth questioning further, although what excuse he could find for doing so he couldn't possibly imagine.

Mike made his way to the duty manager's office. "Who was on last night? I need to check out Mr Watson's movements from when he arrived until he left last night."

"I was on duty until 9.00 and then Pierre took over. I can confirm that Mr Watson ate in the restaurant last night, I spoke to him in reception as he was walking through. That would have been at about 8.30. The waiters in the restaurant will be able to tell you what time he left. Normally Mr Watson went through to Mulligans for a drink after dinner before retiring," Stephan replied.

"Mulligans?" Mike enquired.

"The Irish bar," replied Stephan indicating the entrance on the left-hand side of the reception area.

"Did you know him well?"

"He was a regular visitor. I knew him to say hello to, to pass the time of day."

"And what sort of person was he?"

Stephan chose his words carefully. "He seemed a very pleasant man. He came to stay regularly on business. He was a valued customer."

Mike gave him a look. "Listen, this is a murder enquiry so you're not going to upset your valued customer by bad mouthing him. Anything you say will be treated in the strictest confidence. I need to find out what he was really like, not the public relations version."

"Arrogant. Flash. Very full of himself. I had a drink with him on quite a few occasions. Good company but definitely thought he was a bit special." It didn't take much to open Stephan up.

"And what about the girls? Did he chase the ladies?"

"Very much so. He was always up for it. That's why he stayed here I think. With the bar being part of the motel we get a fair amount of local talent dropping in."

Mike looked over towards the bar entrance. "And who was behind the bar last night?"

"Roberto, Jules and Rick. They'll be on again tonight."

"What time do they come on?"

"Roberto's in there now. He's full-time, the bar's his responsibility. The others come on at 7.30."

"And what about the restaurant? Which staff were on last night?"

Mike enquired.

"Pierre is in charge, he lives on site. He also doubles as duty manager when I finish. He'll be taking his break now as he's due on at 7.00. He'll be able to tell you who was waiting on him."

They found Pierre in his room at the back of the motel. He confirmed that Mr Watson had eaten in the restaurant last night, that he had arrived at about 8.30 and left at 9.30. He couldn't be sure but was reasonably certain that he intended to go into Mulligans for a drink after his meal.

Mike left Pierre and wandered through to the Irish bar. It was early evening and the place was deserted other than for two businessmen propping up one end of the bar. A dark, swarthy man in his early thirties stood behind the bar and Mike guessed that this must be Roberto. Mike showed him his warrant card and Roberto confirmed that Mr Watson visited the bar on the previous evening. He had served him his first drink but other than that he couldn't help. He hadn't noticed him talking to anyone and didn't notice what time he left or who he left with. Mike sat back with his bottle of lager and awaited the arrival of the other bar staff.

Rick was a tall, thin, spotty youth of about eighteen wearing a back-to-front baseball cap, Gap t-shirt and baggy pair of combat trousers. Luckily for Mike he also had a very good memory.

"Yeah, he hit on a chick over at the far side of the bar. I served them. He spilt her drink, deliberate like, to get in there."

"How do you know it was deliberate?" asked Mike.

"He was always doing it, man. I've seen him do that five or six times. It's cool because he has to drop me a decent tip so I don't blow his cover," replied Rick speaking in the gangland slang he'd heard on the videos.

"So, Mr Watson was always chasing the girls."

"And then some. Sad bastard. For an old man he didn't do too bad either," replied Rick.

Mike decided to let the reference to the old man pass. All things were relative, he told himself.

"So, what did this girl look like?" he asked.

"Nothing special. Late twenties, early thirties. Mid-length brown hair, Bit on the weighty side. Dowdy. Boring. Know what I mean?"

"Seen her before?"

"No. I'm pretty sure about that. I remember thinking That's handy, two of them staying in the motel and both up for it. I thought she was just a guest passing through."

"And what was she wearing?"

"Red top, black trousers. Oh, and she's called Jane."

"How do you know that?"

"I heard her introduce herself when I was picking up the glass he'd knocked over."

"What was she drinking?"

"Cuba Libras. Had about three or four, I guess."

"And did you see them leave?"

"No. Once the bell goes you lose interest in who's at the bar. Too busy cleaning up. That way you can get away a bit quicker."

"How many were in last night?"

"Hard to say. It wasn't busy, never is on a Wednesday. Maybe forty or fifty all night."

"And how many of those do you know? How many are regulars?"

"Most of them."

"Right. Well, you, Jules and Ricardo get together and start drawing up a list. I want the names of everyone who was in here last night."

Jules gave him a sideways look. "We don't know their names. Not most of them anyway. Sometimes a first name but that's all. We just know them as punters."

"OK. Tell the other two. I'm going to be sitting in the corner over here. Anybody that comes in that was in last night just tip me the wink."

By the end of the evening he had spoken to eighteen drinkers who had been in the previous evening. Five of them remembered seeing the girl sitting at the bar chatting with Dennis and two of them were pretty certain that the two of them left together.

He left the bar at 11.30 and thought through the day's events as he drove home. Man makes apparently random meeting with girl in bar. Man and girl probably leave together although no confirmation of this fact. Man later found dead five miles away in isolated spot. Man's car and car keys still in motel room. Ditto wallet. Conclusion. Man going for drink in motel where he was staying so doesn't need car keys or credit cards. Just takes enough cash for a few beers. Meets girl who suggests they go on somewhere else in her or accomplice's car. Man lured out of car in remote spot and killed. The question is, Why? What's the motive? Who's the girl?

Mike made one last phone call to Daniels on the way home. The widow would be leaving early next morning and should be with them by 10.00 at the latest to identify the body. The motel room had revealed nothing. The cleaners had already been over it but somehow Mike doubted that Mr Watson and friend had ever made their way back to the room. If they had, why leave again?

Mrs Watson arrived in the unmarked police car early on Friday morning. Early thirties, blonde and extremely attractive, she seemed to Mike remarkably composed considering the news she had received the previous evening. They completed the journey to the morgue in silence and she duly identified the body. Back at the police station Mike seated her in one of the interview rooms and tried, as delicately as possible, to prepare her for what was to come. He knew that details of the case would soon be released in the press and that certain awkward facts were bound to emerge.

"Was your marriage a happy marriage, Mrs Watson?"

She appraised him coolly. "I like to think so, Chief Inspector. Why do you ask?"

God, she made him feel uncomfortable. "It's just that certain facts are bound to emerge during the investigation. It can't be avoided. Once the tabloid newspapers get hold of a story like this they won't stop until they've dug up every last detail."

"Certain facts? Tabloid newspapers? What do you mean, Chief Inspector?" Her voice was haughty, demanding, unemotional.

"Were you aware that your husband might have had affairs with other women?" He felt awful having to tell her this, disrespectful of her dead husband, expecting to see the women opposite him break down as the reality of what he was telling her hit home.

"What other women, Inspector?" she asked, the voice still superior, not a tremor.

"The information we have is that your husband left the motel on the night of his death with a woman he had met in the bar." Christ she's a hard one, thought Mike.

"Really. That hardly constitutes an affair. I don't see what you're getting at."

"We have spoken to other people. The information we have is that this was not an isolated incident. The tabloids will talk to the same people we're talking to. You're going to read it in the press anyway. There may be a perfectly innocent explanation but I would prefer that you heard it from us rather than read it in the paper."

"I'm very grateful for your concern, Inspector. Was there anything else?"

"It may seem a stupid question but did your husband have any enemies? Anybody who would want him out of the way?"

"No. Definitely not. Dennis might have been a bit strident at times but he didn't mix with the sort of people who go round killing each other to settle their scores."

She was probably right, normal people didn't settle their disputes by disembowelling their enemies.

"That's what I thought. What about his financial affairs? I'm afraid we'll have to go through all the records anyway, it's standard practice in a murder enquiry. But it would help if you could give me an idea of any problems he may have had, any debts outstanding, that sort of thing."

"We don't have any debts other than the normal mortgage and a bit on the credit cards. Dennis earned a very good salary. And he had share options. I don't know the exact details but I believe that, as long as the company continues to do well, they will be worth a considerable sum when they mature."

Mike tried to sound casual. "And were you at home on Wednesday evening."

"Good Lord, Inspector. You're not seriously suggesting I had anything to do with this?" Some of the cool was gone. There was definitely an edge to her voice.

"Of course not. It's routine in murder cases. We have to ask," he replied.

"I was at my bridge club from 8.00 until about 11.30. I play every Wednesday. This week it was at Judy Parfitt's house. As I said, I arrived home at 11.30."

"Thank you, Mrs Watson. Perhaps you could let me have Mrs Parfitt's number. We have to check, you understand."

She gave him a look that indicated she considered him beyond contempt, pulled her address book from the black leather bag and wrote the number on the pad on the desk. Mike saw her to the car and bade her farewell.

Chapter 12

Sitting in his office on the Saturday morning Mike was feelingly distinctly subpar. He'd picked up a Chinese on the way home from the motel and then, having consumed the meal, sat back with a large scotch to run over the facts as they now stood. One scotch had led to another and he eventually crawled to bed at 3.00 in the morning. Now he was regretting it. Forrest lay in the middle of the floor, taking up most of the office, tongue out, panting. Dogs weren't allowed in the station but the Super wouldn't be in today and he could rely on the rest of them to keep quiet. Everybody loved Forrest, he'd become a bit of a mascot among the murder team. Daniels stuck his head round the door.

"Morning, Guv. Hello, Forrest, how are you, boy?" he said, bending down and giving the dog a pat. "We might have a bit of a breakthrough with Keith White. Seems some of the bar men up in the Village think they recognize him."

"The Village?"

"It's an area in central Manchester: clubs; bars; plenty of nightlife; very trendy. Originally it was a gay area but now it's a bit of everything. Just generally where people head to for a good time in the evening."

"OK, let's go and talk to them. Where do we find them?"

"There are three of them who think they've seen him before. Bit defensive about it, the gay community isn't too trusting of the local plod. Seems there's been a bit of bad feeling in the past. Two work at a place called the Metz and the other at Via Fossa. They are all working this lunchtime so we can catch them then."

"Good. What about the tyre tracks at the golf club? Any news?"

"Dunlop radials available through just about every tyre outlet in the country. Fit most makes of standard family saloons. The farmer drove through on the tractor in the morning and the car tracks overlaid his tracks so they were made that day. Probably gives us the MO but doesn't help in terms of pointing us at a suspect."

"Anything else from scene-of-crime at the club?"

"Only the footprint. Adidas trainer, size eight. Other than that the whole place is as clean as a whistle. Whoever this is they're careful. Either that or damned lucky."

Mike rubbed his eyes, trying to clear the woolliness from his brain. "I want to check out the widow Watson some more. Don't know why but she just seems too cool about the whole thing. Discover your husband's been brutally murdered and playing away from home to boot, you'd expect some sort of emotional reaction. She was cool as cucumber. Look into her alibi. The details are on the file. Also, check out his financial background, I understand there's quite a bit of money involved. Let's find out how much and who gets the loot."

Mike left Daniels to get on with the legwork and went to the tearoom to make a coffee. He filled a bowl he found in the cupboard with water and put it on the floor for Forrest and threw him a couple of the chocolate hobnobs from the biscuit tin. The cobwebs began to lift as the caffeine entered his bloodstream. An hour later and he was feeling almost human.

They parked on yellow lines in Richmond Street, walked down past the Union Hotel and into the area known as the Village, Forrest Gump on the lead. The left-hand side of the pedestrianized road was taken up by a variety of old buildings, many of whose lower floors had been converted into wine bars, bistros and restaurants, while the right-hand side was bounded by a low wall built of large stone blocks, one side of the retaining walls built many years previously by the Victorian labourers to contain the Bridgewater canal as it flowed through the heart of the city. It was only just after noon and the cafés were comparatively quiet, just the odd few people taking morning coffee at some of the outdoor tables that sat on the pavement over-looking the canal. The Metz was about thirty yards down the street and unlike the other bars was on the right-hand side of the canal, reached by a wooden footbridge that spanned the canal at this point. The stairs from the bridge led to a small wooden deck outside the old converted mill building that housed three small round pine tables. The inside was dimly lit and it took half a minute before Mike's eyes adjusted and he could begin to fully take in the surroundings. He approved of what he saw; the place was pleasantly done out but retained an air of individualism so often lacking in many of the modern themed pubs. The structure of the building dictated the format and style of the decoration and the owners had cleverly used this to create an effect. The large circular cast iron pillars supporting huge oak beams that gave the building its strength were left exposed, as was the pipe work that wound its way around the ceiling. The large wooden bar was to the right, glass tumblers stocked neatly in a pyramid, a line of ornate and brightly coloured beer taps proclaiming the name of the beverages on offer; Staropramen, Grolsch, Red C, Guinness and Virgin Cola.

They sat at one of the large unpolished pine tables and ordered coffee. The two men and girl behind the bar were polishing glasses and talking among themselves. Daniels went over to the bar, had a quick word with the barmen and returned to the table. One of them sauntered over. Mike looked up.

"Hello there. Sit down, please."

The young man in matching black polo shirt and tight black trousers joined them at the table. Mike could see the youth was suspicious of their motives.

"You know what this is about, the murder of Keith White. As far as we can establish there is no gay connection whatsoever. All we're trying to do is to find out where Keith went in the evenings, who he might have met, and what became of him, OK?"

The youth nodded, looking at the dog sitting on the floor next to Mike. "Who's this then?"

"Forrest Gump. He's my dog."

"He's beautiful. Is he a police dog then?" asked the youth, stroking Forrest's head.

"No, just a big, dumb ordinary dog. About Keith White, you think you've seen him here?"

The lad looked at the six by six portrait photograph that Daniels had dropped on the table.

"Definitely. I'm sure it's him. Not regular but maybe once a week or so for the last couple of months. Came in, had a beer at the bar and then went on his way."

"Did he ever have anybody with him or meet anybody?"

"Not as far as I can remember. Always on his own. A bit out of place really, that's why I noticed him. Not just the age thing, we get plenty of old rockers in here, but square. You know, not dressed up at all. Like a schoolteacher or something. "

"Which nights did he come in?"

"Mid-week. Don't remember which nights but definitely mid-week. We're quieter then. Fridays and Saturdays we're rushed off our feet, always two or three deep at the bar. I remember him standing at the bar drinking a beer. You wouldn't be able to do that at the weekend. No room."

"Anything else?"

"Not that I can think of. Didn't really pay a lot of attention. Not my sort, if you know what I mean."

"Thanks. Could you ask your friend to come over?"

The other barman had little to add. While they were talking the first youth returned with a large ashtray full of water and placed it on the floor. Like his friend he had noticed Keith at the bar on a couple of occasions but couldn't recall him talking to any of the other punters. When he returned to the bar the girl came over and started petting Forrest.

They left the Metz, walked back over the bridge and strolled fifty yards down the street to Via Fossa. Mike was unable to place the style at first, there was definitely something Italianate about it but there was something more. Then it struck him. The oak panelling behind the bar was actually a church pulpit. Ethereal music emanated from the stereo system, tapestries hung from the walls and the benches on either side of the wooden tables to his left were old church pews. Clever and effective. The barman told them a similar story; he'd seen Keith a few times but could shed no light on whom he might have been meeting or where he was going.

As they left the wine bar Daniels said, "This dog trick seems to work remarkably well. I've never known young people be so friendly towards the police. You'll have to let me borrow him next time I'm interviewing." Mike gave him a sheepish grin, the huge black mass straining at the lead, nearly pulling him over.

On the drive back to Sale, Mike used Daniels as a sounding board as he reviewed the current situation.

"Given what we've just heard there seems a strong possibility that the reason we found Keith's car in the car park was because he parked there before catching the Metro into town. From there he went to the Village where he visited some of the local bars. At some stage he met at least one other person and was driven from the Village to Knutsford where he was murdered. The MO for Dennis Watson is very similar. He is out on his own enjoying a few drinks, meets up with a girl, is driven to a remote spot and murdered. The trouble is there doesn't seem to be any connection whatsoever between the two men and there also doesn't seem to be any motive."

"Makes it very difficult. If there's no connection between the victim and the murderer then the only way we're going to catch her is if she makes a mistake," replied Daniels.

Mike looked across at him. "So would you like to explain that to the Super on Monday morning?"

The Super was a lot more sympathetic than Mike had expected. The press was now running hard with the serial killer stories and the Super was suddenly aware that it was his cock that was on the block. He'd studied the reports on similar cases, had seen what it did to the health and career prospects of the senior officers involved. And although he'd always been on the uniform side of the force he understood the impossibility of finding a suspect when the killer was acting in a totally irrational and random fashion. With the exception of the mentally deranged and the psycho-pathic, all murderers have some sort of tie-in to their victims. Without that connection the only option was to hope that the killer made a mistake; that he left some vital clue behind that would eventually lead to his undoing.

"Do you know anything about my soup bowl, by the way?" asked the Super.

"Soup bowl?" Mike was totally thrown by the change of tack.

"Yes, I keep it in the cupboard in the tea room. Spot of soup for lunch, nourishing and healthy. This morning I came in and the bowl was on the floor."

Mike shook his head, looking nonplussed. "I can't imagine what could have happened, Sir."

"Quite. Well, I'm sure I'll get to the bottom of it."

At 11.15 the duty sergeant stuck his head round the door of the operations room where Mike, Daniels and two of the detectives were sifting through the evidence and reading the statements for the umpteenth time.

"Sounds like we have another one. Body found on a bowling green at High Lea."

It was the call they had been dreading. It had escaped no one's notice that the first two murders had taken place on a Wednesday night, exactly one week apart. When Mike had arrived at 8.00 that Thursday morning he could feel the tension in the ops room but as the hours ticked away they'd begun to relax; if anything had happened they'd have heard by now. It seems bowlers are not the earliest of risers.

The team knew the routine by now and quickly swung into action with very little instruction required. As they headed out of the police station car park Mike noticed the half dozen cars and three or four motorcycles pull out from their parked positions by the station.

"The press obviously has faith in our killer to keep to his schedule; there are half a dozen of them behind us. Can you lose them?" Mike enquired.

Daniels reached for the radio. "Hello, Control. Get a patrol car to meet me at the junction of Red House Lane and Gorse Lane in ten minutes."

They found the patrol car and after brief instructions it followed them down the narrow lane, pursued by the convoy of press vehicles. After half a mile the patrol car suddenly swung sideways, completely blocking the lane, much to the chagrin of the pursuing pack.

Ten minutes later they found the bowling green set in the corner of a field to the right of the road. To the left of the road, hidden behind a large wall, was an executive housing estate, but on this side of the road there were only fields as far as the eye could see. Shielded by hedging from the road the green was almost completely hidden until one entered the car park alongside it, from where a small gate led through to the playing area. A tent had been erected in the middle of the green and Mike could see an elderly gentleman sitting on the bench in front of the wooden pavilion.

"I understand you found the body," Mike enquired.

"That's right. Horrible it was. A right mess."

"If you could just try to tell me what happened."

"I came over about 11.00 to check up, like I always do. This time of the year no one's playing but I like to just make sure everything is in order. Walked through the gate and there he was. Thought it was a tramp at first, thought maybe the cold had got to him. Then I saw the wounds. Went home and rang your lot."

Mike bent down beside the body. Much older than the other two, mid-sixties at a guess. No means of identification. Set of keys in pocket of grey flannel trousers – one Yale key, one car key – worsted shirt, v-neck sweater and sports jacket. He joined Dr Seymour by his car.

"Same as the others?"

"Certainly looks like it. I'll be able to confirm that once I've completed the post mortem. Time of death between 10.00 last night and 2.00 this morning. More than that I can't tell you at the moment."

Mike remembered their first meeting. The touch of aggression in the air, both men vying for supremacy, who was the alpha male. All that was gone now, both overwhelmed by the awfulness of the situation, aware that a maniac was on the loose, a maniac who was taking the lives of innocent victims and there was nothing they could do to stop it. "Let me have your report as soon as possible please."

"Of course," replied Seymour.

Chapter 13

Mrs Jeffries was confused, she'd said as much to Tom on Thursday night.

"His bed wasn't slept in last night. I'm sure of it."

Tom laughed, "Perhaps he's found a dolly bird, run off with her."

"Don't talk silly. Mr Lister isn't like that, you know he isn't. And he wasn't at home today. He's always at home on a Thursday. He ate his supper on Wednesday – I did him a nice chicken casserole – but then he upped and went."

"Don't worry, pet. Something's probably come up business-wise, and he's had to go and sort it out."

"You could be right. It is unusual though, he always lets me know if he's going away so that I don't prepare food that doesn't get eaten. You know how he hates waste."

"He'll be there right as rain tomorrow, you mark my words."

Mike was also feeling perplexed that Thursday evening. They'd issued a statement to the effect that an unidentified man in his mid-to-late sixties had been the third murder victim of what the press was now referring to as the Cheshire Slasher but were no further in putting a name to the victim. Seymour's report had confirmed that the victim was almost undoubtedly killed by the same person as the previous two and that time of death was around 11.45 on Wednesday evening. The only interesting point was the large bump on the back of the victim's head which led Dr Seymour to surmise that in this instance the victim had been hit on the back of the head with a blunt object at some point prior to death and was possibly unconscious at the time of death. This would explain the lack of his own blood on his hands, a feature noted in both previous killings which occurred when the victims grasped at the bulging wounds in their abdomens.

On Friday morning they had their first break through – it was Daniels who spotted it.

"Guv, remember you asked me to check out Mrs Watson? Well, it seems she's going to be a very wealthy widow. The company records show that her husband held stock and options worth a total of nearly ten percent of the company. At today's figures that's worth just over two million quid. I also rang Mrs Parfitt. Remember, the bridge club?"

Mike nodded.

"Well, she confirmed that Mrs Watson was with her that Wednesday evening. Sounded a bit tense but that's often the way with the general public when they're talking to the police. She also gave me the names of the other three players there that night," said Daniels, the tone of voice suggesting that the statement had implications.

"So?" Mike couldn't see it.

"Mrs Watson plus Mrs Parfitt plus three others makes five. I'm no expert on these matters but I always thought you played bridge with four players, not five."

Mike smiled. "Elementary, my dear Watson. You could be on to something; I think it's time to pay the bridge club a visit. We could be down there by early afternoon if we leave now. Give Mrs Parfitt a ring and tell her we're on our way, that'll give her something to stew over for a few hours. She should be nicely done by the time we arrive."

Mike wasn't far wrong. When they arrived outside the large detached house backing on to the golf course in the early afternoon the door was opened by a very elegant but extremely agitated woman in her early forties.

"DCI Judd and DI Daniels. We rang earlier. May we come in?"

Mrs Parfitt showed them through into the large lounge.

"I think you know why we're here," said Mike, seated now in one of the leather armchairs.

Mike could see the woman was in distress. She sat on the edge of the chair, her hands shaking, her eyes firmly fixed on the carpet. Mike decided to go easy on her.

"You told my colleague over the phone that Sheila Watson was here, playing bridge, on the night of her husband's murder. That's not true, is it?" he asked, his voice quieter, comforting.

"No." The answer was barely audible.

"So, why did you say she was?"

"She asked me to."

"And you often lie for your friends when they ask?" The voice harsher now.

"No. Yes. Oh, this is so difficult. I really don't know what to do."

Mike decided it was time to turn up the heat. "Mrs Parfitt, this is a police enquiry into a murder and at the moment you are in grave danger of being named as an accessory after the fact. This isn't some stupid game we're playing. People are dead. I could charge you with wasting police time at the very least. Now just tell us the truth and stop wasting our time."

The tears were flowing now. She took a minute to compose herself.

"Sheila does belong to our bridge club. Or at least she used to until about three months ago. And then she met some chap. I don't know who he is; I've never met him. Anyway, Sheila started using the bridge club as an alibi for her trysts, asking us to confirm that she was playing bridge with us on a Wednesday night should anyone ever ask. We didn't like it of course, but what can you do? You've met Sheila?"

Mike nodded.

"It's difficult to refuse her, she can be quite aggressive. As it turned out the situation never arose. Her husband's always away on business, or rather was always away," she corrected herself. "And nobody ever asked after her. I'd forgotten about it until last week when Sheila rang and made me promise to confirm her alibi if the police rang up to check. She said it would be terrible for the children if it came out that she'd been with her lover on the night that her husband was murdered. Besides, Dennis was a no good rat. Everybody knew that. He cheated on Sheila every chance he got. I suppose I felt a bit sorry for her really."

"Thank you, Mrs Parfitt. It would have been a lot more straightforward if you'd told us the truth in the first place."

"And will you charge me? For wasting police time, or whatever?"

"Oh yes. You can be sure of that. Good day to you."

Back in the car Daniels looked over. "Bit hard on her weren't you, Guv?"

"You think so? Supposing this Watson woman has something to do with the murders. If we'd known her alibi didn't hold up last week we might have been able to prevent that poor bastard being butchered on the bowling green," Mike replied, the tone angry.

"Fair point, Guv."

Half an hour later they found the deserted Watson house. They sat in the car opposite and waited, Mike reasoning that the kids would be home from school at about 4.00 so she should be home by then. At 5.00 they went off in search of something to eat. At 7.00 they concluded that she'd either done a runner or gone away for the weekend. Mike arranged for Surrey police to keep an eye on the place and headed for home. With a four hour drive in front of them Daniels was far from happy. "My missus is going to kill me when I get home, I was supposed to be taking the kids ten pin bowling tonight."

At about the time that Mike and Daniels were making their way on to the M25 Mrs Jeffries was sitting on the sofa in the lounge of the Lister residence wondering what do next. She'd come in as usual early in the afternoon and had quickly ascertained to her own satisfaction that George Lister had not been home since her visit of yesterday. She had continued with the cleaning and polishing, hoping at any moment to hear the key turning in the lock, an announcement of Mr Lister's safe return from wherever it was he had been. But he didn't appear. She'd stayed on after her normal finishing time saying I'll just give it an extra half hour. Half an hour had turned into an hour and then into two hours but there was still no sign of Mr Lister. It was a difficult situation for her. She was not a decisive women, she knew that. Didn't like rocking the boat, afraid of speaking out of turn, of getting above her station. The kids often chided her about it. They had been brought up in a different world. How she wished she had their self-confidence. She picked up the receiver and dialled.

"Tom, there's still no sign of him. What do you think I should do?"

"Did you ring the depot? They'll probably know where he is," Tom replied.

"No. I didn't think. It's too late now, they'll all have gone home."

"Don't think there's much you can do, love. He's probably just gone away for a long weekend, forgotten to let you know. Why don't you come home? I'll put the kettle on and we'll have a nice cup of tea."

"Right, I'll see you in ten minutes." She sounded happier, reassured by Tom's reasoning.

The weekend was a time of frustration for all concerned. Mike found himself back in the ops room on Saturday morning but could make no progress. The pathologist's report had arrived yesterday and confirmed what he already knew. The only real headway they had made was on the car key found on the third victim. It belonged to a Jaguar XJ12. He'd given Daniels and the rest of the team the weekend off because as things stood there was very little they could do. The Watson woman was definitely a lead worth chasing, although at the back of his mind he was fairly sure that, whatever the explanation for her subterfuge, it was unlikely to get them any nearer to the murderer. In a way that was the problem. He was following the classic murder investigation line: look for someone who is in some way connected to the victim who has a motive. Did that make sense in this case? If this was a serial killer picking his victims at random, and all the evidence suggested that it was, then was there any point in following the traditional lines of enquiry? And the next deadline was approaching. It was always at the back of his mind – Wednesday night was only four days away. But what could they do? Issue a public warning? Mike pondered the thought: 'Cheshire police are warning middle-aged men not to pick up women in bars on Wednesday evenings.' He couldn't see it working somehow. And what about the third victim? They were still no nearer finding his identity. He'd already agreed with the Super that if no one came forward over the weekend they'd issue a photofit on Monday and issue a general appeal on the national news.

Mrs Jeffries was also killing time that weekend. She went in early on Saturday, just to see if there was any sign, and returned again in the late afternoon. Normally she wouldn't go in on a Sunday but she needed to know. Tom could see she was fretting.

"Look we'll phone the depot tomorrow morning. If they don't know where he is then we'll contact the police and report him missing. OK?"

She smiled at him and relaxed a little. "I suppose so."

Sheila Watson's world had been turned upside down. The death of her husband left her in something of a quandary. On the one hand, that the man she had married, the father of her children, had been brutally murdered was undoubtedly tragic. On the other hand, she had already decided that things couldn't go on as they were, that she was no longer willing to put up with his philandering and that the physical intensity of the relationship with Jake was the best thing to have happened to her in years. She was appalled to discover that she felt very little at the death of her husband, that any feelings she may once have harboured for Dennis had long since disappeared. She went to see Jake on the Friday night, leaving the children with her mother, needing to talk to him, to feel him holding her, comforting her, offering succour. That had been her only intention. That they ended up making passionate love on the mat in the middle of the gym, her on top, needing to feel him deep inside her, less inhibited than she had ever been, willing him on, expurgating the ghosts, removing the memory of Dennis from her mind, left her filled with shame. But that was how she felt and no matter how hard she tried there was nothing she could do to change it.

The news caused a cloud to cross over Jake's normally sunny features. Sheila was right to a degree when she assumed that the worried expression was caused by concern, but wrong in determining the cause of the concern. It wasn't Sheila's grief that was upsetting him but the effect the death of her husband would have on her ability to get hold of some serious money. They were seated on the stools, elbows leaning on the counter.

"That's terrible, Sheila honey, absolutely terrible."

"I know, and the worst part is I don't feel anything. Or at least, not what I should be feeling. I feel sad for him obviously but there's none of the pain I should be feeling."

"Don't blame yourself, honey. You said he was cheating on you, had been for years. You can't expect to feel anything for a man like that."

He was so understanding. "I know, but that doesn't stop me feeling bad."

"You've got to look after yourself, honey, make sure you and the kids are alright. What about financially, has he left you OK for money?"

And so thoughtful, she thought. "We're alright for the time being. The company phoned to say they're going to pay his salary for the next three months. And I'll get the house of course – the mortgage is covered by life insurance. Then there's the life insurance cover on his pension, that's worth about half a million. Sounds a lot but invested in blue chips it will only bring in about twenty-five thousand a year tops," she said, the facts gleaned from her accountant over the phone earlier that day.

Jake was perking up. "Still, half a million's a lot of money, you could really do something with that."

She missed the cue. "The share options are the tricky one. We're still working on the legal position but it looks like they pass to me."

He looked up, half-interested. "Worth much?" he asked.

"About two and a half million at yesterday's prices and going up all the time," she said.

Jake did a double take. Two and a half million? Now that was worth having. He turned to her. "I'll be there for you, honey. You know that, don't you?" He gave her his most sincere look.

"I know you will Jake," she replied, her face turned towards him, lips meeting his, her arms folding round his neck.

He forced his tongue into her mouth, flicking the end of hers, gently licking the inside of her lips, his hand reaching up to her breast, feeling her through the silk blouse, his bare muscular leg rubbing against the inside of her thigh. Afterwards, on the mat, she was out of control, like a banshee, nearly ripped his cock off. Jesus, what's got into her, he thought. Still for two and a half million he could stand a little pain.

Chapter 14

The large curtain-sided artic pulled off the N1 and came to a halt in the lorry park of the motorway café. Bill lowered himself from the cab, locked the door and stretched his cramped limbs, feeling the warmth of the sun beating down upon his back. It was at this time of the year that he really appreciated the fortnightly run down to Marseilles. Leaving the drab, cold English climate of late March behind as the truck powered south into the blossoming Mediterranean spring. True, the weather could be pretty unpredictable at this time of the year, even in the south, but as far as Bill was concerned it was like taking a short winter holiday every two weeks. He wandered over to the self-service café, picked up a ham roll and pot of coffee, paid at the cash desk and settled himself down at one of the tables in the outdoor picnic area.

Bill arrived in Marseilles late Tuesday evening, leaving the truck in the depot overnight while he enjoyed a decent meal and a night in a proper bed. L'Hôtel du Sud wasn't much to look at, more of a guesthouse than a proper hotel, but the rooms were cheap and clean and Madam Hoube's beef bourguignon was a work of art. Later he strolled down to the water-front for a couple of beers in one of the brightly lit bars, enjoying the ambience, content to watch the lights reflecting in the still waters of the harbour, searching out the silhouette of the odd trawler as it put-putted back home. Listers had bought out the small French haulage company several years ago when George Lister, the founder and owner, noticed that the international market was growing rapidly and the haulage rates on the long runs made them far more profitable. As well as giving them a local storage and repair facility the depot also gave the company a presence on the ground, making it far easier to arrange the all-important return load, the difference between breaking even and making a decent profit on the trip.

Wednesday was spent dropping off his load and picking up the return loads from various addresses in the Marseilles area. He also picked up the contraband and hid it carefully away. He knew he was taking a risk but he needed the cash, there was always something needed for the house or the kids, the extra money making the difference between surviving and being able to afford a few of life's luxuries. On Thursday morning he completed the last couple of pick-ups and began the long haul home. He'd sleep on the bunk in the back of the cab tonight before catching the early morning ferry on Friday, a couple of drops in London, one in Birmingham and then back to Bolton for Friday evening. As much as anything it was the freedom he enjoyed. Once he'd left Bolton on Monday morning he was pretty much his own man for the week.

The drop at East End Tiles was a regular, rarely missed. They were ceramic wholesalers based in a large warehouse in the East End of London, just off the Old Kent Road. The warehouse was an old wooden structure that fronted right on to the road and Bill pulled the artic straight through the large doors and into the centre of the warehouse, metal racking stacked with pallets of ceramics to either side of him. Mick came over to greet him as he lowered himself from the cab.

"How are you doing, Bill? Good run?" Mick asked, approaching the cab.

"Not so bad. Nice to get a bit of sun on my back."

"Lucky sod. What have you got for us?"

"Two crates. They're back left. I'll sort out the curtain."

"Right, I'll be back in five minutes and we'll go and get a breakfast."

"Hold on a minute." Bill reached inside the small sports bag slung over his shoulder and pulled out a carton of 200 Marlborough. He tossed them over to Mick. "There you go, mate."

"Nice one."

Bill made his way over to the rear of the truck and began undoing the ropes that secured the curtain side to the flatback. The stop was handy for him; his driving hours were up, the statutory one hour break dictated by legislation, so his regular habit was to take breakfast at the greasy spoon around the corner, a welcome return to proper English cooking. Mick invariably accompanied him to the café and always insisted on paying. By way of return Bill brought the occasional carton of cigarettes back for him.

The two crates contained handmade floor tiles produced by a small manufacturing company just outside Marseilles. Having undone and folded back the curtain Bill placed the tips of two extended fingers between his lips and let out a shrill whistle. The man on the forklift looked round. Bill pointed to the two crates at the rear and held up two fingers. The man on the forklift gave him the thumbs up. Shortly after Mick and Bill left the warehouse a third man appeared from behind a large stack of crates wheeling a portable oxyacetylene torch towards the truck.

Bill completed his drops in London and Birmingham and arrived back in the depot just before 8.00 on the Friday evening. He unhitched the trailer, parked the cab up and handed the tachographs in at the office which was deserted apart from Craig, whom he found sitting at a desk reading the paper. One of the managers always stayed until all of the trucks that were due in had returned, just in case of any trouble.

"Hi Bill, everything OK?" asked Craig.

"No problem. You here for the night?" Bill replied.

"No. Al's due in about fifteen minutes and the new guy, John Roberts, is coming up from London. Should be here by 9.00 at the latest. That's all for tonight."

"Well I'm off for a nice hot bath and a couple of beers. See you Monday."

"OK. Goodnight."

The phone rang in the man's office at 10.00 that morning. The voice on the other end didn't wait for any pleasantries to be exchanged.

"Fifteen minutes. OK?"

"OK."

The caller rang off.

Quarter of an hour later the man called a number from a phone box four miles from the office. The number he had dialled belonged to a phone box in the East End of London. The voice at the other end had a distinct cockney ring.

"Usual place, 2.00."

"I'll be there."

He replaced the receiver and returned to the flat.

The black Saab 9000 convertible pulled off the M1 at Junction 15A, turned right down the A43 and after two miles hung a left down the small lane which wound through the flat Northamptonshire countryside, coming to a halt at the side of the lane where a small gravel run-in offered a temporary hardstanding. The man stood by the car and surveyed the countryside, the view unrestricted. He was surrounded by large flat fields offering no hiding place for any would-be interloper, the nearest buildings a small village half a mile away, the lane stretching straight as a die for quarter of a mile in either direction. Five minutes later he heard the low roar of the motorcycle engine as it approached from the west. The large Yamaha pulled up beside him and with no more than a nod of recognition the rider, dressed in tightly fitting blue and white leathers with matching helmet, reached into the pannier at the rear of the powerful machine and handed over the package, the man retrieving his own package from within the Saab and handing it to the motorcyclist in exchange. Within seconds the Yamaha was roaring off onto the distance and the man, looking once more up and down the lane, opened the boot of the Saab. A large metal inset which housed the retractable electric hood when lowered took up a section at the back of the boot. He reached deep within the recess of the boot, pulled down the concealed hinged flap previously cut into the side of the inset, placed the package into the opening, and pushed the flap firmly shut. The sweat was pouring down his forehead. He noticed the shake in his hands as he locked the boot, could feel his heart racing. This was the most dangerous part of the exercise, actually handling the goods. Reaching into the glove box of the Saab he pulled out the small silver phial and poured the white powder into the little silver spoon, snorting the coke deep into each nostril, feeling the fear slowly subside as the effects of the drug took over.

The call was made from a phone box at the Stafford services just over an hour later. It was returned ten minutes later.

"Twenty packages. Usual price. 4.00. OK?"

"We'll be there."

He arrived at the airport with half an hour to spare, found a quiet spot on the top floor of the car park, retrieved the package from the boot and carefully undid it. Each half kilo package, wrapped in thick industrial strength polythene and sealed, was carefully placed in the black Antler briefcase, the lid shut and the locks tumbled. The switch went as planned and by late afternoon he was back in the flat counting the money. The money was becoming a problem. After paying for the goods and sorting out the London end he was still clearing £20,000 cash on each run, a figure far exceeding anything he could reasonably clear through his bank account without attracting the attention of the authorities. Luckily his regular trips to the Spanish Riviera provided the opportunity for shifting the money out of the country and into a less structured regime, one where it was not unusual for foreigners with little visible means of support to arrive with suitcases full of ready cash, where few questions were asked as to the provenance of the money provided the owner kept his nose clean and didn't try to interfere in the local politics. To launder the money he'd decided to buy holiday properties that he could let locally without attracting the attention of the British authorities or Inland Revenue. There were always properties available for cash, no questions asked, and he figured that as long as he kept a low profile, no one would be any the wiser. He'd already purchased two flats in a development just outside Fuengirola. When the time was right he would simply announce he was going to work overseas and disappear from the system.

Surrey police caught up with Sheila Watson on Sunday lunchtime, holding her at Leatherhead for over three hours while Mike drove down from Manchester.

"She's going ballistic in there, Sir, threatening to take us to court. Says she'll sue us for wrongful arrest," the duty sergeant said as Mike checked in at the station.

"Good. Is the canteen open? I'm dying for a cup of coffee."

"No, Sir. But there's a machine at the end of the corridor."

"I'll need a woman officer to accompany me during the interview. Anyone available?"

"I'm sure we can find you someone, Sir."

"Right, tell her to meet me at the interview room, ten minutes."

Mike found the coffee machine and composed his thoughts before interviewing Sheila. She'd certainly given a good display in Manchester; he wondered how tough she really was.

He walked in and approached the table, the policewoman behind him waiting by the door.

"What's the meaning of this, Chief Inspector? When my solicitor's finished with you you'll be back in uniform." She was almost shouting, standing by the table.

"Shut up and sit down," he growled in a voice that told her he wasn't messing about.

"I've never known such disgraceful behaviour, I've been...."

"Shut up and sit down," he interrupted, elucidating the words slowly. She dropped into the chair, watching him. "Unless you want to spend another three hours sitting here you will sit quietly and answer my questions. Do you understand?" She nodded.

"Where were you on the night your husband was murdered?" he asked

"I've already told you, Chief Inspector," she replied, watching him, some of the self-assurance gone.

"You've told me a pack of lies. Now, I repeat, where were you on the night of your husband's murder?"

She didn't know whether to call his bluff, wasn't sure how much he knew.

"I was playing bridge at Judy Parfitt's, I've already told you this."

"You're lying. We've checked your story and Mrs Parfitt has admitted that you were not playing bridge at her house that night. Now where the hell were you?" He was angry now, leaning across the table, shouting at her.

"At the gym," she mumbled.

"Which gym?"

"The Body Beautiful, in Leatherhead."

"So why the hell didn't you tell us this before? What is so secret about working out in a gym that you had to lie about your whereabouts?" he asked, already knowing the answer but wanting to make her suffer.

"I was with my boyfriend, Chief Inspector. Jake Kowalski. He owns the gym."

"What time were you there 'til?"

"Until about 11.30."

"And then you went home?" Mike asked, sensing that he had her, the defences destroyed.

"No, I went back to Jake's flat. The kids were on a sleepover. I stayed until about 5.00 in the morning and then I drove home."

"So why did you feed us a pack of lies?"

"Shame, Chief Inspector," she whispered, looking at the floor, tears trickling down her cheeks. "I wasn't feeling very proud of myself."

He'd put her down as a hard-faced cow, now he wasn't so sure. Or was he just falling for the Barbie doll looks and the feminine wiles, the tears turned on and off as easily as a bathroom tap, to be used when needed? You became so used to dealing with low life it was easy to fall into the trap of tarring everyone with the same brush. He addressed her, his tone gentler.

"You will be free to leave in half an hour, please make sure you are available for the rest of the day, I may want to speak to you again."

"Half an hour, Chief Inspector?" she snuffled, wiping her eyes with a tissue.

"I wouldn't want you contacting Jake before I've had a chance to talk to him now would I?" he replied, letting her know that he still didn't trust her, that a few tears weren't about to get her off the hook.

Before he left the station he checked with a detective he found in the duty room.

"Jake Kowalski, runs a gym called The Body Beautiful, anything on him?

"Not really, suspicion of trading in steroids, nothing heavy," replied the detective.

The gym was in a modern retail unit on a side road off the main street, the large plate glass window covered by a Venetian blind, red neon lettering proudly advertising the name. He judged Jake to be in his late twenties, built like the all-Australian surf boy, six foot two of finely tuned muscle with a deep all year tan, the grey singlet and tight blue shorts designed to show off his assets. The white and green machines were spread around the outer wall of the gym, a couple of rowing machines and three treadmills situated towards the centre, the mirrored walls reflecting the images of the half dozen or so clients working out. Mike couldn't help but notice that all the clients were of the female persuasion, all in their thirties or forties and all sporting the type of hairdos and gym outfits that suggested for them money was not one of life's problems. Mike took an instant dislike to Jake. Was it jealousy, he asked himself, looking at the finely honed body, good looking boyish features and easy smile? No, it was more than that.

The guy was too cocky by half, too sure of himself. A conceited, arrogant bastard who looked out for number one.

"The two of you were here together all evening?"

"That's right."

"The gym closes at 8.00, doesn't it? What were you doing here until 11.30?"

Jake flashed a knowing grin, an all-boys-together look. "She's a good looking babe and between you and me desperate for it. What do you think we were doing?"

Jake was leaning on the pine counter, conspiratorial low voice, keeping his eye on the other ladies as he said this. Mike guessed that Sheila Watson was not the only member of the gym enjoying the extra services and found himself feeling sorry for her. He saw it all the time in his job; vulnerable people exploited by nasty little shits like Jake Kowalski.

"So are you telling me that a week last Wednesday evening you and Sheila Watson had sex here in the gym?" He said it loud enough for some of the closer clients to hear, enjoying the shocked reactions on the faces. That'll spike your guns, he thought.

Jake held his finger to his lips, indicating the clients who were now all ears. "That's right, yes, only keep it down a bit," he drawled in the Aussie accent, the face more worried now, some of the arrogance seeped away.

"And do you make a regular habit of shagging your clients?" asked Mike, in a voice loud enough for the listeners to hear.

Jake was angry now. "Now look, Chief Inspector. I don't have to answer that and you've no right to come here making those sort of accusations."

"I'm investigating a murder, Mr Kowalski, and I'll ask any questions I consider relevant. You, on the other hand, are a suspect in that investigation, no doubt requiring a renewal of your work permit and visa in the not too distant future, possibly running a brothel and whom we have reason to believe may be involved in the supply of illegal substances.

Now, you can either answer my questions or I can arrange for a search warrant, rip this place apart and question all your clients as to any sexual impropriety that may have taken place here." All activity ceased, all eyes on Jake.

"A brothel? What do mean 'a brothel'? Christ, alright, so I may be giving it to one or two of the ladies, but that's all. And I didn't have anything to do with that broad's husband's death." He was on the run now; the earlier cool replaced by the look of a trapped animal, forgetting to keep his voice down, no longer caring about the audience.

"What happened after you left here on the Wednesday night?" Mike continued matter-of-factly, the verbal assault having done its job.

"We went back to my flat," Jake replied, all resistance gone.

"And stayed there all night?"

"Yes. Sheila left about 5.00 in the morning. She had to be back in time to meet the kids."

"Anybody else see you? Anybody able to confirm your story?"

"I guess not."

"Good day to you, Mr Kowalski. Should we require any further information I'll be in touch." With that he turned and headed for the exit. All eyes on him, Jake, a broken man, leaning on the counter, face in hands.

Chapter 15

"Check out this Jake Kowalski, let's see if there are any skeletons in the cupboard," he instructed Daniels on the Monday morning.

Bolton CID came on the line at 9.30. "We've just had a missing person report filed. Fits the description of the man you're trying to ID in the bowling green murder."

After taking the details Mike and Daniels drove over to Bolton where the officer in charge brought them up to speed on the limited background available before directing them to the Lister residence. The small, rotund woman wearing a floral pinafore who opened the door was plainly in an agitated state as was the young man sitting on the expensive looking leather chesterfield in the lounge. He rose to meet them as they entered. Mike experienced a fleeting feeling of recognition, he couldn't place him but felt sure he'd seen him somewhere before.

"I'm Craig Osborne, Mr Lister's great-nephew. This is Mrs Jeffries, my uncle's housekeeper."

Mike walked over to the oak sideboard and picked up the picture in its silver frame. The two men were smiling, faces turned to camera, shaking hands. Behind them a banner proclaimed Bolton Leukaemia Appeal. The man on the right wore the chain of office while the man on the left was the man they had found dead on the bowling green on Thursday morning. He turned to Craig.

"Is this your uncle?" asked Mike, showing Craig the photograph.

"Yes, it was taken a couple of years ago at a fundraising do. Uncle is president of the local appeal fund," replied the young man.

"I'm afraid this confirms it. Your uncle is dead. This is the man we found murdered at High Lea last Thursday."

Craig sank back down on to the sofa, mouth gaping, rendered speechless by the news. Mrs Jeffries, still hovering by the open door, burst into tears, hands to face, shoulders heaving. The policewoman put her arm round her shoulder and ushered her towards the kitchen.

"Come and sit down in here, I'll make us a nice cup of tea," said the policewoman as she sat Mrs Jeffries down at the kitchen table.

Craig was still sitting open-mouthed on the sofa clearly stunned by the news. Mike sat beside him.

"I need your help, Craig. I realize this is a very difficult time for you but I need you to answer some questions. We need to find out who did this."

Craig looked at him, nodding, still in a state of shock. Mike noticed the decanter of whisky on the sideboard.

"Would you like a drink? Something to calm the nerves?" he asked, indicating the whisky.

"No, really. It's just such a shock. I'll be alright in a minute. Perhaps a cup of tea?" Craig replied.

Mike nodded to Daniels who went to the kitchen in search of the tea.

Mrs Jeffries was sitting at the pine table, head bowed, tears still streaming down her face. The policewoman looked up as Daniels entered, her brow furrowed with concern. "I think maybe we should call the doctor out, she's very upset. Her husband works for the council parks department. I've sent out a call for him. Let's get him over as soon as we can."

Daniels nodded agreement. "Wait until the husband gets here, he'll know best. Did you manage to make any tea? The nephew's asking for a cup."

"There's some in the pot on the side there."

Daniels returned with the cup of tea. Craig was looking better, recovering his composure.

"You're Mr Lister's nephew, Craig. Is that correct," asked Mike.

"Great-nephew, actually. My mother is Uncle George's niece." The thought struck Craig like a thunderbolt. "My God, Mother. I'm going to have to tell her. She'll be devastated."

Mike felt for him. "Where does she live, Craig?"

"At the moment she's at the flat in Spain. Spends most of the year there now."

Mike was unsure of his ground, wasn't certain of the procedures in such cases.

"We could arrange for somebody to go round and break the news to her. British Consul, perhaps. It might be easier," said Mike, looking to Daniels for confirmation. Daniels shrugged his shoulders, unsure himself.

"No, it's alright. I'll ring Dave. He and Rose run the bar at the complex. They're good friends of mother, they'll look after her."

"Whatever you think is best. I understand your uncle was a widower?" Mike enquired.

"That's right. His wife died a long time ago, from leukaemia. I never knew her, it was before I was born," replied Craig.

"And he never remarried?"

"No."

"Other relatives?" asked Mike.

"None that I know of, not close ones anyway. I think there are some distant cousins somewhere. Mum would know."

Mike kept prodding. "So he lives on his own here."

"Yes. Mrs Jeffries comes in most days just for an hour or so, cleans the house, gives him a bit of company I suppose. But other than that he's on his own."

"What about friends?"

"I don't know really. He has his charity work. I know he's heavily involved with the local leukaemia appeal. And I think he's a member of the local round table. But other than that, I'm not sure."

"What about personal friends? You know, people he went out with socially."

"I don't think he went out much socially, if at all. Never thought about it really. You just sort of assume, don't you? Old man, stays in, watches television sort of thing. Mrs Jeffries would know."

"What about lady friends? Did he ever mention any lady friends?"

"Not to me. Never seen him show any interest in the opposite sex. Bit old for that sort of thing."

Mike decided to change tack.

"When did you last see your uncle, Craig?"

"Let me think. It must have been on Wednesday at the depot."

"The depot?" Mike enquired.

"The haulage depot. My uncle is the founder and chairman of Lister Haulage. He's semi-retired now, just does a couple of days a week, for board meetings and such. I work at the company as a manager. I remember seeing him early on Wednesday afternoon. He was heading upstairs so there was probably some sort of meeting. Toby would know."

"Who's Toby?"

"Toby Mathews, the managing director. Uncle George is chairman, Toby looks after the day-to-day running of the place."

"And you?"

"I'm European Long Haul Manager. Look after the European depots. We've places in Germany, France and Spain."

"Where do you live?" asked Mike.

"Flat on Salford Quays. Been there a couple of years now."

Mike left Craig in the lounge and wandered through to the kitchen where the policewoman was sitting on one side of the table, Mrs Jeffries and a man he hadn't seen before on the other.

"This is Tom, Mrs Jeffries's husband. We've called the doctor out, she's very upset," said the policewoman as Mike entered the room.

Mike guessed that the man must have entered via the back door while he had been talking to Craig. He sat down on the spare seat opposite Mrs Jeffries and leant forward with his elbows on the table. Tom had his arm around the shoulders of the woman whose face was buried in her hands, guttural noises emitting with each heave of the shoulders.

"Mrs Jeffries, my name's Mike Judd. I'm a detective. I need to ask you some questions." He spoke in what he hoped was a soft and sympathetic manner.

The face appeared from behind the hands, the eyes ringed red, tears still flowing down the cheeks. She dabbed at the tears with a tissue and nodded at Mike to indicate that she understood.

"Now, if you don't feel up to it, let me know. But the sooner I get answers the more chance I have of catching whoever did this." It was part of the crude psychology they taught them as part of the training. Put the onus back on the interviewee, give them the responsibility. He'd have to start slowly and work his way in.

"How long have you worked for George?" Mike asked.

"Mr Lister, it's Mr Lister," she replied. "I must have been here, what, twenty-five years at least, maybe longer." Tom, beside her, nodded in agreement.

"And you came in most days?"

"That's right. Apart from Sundays."

"When did you last see Mr Lister alive?"

The sobbing started again, the face disappearing into the hands. The husband gave him a sharp look. Damn. Stupid choice of words. What on earth had he said that for? He quickly wrote a few words in his notepad and pushed it across the table towards the policewoman. She wrote one word in reply and slid it back in front of him. As the sobbing subsided he tried again.

"Alice, when did you last see Mr Lister? It's important," he asked.

The personal approach, that's what they taught them. Gain their confidence.

"Tuesday. Mr Lister was here on Tuesday. He was usually at the depot Mondays and Wednesdays but he was always here on Tuesdays."

"What time would that have been? When you last saw him."

"About 4.00."

"So you didn't see him at all on Wednesday?"

"No, as I said he was at the depot. But he was here on Wednesday night."

"How do you know?"

"The casserole. I said to Tom, He's eaten the casserole."

Mike looked quizzically at the husband who spoke for the first time.

"Alice said on Thursday how it was strange. The bed hadn't been slept in, she was sure of that. But he'd eaten the casserole she'd cooked him. She was worried, but what can you do? Thought he might just have gone away somewhere on business. Wasn't here on Friday either or over the weekend. So she rang his secretary this morning to find out where he was. That's when the balloon went up."

"What sort of casserole was it?" He tried to make the enquiry as casual as possible.

It was Alice who replied. "Chicken and dumpling. With broccoli."

The pathologist's report had been on Mike's desk since Friday morning. The deceased had eaten a meal of chicken and broccoli at approximately 7.30 on the Wednesday evening, so that pretty much established that he was here in the house at 7.30 on the night of his death. So how the hell did he end up dead on a bowling green thirty miles away four hours later?

"Alice, do you know, did Mr Lister go out much in the evenings?"

"Hardly ever. Just occasionally to one of his charity do's. And sometimes to the Roberts's for a meal. But most of the time he stayed in."

Mike knew he had to tread carefully, but the question had to be asked.

"Can you be sure of that? As I understand it you usually leave by the late afternoon. Would you know if he went out later on?"

The implication was not lost on Mrs Jeffries. That the employer she had served faithfully for quarter of a century had kept something from her. That he had some sort of secret life that he kept from her. There was an edge to her voice. "I would have known. Mr Lister wasn't like that. He was a quiet man, a good man."

But the seeds of doubt had been sown. It was possible of course. She read about things like this in the Sunday papers, people leading a double life. But no, not Mr Lister, it just wasn't possible.

Mike decided to let it drop for the time being. He was convinced she wasn't hiding anything, that she knew no more than she was telling.

"I'm sure you're right, Alice. One last thing, did you notice whether the car was here on Thursday morning?" He'd already sent Daniels to check the garage and he had confirmed that the car was missing.

"I don't think so. I don't know really. I don't normally go to the garage. That's Tom's department."

"What sort of car did Mr Lister own?" he asked Tom, already knowing the answer.

"Jaguar XJ12, absolute beauty," replied Tom.

"You've been most helpful. If there's anything at all you can remember, no matter how trivial it may seem, please give me a ring. It could be important." He dropped his card on the table in front of her.

He found Daniels in the lounge. Craig had contacted the bar owner who was going to break the news to his mother. He'd also booked her on the 6.30 flight from Marbella that evening.

"Let's go down to the depot, see if they can throw any further light on his movements. Have the car details been circulated?"

"Yes, Guv. With any luck it won't take long. XJ12s aren't exactly two a penny."

They found the depot on the outskirts of town, an enormous concrete yard with couple of large corrugated iron sheds at the far end and a modern two storey office block off to the right-hand side. Beyond the sheds a warehouse stretched into the distance. About thirty or forty cars were parked just inside the entrance to the yard but other than that it was empty apart from two flatbed trailers neatly parked on the left-hand side. The doors to the sheds were open and Mike could see the mechanics working on the lorry cab inside each one. He guessed that the rest of the fleet was on the road. They made their way over to the offices where news of George's demise had obviously already circulated. The girl behind the reception desk held a tissue to her nose, her eyes were red and watery. Mike flashed his warrant card.

"Tell Mr Mathews we'd like to see him, please."

The girl buzzed through on the internal switchboard. Two minutes later Toby appeared down the stairs that led off from one end of the reception area looking every inch the high flying young executive; expensive suit, blue shirt, brightly coloured silk tie, in his late thirties, with the confident air of a man who knew what he wanted out of life.

They retired to the MD's office and Toby confirmed Craig's story. George had been at the depot all day on Wednesday, attended a couple of meetings, and had left just after 6.00. He wasn't expected in the office again until Monday so they had no reason to suspect anything was amiss until Mrs Jeffries phoned in this morning. Toby was clearly a no-nonsense sort of man, not given to showing his emotions, but Mike could tell he was upset by George's death.

"What about the business? Was George the sole owner?"

"No. George is the majority shareholder, owns seventy-five percent of the stock. My share options give me a fifteen percent holding, subject to company performance, part of the deal when I came onboard as managing director. The other ten percent is held by the family trust."

"So what will happen now?"

"Good question. Depends on the will. Margaret is his only close relative so I wouldn't be surprised if he's left it all to her. But of course there'll be death duties to pay. At the moment I don't know what's going to happen."

Back in the car, Daniels checked with base on the radio. "They've found the car. Parked in the NCP car park under the G-Mex in the centre of Manchester."

"Good morning to you, Tony," the heavily accented English resounded down the street. He finished locking the door and looked round to see Mr Bangani, the landlord, standing in front of his own house next door but one, the small garden of the terrace protected by a low brick wall, methodically pruning the single rose bush that grew from the sparse patch of soil that passed as a garden. "It is a wonderful day to be alive, is it not?"

"Good morning, Mr Bangani. Yes, lovely day," he replied, for it was indeed, the clear blue sky a harbinger of the approaching spring.

Mr Bangani was in his fifties, dressed as always in the grey suit with the long straight single-breasted jacket with four buttons on the front and a white turtleneck shirt.

"I see you were having a fire yesterday," the Indian gentleman commented, hoping to draw him out, anxious to learn more about the young man renting number 12. In India he would simply have come straight out and asked but in England this was considered rude – people protected their privacy, were unwilling to reveal more than the sparsest details.

"Just burning some old rubbish, you know how it builds up," he replied.

Probably destroying perfectly good merchandise that I could have found a home for, thought Mr Bangani, appalled by the waste he saw all around him, brought up in his early years in a world where everything was recyclable, nothing ever disposed of.

"I noticed you had a young visitor on Wednesday night," said Mr Bangani, trying another angle, for he missed nothing of the comings and goings in the street.

"Visitor?"

"The young lady, very attractive if I might be so bold as to venture." Mr Bangani pressed home the attack.

"Oh, right. You mean Jane. She's a friend of mine," he replied, momentarily flustered, wondering how much the nosey old sod had seen.

"A very close friend," Mr Bangani rejoined, the movement of his eyebrows conveying the unspoken question.

"Nothing like that, Mr Bangani. We're just friends.

"It is not my business," he replied. "But it is a big house for one person. You pay the full rent so it is not a problem if you invite guests to stay." Mr Bangani was a businessman but prided himself on his sense of fairness. He did not like to take so much rent for only one person when he knew the property could comfortably house seven or eight.

"I'll bear that in mind, Mr Bangani. Must be going, things to do." And with that he was off up the road.

Most unsatisfactory, thought Mr Bangani. I forgot to ask him where he was going.

Chapter 16

The meeting had been the Super's idea. Mike wasn't so sure but the Super had insisted, said they needed to explore every opportunity, leave no stone unturned. Covering his back, more like, thought Mike. He could guess at the pressure the Super was under to produce a result; so far they had next to nothing. Three murders and not a clue worth talking about. The Watson woman or her boyfriend were still a possibility but Mike thought it a long shot. The boyfriend was hitting on her for cash and she'd already handed over ten grand but there was no indication that either of them was involved in the murders. The previous week, on the Wednesday night, the couple had been to the pub for a drink with half a dozen of his friends before heading back to his flat in Leatherhead for a spot of extra marital activity. There was no way that either of them could have been anywhere near Cheshire at 11.30 that night, and if they weren't involved in the Keith White murder it was difficult to see how they could have murdered Sheila's husband. After talking to Jake he'd called back at her house, torn her off a strip, warned her about wasting police time. He'd also told her, off the record, that Jake was a piece of scum who was rolling half the women in the gym. Why he'd done it he wasn't sure; whether or not she took any notice, well, that was up to her. But none of this left him any nearer to discovering who the murderer was.

The university buildings were set in their own grounds, the campus surrounded by grassy parkland, some five miles to the east of the city centre. Mike made his way to the reception centre in the administrative building from where he was rerouted to the psychology department, an old stone building some two hundred yards further down the tarmacadam drive. Criminal profiling was the 'in thing' at the moment, particularly in America, and Professor Bleasdale was acknowledged as one of the best in the field. The door led through to a reception hall, on the right-hand side of which was a small glass window set in the wall with an enquiries sign above it. He knocked on the window and announced himself to the lady who appeared from the room beyond.

"I'll let the professor know you're here. Won't keep you a minute."

Mike looked around. The building had no doubt once been grand but was now suffering from the ravages of old age and a lack of sufficient maintenance funds. The floor was a patchwork of diamond shaped black and white stone tiles, although many of the tiles were now chipped and cracked, the plastered walls painted an off-white colour where in places it peeled away to reveal the slightly darker coat below. A harsh phosphorescent light adorned the ceiling, the elegant plaster rose of the original light no longer in use. At the end of the reception hall a wide wooden staircase gave access to the floor above, the railings ornately carved, the banister highly polished – a reminder of a more salubrious past – and two corridors led off to either side of the ground floor. A minute later from the corridor on the right-hand side a blonde girl appeared dressed in blue denims, a grey hooded tracksuit top and pink and white trainers. Mike could see straight away that she was a looker. Flowing blonde hair, pretty face, athletic body, the combination was fatal. As she came nearer he realized that she was older than he had first thought, mid-thirties probably. She walked up to him, hand outstretched.

"DCI Judd?"

Mike nodded.

"I'm Helen Bleasdale."

"Call me Mike, please," he mumbled, momentarily taken aback. This was not what he had been expecting. In his mind's eye he had pictured a middle-aged, wiry-haired, slightly eccentric academic in a worsted jacket with leather patches at the elbows."

"Nice to meet you, Mike."

The touch of the hand was disconcerting, disconcerting in a very pleasant way. Ditto the eye contact.

"Let's go down to my office and see what we've got," she said, leading the way back down the corridor, him slightly behind. The rear view was equally appealing. He forced his mind back to the business in question.

"You've read the files?" Mike asked.

"Yes, they were delivered yesterday by a police motorcyclist. Very impressive. We don't normally warrant the VIP treatment," she replied.

"There's information in there that's highly confidential. I'm sure you can appreciate that we have to be very careful that the details of the case do not become public knowledge. We don't want any copy cats appearing or Yorkshire Ripper tapes."

They were both aware of the tapes that had been sent to the police during the Yorkshire Ripper enquiries purporting to have come from the murderer. The details on the tapes had convinced the police that they were genuine and valuable weeks were wasted chasing a red herring before the police finally realized that the tapes were from a crank.

"Don't worry, I've kept them under lock and key. Coffee?" she asked as they entered the office.

The coffee making equipment was on a tray sitting atop a small cupboard in the corner of the room.

"Thanks. White, no sugar."

Mike noted, and was aware of noting, that there were no rings on the left hand as she handed him the mug.

"So, how long have you been at Nottingham?" he asked.

"It will be four years this summer. Prior to that I was principal lecturer in criminal psychology at UCLA for six years and before that the University of Sussex."

"I'm afraid I haven't read any of your books. Criminal profiling isn't one of my stronger subjects," said Mike.

She gave him a frank look, holding his gaze. "You mean you think it's pretty cranky stuff. Alright for us academics to pontificate about but not much use when it comes down to the real business of catching criminals."

He could feel the colour rising in his cheeks; she'd pretty much hit the nail on the head. He couldn't go completely on the defensive.

"There's an element of truth in that. I think you'll find if you talk to most detectives working on the ground they will display a degree of scepticism about how much benefit there is from profiling in terms of actually producing a result. Plus of course very few of us actually ever handle a case where profiling would apply. Despite what the media would try to have the public believe, it's not very often that we are faced with the serial killer syndrome."

Although he didn't know it he'd just passed a major test; had he denied his doubts she would have put him down as a major creep. She knew from experience that the average working policeman had little time for what they regarded as the 'airy fairy concepts' of criminal psychology, were more comfortable with hard facts than the more abstract analysis of human behaviour, found it difficult to accept anything that they couldn't touch, see or taste. In the male-dominated world of the police detective unless they had experienced it for themselves, actually been involved with a case where profiling had helped pinpoint the killer, then they dismissed it as so much nonsense.

She was used to the scepticism, had spent her working life fighting against it. "Well let's see what we can do to convince you. I've read through the case files and there are certainly some very unusual pointers in this case. Firstly, your suspicion that the murderer may be a woman. Now I don't want you to think I'm going all feminist on you or anything but the fact is that, almost without exception, all murders of this kind are committed by men. Where a woman is involved she's usually involved because of the influence of a man. Myra Hindley is a classic example. Bonnie and Clyde if you want to go back a bit further."

"So you don't think it can be a woman?" asked Mike.

"Statistically it's a non-starter. Of course the only concrete evidence you have that points to a female killer is that the second victim was enticed to his death by a woman, or someone who appeared to be a woman."

"Appeared to be a woman?"

"Could have been a man dressed as a woman."

Mike looked doubtful. "We considered that possibility but they'd have to have been very good. It's one thing passing as a women from a distance, it's quite another being able to talk to somebody close up and get away with it."

"All I'm saying is keep your mind open. Just remember that the chances of coming across a serial killer are about one in ten million, make that a female serial killer and you're looking at one in a billion. It's a hell of a long shot."

"What else?"

"The timing of the deaths is pretty weird, it's too precise. Serial killers kill either because the opportunity presents itself or because the urge to kill becomes so overwhelming that they have to go out and make it happen. A good example of the opportunist killer is Hans Kramer, the engineer who killed all those tramps in America. He enjoyed the feeling of power that killing gave him and knew that he could get away with it with the old hobos because nobody was going to notice them missing. But he didn't know when the opportunity would arise. Sometimes he would kill twice in a week; sometimes he went three or four weeks between killings. Your driven killer, on the other hand, is very similar in nature to a typical multiple rapist. The urge comes upon them and they have to go out and do something about it. But that's a biological thing and the biological clock just isn't that precise. Plus there's no obvious indication of any sexual connotation. There's normally a sexual tie-in somewhere. It's the same with the wounds. They're not similar in each case; to all intents and purposes they're identical. Not what I'd expect to see. As if someone's performing to a script."

"So you think somebody's trying to convince us that we're looking for a serial killer to throw us off the real scent?" Mike enquired.

"It's possible. The whole thing started so suddenly. Geographically the crimes are tied to a fairly small area. I presume that you've checked back through the records for any crimes showing a similar pattern."

"We've checked. There's nothing."

"I'd expect to see some sort of history. These people typically build up to their crimes. It starts as assault and then gets gradually worse as they become braver. The demons build in their heads. Of course the perpetrator may have recently moved to the area which would explain the lack of history."

"Anything else?" Mike asked

"Only the obvious, I'm afraid. You're probably looking for a male, aged between twenty-five and fifty who lives alone, has a manual job and comes from a dysfunctional family." She smiled at him as she said it.

"Terrific."

"That's what you were expecting to hear, wasn't it?"

"Touché," he replied.

They discussed the case for a further hour, taking each murder separately, searching for any small anomaly that might offer a pointer, but were left with the same conclusions. Mike had to admire her professionalism, she certainly knew her stuff, was able to quote examples to either prove or disprove any theory that either of them put forward. He also found his mind wandering away from the conversation on more than one occasion admiring her beauty, speculating on her availability or otherwise, formulating lines that would allow him to probe without giving his intentions away, embarrassed when he realized she was awaiting the answer to a question he hadn't heard, caught not paying attention like a naughty schoolboy. Helen was no fool, she was aware of the effect she had on men and sensed his interest. Would he ask her out? He seemed a bit diffident. Pity, he wasn't bad looking and from what she'd seen so far of his character she wouldn't mind getting to know him better.

"I need to make a quick phone call and then how about I take you over to the canteen for some lunch?" she offered.

The invitation sounded too good to miss. "Where is the gents?"

"End of the corridor on the right."

They walked over to the canteen, situated in the rear of the administration block, helped themselves at the self-service counter and sat at one of the plastic topped tables. The canteen was reasonably busy, most of the tables occupied, and while they were eating a couple of young students came over to the table.

"Hi, Helen. Mind if we join you?"

"Be my guest. Mike this is Yvonne and Declan. Yvonne, Declan this is Mike."

Introductions over they continued with the meal. Mike was a bit pissed off that the other two had joined them. He wanted the professor all to himself but they seemed pleasant enough and at least with the four of them there were no pregnant gaps in the conversation, small talk not being one of his strong points. He learnt that they were both post-graduate students; Yvonne a mathematician from Bristol, and Declan a chemist from County Kildare.

After the meal they strolled down the hill to where Mike's car was parked.

"Thanks for all your help, it's been most useful. If you think of anything else please give me a call," he said, trying to think of a reason to engineer another meeting.

"I will."

"Perhaps I could call you if there are any further developments. Get an up-to-date view of things."

"Please do," she replied. "By the way, what did you make of Yvonne?"

Somehow he knew he was being set up, but he just didn't see it coming.

"She seemed pleasant enough. Why do you ask?"

"His real name is Frank. Our resident transvestite. Brilliant mathematician but a bit confused in the gender department." She smiled at him as she said this, softening the blow.

"That was a bit below the belt," he replied but with a grin that let her know he wasn't taking it personally.

"I know but if I'd told you the experiment wouldn't have worked. Pre-warned you would have convinced yourself that you could tell the difference. Don't forget, I'm a student of human nature, I know how the brain works."

Forrest heard them approaching. He'd been asleep on the back seat, the passenger window left six inches open to let in a cooling supply of fresh air and disperse the infragrant farts he let rip at regular intervals. He clambered through to the front, face peering out of the windscreen, looking for Mike.

"What's that?" asked Helen in amazement, seeing the huge black bulk moving about inside the car.

"Forrest Gump," Mike replied. "He's a Pyrenean Mountain dog."

"He's huge," said Helen, laughing now as she approached the car, able to see the giant dog within.

"I know, he just keeps getting bigger," replied Mike with an apologetic look on his face, convinced that people must think him an absolute berk for owning such a dog, unable to see the funny side of the situation. "Is there a park around here? I could do with giving him a quick run out, he's been sitting in the car all morning."

"Let him out here, the university won't mind. If you hold on for five minutes while I nip and get my coat I'll come with you," she said, warming to the man and loving the dog.

Can't be bad, thought Mike, emptying the Sainsbury's mineral water into the bowl, the dog lapping it up. The walk passed quickly, Forrest supplying the topic of conversation as he galloped around the campus, having the time of his life with all his new-found student friends.

As he drove away Mike thought back to the lunchtime and had to concede it had been a convincing display. He had sat opposite the woman for twenty minutes, conversed with her without having the slightest inkling. He tried to picture her again as he drove back towards

Manchester. Was there anything to give her away, something he'd missed? The dark shadow of a beard covered with make-up, the shape of the facial features, the Adam's apple, the size of the shoulders, the way he talked, the way he walked, the expressions he used, some indefinable maleness that would give the game away? He couldn't think of anything but realized that was not the point. If you weren't specifically looking, as he hadn't been and the murder victims presumably hadn't been either, then it was quite possible to be totally taken in by a man dressed in drag, to have no suspicion that you were looking at anything other than a woman.

Chapter 17

On Tuesday Mike paid a further visit to Mrs Jeffries. The terraced houses that lined either side of the street were pre-war with front doors that opened directly onto the pavement. Mr and Mrs Jeffries lived at number 42, halfway up on the right-hand side, but the house was deserted. He settled back to wait. Twenty minutes later he saw her round the corner at the end of the street, headscarf tied under the chin, long quilted brown coat buttoned against the chill, pulling the wheeled shopping basket behind her. He intercepted her as she reached the front door.

"Just a few more questions, if you don't mind, Mrs Jeffries."

"Of course not, Inspector. You sit down and I'll put the kettle on," she replied, removing the headscarf and coat, hanging them in the cupboard under the stairs.

The inside of the house was much as he had imagined it. Not expensively decorated but everything pristine, not a speck of dust to be seen. Small china and brass ornaments, all lovingly polished, covered every available flat surface, the brass reflecting the afternoon light. He noticed a larger piece on the pine dresser, what he took to be a fairy and two elves under a small tree.

"That's nice," he said, privately thinking pottery figurines grotesque.

"Beautiful, isn't it? My favourite. Mr Lister gave it me for Christmas year before last. He'd seen me admiring it. I told him off, said it was too expensive and anyway I wouldn't dare to look at anything in the house if he thought I was angling for it. He said he wouldn't do it again but I was to keep this one because he knew it was my favourite. That's what he was like."

Mike sat at the small round pine kitchen table the cup of tea in front of him, a plate of biscuits between the two of them. He noticed the quality of the bone china and guessed that she'd brought out the best crockery for a visitor, as his own mother would do, that normally it would be a mug for Tom and an ordinary cup and saucer for herself.

"You said Mr Lister rarely went out, but what about visitors?" he asked.

"Well, there's Jim Roberts of course. He came round every Monday without fail. Mr Lister and Jim go back a long way, Jim was one of the first drivers to work for the company. Retired about four years ago after a bit of heart trouble. Mr Lister looked after him alright, financially I mean, pension and what have you. Anyway they always played chess on a Monday night. I'd leave a supper for them. Fish pie usually, that's Jim's favourite."

"Do you know where he lives?"

"Of course I do," she replied, giving him a look, the question stupid. "Just down the street. Number 16. I usually drop a little something in to him once a week. Meat pie or a stew he can heat up. He's a widower you see, Ethel died two years ago."

"Anybody else? Visitors, that is." Mike interrupted, wanting to move her along.

"His great-nephew, Craig, visited about once a fortnight, stayed for an evening meal. And then there's Margaret, Craig's mother. When she's home she stays at the house. But she spends most of the year in Spain; she hasn't been back since Christmas. Mr Mathews from the depot quite often dropped in, discussing business. Had some rows as well, I would hear Mr Lister shouting at him. And the man from the charity – I don't know his name but he was always calling by with papers for Mr Lister and that, things he had to sign, I think." She thought for a minute. "That's it as far as I can recall. He wasn't a great one for socialising."

"And have you noticed anything at all unusual? Anything out of place?"

"No. Of course I've not been to the house since." She paused, becoming weepy, and then gathered herself. "Well you know, since they found him. There's nobody there. Margaret wouldn't stay when she came over, said it would be too upsetting, so she booked into the Railway Hotel. Understandable really, I feel a bit funny about going in myself but I'll go in tomorrow, have a tidy round. Can't let the place go to pot now can we? Mr Lister wouldn't approve of that."

"I'm sure you're right." He liked the woman, she reminded him of his own mother. Same values.

"Is Margaret still at the hotel?" he asked.

"No, she only stayed a couple of days, gone back to Spain. She's coming back for the funeral next week."

"I could do with having a word with Tom, what time does he get back from work?"

"Finishes at 5.00, usually home by ten past. But if you want to catch him he's only down the road at the playing fields tidying up, I've seen him not ten minutes since." She gave him directions.

"If you remember anything at all please give me a ring. Do you still have my card?"

She nodded towards the mantelpiece where the card held centre stage.

He walked up the street and knocked on the door of number 16. Jim Roberts had clearly been a powerful man in his younger days although now the huge frame was stooped and a large beer gut hung over the waistband of his brown trousers. The layout of the house was identical to Mrs Jeffries's but the ambience was totally different. The whole place was in need of redecoration and the place had a slightly damp, musky smell about it.

"I understand you and George Lister were good friends?" Mike asked now that he was seated in the armchair, part of a leather three-piece suite that had seen better days.

"Been with George nearly forty years. We had some times together I can tell you. You couldn't hope to meet a finer man. I'll miss him, the old bugger."

"What sort of man was he?" Mike asked.

"Like I said, you couldn't hope to meet a finer man. Honest, hard-working, fair in his dealings, enjoyed a drink and a laugh when the time was right. Didn't take any messing round, mind."

"What do you mean by that?"

"With the drivers, expected a day's work for a day's pay and no fiddling. If you did he took you round the back."

"Round the back?" asked Mike.

"Aye, did it to me once, when I first started. Course, I was a youngster then, bit hot-headed. Used to collect oranges from the docks at Liverpool and bring them up to the wholesalers in Manchester. 'Course I nicked a few, took some home for the kids and sold the rest to a lad on the market. Anyway the wholesalers must have complained and George cottoned on, took me round the back of the shed, told me he knew what I was up to and gave me a thump."

"And what happened?" asked Mike, fascinated.

"I flattened him. I was a big strong lad in those days, gave him a right shiner," said Jim, chuckling at the memory.

"So he sacked you?"

"No, I helped him up and apologized. I'd got Ethel at home with two young bairns and you didn't have the social like you've got today. Said I'm sorry I hit you George but you took a crack at me first and I'm sorry about the oranges I shouldn't have nicked them. Said it wouldn't happen again and he could dock one pound a week from my wages to pay for them if he'd keep me on."

"And he did?"

"Aye. Took that pound a week from the wages though until all the oranges were paid for. Ethel nearly threw me out when she heard. But then, later that year, he started buying a crate off the wholesaler, everybody with youngsters got an orange a week for each bairn. That's what sort of man he was."

"But he must have made some enemies, somebody he sacked who would hold a grudge?"

"George hasn't been doing the hiring and firing for five years now, it's a long time to hold a grudge."

Mike had to concede he had a point.

"And I understand you used to visit most weeks."

"That's right, every Monday. Been going for almost four years now. It started when I took retirement, because of my heart trouble. Doctors wouldn't let me drive no more. We were joking about. George says 'You'll have to find something to keep yourself occupied, can't be sitting on your arse at home all day'. So I said, as a joke really, 'I'll take up chess, that'll show you.' I was ribbing George you see, it was a joke we had about how we'd both started as lorry drivers but now George was a bigwig, mixed with the toffs at these charity do's, see? So now I'm taking him on at his own game if you take my meaning. Anyway George says 'You're on'. And that's how it started. We were both useless at first of course but we got better. I used to get books out of the library, have all these fancy openings in them, used to drive George potty." He chuckled to himself at the memory.

"So you played last Monday?"

"That's right."

"And did George say anything unusual, anything out of the ordinary?"

Jim paused for a moment, lost in reverie, recalling the evening.

"Not that I can think of. Just the usual banter. What was happening at the depot, football, that sort of thing. Mentioned something about a bit of trouble at the yard."

"What sort of trouble?"

"One of the drivers smuggling a few fags in. Nothing to worry about. Said they'd sorted it."

Mike left his card, asking Jim to call if he recalled anything else, and thanked him for his help.

Tom was clipping the privet hedge that separated the swings from the rest of the play area. Mike took the opportunity to let Forrest out for ten minutes.

"Hello, Tom. Remember me?" asked Mike, standing on the other side of the four foot hedge, his back to the playing fields.

"Hello, Chief Inspector. What can I do for you?"

"Just wondering if anything has come to mind, anything out of the ordinary that may shed any light on the death of George Lister."

"'Fraid I can't help you. I only did the garden, didn't see much of George. The wife's the one for that."

"I know, but I thought I'd better check. I saw your wife earlier, she seems a lot better."

"She thought a lot of George Lister, something like that takes a lot of getting over."

The two men stood for a minute, either side of the hedge, both lost in their own thoughts. Tom was looking over Mike's shoulder. "What the bloody hell's that dog doing?"

Mike turned to see Forrest prancing round an elderly lady who was berating him with her umbrella. "Oh Christ, that's mine. Excuse me Tom, I'd better go and sort it out." With that he ran off across the playing field leaving Tom with an amused expression on his face.

The next port of call was Smethwick Chalmers, solicitors. He found their offices on the high street occupying the second and third floor of a Victorian building, the ground floor comprising two retail units: a men's outfitters and a video shop. Seated behind the large desk, immaculate blue suit set off by a starched white shirt and blue and maroon striped silk tie, gold-rimmed glasses perched on his nose, Mr Chalmers played the part with consummate ease.

"How may I be of assistance, Chief Inspector?" Chalmers asked.

"I understand you acted for George Lister."

"Correct."

"And you drew up his will."

"I did."

"I need to know what's in it."

"You know the rules, Chief Inspector. I can't release details of the will until after the funeral."

"This is a murder case, Mr Chalmers. It's imperative that I know the details of the will." Mike pressed the man guessing that there were considerable sums involved; he needed to know who would benefit from George's death.

"I suppose you have a point, Chief Inspector," Chalmers conceded. "To be honest it's not a situation I've ever encountered before in thirty-three years of practice, my clients don't make a habit of finding themselves murdered. The information would have to be kept completely confidential of course."

"You have my word," replied Mike.

Chalmers opened one of the desk drawers and pulled out a thin fawn coloured cardboard file tied with a pink ribbon. Undoing the ribbon he opened the file and began to scan the papers.

"I take it you wish me to summarize."

"If you would."

"There are one or two personal bequests. £5000 each to three distant relatives, cousins half removed or some such, £50,000 to Mrs Jeffries – I believe that's his housekeeper – £10,000 to a Mr Roberts and £10,000 to Craig Osborne – that's the great-nephew. The house, its contents and £100,000 to his niece, Mrs Osborne, who will also be the sole beneficiary of the income from the family trust. Under the terms of the will the family trust will benefit from an additional five thousand shares in Lister Haulage.

"The five thousand shares, how much are they worth?"

"They represent five percent of Lister Haulage. Their value will depend upon the valuation placed on the business should it ever be sold. As I said, the shares are held in a trust. The real value lies in the income derived from that trust which in turn depends upon the dividends declared by the company. Based on last year's dividend the shares would yield an income of £10,000.

"What about the rest of the company?" asked Mike.

"The remaining shares in Lister Haulage were transferred into a charitable trust some time ago, to avoid death duties."

Mike was trying to remember what Bill Smith had told him.

"That would represent, what, seventy-five percent of the business?"

"Seventy percent, Chief Inspector," Chalmers corrected him. "Fifteen percent resides in the family trust and the remaining fifteen percent accrues to the managing director, Toby Mathews."

"Who controls the charitable trust?"

"The great and good of Bolton, Chief Inspector. A committee of six appointed by Mr Lister and comprising Mr Lister himself, The Right Honourable Douglas Bradshaw, Mayor of Bolton, Superintendent Hargreaves, one of your own, Councillor Anne Fanshaw, leader of the Labour group, Doctor Crawford, an EN and T surgeon at St Bartholemews and the formidable Jean Smedley, headmistress of Highfield Road Comprehensive. They have complete control over how the trust spends its income.

"And what will happen now? Will the committee carry on?" asked Mike.

"Under the constitution of the trust the remaining committee members will select a new member to replace George Lister. The workings of the committee will continue unimpaired."

"What about Toby Mathews's holding? How does that operate?" asked Mike.

"Mr Mathews attracts share options of three thousand shares, or three percent of the business, per annum over a five year period subject to meeting the performance criteria specified in his contract," replied Chalmers.

"And George Lister's death wouldn't affect that position."

"Only if the business was sold, Chief Inspector. In the event of a change of ownership Mr Mathews would accrue the full fifteen percent immediately. But Mr Lister's death does not constitute a change of ownership, the majority shareholding remains with the charitable trust."

"And could the business be sold?" Mike enquired.

"Firstly, the committee would have to approve the sale. They hold the majority shareholding and could therefore block any sale if they didn't believe it to be in the best interests of the trust," replied Chalmers.

"How much would the business be worth if it was put on the market?" asked Mike.

"Not my field, Chief Inspector. But from what Mr Lister said when we were discussing the trust funds I don't think you would see much change out of thirty million."

Not bad, thought Mike. Toby Mathews's shares were worth a cool four and a half million.

"What about the great-nephew, Craig."

"Mrs Osborne's son?"

Mike nodded.

"As the niece is the only named recipient of income from the family trust this will pass to him upon his mother's death."

One final call and he'd head back to the station. He managed to lose himself several times in the Manchester one-way system before finally finding himself outside the G-Mex centre, the former railway station that was now used as an exhibition centre. Daniels had already checked out the car park but he wanted to see for himself. The car park, situated beneath the G-Mex, was a labyrinth of small tunnels and bow-topped openings, being a former stable block where, until the early part of the century, many of the city's horses were housed. The entrance to the car park was protected by two automatic barriers that issued tickets giving time of arrival while the manned exit was at the opposite end of the car park. The natural point of egress was a set of stairs close to the entrance ramp that gave access to the cobbled concourse in front of the G-Mex from which emanated several streets that led to the centre of the city. The manned exit ramp was on the far side of the car park and thus the attendants would be unaware of their customers until such time as they chose to leave.

Daniels was in the ops room, as Mike walked in, seated behind a desk strewn with papers, his right hand wrapped around a polystyrene cup half-full of lukewarm coffee.

"Where's the list of personal possessions for the Lister case?"

He walked over to one of the other desks where a computer terminal sat and punched instructions in via the keyboard.

"Here we are, Guv. What are we looking for?"

Mike stood by the side of him, both men stooped over the desk surveying the list that now appeared on the screen.

"A ticket for the car park. Nothing there. What about the car?"

"Guv?"

"What was found in the car? Was the ticket in there?"

Daniels looked sheepish. "Don't know, Guv. We checked it for prints of course, didn't find anything unusual. Didn't pay much attention to the contents."

"Where is it now?"

"Still in the pound. We were going to deliver it back to the house tomorrow."

"Right. I want that car searched from top to bottom. If George Lister parked his car at the G-Mex then he should have a ticket, otherwise he wouldn't have been able to get out again."

The ticket was nowhere to be found. Wednesday was spent reviewing the case notes on the three murders, going over the evidence for what seemed like the hundredth time. Wednesdays were becoming a nightmare. Each murder brought not only the inevitable feelings of sadness for the loss of life but also a feeling of hope among the team, the feeling that maybe this time the killer had made a mistake, left some vital clue that would eventually lead to his downfall. By the following Wednesday it was obvious to all concerned that this was not the case, that they had exhausted every line of enquiry and were still no nearer catching their quarry. And the next deadline was fast approaching.

The Super called him in late afternoon.

"Do we have any leads at all as to who it is we're looking for?" asked the Super, eyeballing him over the top of his glasses.

"Not really, Sir. No. He or she is not making many mistakes. We're doing all we can, the teams are out on the street everyday asking questions. Sooner or later somebody's going to remember something."

"What about Professor Bleasdale? Was she able to shed any light on the matter?"

"Her view was that statistically we are almost undoubtedly looking for a man and that we shouldn't necessarily presume this to be the work of a serial killer," Mike replied.

"Not a serial killer? That's interesting. What's her thinking?"

"That the patterns are almost too exact, as if someone's working to a prepared script."

"Interesting, most interesting," the Super mused, considering the possibilities. "Look, I'm sorry, Judd, but there's tremendous pressure for a result on this one. The Chief Constable wants to bring in a more experienced man."

Mike thought about the possibility for a moment. The pressure was getting to him as well; there was no doubt about that. But he couldn't see that anybody else could do any more than he was already doing. The teams were working round the clock, every avenue was being explored. The fact was that in all the similar cases he'd studied catching the culprit had never been simple. It was the nature of the beast; you relied on the killer making a mistake. And now it was getting personal. He wanted this bastard.

"Are you questioning my handling of the enquiry, Sir?" Mike asked, facing down the Super's stare, unwilling to be bullied into submission.

"It's not that, Judd. It's just a change of command, you know, look at things from a different point of view, fresh perspective, that sort of thing," the Super prevaricated.

The Chief Constable covering his arse more like, thought Mike. "I'd like to stay with the case, Sir."

"I'll see what I can do. But you need a breakthrough, Judd, and pretty soon, otherwise I don't think there's a great deal I'll be able to do to stop the Chief Constable having his wish."

Chapter 18

They didn't have long to wait on the Thursday morning. Mike arrived at 7.00. A couple of the team were already at work and the rest drifted in over the next fifteen minutes. The atmosphere in the ops room was tense, everybody pretending to work, sifting pieces of paper between files, entering data on to the computer, waiting for the call. All eyes were on Daniels as he answered the phone. He spoke briefly, jotting a couple of notes on the pad in front of him. "Ashley cricket ground. Sounds like our man. Another bloody dog walker," he said to no one in particular.

The team swung into action and within thirty minutes they were at the scene, area sealed off, house-to-house enquiries under way, scene-of-crime beginning their painstaking search of the area. The pitch was surrounded by fields, being some four hundred yards beyond the railway bridge on the other side of which stood the small village of Ashley. The access was via a short dirt track approximately fifty yards long, the pitch largely hidden from the lane by a low hawthorn hedge. Seymour emerged from the cordoned-off area.

"It's the same man alright. Wounds identical. Victim is white, Caucasian, thirty-five to forty-five. Died between six and ten hours ago. Tell you more once we get him back to the lab."

Mike went over to where the body lay. Beige chinos, blue shirt, leather jacket. The wallet was in the back pocket of the chinos, house keys in the jacket pocket. Chris Grant, forty-one years old according to the driver's licence. Barclaycard and forty quid in notes. Address in Urmston.

"Get all the background you can. Check the electoral register and find out from social security where he works," he told Daniels before walking back up the track to where his car was parked, taking a minute to collect his thoughts. He looked longingly at the glove box where the half empty packet of Marlborough still lay hidden. It was moments like this that were hardest. Was he going to have to go and break the news to another unsuspecting young wife, see the look of fear in the faces of the small children? Five minutes later Daniels joined him in the car.

"According to the electoral register he's the only occupant of the address. They should be coming back with a place of work shortly."

Mike realized that he had actually been relieved when Daniels had told him the man lived alone, had actually experienced a moment's euphoria. The poor guy's had his guts ripped out and here's me celebrating the fact that he lives alone. This was what the case was doing to him. He turned to Daniels.

"Let's go over to the house, see what we can turn up."

The house turned out to be flat in a modern four storey block. The place was clean but cluttered. Mike nearly tripped over the golf clubs as he entered the hall; shirts were hanging on the back of the bedroom door waiting to be ironed; the draining board in the kitchen was stacked with washed pots not yet put away; the lounge floor covered with newspapers and magazines. Mike's heart sank as he saw the silver framed photographs on the sideboard: two young girls posing in party frocks; same two girls in swimsuits playing with attractive brunette on beach; the victim, attractive brunette and two girls smartly dressed at somebody else's wedding. He turned to Daniels. "You start in the bedroom, I'll take a look in the lounge."

A couple of hours later they had a fair picture of Chris Grant's life. The pay slips had confirmed what the enquiry to social security had already revealed and they made their way into the centre of town where the small import export company Chris worked for was located. On the drive into Manchester the station came on the radio.

"A Mrs Jeffries tried to reach you, Sir. Couldn't really make it out. Something about a glass."

He flipped through his notebook, found the number and called. No answer. He tried George Lister's house. Mrs Jeffries answered. The voice was timid, scared almost.

"Mrs Jeffries it's DCI Judd speaking. I believe you tried to contact me."

"I don't know if it's anything really, but you said I should ring."

"What is it, Mrs Jeffries?"

"There's a glass missing." She wasn't explaining herself very well.

"Take your time, Mrs Jeffries. What sort of glass, missing from where?"

"One of Mr Lister's whisky glasses, in the lounge. It's missing."

Mike glanced at his watch. "How long are you going to be at the house for, Mrs Jeffries?"

"I've finished really. There's not much to do. Run round with the hoover and do a bit of a dusting."

"Can you meet me back there at 3.00? I'm tied up on something else at the moment."

Chris Grant's work mates were more than a little concerned when the police appeared. Chris had not turned up that morning and they hadn't been able to contact him at his flat. Now the police were asking all sorts of questions but weren't able to tell them what it was about. Chris was a great lad, had worked there for eight years, recently separated from his wife, Susie. He'd been a bit down about that but he saw the kids regularly and accepted the situation. Bit of a lad since the separation, always out on the town. Didn't like to stay in on his own in the evening. Understandable really. He and Tim had gone for a drink last night after work. They'd finished about 7.00 and gone to the tapas bar on Deansgate for a drink. Tim left at 9.00 by which time Chris was a touch on the tipsy side but seemed fine. Said he was just staying for one more and then he'd head for home. No, he didn't have a car with him, always caught the bus into work. Saved paying for parking, which is extortionate in town nowadays, and it meant he could have a drink after work without worrying about the driving.

The tapas bar was just round the corner from the office. Juan, the owner, knew Chris well.

"Ah, is lovely man, Chris. Is good customer. No trouble, like a drink, but no trouble, know what I mean?"

"And do you remember seeing him in here last night?" Mike asked.

"Sure, was in here last night, with Tim."

"That was early on, Tim left at 9.00. What about after that?"

Juan touched the side of his nose with his forefinger. "He doing alright. He talking to young girl at the table in the corner." He pointed to one of the round tables at the far end of the bar. "They have tapas and a few drinks and then they leave."

"They left together?" Mike felt he was finally getting somewhere.

"Sure they left together."

"What time was that?"

"Not late. Let me see, maybe 10.30, maybe a little later," replied Juan.

"Had you seen the girl before? Was she a regular?"

"No, I never seen her before."

The description matched the girl at Mulligans. Mike turned to Daniels.

"You stay here. Question the other staff and as many of the customers as you can find. We'll need statements off them all. Get SOCO over to have a look at the table. I know it's been cleaned but we may get lucky. I'm going over to see Mrs Jeffries."

He arrived at the Lister residence just after 3.00. Mrs Jeffries was already there.

"I'm probably wasting your time, but you did say to ring," said Mrs Jeffries, unsure of herself now, worrying that she was making a fool of herself, wasting the Inspector's time.

"Not at all, we're grateful for all the help we can get. If you could just show me where the missing glass was," said Mike, trying to soothe her nerves.

She led the way into the lounge and walked over to the side table where the silver tray sat.

"Here. There are only three glasses."

Mike looked at the silver tray containing the decanter and three cut glass tumblers.

"And there should be four?" he asked.

"Oh yes. There have always been four."

"When did you first notice it missing?"

"Today, when I came to dust. That's when I phoned you."

"And when did you last see all four glasses?"

She looked bemused. He could almost see the mental cogs ticking over as she pondered the question. "I'm not sure really."

"Please try to think, Mrs Jeffries. It could be important."

She stood thinking for a couple more minutes, getting things straight in her mind. "Tuesday, there were definitely four glasses there on Tuesday."

"How can you be sure?"

"Because I washed two of them on Tuesday morning. Mr Lister and Jim always have a drink when they're playing chess. I won't let Mr Lister put them in the dishwasher, scratches the surface, so I always wash them by hand." He noticed the way she referred to him as if he was still alive, unable to accept the reality.

"But you only washed two of them. How do you know there were four?" He still wasn't convinced.

"I put them back on the tray after I've polished them. I would have noticed if one was missing."

"Mr Lister could have broken it, later in the week."

"Not Mr Lister, careful he was. I've never known him break a thing in all the years I've worked for him."

Mike thought for a moment. George could have broken it sometime between Tuesday morning and his death. What would he have done if he'd dropped the glass? Clear up the pieces. Put them in the bin.

"What happens to the rubbish? What I mean is, if Mr Lister had broken the glass, where would he have put the bits?"

"In the waste bin in the kitchen. Then I empty the waste bin into the wheelie bin."

"And on what day do the dustbin men come."

"On a Monday."

Damn. Another potential clue disappeared. He guessed that the chances of identifying the contents of one wheelie bin from all the other garbage at the local dump were just about zero. He collapsed on to the chesterfield. Mrs Jeffries could see he was worn out.

"Why don't I make us a nice cup of tea?" Mike nodded gratefully. Five minutes later she reappeared with a mug of tea in each hand. She handed one to Mike. Her mind was methodical rather than quick but, given time, she could work her way through a problem as well as the next person. And she wanted to help the police catch whoever had done that to her Mr Lister.

"You want to find the bits of glass, to see if Mr Lister broke it?"

Mike took a sip of the tea. "That's right."

"But I didn't put the bin out last Monday, what with all the goings on I completely forgot about it."

Mike perked up, his interest once more intense.

"And I didn't put it out this Monday, because I wasn't here. Today's the first day I've been in since Mr Lister was murdered."

Mike jumped up from the sofa. He wanted to kiss her. He knew it may be nothing but his intuition was telling him this was important. He wheeled the bin into the empty garage and emptied the contents of the two black plastic bags onto the concrete floor. No obvious signs of any glass.

Two minutes later he was on the phone to the station. "I need a scene-of-crime officer over at George Lister's house ASAP."

It was WPC Owen who arrived thirty-five minutes later. He quickly explained the situation. She spent less than five minutes in the garage.

"Nobody has put the bits of glass in the rubbish. Not unless they've ground them down into fine powder first. Now let's have a look at this carpet," said Owen.

It took her over two hours down on her hands and knees to complete the search of the carpet. In her left hand she held a plastic spatula, about six inches long and quarter of an inch across, while her right hand held the short microscopic lens screwed to her right eye. She carefully moved the tufts of the beige carpet to either side with the spatula, searching deep into the pile for any hidden evidence. Occasionally she would stop, mark a small circle on the carpet in blue chalk, pick up the pair of tweezers from her bag, extract whatever it was she had found, drop it into one of the small plastic evidence bags and make a note on the label. At other times she would merely draw a small round circle in red chalk on the carpet.

"We'll need to run some tests, check that the slivers are from the same type of glass," she said as she finally rose from her knees. "Judging from the pattern I'd guess it dropped about here." She pointed to a spot on the carpets. "We'll need to run DNA tests on the blood spots, see if they belong to the victim. Should we have a look at the vacuum?"

The vacuum was a Dyson, the dust being collected by centrifugal force into a plastic container that was then emptied, rather than the traditional type with a disposable bag. She found further slivers of glass lodged at the bottom of the plastic dust container.

He met up with Daniels back at the station. The enquiry into the death of Chris Grant was progressing. They had good eyewitness descriptions of the girl he had met from half a dozen people, although nobody knew who she was and nobody could remember ever having seen her before. The house-to-house in Ashley had revealed nothing, the houses were too far away for anybody to have heard or seen anything. They had an address for the wife. In all the excitement at George Lister's he'd completely forgotten about the wife. It was 8.30.

"Let's get it over with. Get a WPC sorted out. I'll be with you in five minutes, I just need to make a quick phone call."

"We have another murder plus some interesting developments in the George Lister case. I'd value your opinion. Any chance of a meeting tomorrow morning?" he asked.

"I'm tied up first thing but I could arrange to be free for an hour from about ten, is that any use to you?"

"That would be great, I'll see you at ten."

"One last thing, Mike."

"What's that?" he asked.

"You will be accompanied by your trusty side kick, Forrest Gump, won't you," she teased.

"Huh," he mumbled into the phone before hanging up. The damn dog was getting more press than he was.

Benjie decided it was worth a second shot. He followed the same routine as on the previous outing, parking outside the club, prepared this time when Tommy appeared in the BMW, certain after the first couple of miles that he was following the same route. Reaching the airport, Benjie sped up the ramp on the left and parked in the departures car park, well away from Tommy, certain that he'd find him back in the arrivals hall. Sitting in the café sipping from the cappuccino, face half hidden behind the paper, he started to worry. Still no sign of Tommy. He checked the gold Pageat on his left wrist, 3.50. No sweat, it would be a 4.00 meet. Five minutes later Tommy emerged from the lifts and Benjie relaxed a little. He watched him disappear from view as he entered the corridor, saw a minute later the other man following him in, briefcase in his right hand. Tommy reappeared, bag slung over the shoulder, and headed for the pay station, Benjie waited. Here's my man, thought Benjie, rising from the table and following him through the short corridor and up the escalator.

The man stopped at the car park pay station situated in the concourse and Benjie sidled up alongside him, using the adjacent machine to pay for his own ticket, paying the man no attention, just another busy commuter trying to get through the working day. Must be my lucky day, thought Benjie, realizing that the man was parked in the same car park as he was.

Benjie entered the lift and pressed the button for the sixth floor, noting that the top floor button was already lit, and stood staring at the doors, as people do in lifts, studiously ignoring the other occupant. Leaving the lift he realized that his car was parked too far from the exit ramp to afford him a decent view so he walked down the length of the car park trying to appear nonchalant, another punter who had misplaced his car among the ranks of parked vehicles. He performed a couple of double backs to kill time, neck strained, searching the rows, ham actor in him coming to the floor. The first car down was a Volkswagen but the driver was a woman. He continued his act. Two minutes later the Saab appeared down the ramp and Benjie turned just long enough to memorize the registration number before turning on his heels and walking back down the car park.

In the alley that night he handed the auxiliary, one of the thousands of civilian police workers who undertake the majority of the day-to-day clerical duties, the piece of paper and three hundred pounds.

"Name and address by tomorrow," said Benjie.

"I'm not on until Monday," replied the auxiliary, looking at the note.

"OK, Monday will do."

Chapter 19

Breaking the news to Mrs Grant the previous evening had been dreadful, a total nightmare. The couple had separated six months ago but, if anything, that only seemed to add to the guilt she was feeling. She went into hysterics, sobbing uncontrollably, the children followed her lead. None of her relatives lived close by. Eventually her sister arrived from Liverpool; more tears. And then Chris's parents had to be told, they lived in Bournemouth. In many ways that was worse. He could sense the pain down the telephone, the disbelieving silence, the loss of all that they held dear, two lifetimes destroyed in one terrible moment, no possibility of life ever being the same again. He finally left the house at one in the morning by which time the two sisters were well into a bottle of brandy and had reached the maudlin state. He arranged for Daniels to pick up the wife in the morning to complete the formal identification and headed for home.

The two hour drive each way wasn't strictly necessary, he could have dealt with the matter over the phone, but he needed the break. And he wanted to see her again. He found his own way to her office. The jeans were the same but the top had been swapped for a white t-shirt with 'Is God an Existentialist?' written across the front. Having considered the matter for several seconds, and, he realized with some embarrassment, stared at her breasts for longer than was strictly polite in the process, he decided that you probably required a PhD in philosophy to understand the joke, if indeed it was a joke. He felt the need to explain.

"Trying to understand the slogan. Bit too deep for me I think."

Helen was not unaware of her assets and had concluded after their first meeting that she wouldn't mind seeing more of the Inspector.

"Very clever."

He looked perplexed. "Sorry?"

"Was that 'Bit too deep for me I think' or 'Bit too deep for me,' a slight pause, 'I think', emphasis on the I?"

Now she'd totally lost him. "I'm not sure I follow." He knew he was out of his depth.

"I think therefore I am. As in existentialist," she explained.

And it was he who had initiated the conversation, he thought. It was always the same. Meet someone you fancied and within minutes you'd managed to make a right ass of yourself. It was time to extricate himself.

"Exactly. How about a cup of coffee?" he asked, remembering his college roommate's adage: When you've got yourself into a hole, stop digging.

As she was making the coffee he noticed The Times neatly folded on her desk, the crossword nearly finished. One smart lady. "I wanted to bring you up to speed on the case, there have been some new developments. I'd be interested to hear your thoughts." He quickly explained the circumstances of the latest murder and the discovery of the broken glass and blood spots at George Lister's house. She was sitting behind the desk, drinking the mug of coffee, giving him her undivided attention. When he'd finished she looked over to where he sat.

"And what conclusions have you come to so far?" she asked.

"Nothing very startling. There are a few significant differences between George's death and the other three that don't add up. Firstly, George was considerably older than the other victims. Secondly, George was given an almighty whack on the back of his head prior to death. Thirdly, we can place the other three as being in bars or clubs prior to the killings and in two of those three cases we are certain that they left the bar with an as yet unidentified third party. We can't definitely prove that George wasn't out on the town prior to his death but it seems highly unlikely. He just wasn't the type, unless he was living a double life that none of his friends or acquaintances was aware of. But what would be the point? It wasn't as if he was cheating on his wife or anything like that. If he wanted to go out and enjoy himself there was nothing to stop him. Call it a gut feeling if you like but from all I've heard and learnt about George I just can't believe that he was the type to go gallivanting around the Manchester hotspots of an evening. My guess is that he was attacked at home, hit over the head and knocked unconscious. From there he was taken to the bowling green where he was murdered."

"And what does that tell you?" she asked.

"That the death of George Lister is the key to this case. That maybe the other murders are, as you suggested, nothing more than cover-ups, red herrings designed to put us off the trail," he replied.

"So, what do you want from me?" Given different circumstances his answer to that question might not have been quite so propitious.

"I have four murders to solve. The generally held view is that I'm looking for a serial killer; a mad man or woman who chooses victims at random and kills for reasons that stem from the demons inside his or her head rather than any of the usual emotions we associate with murder cases. I need your views on that," he said.

"Nothing you've told me today has changed my views on this case; if anything they've rather confirmed what I was already thinking. I said last week that many features of the case didn't fit with the normal patterns we would look for, or in some instances fitted almost too well. I can't rule out a serial killer, obviously, but I'm more inclined, particularly given the new evidence in the George Lister case, to lean towards the view that this is someone deliberately trying to mislead you by creating a false trail."

"Thanks."

After last week's visit, he'd been fairly certain that was the line she would take. (Could have been dealt with in ten minutes over the phone.) Still, he felt better for seeing her and right now he needed anything that could give him a lift.

"There's one other point you might like to think about. If someone is laying a false trail, trying to hide a needle in a haystack as it were, then the chances are that either yesterday's murder or the next one will be the last. That would complete the pattern," Helen said.

He could see what she was getting at. A couple of murders either side of the one they were trying to hide. No need for more than that. And it was getting riskier for them with each additional murder; they wouldn't want to carry on with more than they thought was absolutely necessary to establish the false trail.

"You could be right," he replied.

"I could ask our games theorists to have a look at it if you like. That's their speciality, predictive behaviour patterns."

Mike didn't know exactly what games theorists did but it conjured up an image of young anoraks playing games on computers. He could just imagine the Super's reaction.

"I'll pass on that for the time being. I'd better be getting back to the fray, see what the boys and girls are up to. Thanks for all your help."

"Aren't we taking Forrest for a walk?" she asked, the tone mildly disappointed, the look of a little girl denied her sweeties.

"If you have the time he could do with a quick ten minutes," Mike replied, wondering which interpretation to put on the question: was it just the dog whose company she enjoyed?

They strolled quickly around the campus, Forrest running among the students as they swapped buildings between lectures, the majority making a fuss of him before proceeding on their way, Helen providing a running commentary on the various departments housed within each facility. Completing the circuit they found themselves back at the car.

"Thanks once again for all your help," said Mike.

"Anytime. It was nice to see you again," she said, holding his gaze.

What interpretation do I put on that, thought Mike. I mean, that could be taken as a come on couldn't it? He wasn't the most forward of men when it came to his dealings with the opposite sex, he knew that.

It normally took at least half a dozen carefully contrived casual meet-ings, (of the, 'fancy you being in here tonight' variety), checking out the response, before he summoned up the courage to ask someone out. But it was going to be bloody difficult contriving any sort of meeting with someone who lived a two hour drive away. He couldn't keep popping over the Pennines every week for a quick case update.

"Maybe we could get together one evening, go out for a meal, if you'd like to," said Mike, wondering if he was overstepping the boundaries of professional behaviour, waiting for the brush off.

"Sounds like a great idea. Give me a ring, we'll sort something out," she replied, turning and heading back up the driveway.

It never varied, that feeling of accomplishment when you finally took the plunge, risked the humiliation of refusal and attained the treasured first date. It was exactly the same now as it had been when he was fifteen. What was her name? Janice Morgan, that was it. A night at the Edgbaston Odeon. Mike ruffled the dog's coat between the ears as they headed for the exit. "You're not the only one who can pull the birds, you know," he told the dog. He hadn't felt this good in ages.

The ops room was quiet when he arrived back in the late morning. Most of the team was out on house-to-house following up on the Chris Grant murder. Daniels was sitting behind one of the desks, a mountain of paper-work in front of him.

"Any joy in Nottingham, Guv?"

If only he knew, thought Mike. "Confirmed what we suspected. The professor wasn't prepared to rule out a serial killer but thinks it's odds on that someone's trying to pull the wool over our eyes. How did the identity go?" Mike asked.

Daniels grimaced. "She confirmed it was her husband. Emotionally she's shot to hell. Had a lot of trouble dealing with it. I left the sister with her."

"Poor bastard, and if we're correct in our thinking the guy's death is a total waste. They aren't fooling us anymore. Did anything turn up on Jake Kowalski?"

"Financially he's in a mess," Daniels replied. "He's up to his ears in debt and his suppliers are threatening him with repossession unless he comes up with the money. So far he's just about staying afloat. There have been half a dozen cash payments into his account that can't be accounted for ranging from five hundred pounds up to four thousand. Totals about eighteen thousand so he's finding money somewhere."

"His lady clients is my guess," replied Mike, a look of distaste on his face. "Sheila Watson told me she'd leant him some money and he admitted to me he was hitting on some of the other clients. He implied it was purely sex but Jake's the type who wouldn't think twice about putting the squeeze on them."

"So, couldn't he have cooked something up with the Watson woman? There's a couple of million involved."

"Jake Kowalski loves two things in life; himself and money. I asked Sheila Watson about the money the last time I saw her, when I told her a few home truths about her boyfriend. The fact is Jake knew she was worth a few bob but didn't know anything about the share options until after the murder. Then there's the logistics. It would be damn difficult to plot all this from Surrey, you'd need an accomplice working up here and I don't believe Jake has those sorts of connections. Besides, I don't think Jake has the balls for it. He's all wind and piss, an opportunist who's not averse to taking advantage of the fair maidens, but I can't see him being up for anything like this. George Lister's the one to look at. That's where the key lies. Jake Kowalski may be a nasty little piece of scum but I don't believe he has any involvement with the murders. Lister was worth a fair few bob, the problem being that the majority of the money is tied up in trust funds which doesn't help us much in establishing a motive, but there has to be something we're missing." He paused, reflecting, searching his brain for the missing link. "What is it you're working on?" He indicated the heap of files covering Daniels's desk.

"There's something in here, I know there is. It's been niggling me ever since you updated me about the George Lister case. I just can't put my finger on it but it'll turn up eventually."

Mike nodded. A murder investigation produced a mountain of paper-work – witness statements, pathologists' reports, scene-of-crime reports and a hundred of other bits of information all logged and recorded. That was often the problem, sorting out the wheat from the chaff. Finding the one bit of really useful information from among all the dross.

"Super said he wants to see you as soon as you reappear," Daniels informed him, the look indicating rather-you-than-me.

"Better not keep the man waiting."

The meeting with the Super went reasonably well. True he couldn't think of anybody at this moment in time with a motive for killing George Lister and that, he had already admitted to himself, was a bit of a flaw in his argument. They were going to have to wait a week for a DNA match on the blood samples which Mike still felt was too long, but that was better than the three weeks they had originally been quoted before the Super's intervention. He told the Super about the criminologist's views on the serial killer. He noticeably perked up.

"Can we get anything in writing on that? Something to show to the press? Kill all this Cheshire Slasher nonsense?" he asked. It would also calm the Chief Constable down, thought the Super. If it was just a normal murder case, obviously, absolutely terrible and all that, but a serial killer was a whole different ball game.

"I wouldn't have thought so," replied Mike. "The professor's hardly likely to put her professional reputation on the line just to help us out of a jam."

"Have a word with her, see what you can do," suggested the Super. "Make it easier to keep you on the case as well. Not the same pressures you see. If we don't have a serial killer on the patch, well, there are not the same pressures at all."

Back in the ops room he spent the afternoon catching up on the reports filed by the team over the previous twenty-four hours and trying to think of a possible suspect in the George Lister case. Nothing came immediately to mind. He was going to have to start again from scratch, re-interview everybody, only this time probe a little more deeply. By 8.00 he decided he'd had enough for one day.

"I'm heading for home. Fancy a quick drink? I'll buy you a pint," he said to Daniels.

Daniels was still had his head down, wading through the paperwork. "I'll take a rain check on that, Guv. I'm sure there's something important in here, it's just a matter of nailing it."

"Your wife must be very understanding."

Daniels looked at his watch. "Oh Christ, it's her aerobics night. I was supposed to be home by 7.00 to look after the kids."

Mike gave him a rather-you-than-me-sunshine look and left him dial-ling the number. A hot bath, an Indian takeaway, a couple of cold lagers and an early night beckoned.

Chapter 20

The cab was his pride and joy. The three month old Volvo supertwin had all mod cons: air con; radio cassette; adjustable seats; power steering. She was a beauty. He circled her, the final inspection before climbing on board. The livery was immaculate; it was one of the company rules. The red paintwork glistened in the early morning sun setting off the white lettering with silver outline. Both cab and trailer had to be kept in pristine condition at all times, they told them that at the meetings. The truck was a large, rolling advert for the company, the drivers the company's ambassadors. Load of bullshit really but he didn't mind. They were a good company to work for and he should know, he'd worked for some right dodgy companies in his time, real cowboy outfits. At least at Listers they played by the rules, checked your tachos after each run. If you were over on your hours you were given a warning, told that if it happened again you could be dismissed. Satisfied that everything was in order he pulled himself up into the driver's seat and turned the ignition over, listening to the twelve cylinder turbo charged diesel spring to life.

It always made him feel good, the power of the engine throbbing beneath his feet, knowing that very shortly now he would be off and away, free as a bird, with nobody looking over his shoulder. He glanced through the paperwork as he gave the engine five minutes to warm up, making sure all the export documents were present and correct. He'd read in the papers about how the European Union was going to make life easier, how it would make it all like one big country with no border checks to worry about, no forms to fill in. All he knew was that if you arrived at Calais without all the papers in order then you could spend hours waiting for the correct documents to be faxed through. More trouble than it was worth. It had happened to him a couple of times when he'd first started the south of France run and now he always double checked all the papers before he left.

Satisfied that everything was in order he reversed the cab out of its parking slot and crawled across the yard in second gear to where the curtain-sided trailer lay waiting, the load already on board, the fork lift fetching the crates from the warehouse at the back of the yard and dropping them onto the flatbed. There were just a couple more collections to make on the journey south to Dover; one in the Midlands and one in London. The cab jolted slightly as the large round metal plate on the rear of the cab made contact with the connector on the trailer. He gave it a little more gas and felt the thud as the connector pushed home. Ten minutes later he'd finished connecting the hydraulics and electrics and was heading towards the roundabout on the M62.

Daniels was slumped across the desk, head cradled in his arms, sleeping like a baby. It didn't take a genius to work out that he'd been there all night. Mike placed the mug of coffee on the desk and gently shook his shoulder.

"Wakey, wakey."

Daniels was disorientated for the first few seconds, wondering where he was. Then, as dream became reality, a moment of embarrassment. He'd nodded off at his desk, been found asleep on the job. He'd noticed that recently, mid-afternoon and he could really fancy a quick forty winks. Then he remembered. He'd been going through the files, had finally found the answer. He was dog tired, better head for home. He'd checked his watch. Quarter past four. Cathy would go bananas of course, arriving home with the milkman. He'd just rest his head for a minute before he took off.

"Sorry, Guv. Must have nodded off last night."

Mike indicated the cup of coffee. Daniels had been in the office right through the weekend, working his way through sheet after sheet of paper. It made Mike feel guilty about sloping off on the Sunday afternoon, but there wasn't a lot more he could do until the next set of reports arrived on his desk.

"And did you find whatever it was you were looking for?"

A look of triumph appeared on Daniel's face. "Certainly did, Guv. Remember the missing key at Tatton Park? The Keith White murder? We couldn't narrow things down much because the park wardens had lent it out to God only knows how many people. I asked the marketing manager for a list of all the companies who've used the park for corporate entertainment in the last year, just for the record really, I couldn't see that the information was going to be of any use to us. Guess who's on the list?"

Mike allowed him his moment. "Come on, the suspense is killing me."

"Lister Haulage," he announced. "Had a do there in January of this year."

"Well, there's a coincidence. It seems that all roads lead to George Lister in this case. You go home and get some sleep, I'll go over to Tatton and see what I can find out."

He thought about objecting, he wanted to stay with the case. But he felt like shit, he was getting too old for this staying up all night lark. A couple of hours would see him all right.

"I'll catch up with you later."

"No problem. Oh, and well done Daniels. Good piece of detective work."

He found the entrance to the park without difficulty and, having received directions from the lady manning the pay kiosk at the entrance, drove towards the hall that housed the manager's office. With so many other things on his mind he hadn't really taken in the size or beauty of the park during his earlier visits. The driveway wound through the rolling parkland, a herd of deer grazed in the pastureland to his left, the large mere was on his right and in the distance he could see the hall nestled among a copse of trees. The hall was an imposing Edwardian mansion of substantial proportions, being the former seat of Lord Tatton, who, upon his death in 1958, had left the hall and parklands to the nation.

The manager's office was situated in a small ante-room on the ground floor. He ascertained that there were four wardens responsible for gate security and that three of the four were currently on duty, the fourth not being due on until 2.00. The three on duty, among whom he recognized the warden he had encountered on the day of the murder, were unable to recall anything of significance. The omens weren't good. The marquee had been set up some weeks before by an entertainments company for the New Year's Eve bash and was subsequently hired out to local firms on a nightly basis throughout the first three weeks of January. The tent came ready supplied with chairs, tables and dance floor. It only remained for the companies booking the marquee to arrange the catering and music. He had a couple of hours to kill until the final warden was due and, after taking Forrest for a long walk, spent the time looking round the magnificent museum housed within the hall.

Seated behind the desk in the office that he had commandeered for the morning's work, to the obvious displeasure of the manager, he began the final interview.

"Do you remember a company called Lister Haulage holding a corporate evening here in January?"

The man struggled with his memory. He was one of life's helpers, Mike could tell that. He desperately wanted to be of assistance but couldn't for the life of him recall anything about the company. There were so many of them, you hardly paid them any mind.

"Not that I can recall," the man replied having thought for some moments.

"Please try to remember. There was a marquee over by the children's area for the first three weeks of January. Listers had a company do there on the Thursday night of the third week," Mike tried again.

He was still struggling. He could remember the marquee. There were far too many of these big company dos as far as he was concerned. They may bring in the money, but it wasn't right. Not what the park was meant for.

"I remember the marquee. Made a right mess. Had to replace a load of turf."

"And Listers?" asked Mike.

Something clicked into place.

"Haulage company, you said?"

"That's right."

"There was a lorry came in one evening. Big articulated job, parked right outside the marquee. That was a haulage company, forty years anniversary or something. Wanted the truck there as a sort of symbol to show off, if you see what I mean."

"And was it a Listers truck?" asked Mike, sensing that he was at last making progress.

"Couldn't say, not for sure. Might have been."

"What colour was the truck? Can you remember?"

"Red. Definitely red. Beautifully turned out. That's why I remember it. Paintwork all polished, chrome exhausts, looked an absolute picture."

"What time did it arrive?"

"Couldn't say. It was after I'd gone. We finish at 5.00 in the winter. No point in staying after that, the light's gone."

"But you just said you saw it. You said the lorry came in and you saw it." There was a note of aggression in Mike's voice. He hadn't meant it. It was exasperation, going round in circles, getting to the truth. The warden gave him a look. Here he was trying to help, and this young bugger was getting all uppity. He didn't need this. Mike realized he'd made a mistake, pushed too hard. He backed off.

"Sorry, it's been a long day. Gets to you sometimes. Same in your job I should think?" Mike apologized, trying to get the man back on his side.

"Oh, we have some right fun and games I can tell you. It's the management, haven't got a clue."

Mike cut in. "Let's get a cup of tea, I'll treat you."

He let the man waffle on for ten minutes while they drank the tea. Sensing the moment he nudged him back on course.

"Tell me about the truck again. Exactly how it happened," he asked.

"I saw the truck in the morning when I came on duty. It was parked outside the marquee."

"But it wasn't there the previous evening, when you left?"

"No. I'm sure it wasn't. I remember now, I lent them the spare key. They couldn't bring the truck in 'til later, it wasn't ready."

Something was still niggling Mike, something that didn't quite fit.

"The key you gave them, that's for the padlock on the main gates, right?" Mike enquired.

"That's right."

"What about the pedestrian gates, does the key fit all three padlocks?"

"No, there are three separate keys, one for each padlock. But they're all on the same key ring."

"So you gave them the key ring? The complete set of keys?"

"That's right."

Mike tried to keep the excitement out of his voice. "Who did you lend the key to? The man's name."

"It wasn't a man. It was one of the girls helping set up the tables inside the marquee. Pretty young thing. Didn't get her name."

"And what about the keys? Were they returned to you the next day?"

"No. I told her to drop them off at the office when they'd finished with them."

Mike checked with the manager but he had no recollection of the incident. Happened all the time, it was not something that was liable to stick in the mind. But somebody at Listers had access to that key, somebody could have copied it. He recalled the conversation with Jim Roberts the previous week. Something he'd said about one of the drivers.

Jim was at home. A keen student of the turf, he was engrossed in the Channel Four coverage from Chepstow when the ring of the doorbell disturbed him. Mike eased himself into the armchair. "Tell me again about the conversation on the Monday night prior to George's death. As much detail as you can remember."

"We didn't talk that much, we were concentrating on the chess. As I recall we started off talking about the football and whether or not Bolton would make the play-offs. I didn't think they would, difficult run-in. George reckoned they might, if they could beat Ipswich away. Well they didn't, did they? Drew one each. Unless they can get a result down at Charlton I don't think they've got a prayer."

"It's not so much the football I'm interested in, more the depot. George said something to you about trouble at the depot," Mike interrupted.

"Not really trouble, just one of the lads trying it on a bit, smuggling fags in. Said they'd given him a right bollocking. George had been a bit worried by it, playing on his mind. But now they'd sorted it, I remember that distinctly, said the problem was sorted."

"Did he say who the driver was?"

"He did mention a name, but it wasn't anybody I knew. I've been retired a few years now you know. New faces come in, you lose touch."

"You can't remember the name?" asked Mike.

"Sorry, no. Is it important?"

"It could be. Listen, Jim. If I brought a list of names do you think you might be able to pick him out?"

"It might jog the memory. Worth a try."

Chapter 21

The offices of Marshall Lomas were situated between a dentist's surgery and a play school, the majority of the Victorian detached houses in what had once been an affluent residential area now used for commercial purposes, unsuited to the requirements of the modern family, the upkeep too expensive, designed for an era when servants were plentiful and families large.

"Tell me about Lister Haulage," said Mike, addressing James Marshall who was seated on the other side of the desk.

"What exactly was it that you wanted to know?" he replied, parrying the question.

"How are they doing financially? Any skeletons in the closet? That sort of thing." Mike asked.

"Financially they're fine. Last year's accounts are available for anyone to inspect, Chief Inspector. There are no secrets," Marshall rejoined. Mike felt sure he was holding back; it was nothing he could put his finger on but the man seemed uneasy.

"If the company was put up for sale how much would it be worth?"

"Difficult to say, depends on who was interested. Somewhere between twenty-five and forty million." Marshall replied.

"And has anyone suggested putting the company up for sale?"

"Not to me, Chief Inspector."

Marshall was surer now, the edginess gone. Mike was on the wrong track.

"What do you know about Toby Mathews?" Mike asked.

"Toby Mathews, Chief Inspector?"

"Yes, Toby Mathews. The managing director of Lister Haulage. I take it that as their accountants you are not unaware of the man," Mike said, pushing Marshall, keeping the pressure on.

"Right, yes, Toby Mathews. Embarrassing situation. We recommended Toby to George, that would be about eighteen months ago. George was looking to take more of a back seat role. We knew Toby from our dealings with Kennedys; they are another of our clients, a large haulage company based in Macclesfield. We recommended George take a look at Toby, thought he might fit the bill. Nothing official of course, just a friendly word in the ear."

"Why did you say 'embarrassing'?" asked Mike.

"Toby hasn't performed up to standard, failing to meet the targets. Seems there was also a bit of a character clash between him and George, different ideas on how to take the company forward. Always a problem when the founder hands over the reins. Used to having things their own way you see, find it difficult to let go. Between you and me George came to see me about a month ago. Wanted to find a replacement. Didn't think Toby was up to the job," replied Marshall.

"And did Toby know this?"

"Shouldn't have thought so. I imagine George would have kept his own counsel until he'd found a suitable replacement."

"But you said not five minutes ago that they were doing all right financially."

"They are. No danger of going under or anything like that, still making a healthy profit. But George set some fairly ambitious targets, particularly on the European front, wanted to keep growing the business. He could see that the proposed expansion of the European Community and the continued growth in trade between EEC members presented a unique opportunity. By establishing an EEC wide presence he could steal a march on the competition."

"And Toby didn't agree with him?" asked Mike.

"Not so much that he didn't agree, more a question of priorities. Toby wants to concentrate resources on centralized computer booking systems and a new Internet-based load clearance system. It's something a consortium of the larger haulage companies is working on. George thought it was a load of baloney. He was from the old school, not into computers, thought Toby was wasting the company's money."

"And was he?"

"Your guess is as good as mine, Chief Inspector. Predicting the future is never easy. But on balance I would say, looking at the way the world is progressing, Toby's strategy is pretty sound. The real problem is that Listers is too small to compete in the modern world. They don't have the flexibility of the small one or two truck operators and they don't have the financial muscle to compete with the big boys. A takeover may well be the best option for them in the long term."

"Mathews has some pretty healthy share options, doesn't he?" asked Mike.

"That's right, and that was one of the problems. George was worried that if he left it any longer it would cost him an arm and a leg to replace Mathews. He'd have to buy out his options."

"How many options does he own at the present time?" Mike asked.

"None, he didn't qualify. The options only come into effect if he meets his targets. That's why George was keen to move quickly."

Mike and Daniels went to see Mathews the following morning.

"Did George ever mention to you that he'd discovered one of the drivers smuggling cigarettes?" asked Mike.

"Not a thing. It would mean instant dismissal of course. Any suggestion of anything like that and customs and excise would be down on us like a ton of bricks," replied Mathews.

"But he mentioned it to Jim Roberts. Said it had been 'sorted', to quote his exact words."

Mathews shook his head slowly from side to side, a resigned look upon his face. "Doesn't surprise me. George was very hands on for a chairman. You have to remember that he built the company up from nothing, it was his baby, and he sometimes had difficulty letting go. Things were very different in the old days; it was a tough old game and there wasn't the mass of regulations to deal with that there is today. All the drivers were at it in those days, give them an inch and they'd take a mile. George was a tough old bastard; he knew how to look after himself. The old ones still talk about it in the canteen: 'George caught me nicking diesel. Used to siphon a few gallons off and sell it to old John Watson. He ran a tipper in those days. Anyway, George took me round the back of the shed, gave me a right hiding.' That was the way it was. Of course, you can't run a modern business in that way, but George couldn't always see that."

"So you think that's what happened. He dealt with the problem in his own way."

"I guess so. He certainly never raised the subject with me," replied Mathews.

"I'll need a list of all the drivers that have been on any of the continental runs over the last three months."

Mathews spoke briefly into the phone. Mike changed tack.

"You had a company do at Tatton Park in November?"

"That's right. Fortieth birthday. Thought we'd push the boat out a bit. Reward the staff for their hard work."

"Who organized the do?" Mike asked.

"I put Craig in charge. Wasn't that much to do really, once we'd decided the venue."

"But you had some people on site, helping to set it up."

"You mean Linda and Jean from reception. They went down in the afternoon to give it the woman's touch. Flower arrangements for the tables, folding the napkins into pretty shapes, that sort of thing," replied Mathews.

"And what about the truck that you took over? Who drove that?"

"That was the new Volvo, only took delivery a couple of weeks earlier.

That's Bill Fenwick's cab. I remember joking with Craig about it in the afternoon. Bill was on a London run, supposed to be back mid-afternoon so that we could tart the truck up. Of course, sod's law, there's a pile up at Birmingham. M6 is at a standstill. Anyway, luckily things started moving again and we managed to get it over there with about half an hour to spare."

Mike looked Mathews straight in the eye. "When I spoke to you last week you said that you had share options giving you fifteen percent of the company."

"I said that my holding would eventually be worth fifteen percent, subject to performance," Toby answered.

"But that's not strictly true, is it? According to our information you haven't received any options to date because you didn't make the financial targets." Mike pushed the dagger home, looking for a reaction.

Mathews didn't miss a beat.

"That is true, Chief Inspector, but it takes time for plans to come to fruition. I am confident that in the fullness of time the restructuring I have put in place would have paid dividends."

"Did you know that George Lister was planning to replace you?" asked Mike.

He seemed genuinely shocked. While he had accepted the news of George's death with equanimity this personal assault upon his self-esteem was far harder to take.

"No, I didn't, Chief Inspector," Mathews replied, sitting back in his leather executive chair, a look of disbelief on his face.

Jim Roberts sat at the kitchen table, the list lay in front of him. He'd crossed out a dozen of the seventeen names straight away.

"It wasn't somebody I knew. It must be one of these five but I'm buggered if I can remember which." Daniels was behind him, looking over his shoulder.

T. Butler

B. Riley

A. Jones

W. Fenwick

S. O'Malley

Daniels took hold of the list. "Give me two minutes, Jim. I just need to make a quick phone call."

He disappeared into the hall and returned momentarily with a new list that he placed on the table.

Tom Butler

Ben Riley

Alan Jones

Bill Fenwick

Sean O'Malley

"Does that help?" asked Daniels.

Jim studied the new list. "Bill Fenwick. That's him. I'm sure of it. Aye, Bill Fenwick."

They headed back once more to the depot.

"I think it's time we had a word with Mr Fenwick." Mike was convinced that they were on to something. Trouble was, he wasn't sure what.

"We've not much to go on, Guv," said Daniels.

"I know, but let's see if we can rattle his cage a little, see if it produces a reaction."

The girl behind the counter was the same one he'd seen earlier. Seventeen or eighteen, he guessed, not bad looking, but a bit on the tarty side. A little too much make-up, the blonde streaks too vivid, the blouse a touch tight across the chest. The nametag attached to the blouse proclaimed her to be Linda.

"Hello again, Linda. I'm trying to find Bill Fenwick."

"He won't be back 'til Friday. He's doing the Marseilles run. Left on Monday."

Damn, thought Mike, momentarily caught off balance. He couldn't have him recalled, not enough evidence for that at this stage. On the other hand, waiting three days to interview the man could potentially waste a great deal of valuable time.

"What time is he expected back on Friday?"

"Friday evening. He never gets back till well after I've finished, about 9.00 I think."

Even worse. Not a lot he could do though. He'd have a word with the Super, see what he thought.

"Thanks Linda."

"Any message?"

"No, that's OK. Thank you."

Ten minutes later Craig sidled down the stairs from his office on the first floor. She quite fancied him but in the ten months she'd worked there he'd never shown much interest. Plenty of talk but no action.

"How are you doing, gorgeous?"

"OK. It's quiet this afternoon though."

"Time for a quick snog behind the filing cabinets, then?" he asked, eyebrows raised.

She giggled. It was one of his standard lines. Nothing ever came of it, but she couldn't help but feel flattered. "You wouldn't dare."

He put on a broad Lancashire accent. "Just you wait 'til works outing lass, thou and me on't back seat of charabang."

He wasn't at all like a boss, always playing the fool, always messing about.

"Was that Chief Inspector Judd I saw leaving a minute ago?" he asked.

"That's right. Looking for Bill Fenwick. I told him he wouldn't be back 'til Friday."

"And what have you got planned for tonight? Clubbing it in town?"

"No, not tonight. Quiet night in. Watch the TV."

"Oh well, I suppose I'd better head back to the grindstone, somebody has to keep the company going," he said, heading back upstairs.

God, he never takes the bait, thought Linda. I'll have to try harder.

Back in the ops room Mike and Daniels reviewed the situation. Despite the fact that he was now convinced that a serial killer wasn't at large, and that all the murders were somehow linked to the death of George Lister, Mike nevertheless could not ignore the looming Wednesday night deadline. He had agreed with the Super to put out a press release, although they both thought it sounded faintly ridiculous.

"Following the recent spate of murders in the Manchester area police are warning single males in the area to be wary of accepting a lift from a young, white woman in her mid-twenties with medium length brown hair. It is thought that the woman may be a transvestite and is believed by police to be heavily implicated in the crimes."

"What's your thinking on Bill Fenwick, Guv?"

"I'm not sure exactly. It's just a gut feeling that he's involved somehow. Everywhere we turn his name crops up."

"But he couldn't have murdered Dennis Watson, he was in France at the time."

"I'm not saying he's the murderer just that he's involved. My guess is that the girl, or boy, in the bar is doing the actual killing. What I'm looking for is motive."

"Which is the smuggling racket?"

"Could be. Marseilles is one of the main shipment centres for narcotics in Europe. There's a hell of a lot of money in that game and in my experience that equals a hell of a lot of motive. The truck gives them the perfect cover for shifting the stuff. Then George stumbles upon the hiding place so they have to bump him off. But they don't want anybody putting two and two together so they try to make it look like a random killing."

"How do they get to George? He never goes out."

"Precisely. That's why they have to visit the house. George knows this driver from the depot. He's just given him a right ticking off because he thinks he's smuggling fags so he's not too surprised when he turns up at his house one night. The guy makes up some cock and bull story, come to apologise or whatever, and George invites him in for a drink. He's that sort of bloke, doesn't bear a grudge. While George is pouring the drink he has his back to Bill who uses the opportunity to whack him over the head. George drops the glass and it breaks so Bill clears up all the bits and takes them with him. His accomplice is waiting outside somewhere. They drive him to the bowling green and finish him off. Then they drive George's Jag to the G-Mex to put us off the scent. That's why we didn't find a parking ticket among George's possessions."

"It certainly fits," said Daniels.

"All we have to do now is find some evidence to prove the theory. I also want you to take a look at Toby Mathews, see what we can dig up. The guy's too full of himself. Personally, I wouldn't trust him an inch."

The Super was noncommittal. "This is all conjecture, you don't have a shred of evidence to back it up. You need hard evidence. Look into his background; see if this Fenwick chap has any skeletons in the cupboard. Where's all the money going? Talk to the drugs squad and see if they've had any dealings with him. A magistrate wouldn't even consider a search warrant with what you have at the moment."

Chapter 22

Two collections to complete and then he would be on his way. It was one of those mornings when he felt glad to be alive; the sky was blue with hardly a cloud in sight promising a fine day to come and the first signs of the sun were showing on the horizon. Although the March morning was still cool as he left the depot at 7.15, the sleeveless quilted jacket was sufficient to keep the morning chill from his body and he knew that in a few hours the Mediterranean sun would raise the temperature into the low seventies. He gunned the engine into life, wandered over to the office to pick up the paperwork while he waited for the engine to warm up, said his au revoirs and headed out on the Avignon road. The first stop was at a small factory on the outskirts of town. The forklift loaded the two crates of electrical components onto the flatbed and, after signing for delivery and tying down the curtain, he headed out to the final call at the tile factory.

On the first visit he'd had a hell of a job finding the place; it was situated in a disused quarry about five miles outside of Marseilles and was serviced by an unmade road that ran for nearly two miles into the surrounding hills. The turning off was easy to miss if you didn't know what you were looking for, the only indication that the track was anything other than a dead end being a small wooden sign, bleached by years of exposure to the Mediterranean sun, on which he could barely read the name of the tile company that now owned the quarry. He dropped down into third gear and pulled off the highway onto the white stone road. Although unmade the surface was firm and the Volvo made short work of negotiating the track. After a mile and a half winding through the sparse vegetation the track turned to the right and dropped down into the quarry, a large hole in the side of the hill surrounded on three sides by the sheer cliffs of white stone created by the excavations of the previous tenants. The factory was no more than three large sheds situated on the quarry floor, a small family affair turning out hand-pressed, high quality terracotta floor tiles for use in the kitchens and conservatories of the more discerning home owner.

As he parked up and climbed out of the cab, Eric sidled over from the direction of the caravan, a large bull of a man dressed in a washed-out red checked woollen shirt and denim dungarees with the face of a prize fighter, a day's dark growth on his prominent chin.

"Bonjour, Bill. a va?

"Bien, merci. a va Eric?" Bill replied.

"Oh, pas mal."

They always completed the initial cordialities in French; after that it was a combination of Bill's pigeon French and the Martines' pigeon English, but they got by.

"Où sont Jacques et Pierre?"

The older man gestured towards one of the sheds. The father and two brothers ran the factory. Bill had never actually seen any other workers on his visits to the factory and wasn't sure whether indeed there were any. Eric led him over to the caravan that served as the general office and mobile canteen and bade him sit down at the rough wooden table beside it.

"Petit déjeuner, oui?"

"Ah oui, merci."

He disappeared into the caravan and Bill could hear the sounds of plates and cutlery being collected together. He was looking forward to the fresh bread and coffee, always enjoyed the camaraderie of sitting out in the open sunshine with his friends, the breaking of bread in this way somehow so symbolic of the idealistic Mediterranean lifestyle that he pictured in his mind.

"Bonjour, Bill. Ça va?

He looked round, unaware of his approach.

"Bien merci. Bonjour Pierre, ça va?"

Pierre walked round the table and sat opposite him.

"Bien merci. Your trip, is good?"

"Oui, bonne, très bonne."

The old man appeared and placed the plates, knives, forks and mugs on the table. As he returned to the caravan Pierre reached into the top pocket of his light blue denim shirt and pulled out a roughly folded piece of paper. He carefully unfolded it and flattened it with his large hand on the table. He spoke with a strong French accent.

"We have two pallet today, for going to London." He indicated the piece of paper. "You sign for collect, oui?"

"Oui." Bill reached into his own jacket pocket for the biro and scrawled his signature across the bottom of the docket.

The old man appeared with a large baguette, some cheese and small bowl full of tomatoes. He returned once more to the caravan emerging seconds later with a steaming coffee pot. Seating himself at the head of the table he indicated to Bill to tuck in.

"Bon appétit."

In the first fleeting half-second he thought it was an illness, a heart attack of the neck was the best he could manage. A searing pain, far worse than anything he had ever experienced in his entire life, gripped his neck, choking the life from him; the half masticated white dough falling from his mouth. His hands automatically reached up to try to free whatever it was that was causing the agony but there was nothing to get a grip on, the wire already buried deep in the skin, throttling the life from him, the pressure unrelenting, closing the windpipe, forcing the life out of him. His body writhed from side to side on the small wooden chair, the efforts of a man who was quickly beginning to realize that these were his last moments on earth, but the strength of the man applying the garrotte kept him locked firmly in position. His eyes were bulging from their sockets. The two men sat looking at him motionless. What were they doing? Couldn't they see that he was being attacked? Why did his friends not help him? These were his dying thoughts.

They quickly moved into action. The body was wrapped in an old tarpaulin that lay nearby and left to rest by the side of the caravan. Moving over to the truck Pierre disconnected the hoses joining the cab to the trailer, unhooked the flat bed and drove the cab into the nearest shed. Eric and Jacques were already at work on the trailer, undoing the nylon ropes which kept the curtain attached firmly to the side of the flatbed. The work was tedious, pulling the rope through each eyelet in the thick sheeting before unwrapping it from the metal cleat attached to the side of the trailer, and it was thirty minutes before the lower part of the curtain was completely free. They fetched an old wooden extending ladder from the side of the shed, and, taking one section each, began undoing the top of the curtain from its frame.

After parking the truck Pierre wandered over to the far side of the quarry floor where the remnants of a fire still smouldered, the grey ashes hiding the intense heat below. He roughly smashed up a couple of the wooden pallets that lay nearby and threw the broken pieces on the fire, watched for a couple of minutes to be sure that the fire would take hold, and then returned to the shed. Everything was to hand, the plan had been carefully thought out. He donned the paper facemask that kept the dust of the terracotta clay from clogging the lungs, plugged the Bosche sander in, and began work on the cab. Having roughed up the immaculate paintwork he quickly covered the windscreen, side windows, exhaust, bumper and door handles with newspaper held in place by half inch masking tape. The job didn't need to be perfect, just so long as it was adequate for the purpose. The electric spray gun was already prepared, the plastic reservoir filled with dark green paint. He worked his way carefully round the truck making sure the fine spray entered every nook and cranny of the cab's bodywork, obliterating all traces of its previous existence.

The men in the yard had completed the task of undoing the curtain and the two large sections of nylon coated sheeting emblazoned with the Lister Haulage logo now lay flat on the quarry floor, the trailer naked, its load exposed to the world. They took one corner each of the first piece and began dragging it towards the blazing fire on the far side of the quarry. Bundling the sheet onto the fire didn't prove easy: the sheet was stiff and unwieldy and it took them several attempts before they were satisfied with the results.

They were returning for the second sheet just as Pierre emerged from the shed. He shouted to them, they gestured in acknowledgement. The older man brought out fresh bread and they ate with gusto, the conversation totally unaffected by the morning's work or the grisly contents of the tarpaulin that lay not ten feet from them. Jacques, who was seated with his back to the caravan, pointed across the yard. "A problem, you think?"

The other men turned to look. A large pall of black smoke rose slowly from the fire as the flames melted the plastic content of the sheet. It was Eric who spoke. "Don't worry, if anybody asks we were burning some old tyres."

The conversation resumed.

After breakfast the three of them went to the second shed, pulled the two large pieces of dirty brown canvas to the side of the trailer and began the task of attaching the sheets to the tubular metal frame. By mid-morning the work was complete. The original sheeting was reduced to a fine grey ash, the trailer sat in the middle of the yard clad in its new colours and the dark green cab stood nearby. Jacques backed the cab onto the trailer and connected the umbilical cords which provided power and electrics before setting off down the track with a final wave.

The Northern Star cast off at 11.30 that morning and moved sedately towards the open sea, Captain Andreus standing at the bridge, mindful of the two trawlers on his starboard side but satisfied that they were well out of harm's way. The turbines were barely ticking over as she proceeded at quarter speed, staying well within the six knot speed limit that was mandatory within the confined waters of the port. He looked at the clear blue sky and felt glad that the winter months were all but over, the cold and the salt spray playing havoc with the rheumatism in his knees leaving him almost crippled on the bad days, and anticipated the soothing effects of the spring sunshine on his aching joints.

He had come a long way in the last two years; he was no longer the old soak with unkempt appearance and the wardrobe of a vagrant. True, he was still no movie star but he moderated the drinking now, had lost a couple of stone in weight, dressed with a modicum of decorum, bathed on a regular basis and generally tried to conduct himself in a manner that he thought was more fitting to his status. All this he owed to his new friends for they had given him both a reason to live and provided him with the means by which he might do so. Oh he knew they were up to no good and years ago his morality might have got the better of him. But what had morality ever done for him? The meek shall inherit the earth, the Bible said. It seemed to him that the fraudsters and the criminals and the capitalists who exploited a man when he was down were the people who inherited the earth and what he was doing was no more than collecting his due. It was easy to moralize when you were young and well-paid with a rosy future in front of you; moralizing should be left to those who had lived a little, who understood how unfair life could be.

They would make Barcelona by tomorrow morning, the forecast was set fair, and barring any last minute changes of schedule he would be back in Tunis by Tuesday. With his new-found status had come a return of some of the old self-confidence, the owners surprised and caught unawares when he demanded proper days off for himself and the crew, rather than the ad hoc arrangement that had often seen them working for weeks without a break. But Greece had made a fatal error; beguiled by promises of increased wealth and European fraternity it had joined the EEC and the Northern Star was Greek registered, subject to the myriad of rules that dictated almost every aspect of the working day. At first they had threatened to pull the plug, arguing that it would not be worth their while to re-register the old crate in Panama, but Nicholia was reasonableness itself, explaining how they could still keep to the schedule with a few minor alterations and allow the crew a three day stopover in Tunis every fortnight. But the crew will not want to stay in Tunis, they had complained. We will get new crew then, countered Nicholia, and think how much cheaper the Arabs are to employ.

He had known Anita was on the game, had known it as soon as he left port that day, and perhaps even before then. But they had reached an understanding; whenever he was in port she was exclusively his. And they had a good time together, behaving more like courting couple than prostitute and client: shopping in the market; promenading on the waterfront; enjoying a meal in the evening; he living at the apartment. In return he paid her 'housekeeping' to help with the expenses.

The truck reached the intersection with the main road and turned right, following the road for two miles before taking the left-hand turn at the intersection, signposted Marseilles, gathering speed down the slope of the slip road and joining the dual carriageway that led into the heart of the great city. Jacques knew the area as only one who has spent his entire existence in a place can. He swung the truck off the dual carriageway and negotiated the backstreets of the old French Quarter, passing through the residential streets and into the working area beyond. No town planner had influenced this development, a mixture of junkyards, builders' merchants, second-hand car plots and small factories that acted as cover for the activities of the Marseilles underworld. He turned the truck in between the large tubular steel gates covered in wire mesh and topped off with a spiral of razor wire and came to a halt by the small hut. After a brief conversation he pulled over on the far side of the yard beside the small warehouse where two of the workers immediately set to work undoing the tarpaulin, the fork lift truck unloading the exposed load and carrying it into the warehouse. The trailer emptied the men quickly secured the curtain and Jacques was on his way once again, taking the route to the north via Avignon, knowing that he faced a long drive if he was to make the timetable. They would dispose of the load tomorrow; that was the deal. Anything with a price would find its way onto the thriving black market economy, the rest would be discreetly disposed of.

Jacques headed on up the N1 keeping strictly to the speed limit, resisting the temptation to push on as he made his way gradually north, the countryside imperceptibly changing from the sparse vegetation of the Mediterranean to the lush green of the temperate region, the temperature dropping as the sun lost its strength, boredom the main enemy as the truck trundled remorselessly on. The motorway, a never changing sea of grey before his eyes. Allowing for a couple of half hour breaks and barring any major hold-ups he reckoned he could complete the journey in sixteen hours, leaving him a couple of hours to spare if he was to catch the morning ferry. Passing Dijon in the early evening he stopped for a large pot of coffee at the service station but resisted the temptation of food other than to purchase half a dozen chocolate bars and two tubes of glucose sweets, knowing that the combination of caffeine and glucose would help keep him awake during the long night ahead. And the timing was on his side. He hit the Périphérique minutes before midnight by which time the ring road was relatively quiet allowing him to make good time as he took the western route around the capital. He spat out of the window as he passed under the large motorway sign advertising the turn off for central Paris being no fan of the politicians, bureaucrats and corrupt capitalist who lived and worked there, interfering busybodies who thought that Paris was France and had little comprehension of, or time for, the real France, the one he knew and loved.

North of Paris he took a further break, satisfied that he was ahead of schedule, and downed another half litre of strong coffee but once again ignored the complaints of his stomach knowing that a hot meal and full stomach would find him craving sleep within the half hour. He finally arrived in Calais at 4.45 and was grateful to find an enterprising hot dog salesman plying his trade at the entrance to the ferry terminal, taking advantage of the trucks and cars arriving for the early morning ferry. He purchased two and greedily ate them, soothing the pangs in his stomach, before climbing into the bunk at the rear of the cab for a short sleep.

The banging on the cab and shouts of the loader woke him and for a few seconds, before he recovered his senses and remembered where he was, he was totally disorientated, the strange surroundings of the small bunk hideyhole confusing his mind. Handing over the ticket he drove the truck up the ramp, following the signals as the loader manoeuvred him into position before abandoning the truck and making his way to the rear deck to make a short call on the mobile. Satisfied that all was going to plan he settled into one of the large recliner seats in the aft cabin and was quickly asleep once again.

Waiting until the sun was well down and the evening's darkness engulfed the quarry, Pierre and Eric loaded the tarpaulin containing the body into the back of the Toyota and Pierre followed the route taken earlier by Jacques but ignored the sign for Marseilles. He continued instead along the road which traversed the north of the city until he came to the temporary construction yard that housed the materials and equipment required to build the new bypass that would route the heavy traffic around the village of Rouisson. The charge hand appeared from the shadows by the entrance to the yard and jumped into the passenger seat, directing Pierre a further hundred yards down the road and then off to the left, following the tracks cut into the field by the heavy earth moving equipment. They followed the tracks for quarter of a mile before coming to a halt beside a large hole with steel reinforcing bars protruding from it, the foundation for one of the columns that would support the bridge.

The two had known each other since their school days and he trusted Henri completely. They stood either side of the hole, which was about eight feet square and nearly as deep, and lifted out the cage of reinforcing steel. It was a struggle but they finally had the cage safely parked by the side of the hole. Henri picked up a short ladder that was lying nearby and dropped it into the hole before picking up the spade that lay nearby and climbing down. It took him less than fifteen minutes to dig the shallow grave. The two of them manhandled the tarpaulin off the back of the Toyota and swung it over the side of the hole, and Henri climbed down one last time to place the body in the shallow grave and cover the evidence. Finally he emerged and the two of them replaced the reinforcing as best they could manage. The four trucks were scheduled for 7.30 the following morning and would seal the grave with twenty-four cubic metres of high strength concrete. He dropped Henri back at the entrance to the yard, handing him a large wad of francs as he wished him bon voyage.

Pierre arrived back in the French Quarter just after 10.00. The bar was not one that any tourist would ever visit. Should they inadvertently happen upon it the looks of the men sitting at the tables would quickly tell them they had made a grave error of judgment and they would beat a hasty retreat, looking for a less threatening environment in which to soak up the real flavour of Marseilles. Eric was sitting alone at one of the tables, Pernod in hand, when he entered.

"Salut."

"Salut, papa."

Chapter 23

Mike was feeling more relaxed than he could remember in a long time. The case was barely four weeks old but it felt like an eternity. Every single waking moment over the last month had been dedicated to trying to solve the murders, beating his head against a brick wall, reading and re-reading the reports, searching for the missing link, looking for the answer to what seemed an insoluble problem. That had been the worst part about it, the lack of progress, but now he had a lead, something to get his teeth into.

The atmosphere was tense that Thursday morning in the ops room. People pretending to be busy, finding excuses to hang around, lifting their heads at every phone call, eyeing the recipient, watching for the reaction. But as the morning wore on and the call never came Mike became convinced that Helen was correct; there was no serial killer. And what about Helen? It had been nearly a week and he hadn't phoned her. Why not tonight? God knows, he could do with a night off, a night away from the constant pressures, and with no further murders reported and the chief suspect not due back home until tomorrow night it couldn't do any harm to take the one evening off.

He went back to his own room further down the corridor to make the call; he needed the privacy. He'd hardly been in the room for the last four weeks – the ops room was the nerve centre of the operation and that was where he was invariably to be found. By the time he made the call he'd convinced himself that the chances of success were remote, that an attractive woman such as Helen would be much in demand, the diary booked weeks in advance. She probably wasn't really interested anyway, just being polite. He was pleasantly surprised when the arrangements were successfully completed and he walked back down to the ops room with a spring in his step and a smile on his face.

There was somebody else with a smile on her face that Thursday. Craig checked carefully from the top of the stairs before bounding down into reception.

"Whoa, sexy top."

Linda had bought the bright crimson crop top with a small butterfly picked out in sequins just below the left shoulder at the weekend. She didn't normally wear the new gear to work, it was reserved for clubbing at the weekends, but almost subconsciously she'd found herself taking more care with her appearance on workdays, wearing the newer and more outrageous clothes, taking a little more care with the make-up.

"Do you like it?" she asked, pleased by the attention.

"Terrific, yea. Really makes you look, well, sexy."

He'd used the word twice; she was definitely making an impression. Craig slumped with his elbows on the counter, chin resting in his cupped palms.

"God I'm bored. I could really do with a fun night out. Blow away the cobwebs, have a few laughs," he said.

She joined in with his mood, she wasn't about to upset the apple cart.

"I know what you mean, I feel the same. It's been ages since I had a really good night out."

Craig smiled to himself. This was too easy; he could play her like a violin.

"Think I'll go out tonight, have a few lagers, maybe do a club."

This was her big chance.

"Wish I could, but I've nobody to go with. It's alright for you blokes, go out on your own no bother. It's not the same for us girls."

"Get away, you must have loads of mates. I'll bet you get asked out all the time," he said, playing the innocent.

"Well I do but it's not the same, is it? If I wanted to go out tonight then my mates might not want to go out, or they may already be doing something else. And most of the lads are right sad cases."

"What about your flat mate, what's her name?" queried Craig.

"Annie. She's on lates this week."

"Where is it she works?" he asked.

"Over at the airport. Good job it is, wouldn't mind working there myself, apart from the shifts."

He affected an air of mild indifference, of someone just passing the time of day.

"So what time does she start when she's on late shift?"

"6.00. It's 6.00 'til 2.00."

"Oh, right. See what you mean." It was time to go for the jugular. He put on his this-brilliant-idea-has-just-occurred-to-me face. "You could tag along with me if you like. I haven't arranged anything yet. We could go out for a few drinks somewhere."

She wasn't overly impressed with the 'tag along bit', but it was a start.

"Yea, why not? Might be a laugh."

As they were making the arrangements he heard the clatter of footsteps on the stairs and turned to see Marjorie, Toby's secretary, appearing. He turned back to Linda, winked, and put his finger to his lips. He changed the subject and started talking about a programme on the television the previous evening. Linda followed his lead. Marjorie walked through to the back of reception, opened one of the filing cabinets, found whatever it was she was searching for and disappeared back up the steps.

"What's wrong?" Linda asked him

"Oh nothing, but you know what they're like round here. Any gossip and it's all over the building within five minutes. One night out together and they'll have it down as the greatest romance since Romeo and Juliet given half a chance. Let's just keep this between ourselves for the time being."

Interesting, thought Linda, so does that mean it is a date after all? Craig was certainly difficult to read.

"By the way, what are you wearing this evening?" he asked.

The question took her totally off guard; it wasn't the sort of things blokes usually asked. Besides, she couldn't possibly know until she'd spent at least an hour trying on a dozen or so of the more recently purchased outfits that filled her wardrobe.

"Why?"

"It's just that I don't want to clash. I hate that, when you see couples out together and their clothes totally clash. It's really naff," Craig replied.

'Couples out together', things were looking up, thought Linda.

"I hadn't really thought about it. What are you wearing?"

"Don't know really. What about my Armani, the dark blue one? I know, have you got anything in black? That would be cool."

Her mind was racing; she liked this, being part of his world. "I've got a black skirt, knee-length. What about that?" She was feeling disappointed even as she suggested it, the skirt being by far the most boring and possibly only sensible item in her wardrobe.

"Yea, cool, great. And what about the top? Do you have a black blouse? All in black, that would suit you."

She had a blouse she'd bought a couple of months ago. It wasn't her favourite but she supposed if that's what Craig wanted, well, that was OK by her.

Having finalized the arrangements Craig made his way back upstairs. It had gone better than he dared to hope for. The empty flat was a bonus and with any luck she'd tone the outfit down a bit. She wasn't bad to look at but some of her clothes were way over the top, made her look like a bloody tart. And he wasn't convinced about her ability to keep her mouth shut but he'd just have to take a chance on that.

He was right; Linda was desperate to share her news with someone if only she could find a suitable friend to confide in. Jean had finished for the day, she knew that Annie would be long gone before she arrived home and there was no time to phone her mates. He was picking her up at 8.30 which only left her two and a half hours to prepare.

By coincidence Mike had arranged to meet Helen at 8.30 that evening. Her flat was located on the first floor of one of the old university buildings set within the campus grounds. He'd left the eating arrangements to Helen, having no knowledge of the area, and she had booked a table at a bistro in Beeston, the small town adjacent to the campus.

"Let's walk down, it only takes fifteen minutes and I could do with some fresh air," she said.

It was a cold, clear evening and after the two hour drive he could do with stretching his legs so readily agreed with her suggestion. She was wearing black trousers, a cream coloured blouse and low-heeled black shoes, adding a dark blue duffel coat as they left the flat to guard against the chill of the March evening. The bistro was pleasant but nothing special and the food fairly standard fare. He couldn't help wondering whether she had picked the venue with his pocket in mind. She struck him as the type of woman who would be equally at home, and equally as happy, dining in the classiest of restaurants with the top echelons of academia or sharing a pub meal with a few of her students. The waiter came over.

"White or red?" she asked him.

He held up his hand. "You go ahead, but it's water for me, I'm afraid." She gave him a look.

"Wouldn't look too good I'm afraid. DCI in Cheshire Slasher case arrested on drink drive charge. Seriously, I daren't risk it. It's the end of the career if you fall foul of the drink drive boys nowadays."

She ordered a carafe of house white. She was disappointed. He looked like he could use a drink; she could guess at how much pressure he had been under for the last few weeks. Besides, first dates were difficult enough as it was and a little alcohol was wonderful for freeing up the inhibitions, breaking down the barriers. She knew there were people who said they could have just as much fun without alcohol, that they didn't need the stimulus of unnatural chemicals, but in her experience they were pretty rare. Whenever she attended dinners or parties where she couldn't drink she inevitably found herself bored stiff and hating every minute of it after the first hour or so as the other guests inevitably became more garrulous from the effects of the booze while she became more and more withdrawn.

"Look, don't take this the wrong way, but you look like you could use a few drinks. If you want to sleep on the sofa at my place tonight I don't have any objections. I take it I can trust you to behave like a gentleman." She said the latter with raised eyebrow and funny accent to ensure he understood it as a joke. He raised a feeble objection but knew he would accept the offer without too much persuasion. She was right; he did need a few drinks.

They got on like a house on fire; he couldn't remember when he'd enjoyed another person's company so much. In retrospect he put this down to four factors. Firstly, she was naturally very good company; secondly, the release of tension was having an Einstein-like opposite and equal effect on his brain; thirdly, by the end of the meal he was fairly pissed; fourthly, he was falling in love. He had to admit that the last one was a bit of a shocker but there wasn't a lot he could do about it.

The only sticky point had come at the end of the meal. When the waiter arrived with the bill he reached inside his jacket pocket without thinking, extracted his wallet and placed the credit card on the saucer. For the first time he detected a note of anger in the voice.

"What do you think you're doing?"

"Paying for the meal." His tone was neutral, he was a bit tipsy, didn't cotton on to the problem. The waiter hovered, embarrassed. She waved him away.

"Come back in five minutes." He was glad to be out of it. "What gives you the right to decide that you're going to pay? Would you do that if you were sharing your meal with one of your male friends?"

He was beginning to get the drift.

"Hold on, it's no big deal."

"Perhaps it's no big deal for you but it is for me. I don't like being taken for granted."

"I wasn't taking you for granted. I just offered to pay for the meal, that's all. Look, how about I get this one and you pay next time?"

Why did she always have to ruin it, she thought. She knew he was no bigot but she had spent so many years fighting for acceptance, everyday a battle against male-dominated institutions that thought that little blonde girls were there to make the coffee and see to the post. But why have a go at him over something so trivial? She softened her tone.

"Sorry, maybe I over reacted a bit; I'm a bit touchy about protecting my space. You're right, you pay for this one and I'll pay next time."

Storm over and it sounded like he'd landed himself another date.

Leaving the restaurant he'd put his hand on her shoulder to guide her through the door and it had just sort of stayed there. She'd reciprocated by wrapping her arm around his waist and they had walked back to the campus entwined but not speaking, both lost in their own thoughts. They'd stopped at the large stone pillars that had once supported gates long since disappeared to gaze at the stars. The kiss had been inevitable. Later, as they lay in each other's arms, he staring at the ceiling, left arm wrapped around her shoulders, hand resting lightly on the blonde hair, her head lying on his shoulder, he knew that for him this was more than a casual infatuation, that she was already getting under his skin, that he already wanted more from her than she might be prepared to give.

"Do you think Forrest will mind?" she asked, brown eyes staring up at him.

"Mind what?" he asked dreamily, his mind still reeling from the arousal he had felt minutes earlier.

"Sharing you with me," she replied, wondering whether she was pushing it too far too fast. For all she knew this could be a one-night stand. She didn't have any firm rules about who she slept with and when, preferring to play it as the mood took her, but realized this had all happened terribly quickly. But it had seemed so right.

"I don't know, I'll have to ask him," he replied, teasing her, pleased by the implication of the question.

"I think he likes me," she responded.

He remembered, sitting bolt upright, a frown on his face. "Oh no, Forrest alone in the flat all night," he groaned.

"Is that a problem?"

"He'll wreck the place and it's not even my furniture."

She reached up and pulled him down to her, breasts pushing against his chest. "Too late to worry now, lover boy. Perhaps you should have settled for a budgie."

The feel of her was enough to arouse him again. "Oh you wicked woman, have you no shame?" he said jokingly, melting into her as their lips met.

She was beginning to worry; she'd fed the kids, let them watch TV for a while and then sent them off to bed and there was still no word from Bill. His mobile was switched off and she hadn't heard a thing from him since Wednesday night. She tried to remember: would he catch the overnight ferry or would he wait until Friday morning? Had they caught him, that was her biggest concern. She'd told him he was taking a stupid risk, was bound to get found out sooner or later, and what would happen if they did? She fretted all night, worrying about what was happening to him, hardly got a moment's sleep.

Chapter 24

The dark blue Vauxhall Cavalier pulled up outside the semi-detached house just after 8.30. The house was originally built as a single residence but had been converted by a former owner into two self-contained flats, one on the ground floor and one on the first floor, the latter now rented by Linda and Annie. He checked up and down the street, the evening dimly lit by the orange glow of the sodium streetlights, before leaving the car and walking up the path to the small porch that protected the front door. The two door bells were situated one above the other and he rang the higher of the two, waiting as he heard the door closing inside, saw the outline of the figure descending the stairs through the frosted glass. His prompting had worked; she looked quite presentable in the black ensemble and wouldn't stand out in a crowd. Once inside the car her initial reaction was one of disappointment.

"Where's your car?"

"The exhaust blew on the way home tonight, sounds like a tractor. I'll have to take it down the exhaust place tomorrow and have a new one fitted. Lucky I managed to borrow this or tonight would have been a blow out"

She had looked forward to riding in his car, the Cavalier was a bit of a come down. Still, like he said, thank goodness he'd found an alternative, it would do for the time being. She noticed his clothes.

"I thought you were wearing your Armani?"

He pulled a face. "Stinks of tobacco. Forgotten I wore it down the pub the other week. Needs cleaning. I'll do, won't I?"

He was dressed in grey flannel trousers, a long-sleeved dark blue polo shirt and a blue fleece jacket. She gave him the once over.

"Yea, you'll do."

While they were talking he made his way on to the A58 heading south out of Bolton and joined the M61 at Junction 5. She looked out of the window.

"Where are we going?"

"Little pub I know, out in the country. Have a drink there and then decide what we fancy doing."

He flipped open the lid of the central console revealing half a dozen cassettes.

"See if there's any decent music."

She rifled through the cassettes, selected one, and pushed it into the slot in the player. They sped on through the night in silence, the cassette player blasting out the Fleetwood Mac Rumours album. The drive seemed to last forever but she didn't mind. It was intimate in the car, the two of them and the music, cocooned in its shell, surrounded by the dark night. Eventually he dropped off the motorway and navigated through the countryside, turning first left and then right, each road seemingly more rural than the last until they finally found themselves driving down a small winding lane with high hedges on either side. She didn't have a clue where they were. She knew Bolton, she knew central Manchester, she knew Benidorm and that was about it. The car turned off the lane and up a cobbled driveway.

She came to life as the car drew to halt in the large car park. They were out in the countryside, that was for sure. The car park was surrounded by wooded scrubland and the only buildings she could see was the back of the large pub and what she took to be a barn off to the left of it. They walked across the car park and round to the front of the pub where a small paved courtyard gave straight on to a graveyard, at the far end of which stood the church. The entrance was via a wooden porch, its wooden supports entwined with the branches of an ancient wisteria that covered the front elevation of the pub. To the right was a small bar, to the left a room containing seven or eight tables of various sizes and shapes, and in front a doorway leading to further rooms at the rear. Craig looked in the room to the left. Two of the tables were occupied but other than that the room was empty. He ushered Linda into the room and chose a table in the far corner, as far away from prying eyes as possible.

"What will you have?"

"A raspberry Hooch" she replied.

He left her seated at the small round oak table and went to the bar to order the drinks. Surprisingly the request was not met with a look of admonishment as he had expected, the young barman fetching a small bottle of pink fizzy liquid from the cool cabinet without batting an eyelid. He ordered a pint of shandy for himself and sat down next to Linda on the oak settle. The conversation was fairly strained at first but became easier as she poured bottle after bottle of the pink liquid down her neck. After the fourth bottle she leant her shoulder against his, right hand rested lightly on his thigh, and by the sixth she was giving him the unexpurgated version of her assessment of the characters of her work colleagues. None of this worried him, but she was getting louder and the other people in the room were beginning to notice them. At the bar he had a quiet word with the barman who was happy to supply two bottles of the Hooch, top loosened, for take-out. Back in the car he handed the bottles to Linda and drove out of the car park.

"Where are we going now?" The voice was slurred.

"Heading for home. What did you think of the pub?"

"Very nice." Bloody boring old pub, she thought, bloody boring old night.

"I think I'm going to be sick," she said.

They had travelled less than two miles from the pub. He pulled to the side of the lane; she fell out of the passenger door, clutching the bottles.

"For Christ's sake you stupid tart, why don't you learn to hold your drink?"

"Fuck off, mummy's boy. Who do you think you're calling a tart?"

"Look at you, you're disgusting," he said, appalled by the spectacle.

"Oh piss off, you wanker," she spat back, slurring the words.

"For Christ's sake get a grip of yourself," he said, her language upsetting him.

"Fuck off telling me what to do, wanker." She was shouting now.

"Will you just bloody well calm down?"

"Go screw yourself, motherfucker. I'll show you who's a fucking tart. Thought you'd get your fucking hand in my knickers, did you?" she shouted, all control gone, the alcohol taking over.

"Look, calm down or I'm leaving," he warned her, worried by the noise she was making.

"Fucking leave then. Go on. Fuck off home and play with your dick, wanker."

That was it, he'd lost his nerve, couldn't carry on with it. He drove off, leaving her by the side of the lane.

She presumed they were going in the right direction, but since she was totally lost and half cut, actually had no idea whether this was true or not. In fact they were driving deeper into the countryside, he wanted to put some distance between himself and the pub. After about an hour he pulled in at an isolated spot on the deserted country lane. Linda had consumed both bottles by now and sat, slightly befuddled, staring out at the star lit night.

"What've we stopped for?" she asked.

"To look at the stars, aren't they beautiful?" he replied.

Even in her inebriated state Linda could see that the situation had romantic possibilities and she slouched back in the passenger seat, face turned towards him, waiting for the inevitable approach. He slid his left arm round the back of her neck and leant his face into hers. After ten minutes of kissing she was feeling a touch disappointed; he wasn't responding to her enthusiasm and nothing much seemed to be happening. Her romantic experiences to date had been of the 'wham, bam, thank you mam' variety and she couldn't understand why it was taking him so long to get down to business. She decided he needed some encouragement. Releasing her left hand from his shoulder she deftly undid the front of her blouse and slid her finger along the top of the bra, forcing the black lace material down and releasing her left breast from the restraining cup. Reaching down she found his right hand resting loosely on her thigh and lifting it, pushed it inside the opening of the blouse and over her breast. The nipple hardened as his hand squeezed her breast; she arched her back, forcing her body up to meet him, her tongue darting deep into his mouth. This was more like it, she thought, as his fingers tweaked the nipple, rolling the hard protuberance between forefinger and thumb. The hand slowly slid upwards and she felt the fingers caress the nape of her neck. The grip around her neck tightened as his left hand came into play. It was beginning to hurt, she pulled back from his kiss, about to give him a mouthful, but no words came. The hands were tightening their grip, the thumbs pushing deep into the windpipe, stopping the flow of oxygen to her lungs, the compression of the larynx preventing the vocal chords from issuing the verbal reprimand. What was he playing at? She was panicking now, hands thrashing wildly, trying to break his grip. He was too strong for her and the look on his face, staring eyes and a half smile, told her that nothing would stop him now.

It was almost 1.00 when he returned to the flat in Salford Quays. The car was still parked in his reserved parking bay by the side of the block and he checked that the entrance hall was deserted before sliding his key into the lock and carefully closing the door behind him. He climbed the stairs slowly, placing his toes on each step and then gradually transferring his weight. On the landing he tumbled the Yale as quietly as he could and entered the flat letting the door close gently shut behind him. The lights were on and he could hear the voice on the television reaching him from the lounge.

Unusually for Mike he awoke at 7.30 on the Friday morning without the aid of an alarm clock, some internal body clock taking over, the thought of what Forrest might do to the flat enough to force him into action. He quickly dressed and, deciding not to wake her, left a short note explaining why he'd shot off and promising to call her.

The alert reached Mike in a round about way. The driver of the milk tanker, making his way to one of the outlying farms for an early morning collection, had spotted the girl's leg sticking out from the lush undergrowth that grew along the side of the lane. At first they thought it was a hit and run case; the pathologist had told them different. Stafford contacted Bolton and asked them to check out the address. Uniform had duly visited, confirmed that the girl lived there, dealt with a distraught Annie and provided the contact information they required. As luck would have it Daniels was visiting Bolton nick that morning, checking the records for any incidents involving Lister Haulage. On arriving he called in on Dick Whelan, an old colleague he'd worked with for many years, and was drinking coffee, chewing the fat, when he noticed the picture of the girl uniform had borrowed from the flat lying on the desk.

"Linda what's her name?" he said in a mildly enquiring tone, apropos nothing in particular.

"Linda Walker. You know her?" asked Whelan.

"Not really, bumped into her a couple of times on this enquiry we're working on."

"Well you won't be bumping into her anymore."

"Why not?" He was surprised. His immediate thought was that she had been arrested in connection with some criminal activity and Dick was alluding to the time he expected her to be serving at Her Majesty's Pleasure. She didn't seem the type.

"She was found dead this morning, strangled."

The mug shattered as it hit the floor, coffee staining the trousers of his suit.

Daniels couldn't get hold of the governor: he wasn't answering his phone at the flat and the mobile was switched off. He'd already spoken to Stafford and explained the situation with their own enquiry. The DCI in charge agreed that there could well be a link, that they needed to pool their knowledge, but Daniels couldn't do anything without the governor's say so – he didn't have the authority to allocate resources. The police force could be funny like that. He'd been burnt a few times before and he was too experienced to let it happen again. Where the bloody hell was he? It was nearly 8.00. He tried the mobile again, success at last.

"Where are you, Guv?" To Daniels it was an innocent enquiry, to Mike a potential minefield.

"Just outside Derby, why?"

Daniels explained the development.

"Right, put whatever resource you need on to it. You'd better get yourself down to Stafford, see what you can dig up. I'll get back to you in ten minutes." He needed time to think.

Daniels smiled wryly to himself. Now what was the boss doing in Derby at 8.00 on a Friday morning? He wasn't vindictive, had no interest in office gossip, simply a natural detective, on duty and off. The information was stored with the thousand other little titbits that resided in the depths of his prodigious memory.

"Papers please," said the customs man, a look of bored indifference on his face.

"I'm empty," replied Jacques.

"Let's take a look."

They walked to the rear of the trailer where Jacques undid the corner of the curtain, the customs man taking a quick cursory glance, using his torch to light the furthest reaches of the trailer, no more than a standard procedure to be followed, not expecting to find anything.

"On your way then," he told Jacques, satisfied that all was in order.

Two miles outside Dover he saw the Transit van sitting in the layby, the rendezvous previously arranged, the timetable not allowing him the luxury of driving to London. He followed the Transit for a few more miles until it pulled into a service area and parked at the far end of the truck park, the area largely deserted, the truck drivers preferring the bays nearer the café where minimum effort was required to reach its welcoming tables. They parked the van alongside the trailer, blocking the view from any prying eyes and the van's passenger quickly went to work with the oxyacetylene, Jacques and Mick leaning on the front of the truck, casual, keeping a lookout, ready to intercept any interfering busy bodies that may have felt like lending a hand. The precautions were unnecessary, within fifteen minutes the goods were unloaded and nobody had taken a blind bit of notice of them. As they were saying their goodbyes Mick reached into the Transit.

"Nearly, forgot," he said, handing over a bottle of single malt Glenlivet. "For you and the family. Nice to meet you at last."

Jacques was temporarily embarrassed; he had brought no petit cadeau for the man. He mumbled his thanks and climbed back into the truck, following the Transit north as far as Barham before turning back on himself and heading down the A260 to Folkestone. There was room on the 11.30 ferry, he bought a ticket and settled back to wait, satisfied with the day's work.

Chapter 25

Mike sat in the car for several minutes but finally concluded that he could think of no possible reason for the death of Linda Walker. He checked the map and followed the signs out of Nottingham for the A50. Forrest will have to wait, he thought, his mind picturing the terrible carnage back at the flat. Stafford nick was very much like their own, modern seventies building of glass and concrete on three levels. He was directed to DCI Godfrey's office where he found a thickset man, short grey hair, obviously at the other end of his career to Mike, sitting behind the desk. They made their introductions and Godfrey brought him up to date.

"Preliminary pathology report says she died of strangulation between 10.00 last night and 2.00 this morning and that she had a considerable quantity of alcohol in her bloodstream," Godfrey told him.

"Sexual activity?" asked Mike.

"Doesn't look like it; we'll need the full report for confirmation."

Daniels had already briefed Godfrey on their own enquiries and of course the press coverage had not escaped his attention.

"I can't see the connection. Where does she fit into the case?" Mike mused as they sat drinking coffee.

"Perhaps she doesn't. It's a hell of a coincidence but it is possible that your enquiries and the death of Linda Walker are in no way connected. On the other hand...."

Mike looked up, interested.

"DI Daniels informs me that you are of the opinion that your case is in some way connected with a smuggling operation?"

"Correct."

"That could mean the heavy brigade. If Linda Walker was in some way involved, perhaps tipping them as to which trucks were due on which run, the insider as it were, and they knew that you were sniffing around, well, maybe they saw Linda as a weak link, somebody they couldn't rely on who knew too much."

It made more sense than anything he had come up with so far, thought Mike. Godfrey is no fool, he knows his stuff.

They agreed that given the nature of the enquiry they would split the case; Mike and his team would deal with the background and house-to-house at the Bolton end while Godfrey would concentrate on piecing together how she came to be in the isolated lane that night. On the drive back to Sale it struck Mike that he may well have been the trigger that caused Linda's death. He remembered the last time he'd spoken to her, asking after the whereabouts of Bill Fenwick. If she was involved then she might have tipped them off that the police were looking for Bill. Perhaps that's what caused the panic, that's when they decided they had to shut her up permanently. He was angry, the guilt of the realization getting to him. He couldn't wait to get his hands on Fenwick.

He entered the flat to find Forrest happily snoozing on the settee, the only signs of any mishaps being a large pool on the kitchen floor. He cleared up the mess and took him out for half an hour in the park down the road, the fresh air clearing the cobwebs from his brain, the peace and quiet affording him time to think.

Daniels' enquiries in Bolton revealed very little. The elderly couple in the ground floor flat remembered the doorbell for the upstairs flat ringing at 8.30, remembered hearing the footsteps on the stairs and remembered the front door closing. But that was all. They hadn't taken a sneak look through the net curtains to see who it was, they weren't that type, more's the pity.

After exercising Forrest Mike made his way to the depot and after questioning all the staff established that the last people to see Linda alive were Marjorie and Craig.

"It would have been about 4.00. Mr Mathews wanted to look at the diesel figures for February. The file is kept in the cabinet behind reception. I went to fetch it and remember Craig standing at the counter talking to Linda," Marjorie told them.

A red-eyed Craig confirmed the story.

"That's right. I was just passing through reception, stopped for a chat. We got on alright, Linda and I. I suppose I was there for about ten minutes or so and then I returned to my office. I didn't leave until gone 6.00 and Linda had left by then. She finishes at 5.30."

As he was leaving Craig's office Mike remembered his other appointment.

"Bill Fenwick's due back tonight, isn't he?"

"That's right."

"What time will he be in?"

"He's normally back by 9.00 at the latest, depends on the traffic."

"I need to speak to him when he returns, will the office still be open?"

"We always keep the office open until all the drivers are in. Just a moment."

He turned to look at a rota pinned on the corkboard behind him.

"Roger's on tonight."

"Roger?"

"Roger Whitehead. He's the transport manager."

"Tell him I'll be down at about 7.00, will you?"

"No problem."

He spent the rest of the day filling in background on Linda Walker. Nothing to indicate any connection with anything illegal. Should show in the finances if she was up to anything but there was no indication that she did anything other than struggle to survive on her meagre wage.

Jacques disembarked on the French side without any problems and started the long run back to Marseilles, judging that he could make Dijon at worst before having to pull in for the weekend, the French regulations allowing no commercial traffic on the road between Friday midnight and

Sunday midnight, the legislation designed to keep the roads clear for the families and the tourists, the law also conveniently ensuring the drivers a work-free weekend. Passing through the tollbooth he put his foot down, pushing the truck up to the seventy kilometres per hour mark, willing to risk a pull now that the contraband was no longer on board, the extra risk worth the time saved. He hit Paris in the early evening and lost an hour as the traffic ground to a halt on the Périphérique, Jacques cursing the other drivers, frustrated by the delay but unable to do anything about it. He finally emerged from the chaos at 8.00 with seven hundred kilometres still in front of him, the truck now hitting the eighty kilometre per hour mark where traffic allowed, time the critical factor.

The traffic had all but disappeared by midnight and, after consulting on the mobile with Pierre, he put his foot to the floor, the diesel engine easily taking the empty truck up to one hundred kilometres per hour, Jacques keeping an eye on the mirrors for approaching headlights. He knew that despite the regulations he was safe until about 6.00 on the Saturday morning, the gendarmes lenient with the odd latecomer as long as they were off the road before the early morning shoppers began the weekend ritual. By 2.00 in the morning the traffic had all but disappeared and he pushed the accelerator to the floor, the diesel screaming, the empty trailer bouncing along behind him, skittish with no load to dampen the suspension, the thrill of the ride helping to keep him awake, the speed forcing him to concentrate. It would be tight, but he reckoned they could make it; he gave Pierre a call on the mobile.

In the evening Mike returned to the depot accompanied by Daniels. They found the transport manager in the main office.

"Surprised Craig didn't mention it to you. Very strange, haven't heard a thing from him since Wednesday night. Mobile's on the blink, I suppose. Still, you'd think he'd have made the effort to phone in."

Daniels gave Mike a look. They waited until midnight before deciding to call it a day. Once in the car they were free to talk.

"Do you think he's done a runner?" asked Daniels.

"It's possible, if he's got wind that we're after him. Fits in with the Linda Walker theory. Maybe she contacted him to warn him, that's when he arranged to have her bumped off."

It all fitted.

"Nothing more we can do tonight, let's see what tomorrow brings," said Mike.

Approaching Marseilles Jacques checked his watch and dropped the speed down to seventy, taking the exit marked Ville Français, the empty streets echoing to the sound of the diesel as he made his way between the old tenement blocks. He knew the area as only one who has spent his entire existence in a place can, negotiating the back streets of the old French Quarter with ease, passing through the residential area and into the industrial region beyond. He turned the truck in between the large tubular steel gates covered in wire mesh and topped off with a spiral of razor wire and came to a halt by the small hut. After a brief conversation he expertly backed the trailer into the space the man had indicated, disconnected the hoses, unhooked the trailer and parked the cab in the centre of the yard.

Pierre went to work removing the number plate from the trailer and throwing it in the cab, crawling under the rear of the flatbed and levering off the small brass plaque stamped with the maker's build number which he placed in the breast pocket of his denim shirt before finally scratching off the GB sticker from the rear bumper. The trailer now stood among a dozen or so Crane Frauhaufs parked in the yard, the German firm having the lion's share of the market for flatbed trailers in Western Europe, thousands of their products plying the highways and byways of the European Nations on a daily basis. The trailer was now one of the fleet, indistinguishable from the other trailers that lined the edge of the yard.

A final shake of the hand and he was on his way, Pierre following in the Toyota. He drove the cab on through the outskirts of the city until finally all evidence of economic activity was left behind and he was driving through the arid Mediterranean countryside, the cab now free of its burden like a frisky stallion finally let loose from the stalls as he pushed the accelerator to the floor, the quartz halogen headlights cutting a swathe through the darkness, his hands expertly jiggling the wheel as he negotiated the bends on the twisting road. Deep in the countryside he turned off the road and down the short track that led to the junkyard. The crane stood in the clearing at the centre of the yard, rusting heaps of precariously balanced cars piled four or five high all around, the spotlights illuminating the whole scene. The man who emerged from the Portakabin had clearly been expecting him. Jacques took one last look around the interior of the cab and, having satisfied himself that nothing of any import had been left behind, climbed down to the ground and walked over to the office.

The man looked at Jacques and nodded; Jacques returned the nod. The man gave the crane driver the thumbs up, right arm extended in front of him. They could hear the roar of the diesel as the crane whirled into action. The pulleys reeled in the thick steel hawser, lifting the large metal grab off the floor and high into the air, the driver swinging the arm around slowly until the grab was directly over the cab, ten feet above it. Suddenly the grab dropped like a stone as the driver released the clutch on the winding gear, the jaws smashing into the roof of the truck. He pulled another lever and the jaws of the giant crab closed on the cab, holding it in a vice-like grip. The winding gear started to creak and strain as the truck slowly lifted from the ground; first the front wheels and then the rear until finally the cab was clear of the ground, suspended on the end of the hawser. As the truck rose higher in the air the arm of the crane proscribed a slow arc to the left until the cab was suspended three feet above the open jaws of the huge crusher that dominated one side of the yard. He lowered the truck into the crusher and released the jaws, swinging the grab clear.

Jacques and the man had stood in silence, watching the crane perform its task. Now they set off across the yard to the small hut raised on stilts at the side of the crusher that housed the controls. The man pushed a couple of buttons and the two ton hydraulic rams on either side of the crusher began their inexorable journey, powered by the twin five hundred horse power Perkins diesel hidden deep within the bowels of the machine. Within ten minutes the crusher had reduced the cab and its contents to a five foot by three foot square cube of unidentifiable scrap metal. The damper pushed the cube out of the crusher where it landed among a heap of similar objects awaiting collection for their final journey to the smelting plant. Jacques joined Pierre in the pick-up and they headed back to the quarry.

The morning brought no salvation. There was still no sign of the missing driver and enquiries at the Fenwick household had only increased the anxiety of his already frantic wife. He found, via Toby Mathews, the home number of the Marseilles depot manager who, luckily for Mike, spoke fluent English. He rang back from the depot thirty minutes later, confirmed that Fenwick had departed as planned on Thursday morning and faxed over his schedule of collections and drops for the return leg. Mike checked the deliveries first. There was no answer from the first name on the list but the second brought a reply.

"No sign of him. He was supposed to be here yesterday, I've got dead-lines to meet. I've told those buggers at Listers they can stuff it if this is the best they can do," the man told him, clearly an irate customer.

Time to check out the French end. An unusual call went out on the police radio that morning.

"Control to all cars. Chief Inspector Judd would like to know if any of you morons out there parlez-vous français."

Twenty minutes later the young constable, having been briefed by Mike, was on the phone. It didn't take long to complete the task.

"Oui, merci. Au revoir monsieur."

Both companies confirmed that the collection had been made as per schedule.

Mike left Daniels to check the ferry company while he pondered his next move. If Fenwick was on the run then where would he head? And what about his wife and kids? Had he arranged to meet them somewhere at a later date? That wouldn't be easy. Fenwick would know that the police would watch them, waiting for them to lead the police to him. And there weren't many hiding places left nowadays. The extradition laws ensured that, one or two banana republics aside, there were very few places that a man could escape from the clutches of the law.

The ferry company was able to confirm that the truck boarded the early morning ferry: they had the ticket stub and the computer confirmed the details.

"Looks like he's on the run," said Mike. "Put out an all-points on the truck and a watch on the house, he's bound to turn up sooner or later."

In the meantime there was nothing they could do but wait.

Chapter 26

Mike was sitting at his desk, feet up, frustrated by Fenwick's disappearing act, annoyed that they were so near and yet still couldn't nail the bastard, the cheese and pickle sandwich all but consumed, the crisps largely eaten by Forrest who now lay sprawled in an ungainly fashion on the floor, when Daniels entered.

"Something strange happening here, Guv," he said.

"What's that?" asked Mike, unable to muster any great enthusiasm.

"I checked with customs at Dover. There's nothing much else to do and I thought it would help pass the time," Daniels said by way of explanation, aware that many of the other detectives considered him overly pedantic, forever triple checking the obvious.

"And?" asked Mike.

"According to them the truck didn't arrive on the ferry," Daniels replied, eyebrows raised, his face indicating that he didn't know what to make of it.

"What do you mean? Explain." Mike was alert now, feet off the desk, sitting forward.

"Exactly what I said. The customs people at Dover check the documentation of all trucks arriving, keep copies of the load manifest, but there's nothing for Fenwick's truck. He didn't go through customs."

"So according to the ferry people the truck definitely boarded the ferry but according to the customs people it never arrived at the other side," surmised Mike.

"That's what they're telling us," said Daniels, throwing his hands in the air.

Several minutes passed in silence, both men considering the implications of the latest development. Mike finally spoke.

"Doesn't make sense, a bloody great artic can't disappear into thin air. Somebody has made a cock up somewhere. Either the customs people have missed him or the ferry company is giving us duff information. Do the ferry people run Dover-Folkestone from Calais?"

Daniels shrugged his shoulders. "I don't know, Guv. Want me to check?"

"No, I'll have a word with them, you get back onto customs and get them to double check. Find out if there's any way he could have disembarked without them being aware of it. Also check with customs at Folkestone, see if they know anything."

Mike was connected to the operations manager at the ferry company's headquarters.

"Explain to me how the system works," said Mike.

"The loaders collect the tickets from the vehicles before they board, no ticket and you won't be allowed on. Standard procedure. Once the ferry is loaded and out of the way they take the tickets to the office and scan them into the computer and the information is transferred by leased line to the central database at head office," the manager explained.

"So you have access to all the information at head office?" Mike asked.

"That's right."

Mike read the ticket number from the piece of paper Daniels had left.

"What about this ticket, can you tell me the details?"

"Hang on a minute." Mike could hear the man punching in the number.

"Let's see, 6.30 Dover-Calais Friday morning, twenty-four ton artic." The manager read the details from the screen back to Mike.

"Is there any way the data could be wrong?" Mike paused, trying to think of the term. "Corrupt or whatever."

"I shouldn't think so," the manager replied. "Everything seems to be in order. But I'm no boffin, our IT people would be able to tell you better than I."

"Could I speak to someone in IT?" he asked. "It's important."

He explained the problem to Darren. "Is there any way you can check if there's anything strange about the ticket information?"

"Hang on a minute," replied Darren. "I'll bring up the raw data."

Mike could hear the keyboard tapping in the distance.

Darren typed in the SQL statement, the query language that would retrieve the raw data from the Oracle database:

SELECT ALL from TICKET_MASTER where DEP_DATE = "25/2/99" and REG_NO = "ERV548 V"

The statement would return all occurrences of data where the departure date was Friday and the registration number of the vehicle was that of Fenwick's truck.

"Won't be a minute, she's churning and burning," Darren assured him.

"Here we go. I've got 6.30 Dover-Calais and 11.30 Folkestone-Boulogne. Looks straightforward, updates completed successfully, no sign of any glitches."

Mike nearly fell off his chair. "Give me that again, slowly."

Mike arranged for Darren to fax him the details and went to find Daniels.

"Interesting. There's no record of him arriving at either port. Customs say the only way he could have entered without them having a record is if he was empty, wouldn't have a load manifest to check," replied Daniels on hearing Mike's news.

"So what we're saying is that Fenwick knows we're hot on his tail. He picks up his load as normal and starts on the return journey. Somewhere along the way he loses the load. Catches the ferry and spends one hour in England and then high tails it back to France. Why? Trying to lay another false trail? Didn't think we'd find out about the return journey? Or maybe he was making a delivery. Linda only warned him on Tuesday, he might not have been able to cancel the shipment. Supposing he came over to drop the goods off and then headed straight back to France." Mike was thinking aloud. "He must be working with someone in France. He has a supplier over there and somebody must have helped him dispose of the load. That's where the trail starts."

The fourteenth tee afforded a superb view of the surrounding countryside, being slightly elevated and at the top end of the course. The fairway fell away in front of them for the first hundred yards before gently rising to the green, its circle of defensive bunkers clearly visible, four hundred and twenty yards away. Frank had just begun his down swing, the head of the big Bertha driver cutting through the air, when the bleeper sounded. He scuffed the ball forty yards along the ground and into the rough on the right. Nigel wasn't easily embarrassed but it had taken him several years on the waiting list and a great deal of networking to finally be offered membership of the exclusive club. Frank glowered at him as he fumbled in the zip pocket on the golf bag, trying desperately to retrieve the offending pager from among the detritus of tees, toffee papers and other assorted paraphernalia.

"Bloody sorry, Frank. Look, take a Mulligan. It was my fault."

He found the pager. Phone the office. Immediate. Bloody hell. He was one of only three members permitted to carry a bleeper on the golf course, the other two being a heart surgeon and a colonel in the army, reputedly currently on secondment to the SAS but unconfirmed of course. At the time he had felt it gave him a certain kudos, a member of an elite within an elite; right now he was wishing he'd never seen the bloody thing. He turned to his three playing partners.

"Terribly sorry and all that but I'm going to have to return to the club-house, urgent phone call to make."

The committee had reluctantly agreed to the bleepers but drew the line at allowing mobile phones on the course.

He was in a foul mood when he finally arrived back at the clubhouse. Apart from the embarrassment of abandoning his playing partners he had to endure the quizzical looks of the other four balls as he made his way back down the course, trolley pulled resolutely behind him.

"Couldn't it wait, Judd?" he barked down the phone. They were back in Mike's office, Daniels playing with Forrest, teasing him with an empty polystyrene cup, pretending to throw it, the dog enjoying the game.

"I need a contact, and I need one today." Mike was in no mood to back off.

"This driver chap going missing doesn't necessarily tell us anything."

"He's key to this case, Sir, I'm sure of that. The longer it takes us to get on his tail the more difficult it's going to be to track him down."

The Super was beginning to regain his composure. Young Judd was right, and he desperately needed to crack this case. The Chief Constable had made that plain at their Friday meeting.

Forrest barked, jumping up at Daniels and trying to wrench the cup from his hand.

"What was that noise, Judd?" asked the Super suspiciously. Mike frantically waved at Daniels, mouthing silently for him to shut the dog up.

"What was that, Sir?" he asked innocently.

"Thought I heard a dog bark."

"That's Daniels, Sir. Whooping cough, had it when he was a kid, comes back now and again," Mike replied, ad-libbing for all he was worth.

"Whooping cough you say. Never knew about that. So what is it exactly that you require?" he asked.

Mike explained.

The tarmac glistened in the late afternoon light, the sun's rays reflecting from the moisture deposited by the earlier shower. As the plane taxied to a halt Mike looked though the small oval window at the buildings lining the side of the airport, watching the small figures scurrying about inside the glass-fronted terminal. There was no scheduled service direct from Manchester direct to Marseilles; the best they could do was the British

Airways daily service to Lyon. This still left him one hundred and fifty miles short of his destination but on the high speed train the remainder of his journey would take less than two hours.

The Super had left a note of apology and a round of drinks behind the bar for his playing partners before departing the golf course. Arriving home he had used the many connections established over years of attending seminars and conferences to make the arrangements. This was what these gatherings were really all about. The joint Anglo French conference on comparative manning levels for community policing in urban areas he attended last year had done little to enlighten him as to the appropriate policies for his own beat but the contacts he made during the informal evening sessions were now proving invaluable. Commissioner Dubois' response was guarded at first but when Anderson mentioned the possible drugs connection he became far more cooperative. Drug trafficking was a major problem in the Marseilles area and he was desperate for any information that may assist him in identifying the culprits. The French policeman phoned through to the station in the early afternoon. His English was perfect.

"Commissioner Dubois has instructed me to provide any assistance that you require."

Mike quickly explained his plans. The officer phoned back ten minutes later with the name of the small hotel and arranged to pick him up the following morning.

Mike guessed that Jean Paul was about his own age, perhaps slightly younger.

"It will be difficult on a Sunday, we French like a day avec famille," said Jean Paul.

Mike shrugged. "The manager of the depot will definitely be there. I spoke to him on the phone last night. The others we'll have to play by ear. Did you put the all-points out?" he asked.

"Oui, every gendarme in France is now looking for your Mr Fenwick. It cannot be easy to hide a large red truck, I think. If he is out there we will find him. Of course he may have gone over the border to Italy or Switzerland. He could be anywhere by now. Austria, Germany maybe even Spain."

Mike was painfully aware of the possibilities.

The manager of the depot confirmed the details he had given Mike over the phone. He also gave them several sheets of paper containing details of the goods loaded on the truck prior to it leaving the depot. Jean Paul faxed the sheets through to police headquarters.

They found the first pick up point but the small factory was deserted, the gates firmly locked.

"Let's try the next one," said Mike.

"Les Martines."

"Who are Les Martines?" Mike asked.

"The family that own the tile factory."

"You know them?"

"Oh oui, I know the Martines," Jean Paul said this with a tone that suggested his previous encounters had not necessarily met with successful conclusions.

"Father Eric and sons Pierre and Jacques. They are, what is the English phrase, the criminal petits."

"Petty criminals?"

"Oui, correct. Petty criminals. Nothing substantial, fencing stolen goods, ringing the odd car. We can never make anything stick but we know they are at it," replied Jean Paul.

They turned off the main road and followed the track down into the quarry floor. Mike's first impression was that the place was deserted as he stood on the hard white stone surface taking in the layout of the place but as he looked around a man appeared from one of the sheds and walked towards them. A look of recognition flashed across the man's face as he approached.

"Inspector Delon. What brings you out here on a Sunday? Don't they give you a day of rest anymore?"

"Bonjour, Eric. We just want to ask you a few questions. We're trying to trace the driver of the truck that called here on Thursday morning. This gentleman with me is an English policeman."

The conversation had been conducted in French and Mike understood little of what was said. The man looked at him.

"Le gendarme Anglais?"

"Oui, Eric. Le gendarme Anglais."

Jean Paul looked at Mike.

"Ask him if we can see the docket. They should have a collection note," said Mike.

Jean Paul interpreted. The man shrugged and gestured towards the caravan.

The three of them made their way across the yard, Eric and Jean Paul entering the caravan to retrieve the docket while Mike waited outside. He stood by the van, kicking his heels, waiting for the men to emerge. It was then that he noticed the small brass plaque lying in the dust at his feet. Picking it up he read the inscription and casually placed it in the pocket of his chinos as Eric returned with the docket. After checking the signature and asking a few further questions the two policemen departed.

"Everything looked to be in order," said Jean Paul, as they drove down the unmade road.

"Look what I found on the ground by the caravan." He retrieved the plaque from his pocket and handed it to Jean Paul.

Jean Paul briefly inspected the plaque.

"So?"

"Notice the name. Crane Frauhauf. I've seen that before, on the back of the trucks in Listers yard."

"And on the back of just about every other truck you've ever seen in your life," replied Jean Paul.

"What?"

"Crane Frauhauf. They're the biggest manufacturers of trailers in Europe. Next time you're passing a queue of articulated lorries take a look at the back end. You'll find Crane Frauhauf on the majority of them."

Mike felt deflated and slightly stupid. He'd thought finding the plaque was significant. One of those strokes of luck you needed in a case like this.

"Probably not even off your truck."

They arrived back at police headquarters in the early afternoon. Mike called Daniels and sat back to wait. Daniels was back to him within the hour. He found Jean Paul in the corridor talking to a colleague.

"It is off my truck!" he triumphantly told Jean Paul.

Jean Paul didn't twig at first.

"The plaque. I've just had confirmation. They checked the build number. That plaque is off Fenwick's trailer."

"But what does it prove? We know Fenwick's truck was at the quarry. The plaque fell off his trailer. So what?"

"Bit of a coincidence, don't you think? Presumably Crane Frauhauf attach the plaque in such a way as to make sure it doesn't fall off. Let's find out. You said there are thousands of these on the road. Find me one."

Jean Paul looked at him. "Not on a Sunday. Commercial traffic isn't allowed on the road at the weekends in France."

Mike wasn't letting him get off that easy. "OK, so where do they all park up?"

The lorry park was on the outskirts of the city. An inspection under the rear of a couple of the trailers confirmed Mike's suspicions. It would take more than a gentle buffeting to dislodge the rivets that held the plaque in place.

Mike caught the first train on the Monday morning back to Lyon and boarded the 10.00 flight. He was still puzzled by the plaque and its significance. He felt sure that something had happened in the quarry that Thursday morning and that the Martines were in some way involved. The obvious reason for removing the plaque was to hide the identity of the trailer. Were the Martines in league with Bill Fenwick? Had they disposed of the load? And where was Bill Fenwick?

He arrived back at the station to find that little progress had been made on the Linda Walker murder. The Stafford police had circulated her picture around all the local bars and clubs but nobody recollected seeing her on the Thursday evening. Their own enquiries had revealed nothing more than a list of friends and acquaintances, some on more intimate terms than others, but none with any motive for, or inclination towards, murder. A copy of the pathologist's report lay on his desk that confirmed much of what he had already been told. She had died by strangulation, most probably, from the pattern of bruising, by somebody using their bare hands. In the three hours prior to death she had drunk a large quantity of a raspberry flavoured alcoholic drink, the last drink being consumed not more than fifteen minutes before her death. The time of death was between 11.00 and 11.30 on the Thursday night. The report reminded him to ring DCI Godfrey.

"Mike Judd here. I've just been reading the pathologist's report. When are you releasing the body?"

"Tomorrow, probably. We have no further requirements and the family are anxious to proceed with the funeral arrangements."

"How would you feel if I asked for a second autopsy? Had our man up here have a look at her," asked Mike.

"What are you suggesting?" Godfrey replied. Mike could hear the edge in the voice.

"Nothing at all. I'm sure your man has done a first class job. It's just that Dr Seymour conducted the autopsies on all the other victims. If our killer's the same man Seymour may spot some similarity, something your man wouldn't know about."

Whelan had to concede it made sense, the kid wasn't stupid.

"OK. I wouldn't have any objection. One other point while you're on.

Remember you were asking me on Friday why anybody would want to kill Linda?"

"Yes."

"Well there's another possibility, isn't there."

"Is there?" Mike had been wracking his brain for two days and he couldn't come up with one.

"Struck me at the weekend, while I was pruning the roses. Somebody at the depot has to be in league with Bill Fenwick, otherwise how did he know you were after him? But supposing our Linda is an innocent party, not involved in the smuggling. Quite frankly from the background information I've picked up I don't think she'd have the brains for it and there's no indication of any financial irregularities. Supposing a third party saw you visiting the depot on Tuesday, asked Linda what you were after, and she told them you wanted to talk to this Fenwick chap. Now if Linda was still alive the first thing you would have done when Fenwick disappeared would have been to ask her who she'd told about the police wanting to talk to Fenwick. Am I right?"

"Right." The penny was beginning to drop.

"So whoever asked her had to get rid of her, otherwise she would have pointed the finger straight at him."

"You're a genius."

"I have my days."

"Thanks, Bob. I'll treat you to lunch next time I visit."

Dr Seymour conducted the second autopsy on the Tuesday. He was able to add little to the previous report.

Mike received the call from Jean Paul later in the afternoon. They'd had a bit of luck. One of his snouts had been offered half a dozen of the blue glazed lamps produced by the small ceramics factory in Marseilles at a knock down price. Two crates containing sixty of the lamps had been on the truck, destined for The Lighting Emporium, a specialist shop in

Knightsbridge, when it disappeared. Mike made a suggestion to Jean Paul. He desisted; Commissioner Dubois would never buy it. Mike urged him to give it a try.

Daniels had not been idle while Mike was away.

"Fenwick is definitely up to something. The house is the giveaway. Nothing provable, but I know what I can afford on my salary bringing up two kids and there's no way they can afford the lifestyle they have on what Fenwick earns. New fitted kitchen, conservatory built on to the lounge, bathroom recently installed. And then there are all the appliances. Dishwasher, washing machine, microwave, hob cooker. All top quality. And as for the kids' stuff. Computers, Sony games consoles, mountain bikes. I've put a team onto it, ask some questions, find out what he's up to," he told Mike.

Chapter 27

The Super arranged the interview with Jack Hargreaves. It was extremely sensitive, politically, and he didn't want to cause any bad feeling. They were both colleagues and competitors, both with their eye on the Chief Constable's job and Anderson was aware that if not handled sensitively the request could be misinterpreted.

"I understand you serve on the committee that administers the Lister charitable trust, Superintendent." Mike said.

Hargreaves sat opposite him, a large boned man with a face of granite, grey hair cropped short, not the sort of man you would want to mess with. A proper old style northern copper, thought Mike.

"That's correct."

"The trust is the major shareholder in Lister Haulage. Has any member of the committee ever raised the option of selling the business?"

"The situation wouldn't arise. Certainly while George Lister was alive there was an unwritten rule that the business was sacrosanct. The committee would never have considered the option," replied Hargreaves.

"And now that George is dead?" asked Mike.

"I suppose it's possible. If we believed that by selling the haulage business and reinvesting elsewhere we could achieve a better return, then yes, we would be duty-bound to consider the matter."

"But none of the committee members has ever suggested such an option."

"Not to me, Chief Inspector."

Mike revisited George Lister's house on the Tuesday, killing time while the hunt for Bill Fenwick continued, going over old ground, making sure every angle had been covered, checking that he hadn't missed anything first time round. The door was answered by a woman in her late forties who introduced herself as Margaret, George's niece. They hadn't met previously; she was in Spain at the time of the murder and Daniels had interviewed her on her return.

"I understand you spend much of the year in Spain now," Mike said once they were seated in the lounge.

"That's right. I bought an apartment out there several years ago, close to Fuengirola. I'm back for the funeral on Thursday."

Mike offered his condolences.

"It must be nice, living in the sun all year round."

"It is, although the weather in winter can be quite changeable. But you don't get the cold and the damp that you get over here."

"And I should think the scenery is a little more attractive than it is in Bolton."

"That's true, although we didn't live in Bolton, of course."

"Sorry, I'd presumed that you did." Mike had never given the matter any thought.

"No, the family house was in Hale. It's a lovely little village. But after Craig's father died I was never comfortable in the house, too many memories. When Craig went to college I sold it and bought a flat, used the rest of the proceeds to buy the apartment in Spain. They fetch a very good price you know, Chief Inspector, houses in that part of Cheshire."

He supposed they did. It looked like he was in for the whole life story.

"Anyway, I found myself spending more and more time in Spain and George said it was stupid keeping the two places when I was only over here for a few weeks a year and he had plenty of room to put me up. So I sold the flat and whenever I visit now I stay here, at George's place." She became a bit weepy at this point.

"Of course the house passes to you, doesn't it? Will you keep the place?" Mike asked.

"I don't think so. It's very difficult. I know George loved it here but what use would I have for it? It's far too large for my needs. And then there's Mrs Jeffries of course."

"How's she bearing up? She was very upset," he asked.

"She still is, she and George became very close over the years in a strange sort of way. She was in cleaning yesterday. I told her There's no need, Mrs Jeffries, but she insists. At least George left her a nice little nest egg so she'll be alright financially."

"What about Craig? He seems to be handling it alright."

"Yes, well of course they weren't that close really, Craig and George. Don't get me wrong, they got on fine together but I think the age difference was a bit too much. Nothing in common."

"And when are you planning to go back to Spain?"

"On Friday. The flight's booked. Just need to sort out a few things at this end before I go."

Mike was halfway back to the station when the significance of it hit him. It made sense, certainly a strong possibility. There was something else, something that had struck him the previous day when he'd been going over the statements. He turned the car round and headed back towards Bolton. There was no answer at Jim Roberts's house. He was on the point of putting a note through the letterbox when Mrs Jeffries appeared at the end of the street, shopping basket on wheels in tow.

"Hello, Chief Inspector. Are you looking for Jim?"

"That's right, I need to ask him a few more questions."

"He'll be down at the allotments. Always goes on a Tuesday."

Mrs Jeffries gave him directions and he set out in pursuit of Jim.

The allotments were alongside the railway, a long thin stretch of ground, the individual plots separated by hard packed soil paths, with sheds of all shapes and sizes apparently randomly placed throughout. At first glance the allotments looked a mess – sheds, canes, compost heaps, wheelbarrows, water butts, and vegetation of all shapes and sizes scattered in a haphazard fashion – but closer inspection revealed that each plot had its own pattern, the canes placed in lines prepared for this year's crop of runner beans or sweet peas, the winter cabbage in strict regimental order, the tilled soil of the raised bed growing the early potatoes. Many of the plots were unattended but Mike found an old man pottering about on one near the entrance gate.

"I'm looking for Jim Roberts."

The old man pointed. "Down the far end on the right," and continued with his work.

He made his way to the far end of the plots but found no sign of life. He was just about to leave when he thought he detected movement within the shed close by. He couldn't see inside the darkened interior through the open door but was certain there was someone in there. He wandered over and as he approached Jim Roberts appeared from within.

"Inspector Judd?" he called.

"Hello Jim, need to ask you a few more questions if you have a minute."

Jim was looking a little flustered and as Mike approached the open door he caught the unmistakable smell of marijuana drifting from the shed. He threw him a look; Jim knew he'd been found out.

"It's for me rheumatism, Inspector, some days I can hardly walk with the knees. It's the only thing that does any good. My nephew gets it me."

"Let's pretend I didn't hear that, OK?" Mike replied. Although against the law Mike could see little harm in the old man relieving his pain by smoking the class C drug. "There's something you said in your statement I need to clarify."

"I'll do my best," replied Jim.

"We talked about the trouble at the yard. Somebody smuggling cigarettes."

"That's right."

"And you said George told you 'They'd sorted it'. What did you mean by that?" Mike enquired.

"You know. Sorted it out. Given the driver a telling off. Marked his card."

"But who are 'they'. That implies more than one person."

"That's right. George and Craig."

"How do you know it was George and Craig?" asked Mike.

"Because George told me before, when he first found the compartment. Said he'd told Craig to find out what the bloke was up to."

"When was that? When did he first tell you about it."

"Let me see now, must have been five or six weeks ago. Yes, that would be right, about six weeks ago. George had been down at the yard, found the compartment. Said he didn't want to show the lad up. Said it would make Craig look a bit daft if the drivers were smuggling stuff and he didn't know anything about it, so George kept it quiet. Tipped Craig the wink when he came round for his dinner that week. Give him a chance to sort it out. That way he doesn't lose face."

"And it was Craig who was going to have words with the driver, not George?" asked Mike.

"That's right."

"Why did it take such a long time?"

"Trying to catch him at it. Bill only does the Marseilles run once a fortnight. Craig wanted to catch him at it. But the first couple of times he checked the compartment was empty. I suppose he was stopping somewhere on the way up from London and retrieving he fags. Anyway George was losing patience, told Craig it had to be sorted."

"So when George said they'd sorted it what he really meant was that Craig had sorted it."

"Yes, I suppose he did. George had found the compartment and Craig dealt with the driver," replied Jim, perplexed as to why the young policeman was so excited.

Back at the station he called Daniels into his office.

"I've a fair idea who murdered Linda Walker and who's either involved in or responsible for the other murders, now it's just a matter of proving it," Mike told him.

Daniels looked at him, eyebrows raised.

"It's Craig Osborne. He's in this with Fenwick.

One, Jim Roberts confirmed this morning that George Lister told Craig about the compartment in early January, before the killings started, at one of their dinners but agreed to keep it between the two of them.

Two, Craig was responsible for organizing the do in Tatton Park. We know that one of the girls borrowed the keys but it was Craig and Toby who waited behind at the depot for Jim to arrive back from London so one of the two of them must have been in possession of the keys at that point. As I said, Craig was already aware that George knew about the compartment by this time and Craig was either already planning the murders or else maybe seeing the park gave him the idea. Either way he had a copy of the keys made at some stage during the afternoon.

Three, it was Craig, not George, who tackled Fenwick about the compartment, or at least supposedly tackled him. If Craig was an innocent party then Fenwick should have arranged to have him bumped off at the same time as George Lister if the smugglers wanted to maintain the secret.

Four, he visited George quite often. George would have found nothing particularly unusual in Craig appearing on his doorstep on the night of his murder and whenever Craig visited it was their custom to have an early evening drink. Mrs Jeffries said she bought in lager especially for Craig's visits. My guess is that George went to pour himself a scotch and while his back was turned Craig bashed him over the head, hence the broken glass.

Five, he was very friendly with Linda Walker. If Bob Godfrey's theory is correct, and I think it is, then he killed Linda because he saw us visiting on the Tuesday and asked Linda what we were after. Linda told him we were looking for Bill Fenwick and that's when the balloon went up.

Six, it was something Helen said last week, sorry, Professor Bleasdale said last week. The motive for the crime is apparently based in Bolton but all the killings, apart from Linda Walker's which is in many ways different to the others, took place in a fairly confined area over thirty miles away. Why would that be? The answer is that the killer knows that area well, feels safe operating there. And Craig's mother told me this afternoon that the family house where Craig was brought up was in Hale, four or five miles from where the murders took place."

Daniels thought for a moment, looking for a hole in the argument.

"The facts certainly point towards Craig being involved, sounds like we need to have a word with the young man."

"Yes, but not quite yet. Put a team onto him. I want all the background we can get before I tackle him."

"There's something else we turned up today, rather blows a hole in your theory I'm afraid, Guv", said Daniels. "I spoke with Fenwick's wife this morning. She's worried sick, can't think what's happened to him, and either she's a damn good actress or it's genuine. I put the heat on, told her we suspected her husband of being involved in a major drug smuggling operation. That did it; she broke down, spilled everything. Told me she knew it was wrong but all Bill was doing was smuggling a few cigarettes in and he'd never get involved in anything like drugs. She gave me the name of his contact, a small time operator in Bolton, known by the local police as a fence, but not into anything heavy. He buys the cigarettes off Fenwick. We tracked him down and I offered him a deal to tell me the truth on this one, figured it was worth losing a receiving stolen property to get to the truth." He looked at Mike who nodded, agreeing with his assessment. "Fenwick brings in a hundred cartons each trip, that's one thousand packs. Sells them to the fence who distributes them to various small shops, pubs, that sort of thing, around the Bolton area. I checked with Jean Paul and based on what the fence is paying him Fenwick makes about five hundred pounds a trip, not a bad little sideline," Daniels told him.

"But not enough to kill someone for," replied Mike dejectedly, thinking for a moment. "But if Fenwick's only into cigarettes then why do a disappearing act? He's got no previous. The most he'd get for smuggling fags is a hefty fine."

Daniels nodded. "I know, it just doesn't add up."

"I still want to have a good look at Craig, see what turns up."

"Will do, Guv," replied Daniels. So the professor's a lady and we're on first name terms, he thought as he left the office, a smile playing on his lips. That could explain where he was on Friday morning.

Commissioner Dubois had been sceptical at first but Jean Paul convinced him that the disruption would be minimal and that while it was something of a long shot he could see no other means of discovering the whereabouts of the missing truck. Certainly it may be well gone by now, parked up in some haulage yard in God only knows where, but the discovery of part of the load for sale on the black market led him to suspect that this was a local job and that the cab and trailer might also have been sold onto one of the less reputable hauliers in the area. The task was made easier by the fact that, with the Mediterranean covering the back door, there are only three major trunk roads out of the city to cover; the road running east to Toulon, the road heading north-east to Aix-en-Provence, and the road to the west leading to Avignon and the north.

The truck drivers thought little of it as the gendarme waved them in to the side of the road, cursing mildly at the officialdom that seemed to have nothing better to do than harass an honest man trying to earn a day's pay with their never ending regulations, spot checks and forms to fill out. They were pleasantly surprised when, almost as soon as the air brakes brought the truck to a halt, the gendarme sent them on their way again after no more than a cursory enquiry as to their final destination. From their position in the cab they couldn't see the technician who quickly bobbed his head under the rear of the truck to check for the small brass plaque that denoted the trailer's providence. One or two weren't so fortunate and found themselves detained for further questioning. Of the thousand plus lorries they stopped over the two day period thirty-five were found to have been missing the maker's mark. Further enquiries over the next two weeks resulted in over twenty prosecutions for receiving stolen property and, Jean Paul reflected, although not the original goal of the exercise, the results would provide a healthy boost to this month's clear up rates.

Eighteen of the thirty-five could be discounted immediately, having only a single rear axle, and examination of the six inch high metal band that made up the outer frame of the flatbed accounted for another nine. That left eight with the potential to be the missing trailer. The technician used his penknife to remove a sample of paint from each of these, carefully sealing and marking the small plastic bags that contained the loosened paint flakes. The lab already possessed a sample of paint provided by Listers and after completing the chemical analysis and comparing the results they were able to confirm that they had a match with the paint from the trailer being pulled by the Peugeot cab belonging to Bresson Haulage, stopped on the Avignon road as it headed north with a load of tin cans destined for the Jesta fruit drinks factory just outside Lyon.

Bresson Haulage proved to be something of a dead end for Jean Paul.

"Where did you obtain the trailer?"

"Can't remember."

"When did you obtain the trailer?"

"Can't remember."

"How long has the trailer been in your yard?"

"Can't remember."

The trailer would be confiscated and returned to Listers, the brothers would be looking at a ten thousand franc fine and a black mark on their record, of which there were several already, but other than that there was nothing further he could do.

Chapter 28

The interview room was empty apart from the table, four chairs and tape machine sitting on the shelf. Mike and Daniels were seated on one side of the table, Craig on the other. The initial background checks had revealed nothing of any apparent consequence about Craig: twenty-six years old; attended a local private school as a day boy; undistinguished academic record; scraped together two A levels; studied design at the former polytechnic, now university, of Walsall; left with a pass degree; bummed around Europe for six months before joining the family firm. Flat in Salford Quays, mortgage with Abbey National, no signs of any financial irregularities. Craig had expressed surprise and a certain amount of indignation when they'd collected him from the depot that morning but Mike had assured him it was routine in murder cases; they had to question anybody with the slightest connection to the case.

"We wish to ask you some questions in connection with the death of George Lister. You are not under arrest and are free to leave at any time, do you understand that Craig?" asked Mike.

Craig nodded.

"Where were you on the night of George's death?"

"I returned from work at about 6.30. Had something to eat, watched TV. Then I went to play football. Left the flat at about 8.30, game was at 9.00, finished at 10.00, went with some of the lads to the Bull for a pint after the match, we were there 'til about 11.30 and then I went home to bed."

"Where did you play football?" Mike enquired.

"Urmston Leisure Centre. We have a regular booking on a Wednesday night."

"We'll need the names of the people you played with," Daniels interrupted.

"No problem."

"What about the Wednesday before that? Where were you then?" Mike interjected.

"Same routine, playing football. The team has a regular booking, play every Wednesday night at 9.00, have done for the last three or four years," Craig replied.

"Where were you last Thursday night?" asked Mike.

Craig thought for a minute. "Stayed in. That's right, I arrived home from work at about 7.00 and stayed in all night."

Mike decided on a change of tack.

"There was a problem with Bill Fenwick's truck wasn't there, Craig? Tell me about that."

"You're referring to the hidden compartment?"

"That's right."

"Uncle George found a hidden compartment under the truck, asked me to find out what was going on. Well, Bill's a regular on the Marseilles run so the chances are he's trying to smuggle in a few extra fags."

"When did George tell you about the compartment?"

"That would be in January sometime, I can't remember exactly when," replied Craig.

"What did you do about it?"

"I checked it out. Made sure the compartment was there and then tried to catch him at it."

"So you saw the compartment?" asked Mike.

"That's right. Under the trailer, between the axles."

"And when did you speak to Bill Fenwick about it?"

"Must have been about three weeks ago."

"What did Bill say?"

"Wasn't a lot he could say, I'd caught him red-handed. Told him if it ever happened again he'd be for the high jump."

Mike thanked him for his assistance and left Daniels to take the names of the football players who would provide his alibi.

Back in the office Mike looked over to where Daniels stood.

"He's good, isn't he?"

"Didn't bat an eyelid," replied Daniels.

"The football alibi will hold up. I knew I'd seen him somewhere before, I was playing against him that night. Convenient though, isn't it? The night of the week when all the murders are committed is the one night of the week when he has a cast iron alibi."

Daniels nodded. "So where do we go from here?"

"I still say he's involved. We need to find the woman, his accomplice. Check out the football players. Make sure he definitely went for a drink with them afterwards and find out how long he stayed. Ask them about his friends, whether he has any romantic attachments. I'm going to take a poke around in Salford Quays, see if anybody remembers seeing him last Thursday night."

The block of six flats was one of four built around a central courtyard by the side of the disused docks. The whole area was undergoing regeneration, a mixture of futuristic office blocks clad in reflective glass and small residential areas such as the one he was now looking at. Paved walkways and modern street furniture were everywhere and Mike guessed that none of the buildings in the area was more than two or three years old. Each block contained three levels with two flats on each level. Craig's flat was on the first floor, to the right of the central stairwell. He began the wearisome task of knocking on doors. The immediate next-door neighbour didn't know Craig well, she'd only moved in three months ago, but thought he seemed a pleasant enough chap and no, she couldn't remember seeing him last Thursday. Similar results from the other flats in the block other than the flat immediately below Craig's where the couple were sure that his car had been there all Thursday evening, the side window of their lounge overlooked the parking bay, and they remembered his TV being on until quite late, the husband working in the study until after midnight, the background noise making it difficult for him to concentrate.

Mike tried the block of flats to the left, no joy. Same at the block on the right. He rang the doorbell of the top right-hand flat of the block opposite, resigned to the fact that the morning's work was in vain. The man that opened the door was in his seventies, smartly turned out in blue blazer, white shirt, paisley cravat and grey slacks, back ramrod straight, a clipped accent.

"Yes, young man? What can I do for you?"

Mike explained who he was and the purpose of his visit for the umpteenth time that morning.

"Identification, please?" the man asked. Mike showed him his warrant card which the man took from him and studied for several seconds before handing it back.

"Everything seems to be in order. You'd better come in, young man."

Mike followed him through into the lounge that ran the whole width of the building. The French windows at one end led onto a small balcony that overlooked the docks, the picture window at the other end looked onto the courtyard and the other flats. The man walked over to the coffee table and picked up a notebook.

"Now, who's the blighter you're interested in?" he asked. Mike explained again.

"In a spot of bother is he? Up to no good?"

"Nothing like that, Sir. Just routine enquiries."

The man flipped through the notebook. "Target O1R, let me see."

Mike gave him a quizzical look.

"O1R. That's opposite, first floor, right-hand flat. Do you see? RGL. That would be the right-hand block, ground floor, left-hand flat. Getting the hang of it? Now it gets a bit more complex with the couples. O2LW for instance, that would be opposite, second floor, left-hand flat, but the woman. O2LM, same flat but the man. Easy enough once you know how it works. Thought it up myself, keep it simple, that's my motto."

Mike nodded. He noticed the binoculars on the windowsill.

"Now, last Thursday evening you said. Let me see." The man flicked back a couple of pages. "Here we are. Target O1R arrived home 6.32. Left at 7.48. That what you want to know?"

"You keep a record of all the movements?" Mike asked, incredulous.

"Absolutely. Gives me something to do you see. Ex-Navy. Used to working by the book. Moved here to be by the water. Not comfortable if I can't see the water, all those years at sea I suppose. But we've had a spot of trouble, burglaries, mindless vandalism, that sort of thing. Kids mostly, young rascals who don't give a damn, makes you wonder what their parents are like. So we formed a neighbourhood watch. I'm secretary. Keep an eye on things. Make a note of any movements, that's what they tell you to do."

One of the less sought after but unavoidable jobs in the force was serving on the crime prevention committees, the link between public and police, spending hours in endless meetings discussing the locks to be fitted to pensioners' front doors, whether funding is available for CCTV cameras and briefing neighbourhood watch schemes on how to combat crime. The briefings stressed the need to make a note of any unusual movements in the neighbourhood, any cars that seemed out of place, any strangers acting suspiciously. Mike was sure that in all the briefings he had given over the years he had never once suggested that keeping detailed records of one's neighbours' movements would help reduce the local crime rate, but he decided to let the matter go.

"You're certain that Mr Osborne left the flat at 7.48 last Thursday evening."

"Definitely."

"The people in the downstairs flat said his car was here all evening," he said, testing the man.

The man consulted the notebook.

"It was. Unusual that. Subject normally drives, never known him not to take the car. But that night he walked. Noted it down in the book."

"And what time did he return?"

He consulted the notebook again.

"He didn't, at least not on my watch. Finish at midnight you see. Not one for staying up late."

He found Craig in his office.

"At the station you said you stayed in last Thursday night."

Craig nodded, unconcerned. "That's right."

"You sure about that?"

Craig's mind was racing, what did the Inspector know? He'd bluff it out, see what happened.

"Absolutely. Stayed in all night. Did a bit of ironing, watched the box, generally lazed about."

"We have an eye witness who says he saw you leave the flat."

Craig gave a ham performance of a man searching his memory.

"I remember now, I went out for a walk, if that's what you mean? Left about 7.30 I suppose, perhaps a bit later. It was a pleasant evening, thought I'd get some fresh air. Walked around the dock and returned about half an hour later."

"Why didn't you mention this before?" asked Mike.

"I'd forgotten all about it until you mentioned somebody seeing me leaving. Why? It's not important, is it?"

"No Craig, it isn't important."

When he returned to the station he found Daniels already in the ops room.

"Any joy with Craig's friends?" asked Mike.

"They confirm that he played football that night and that they all went back to the Bull afterwards, including Craig. They didn't leave until gone drinking-up time, at least 11.30."

Mike interrupted, "Which puts Craig well in the clear for murdering George. What about his social life?"

"Bit of a dark horse really. The lads only know him through the football, have a drink on a Wednesday night but that's about it. They've never seen him out and about with anyone and he's never mentioned anything about a girlfriend in conversation. Same story whoever we talk to. Keeps himself to himself. We can't find anybody who knows him socially or knows anything about any of his relationships."

"Well let's keep digging, someone must know where he goes of a night. Anything else?"

"Superintendent Hargreaves rang. Asked you to contact him."

Mike dialled the number.

"The matter we discussed on Tuesday. Thought you might be interested to know that the committee met last night to discuss electing a new member to replace George and catch up on one or two administrative duties. The question of the future of Lister Haulage was raised."

"Who raised the idea, Sir?" Mike asked, hanging on to his every word.

"Elaine Smedley."

"What exactly did she say, Sir?"

"Nothing very much really. The chairman moved to 'Any Other Business' and Elaine asked that the committee give consideration to the option of disposing of some or all of our shareholding in Lister Haulage and diversify our investments so as to provide a more balanced portfolio and maximize the income potential."

"And what action will the committee take?"

"We shall have to look at it. Fact is that she has a point. Obviously as long as George was at the helm then we were all quite happy to leave things as they stood; it's by his generosity that the trust existed and nobody would have dreamt of suggesting anything that might have upset him. But now that he is no longer with us we have to be realistic. It would make far more sense to spread the investments."

Mike thanked the Superintendent and rang off.

"Couple more names for you to look into," he said, handing Daniels the sheet of paper.

That evening Mike drove over to Nottingham. Helen cooked them a simple meal of tuna pasta with a green salad and garlic bread on the side, Mike provided the bottle of Chardonnay. Lying on the sofa afterwards, her head resting on his chest, Forrest happily snoozing on the floor, he brought her up to speed with the latest details.

"It must be a very strong relationship," Helen opinioned.

"Why's that?"

"Imagine the trust you would need to have in one another, it's one of the features of cases like this. Usually there is one very dominant and manipulative character and one obsessive but mentally weak, that how it works. Just think about it for a minute. Have you ever been in love?"

She looked up at him, big brown eyes enquiring. Bachman-Turner Overdrive sprung into his mind. He presumed she meant apart from now. It was too soon in the relationship to drop that little bit of news on her; he didn't want to frighten her off before things had a chance to develop.

"I think so, maybe, once."

"What sort of wimpish answer is that, either you've been in love or you haven't?"

Christ, she could be tough when she wanted to be. He remembered back to the girl he'd met in his final year at university. Yes he'd been in love, God how he'd been in love. They'd been together for four years, she going on to be a teacher, him working his way up through the promotional ladder. But he'd never been able to commit and finally she'd gone off with another teacher from the school. It had taken him years to get over the loss; maybe he was still getting over it. He spoke quietly.

"Yes, I've been in love."

She sensed the hurt in his voice, knew that she'd hit a raw nerve. That hadn't been her intention, she just wanted to demonstrate the point. Well, there was no undoing what had been done. She ploughed on.

"And if, at the height of that relationship, when you were totally and absolutely infatuated, your partner asked you to do something that you considered to be totally abhorrent, something that went completely against your moral code, such as rob a bank or murder someone, how would you have reacted?"

He tried to think back. How had he felt, how would he have reacted? It was easier to think of Helen. She was right. He was in love but if she suggested anything like that he'd conclude that he had made a terrible mistake, that the person he was with wasn't who he had thought she was. The relationship would be over. "I'd end the relationship, walk away."

"Exactly. That's what most people's reaction would be. You need to be incredibly sure of your hold over the other person before you'd dare to draw them into you web."

She was right, as usual.

Chapter 29

The drive down to Walsall took nearly three hours, the three lanes of the M6 being stationary, bumper to bumper, on the approach to Birmingham, and Mike was in a foul mood by the time he arrived at the university. Parking the car outside the reception block, deliberately ignoring the sign indicating the space was reserved for the treasurer, he pushed through the glass doors and informed the receptionist in a gruff voice that he wished to see the bursar. A thin, bald headed man in his fifties wearing a woollen shirt, knitted tie, green cardigan, brown corduroys and, rather incongruously, thought Mike, a pair of black trainers appeared from the door on the right, a sign indicating that this was the entrance to the administration office, and after conversing briefly with Mike disappearing once more through the door. Mike had been waiting in the reception area for nearly twenty minutes and was on the verge of creating a scene when the bursar returned clutching a thick sheaf of papers.

"Sorry about the delay. The records are archived at the end of the academic year, had to go and dig them out of the storeroom. Now let me see, there may be something in here, depends where he stayed really," he said, thumbing through the papers. "We keep records for all the halls of residence, obviously, and quite a few of the flats are what we call controlled tenancies which means that although we don't own the buildings we allocate the students and are responsible for collecting the rents. Makes it easier all round; the landlords don't have to concern themselves with any of the administrative grind and we can keep an eye on the health and safety aspects, make sure the gas heaters are up to standard and that sort of thing. We have records for those. But a great many of the flats and houses in the area are beyond our control, landlords advertise in the local rag and deal direct with the students. Those we wouldn't be able to help you on."

He continued flipping through the papers, peering briefly at each sheet through the lower lens of his bifocals.

"Let's see now. Between four and seven years ago, you said."

"That's right."

"And we're looking for a C. Osborne."

Mike nodded "Correct."

Several more minutes passed as he continued to work methodically through the papers, refusing to be hurried, a man for whom the concept of pressure was an anathema.

"Ah yes, here we are. Highfields, two years on the trot. Probably his last two years unless I'm mistaken. A lot of the students take that route. We encourage them to stay in halls the first year, helps them to settle in, get to meet plenty of people. Second and third year they team up with their chums, rent a house. Highfields is on Garston Road, about three miles from the campus. Nice house, or at least it could be if it had a bit of money spent on it. Four bedrooms. Detached. Good sized gardens."

He was lost in his own world, eyes staring into the distance, his mind picturing the residence. Mike interrupted his thoughts.

"What about the other students who stayed in Highfields for those two years, do you have their names?"

"Let me see now. Wilson, Bennett, and Khan."

"And do you know where they went to, after they finished at the university?"

"Not my department I'm afraid. I look after them while they're here, once they leave they're no longer my responsibility. You need to speak to Mrs Hurst, in charge of careers advice. She might be able to help you."

Mrs Hurst was equally as helpful. She delved into one of the rows of green filing cabinets that lined the back wall of her office and returned with several buff folders.

"It isn't compulsory of course. We try to keep track of our former students, at least in the early years, but we rely on them to keep us up to date. Useful for compiling statistics: how many are in work; what sort of jobs; how much they're earning. But there's nothing we can do if the students don't return the forms. Let's see what we have. She opened one of the folders, looking through the contents. "P. Wilson. Here we are. Chemist, lower second class honours, joined ICI, haven't heard from him since. Now, D. Bennett you say." She picked up the second file. "Ah yes. Economics, pass degree. Don't know what happened to him. He didn't avail himself of our services, didn't have a job when he finished here as far as we are aware, and we haven't any news of him since. And A. Khan, wasn't it?" She opened the third folder. "My word, yes. Another Chemist. A first no less. Joined Shell oil. Still there as of last September. Sends back the form regularly every year."

Mike borrowed an office and a phone. The personnel officer at Shell confirmed that Mr Khan was still in their employment but was currently working on a project in Saudi Arabia, had been there for two months and wasn't due back for another four. Wilson had moved on from ICI two years ago and joined a small specialist chemicals company based in Runcorn.

The factory was in a modern industrial estate on the outskirts of town. Phil sat behind the desk, chubby faced, waist straining over the belt of his trousers, already two stone overweight and growing bigger by the year courtesy of an affection for junk food and too many nights propping up the bar at the Red Lion.

"You shared a house with Craig Osborne for two years."

"That's right. What's happened then? Old Craig in trouble with the police? Doesn't surprise me."

"Why do you say that?" asked Mike.

"He was a right idiot, Craig. Up for anything, totally out of control."

"Did you keep in touch with the other people in the house after you left university?"

"I speak to Ali occasionally on the phone, meet him about twice a year for a beer. Saw Dave a couple of times for a pint when we first finished, he went off bumming around Europe and I've never heard from him since. Probably holed up in a Greek taverna enjoying la Dolce Vita knowing Dave. Never spoke to Craig again, we weren't exactly best of chums by the end. He never really was a friend of mine, Dave knew him better."

"What about other friends? Was there anybody else Craig was close to?"

"Not really. He was a bit of a loner. Apart from Tony of course; they were inseparable. Started going together at the end of the first year, you rarely saw them apart for the next two years."

"What's Toni's surname, do you know?"

"Now you're asking," said Phil, ends of the fingers drubbing his forehead as he forced his mind back four years. Suddenly he looked up, clicked his fingers. "Mellor. That's it."

"I don't suppose you'd know where she went after she finished at Walsall?"

"Not a 'she', Inspector. It's Tony with a Y. Craig isn't in to the girls, he's strictly a man's man."

"Craig's gay?"

"Queer as a nine bob note. That's why we didn't get on too well. Not that I'm homophobic but Craig used to flaunt it."

"How did you all end up sharing the house?"

"Ali and I were on the same course, or at least on paper we were. In practice Ali was in a different world to me academically but we still got on alright. He's like that, Ali, really good lad. Bloody Einstein really but he never put any side on, didn't mind mixing with the rest of us plebs. Ali and I decided at the end of the first year to move out of halls and rent a house. We needed four to make up the rent on Highfields and I was pally with Dave, knew him from the rowing club and Dave knew Craig, had the next room to him in halls. So it all just sort of fitted. Dave never forgave himself but it wasn't his fault. Craig was OK at first but then he met Tony and the two of them started doing a lot of drugs. That's when he became totally obnoxious. Used to sit on the settee when we were there and he'd be stroking Tony's crotch, start snogging with him, deliberately to annoy us." His face puckered at the memory.

"What drugs was Craig doing?"

"I don't know really, not my scene. Dope, I suppose. He was always wired. Became hyperactive, charging round the house like a wailing banshee, used to drive us all nuts. By the end it was a relief to get out of the place."

"And do you know what happened to Tony?" asked Mike.

"No, but I presume he went wherever Craig went. Like I said they were very close."

"Thanks for your help."

"Anytime, Chief Inspector."

He checked back with Mrs Hurst but Tony Mellor was another one who had left the university without revealing his future plans. Daniels and his team spent the next two days checking every conceivable source for information but drew a blank. According to the records the Tony Mellor they were looking for had never had a job, never paid national insurance, never filled in a tax return, never registered with a doctor, never paid poll tax, never applied for a TV licence, never had a phone, never paid a gas bill, never paid an electricity bill, didn't have a bank account, didn't have a building society account and had never applied for a credit card. Zilch. Nothing.

Daniels fared better with the other names Mike had asked him to check.

He read from his notebook. "Toby Mathews, thirty-nine, married to Christine, two children, Charlotte, twelve, Caitlin, ten. Educated Durham, upper second in History. Career path seems OK. Big break came when he was headhunted by Listers. Big mortgage. Kids both at private school, bank account strained but nothing out of the ordinary, credit cards ditto. Elaine Smedley, forty seven, divorced six years ago, no kids, lives alone, bank account and credit cards OK."

Mike looked at him. "Great, clean as a whistle."

Daniels smiled his triumphant smile. "Haven't finished yet, Guv. She remortgaged the house three years ago. Took out an additional sixty thousand."

Mike let out a low whistle.

"Thought it was worth finding out why. Took a bit of digging but," he waited, stretching out the drama

"Come on, get on with it." Mike said, irritated.

"She needed it to pay off the bookies. It seems our headmistress has the gambling bug, can't shake it off. She's an irregular member of Gamblers Anonymous, goes for a few months and then falls by the wayside. She has an account with Laskys. Currently twenty thousand in the red and on stop."

"Keep practising and one day you'll make a decent detective, Daniels," Mike ribbed him as he left the office.

Jean Paul waited in the half light, leaning against the workman's hut, looking up and down the deserted dock. To his left, not two hundred yards away, he could see the lights of the bars and cafés of the old port, hear the music and babbling voices wafting across the still waters as the tourists took their evening promenade, peering at the menus, deciding which venue they would sample this evening. To his right three container ships lay at berth, the massive hulls dwarfing their surroundings, giant ropes tethering them to the dockside, everything larger than life. Several fishing boats were tied up to the jetty jutting out in front of him, rigging silhouetted against the evening sky, but the crews had long since departed for the back street bars where anise was cheap and the conversation robust. A shabbily dressed man sporting several days' grey stubble, the neck of a bottle protruding from the pocket of the filthy overcoat, appeared from the shadows behind him, huddled against the wall of the shed, keeping to the shadows, invisible to prying eyes.

"What's the word on the street?" asked Jean Paul.

"The truck was disposed of."

"And the driver?"

The man pulled a finger across his throat.

"You sure?" asked Jean Paul, disbelief in his tone.

"That's the word."

Jean Paul reached into his back pocket and handed the man the three one hundred franc notes.

"Go carefully, Philippe." The man disappeared into the shadows whence he came.

Mike requested a meeting with the Super first thing Monday morning.

"Have you any idea how much surveillance costs? We're talking teams operating around the clock. I'm under pressure to curtail overtime and you're asking me to blow the entire year's budget on one operation."

"I don't see any other way of progressing the case. I'm sure Craig's up to his neck in it and I wouldn't mind betting that this Tony Mellor is his accomplice. If they're as close as we're led to believe then Craig will lead us to his boyfriend sooner or later."

"It had better be sooner rather than later. I'll agree to one week's surveillance; if there's no result by then I will have to review the situation, see what further steps are necessary."

"I need phone taps as well. On Toby Mathews and Elaine Smedley. Toby stands to make three million upwards if Elaine manages to convince the committee to sell Listers. In my book that's possible motive."

"I'll put in a request but without further evidence I doubt whether we'll be given authority." Superintendent Anderson picked up his pen and continued working on the papers on his desk. The meeting was over.

Seymour rang at 10.30 that morning.

"The Linda Walker autopsy. Did some further work on the stomach contents. Thought you might like to know we've been able to identify the drink. Something called raspberry Hooch. Surprisingly pleasant actually. Tried a bottle myself, strictly in the course of furthering medical knowledge you understand."

Godfrey's enquiries in Stafford produced no information as to the possible whereabouts of Linda Walker on the Thursday evening. Mike suggested he ask the nationals to run the story with a request for information, spread the net wider.

Chapter 30

Elaine walked through to the hallway of the modest bungalow reflecting, as she always did upon seeing the faded wallpaper and threadbare carpet, upon how her life might have turned out had it not been for the obsessional curse that forever kept her one step ahead of the bailiffs, and picked up the phone.

"When's the next committee meeting scheduled?" he asked.

"Tuesday evening. Special meeting to discuss George Lister's replacement."

"What about the Omega plan? How are we progressing?"

"I've spoken to Anne Fanshaw. She agrees it's a good idea. She was never too keen on George, thought he was a capitalist, exploiting the workers, usual socialist claptrap. With two of us beating the drum the others will have no choice other than to start giving the matter serious consideration. It's going to take a few weeks but I think we can swing it."

"Can you raise the issue on Tuesday, run it up the flagpole, see if it flies?"

"I suppose I could introduce it under Any Other Business," she replied.

"Good. Keep pushing. We only have a limited envelope of opportunity. This needs to happen sooner rather than later." He hung up.

The call from Jean Paul left Mike perplexed. If his informant was correct then who had murdered Fenwick? Why, where and when? Why did Fenwick return to Britain and then turn on his heels and head straight back to France, if indeed it was Fenwick that was driving? What was the connection between George Lister, Fenwick and Linda Walker? If Fenwick was only smuggling cigarettes then why kill him? And what about Toby? Three million was the best motive he could come up with at this point in time.

By the Friday morning Mike was a worried man. Craig's routine suggested nothing other than a man going about his daily business and the Super's time limit and patience were fast running out. There had been nothing: no clandestine meetings; no outings to unexpected locations; no phone calls to suspect numbers. Roy Simmonds, the ex-naval man, had readily agreed to them using his flat for the evening surveillance work, had been excited by the prospect, which proved a huge bonus. It allowed Mike to reduce the watch team to two overnight, which was at least keeping the overtime to a minimum. During the day they put three teams of two on him and swapped the vehicles daily.

Just after 11.00 on the Friday Craig left the office, the three cars tailing him, drove four miles across Bolton to a phone box situated at the entrance to a housing estate on the other side of town and made a brief call lasting no more than two minutes before retracing his route and returning to the office. Mike and Daniels were in the ops room, monitoring proceedings.

"What do you think that was all about?" asked Mike.

Daniels shrugged his shoulders. "Perhaps he's spotted the tail, guessed that if he's under surveillance his phone is probably tapped. Making a call to lover boy maybe?"

"He's obviously making some sort of arrangement, but for what?"

"Your guess is as good as mine, Guv."

There was nothing to do but wait.

At 12.15 Craig left the depot, joined the M61 at Junction 5, dropped on to the M62 heading towards Liverpool, and from there joined the M6 southbound. Using the three cars the tail on the motorway was straight-forward. They put one car in front of him, far enough out so as not to raise any suspicions but just close enough for the passenger to keep him in view in the additional rear view mirror. The other two cars kept half a mile back, the lead car feeding them instructions over the radio. They lost the lead car whenever Craig changed motorways but that wasn't a problem. One of the backup cars would take its place while the errant car double backed at the next junction, piling on the speed until it finally regained its place in the convoy. At 2.25 they were through Birmingham and still heading south.

Maybe he's visiting friends in London for the weekend, thought Mike. That's all I need. Three teams down in London for the weekend claiming meal and lodgings allowance, not to mention the overtime. He rang Marjorie, Toby's secretary, on the pretext of needing to have a word with Craig to clear up a few loose ends. Craig had left early, told Marjorie he was going away for the weekend, wanted to make an early start to avoid the traffic.

At 3.10 Craig took the slip road at Junction 15A. Slowing for the roundabout at the end of the slip road he noticed the two Rover 800s beginning the ascent. The chase team had nearly been caught unawares by his sudden manoeuvre. Lulled into a false sense of security by mile after mile of motorway the two detectives were engaged in a heated debate on the relative merits of McDonalds versus Burger King when the passenger, glancing occasionally at the additional rear view mirror, was just in time to see Craig, without any use of the indicators, veer from the outside lane across all three lanes and up onto the slip road. The two chasing Rovers gunned their engines in a frantic effort to catch him before he disappeared from view, the lead car accelerating through one hundred and twenty miles per hour as it hit the bottom of the slip road, the detectives catching a glimpse of Craig as he turned right at the roundabout. The driver decelerated, using the slope of the slip road to reduce the speed of the car.

Craig drove straight past the entrance to the lane, bringing the car to a standstill by the side of the road one hundred yards further on, watching as the two Rovers passed him without any apparent interest from either the couple in the first car or the two men in the second. The road prescribed a long bend to the right and he continued watching as the cars drove steadily down the road, able to see the roofline over the low hedge long after the rest of the body had disappeared from view. His eyes never left them until they finally passed behind the row of stone terraced houses that marked the beginning of the village some half a mile down the road. Still he waited, gaze firmly fixed on the distant village.

As soon as the Rover passed the cottage the female detective in the lead car went into action.

"Pull over. I'll take a look from behind the house, see what he's up to. You'd better move the cars out of sight in case he comes through."

The terraced houses fronted straight on to the pavement. She ran back to the end cottage and, peering around the gable end and across the recently ploughed field, could see the roof of Craig's car in the distance with Craig standing beside it. It was a stalemate. Her looking at Craig, Craig looking at her. That was how it felt. Nothing happened for five minutes.

"He's just sitting by the side of the road, Guv." The voice came over the radio.

"In Northamptonshire?" Mike asked.

"That's right. Pulled off the motorway like he was trying to lose a tail, now he's just sitting there."

"Can he see you?"

"No, we're in a village up the road. Blake's keeping an eye on him. Hold on, Guv. Looks like something's happening."

Suddenly Craig was on the move again. A quickly executed three-point turn and he was heading back towards the motorway. Gesturing franti-cally to Pete, who was standing at the top of the side road down which the two Rovers waited, she watched as Craig drove off into the distance. But he was no longer moving away from her. She guessed that he must have turned down another lane as she watched the black roof move from right to left across her field of vision. Come on, get those bloody cars up here, she thought, aware that he was getting away from them. The Rover pulled up alongside and she was about to give chase when she realized that Craig had stopped again. At the same moment an old man appeared from the front door of the house.

"What's your game then?" he asked in a voice that suggested he wasn't prepared to take any nonsense from the strangers messing around in front of his house. Blake flashed her warrant card.

"Is there an upstairs window that looks out from the back of the house?"

"Aye, the back bedroom, that looks over yonder field."

"Could I take a look through it, just for five minutes? Please, it's important." She was using all the charm she could muster.

It had been many years since any pretty young woman had visited the old man.

"Go on then. Up the stairs and straight on." She nearly knocked him over in the rush as she pushed past him into the hallway, faintly aware of the musty odour as she bounced up the stairs and into the bedroom.

Mike was going frantic in the ops room, the frustration of relying on second-hand reports driving him up the wall.

"What the hell's going on now? Where's Craig?" he shouted at the radio.

"Still in the lane, Guv. He moved down the road a bit but now he's stopped again."

The window had clearly not seen a wash-leather for some time but even through the dust and grime she could now see the whole of the top half of the car parked eight hundred yards away with Craig standing beside it. Within seconds of entering the bedroom she noticed the helmeted figure approach from the left, saw the motorcyclist briefly stop, exchange words with Craig, and then continue on down the lane.

She spoke into the radio. "Where's Charlie two?"

Charlie was short for Charlie Alpha Roger, the simple code being car one, car two and car three.

"On his way back up the M1, approaching the junction."

"Right, tell him to park up on the roundabout. There's a motorbike on its way, should be with him in about two minutes, rider wearing blue and white leathers. Tell him to get the number."

She saw Craig open the boot and spend some time with his head under the opened lid. What he was up to? She had no idea. Then he was on the move again, turning the car around and retracing his steps. She rushed back down the stairs, thanked the old man profusely, gave him a peck on the cheek that produced a toothless grin, and jumped into the Rover. She was on the radio again.

"Did you cop the motorbike?"

"Yep, he's going south."

She had to take a gamble. She didn't think that Craig had rumbled them, but if he saw the Rovers on his tail again he would certainly twig.

"Get on the move now, head north. The bandit's on his way back to the roundabout. See if you can pick him up but stay in front. He's cute, try to tailgate him and he'll suss you. We daren't get close, he's already taken a good look at us."

"What's going on for Christ's sake?" The voice on the radio was frantic.

"Looks like we're heading for home, Guv," Blake replied, and filled him in on the details.

She had guessed right. Charlie two spotted Craig in the rear view mirror five minutes later. The crisis came an hour later.

"Charlie two to Charlie one. Bandit has pulled into Stafford services. What do you want us to do?"

"Keep going. Give yourselves a couple of miles and then pull onto the hard shoulder. Charlie three pull onto the hard shoulder and await further instructions." She contacted control and explained what she required.

"Go with it, I'll see what I can organize," replied Mike.

The entrance and exit roads to the services were about half a mile apart. The Rover passed the entrance and pulled to a halt on the hard shoulder about mid-way between the two. The driver immediately jumped out and opened the bonnet. As he did so the police Range Rover pulled in front of them, blocking the view of the Rover from anybody leaving the services.

"Well done lads, good timing," she said as the motorway traffic cops walked back to meet her.

"Always pleased to assist our fellow officers," said the one on the left with a touch of sarcasm. "What's it all about, been a big heist has there?"

"Something like that. Make as if you're inspecting the engine. This shouldn't take long." She leant on the back of the Range Rover peering through the rear window, her eyes glued to the exit road. Sure enough Craig was on the move again ten minutes later.

"Charlie two, he's on the move again. Should be with you in a couple of minutes. Charlie three, you can start rolling again, but stay behind me."

In the ops room Mike and Daniels were still trying to figure out what it was Craig was up to.

"It certainly looks like a rendezvous. But with whom and for what purpose?" asked Mike rhetorically.

"God knows what he's up to," Daniels rejoined.

"What about the motorcycle?"

"Registered to a Mick O'Rourke. Address in the East End of London."

"Run a background on him. See if he has any form."

As luck would have it they arranged for the two replacement cars to pick up the chase at Knutsford services. Even as the Mondeo and Cavalier left the services the radio sprang into life.

"Charlie two to Charlie one. He's taken the slip road at Junction 19."

The services were less than half a mile from Junction 19, the exit road from the services almost joining the slip road for the junction.

"Charlie four, where are you?"

"About half a mile behind him, we're on our way."

Craig was in the middle of a dozen cars and lorries waiting on the red light at the top of the slip road when they spotted him. The lights changed and he headed off round the large roundabout but the two police cars were stuck behind a slow moving tanker crawling towards the lights in second gear.

"Come on you bastard!" the driver of the Mondeo shouted, seeing Craig disappear into the distance. The lights turned back to red, the tanker driver pulled up, the two cars stuck behind him.

"We've lost him, Sir. We're stuck at the lights."

"Jump the fucking lights, just get on him." Mike shouted back down the radio.

The Mondeo swung to the left, mounting the high kerb and on to the grass verge, the driver aware of the sickening thump as the sump crashed into the kerb stone, but carried on up the verge, past the inside of the tanker before dropping back onto the road, the Cavalier in hot pursuit. He could hear the horns of the other drivers, irate at his effrontery, as he put his foot to the floor in second, the front wheels digging into the camber of the roundabout, squealing in protest, seeing Craig in the distance as they took the third exit.

"Got him again, Guv."

"Good, stick with him, whatever it takes."

They followed him down the A56, through the lights at Mere and on down to the junction with the M56, the traffic heavy enough to afford decent cover as they tailed him towards Manchester. Craig moved over to the filter lane and followed the signs for Manchester Airport, sticking to the inside lane of the dual carriageway as it swung back over the motorway and past terminal two on the right before culminating in a large round-about, the imposing façade of the Hilton Hotel opposite. He took the third exit and followed the signs for international departures. The traffic was much lighter here and the couple in the Mondeo found themselves directly behind him with the Cavalier one hundred yards further back as he stopped at the automatic ticket dispenser by the entrance to the short stay car park, waiting for the machine to issue its ticket and raise the barrier. The Mondeo was too close, he might see them. They carried on past him and pulled up further down the road in the temporary drop zone among the several cars and taxis that were unloading passengers and their luggage. The Cavalier pulled up at the ticket machine as Craig made his way under the raised barrier and into the car park.

They caught glimpses of the rear end of Craig's car as it spiraled up the ramps of the multi-storey car park. The first seven floors were full and presented no problem but several spaces were visible between the parked cars on the eighth and by the ninth floor only a sparse scattering of cars littered the concrete floor, making it impossible to go any further without risking attracting his attention. The detectives pulled into one of the empty bays and the driver radioed in while the passenger made his way towards the ramp that led to the next level. The car park was effectively split in two with each side half a level above its neighbour, each slightly higher adjacent level being visible through the three foot gap in the concrete walls surrounding each level and the overhanging roof of the next level. The detective carefully scanned each floor through this gap before climbing the ramp to the next level. Finally reaching the top floor ten minutes later he found only three cars parked on the vast expanse of concrete, Craig's car being closest to the doors of the two lifts, but Craig was nowhere in sight.

"He might be on his way down to you, no sign of him up here."

The two detectives from the Mondeo were positioned either side of the entrance to the booking-in hall, keeping a watchful eye on the steel doors of the car park lift. Two minutes later Craig appeared from the left-hand doors and walked through the hall and on down the concourse, unaware of the two shadows ten yards behind him as he picked his way through the crowds and into WH Smith's. Row after row of chairs, provided for weary passengers as they awaited the tannoy announcement calling them to their flights, lined the middle of the concourse and the woman on the far side slipped into the first empty seat she saw and busied herself with the contents of her handbag, the man walking past the front of the newsagent, stopping to examine the window display of the adjoining boutique. Five minutes and they were on the move again. The other two detectives were now in position; Craig was boxed from all sides.

He retraced his steps, turned right down to the lift that led to arrivals, walked through the corridor lined with bureau de change and airline enquiry desks and on into the main arrivals hall. The woman was behind him as he walked straight to the left-hand side of the arrivals area and disappeared down the short corridor clearly signposted as a gentleman's toilet, the others having dropped back slightly for fear of crowding him. Unable to follow, she turned around to look for support, saw her partner nonchalantly leaning on one of the enquiry counters, and signaled him forward. She never saw the short, squat, dark haired man, a large blue holdall thrown over his shoulder, emerge from the corridor just fifteen seconds after Craig had entered it, though even if had she done so she would have set no importance by it.

Benjie watched Tommy leave with the merchandise from his seat in the coffee bar and waited for Craig to reappear. Mr Craig Osborne he thought, the name provided by his snitch from the police station. Now what should I do about you? He was undecided as to how to handle the situation. Short of blowing Tommy away he couldn't see any way of cutting him out of the loop without starting serious aggro. For the moment he was content to bide his time, keep an eye on things, make sure he understood exactly how the system operated.

Her partner entered the toilets a minute later, noted that the small room was empty apart from one of the three stalls to the left where he could clearly see a pair of shoes under the six inch gap at the bottom of the door, emptied his bladder at the urinal, washed and dried his hands, walked back out, and gave a discrete thumbs up sign as he emerged from the corridor. They tailed Craig back to his car, watched with some envy as he stopped off at the Chinese takeaway, emerging ten minutes later with a small brown paper carrier bag, and from there followed him to his flat.

Chapter 31

The debrief was scheduled for 8.00 the following morning, despite moans from some of the team about having to rise at such an unearthly hour on a Saturday morning. Each team leader spoke in turn, calling on members of the team as appropriate to fill in specific details. The end result was that nobody was any the wiser. Northamptonshire was definitely a meet but for what purpose they didn't know. No apparent meeting took place at the airport and none of the detectives could throw any light on the reason for the visit.

"What about the motorcyclist?" Mike asked, looking at Daniels.

"Still working on him, Guv. Nothing to tie him in as yet."

Later, when they were alone in the office, they ran through various scenarios.

"I still say it had to be some sort of drop in Northamptonshire. He drives the best part of two hundred miles, has a two minute meet with our motorcyclist friend and then drives back. You don't do that to swap phone numbers. Then on the way back he stops off at Stafford. You said there was nothing on the mobile?" Mike asked.

"No, checked with Vodafone. No calls on his mobile at all after lunchtime Friday."

"We know he's a careful sod. My guess is that he stopped off at Stafford to use a pay phone. Maybe to report that the drop was successful, who knows? But where's he sourcing the stuff? And what was he up to at the airport? We know the truck crossed the channel. Supposing Fenwick somehow passed the merchandise on to Craig, then Craig makes the drop to this chap on the motorbike, but then why the airport? The surveillance team reckons he didn't make any contact but he was out of sight for several minutes in the car park, they could have missed it."

"So where do we go from here?"

"We'll keep surveillance on over the weekend, the Super's given me until Monday so I might as well use it. In the meantime I'm going to take a well-earned break, drink a few lagers, put my feet up for a few hours, watch the rugby and generally chill out. What about you? Anything planned for what's left of the weekend?" asked Mike.

"Promised the wife I'd take the kids to watch the football this afternoon. Couple of things I want to check and then I'll be on my way."

When Daniels phoned Mike was walking along the banks of the river Trent, arm in arm with Helen, Forrest scrambling among the bushes, greeting his fellow canines with a wag and a sniff, and generally making a nuisance of himself. He'd driven over on the Saturday evening, enjoyed a quiet dinner in the local bistro, knocked up scrambled eggs for the two of them in the morning, his one and only culinary speciality, and was contemplating a relaxing pub lunch and afternoon in front of the TV.

"Sorry to disturb you, Guv, but it could be important. Remember our motorcyclist, Mick O'Rourke?"

"What about him?" asked Mike.

"He works for a company called East End Tiles."

"And?"

"They were on the list of Bill Fenwick's drops on the trip he went missing. That's what was niggling me. I knew I'd heard the name somewhere before."

"Interesting," said Mike.

"It gets better. I've been checking back through the rotas for the Marseilles run. The collections and drops vary. Some are one-offs, some are there for some trips and not for others. But for the last ten months there have been two constants. On every single run a collection has been scheduled for the Marseilles tile factory and a drop has been scheduled for East End Tiles."

Mike could hear the note of triumph in Daniels's voice. And why not, he deserved it. Mike was willing to bet that Daniels and his kids had never made it to the football, that he had spent the rest of his Saturday and half of Sunday tracking down this morsel of information. It made him feel guilty.

"Brilliant. Look, Jack. Go home and get some rest. We'll pick this up tomorrow morning and see what the implications are."

"Will do, Guv. Enjoy the rest of your weekend."

Mike noted a hint of irony in Daniels' voice as he said this; the cunning old bugger had put two and two together and come up with Helen. Mike smiled to himself as he replaced the phone.

Something was also niggling Mike that Sunday afternoon. Nothing fitted and yet everything fitted. Take out one fact and everything started to make sense. He rushed down stairs and retrieved the half-full pack of Marlborough from the glove compartment.

"I thought you were supposed to have given up?" Helen said disapprovingly.

"I have. No time to explain. Ruler, pen, paper, calculator, quick woman quick." He said it jokingly, with a smile on his face.

She joined in the joke, intrigued. Rushing around the flat she found the items and laid them on the table, and sat on the floor on the other side of the coffee table, knees tucked under her, watching him. He started by measuring the cigarette packet and then went to work with the calculator, scribbling figures on the piece of paper. Five minutes later he looked up.

"That proves it," he declared, teasing her.

"Proves what?"

"Bill Fenwick was smuggling cigarettes, Craig is smuggling something a lot more powerful."

She had seen all the files and he kept her up to date with developments. She understood the conflicts in the case but couldn't see the significance of the cigarette packet.

"OK, Clouseau, I know when I'm beaten, what have you found?"

"As I just told you, Bill Fenwick was smuggling cigarettes. One hundred cartons of two hundreds on each run to be precise. Give or take the odd cubic inch that equates to seven thousand seven hundred cubic inches. The secret compartment is two foot square by six inches deep, Jean Paul's report told us so. That equates to approximately three thousand five hundred cubic inches. So Bill can't have hidden the cigarettes in the compartment, it wasn't big enough. My guess is he hid them in the cab somewhere. That of course leaves the compartment free for Craig to conceal the drugs."

"But why kill Fenwick, where does he fit in?"

"He doesn't, at least not in the big picture. Fenwick was smuggling his fags and that was all he was doing, he didn't know anything about the compartment or the drug smuggling. George Lister found the compartment and told Craig to sort it out which Craig pretended to do. George had to be killed because he knew about the existence of the compartment and had asked Craig to deal with it, putting the future of the smuggling operation in jeopardy. Then I visited the depot and spoke to Linda, who tells Craig what it was I was after and seals her own fate in doing so. But why kill Fenwick, that's what I couldn't figure. The answer is that Fenwick knew nothing about the drugs or the compartment and therefore had to be stopped before we had the chance to speak to him. Craig puts two and two together, guesses that I've found out about the secret compartment, and arranges to have Fenwick removed so that he can't deny that Craig tackled him about the smuggling. As DCI Godfrey explained to me, Linda knew that Craig was the only person other than herself who knew that we wanted to talk to Fenwick and which would have pointed the finger at Craig when Fenwick disappeared. But the smugglers still have a load of merchandise to deliver so one of them drives Fenwick's truck over the channel with the drugs in the compartment and then returns to

Marseilles where the truck is disposed of. And that pretty well wraps it up."

She gave him a short round of applause.

"Bravo, monsieur inspector."

He took a bow.

He wanted to be absolutely positive there were no holes in his theory before he spoke with the Super. Roger Whitehead, the transport manager, had listened to his request, grunted down the phone a couple of times as Mike explained his requirements, and agreed to meet him at the depot later that evening.

"Who's taken over Fenwick's Marseilles run?" asked Mike as they stood in Whitehead's office.

"Frank Jones."

"Tell me about him."

"He's been with us for fourteen years. Good driver, model employee, doesn't skive and gets the job done."

"And what about as an individual?"

"Family man, lives in Bolton. Married about eight years ago, I went to the reception, two kids, the daughter will be about six now and the son about four."

It pretty much confirmed what Mike had strongly suspected.

"Show me Frank's rota for last week's run."

Roger handed him the sheet of paper, both the suspect drops were on the list. Mike just required one last piece of information. Out in the yard the mechanic Mike had borrowed from the police garage stooped under the trailer, torch in hand, and emerged two minutes later.

"It's there alright, measurements are spot on, two by two by six inches."

"It's one hell of an operation, require some coordinating." The Super was seated behind his desk, starched white shirt immaculate as always.

"It's the only way we're going to nab him, plus this way, with any luck, we wind up both ends of the operation at the same time," replied Mike.

"Perhaps we should involve the drugs squad?" mused the Super.

After the sweat of the last few weeks he wasn't about to let anybody else muscle in on the action.

"I don't see why, Sir. It's a murder enquiry, drugs just happen to be involved."

The headlines would make good reading, there was no doubt about that, thought the Super. He could imagine them even now. 'Cheshire police lead raid on International Drugs Gang.' Ah yes, that certainly wouldn't do his prospects any harm. Repair a bit of the damage at the golf club to boot.

"What about the murder investigations? Any developments?" asked the Super, emphasis on 'the murder'.

"The four serial murders, and I use the term loosely, were committed by Craig Osborne's accomplice, quite possibly a Tony Mellor. Mr Mellor seems to have disappeared off the face of the earth but hopefully if we pull Craig on the drugs trafficking it might flush Mellor out of the wood-work. Craig murdered Linda Walker. We've no solid evidence as yet but Stafford are working on it. Bill Fenwick was murdered by person or persons unknown in France."

"Bill Fenwick was murdered. You sure?" asked the Super.

"Neither Bill nor his truck have been seen since he visited the tile company in the South of France a week last Friday. We've found his trailer but no sign of Bill or the cab. Word on the street is that the cab has been destroyed and Bill murdered."

"But why kill Fenwick? I thought you were certain that the drivers are innocent victims with no knowledge of the contraband hidden under their trucks," the Super enquired.

"That's correct. But then Craig found out that Jim Roberts had told me about George finding the compartment and asking Craig to deal with the matter. According to Craig's story he was supposed to have confronted

Fenwick. Had Fenwick returned from France then obviously when I questioned him he would have denied all knowledge of the compartment and that would have pointed the finger of suspicion firmly at Craig."

"So they got rid of him?" asked the Super.

"Looks that way, I'm afraid."

"Nail these bastards, Judd." For the first time Mike noticed the emotion in the eyes, the fire in the belly.

He spent an hour on the phone to Jean Paul, explaining what was required, how the operation would work. Jean Paul was enthusiastic.

"So you think the commissioner will approve the resource?" asked Mike.

"I am sure of it," replied Jean Paul. "The Mayoral elections are in one month's time and drugs is a big issue. The Mayor's campaign is running into stormy waters, he needs a big story to get the voters back on his side. And of course the Mayor is highly influential in determining the Commissioner of Police. Marcel and the Mayor go back a long way."

The phone call he received from Godfrey on Tuesday nearly turned the entire operation on its head. The nationals had run the story on Sunday, not front page news but a reasonable sized splash nevertheless. Her parents had found a recent portrait photo which the police issued along with the statement and request for information but it was the photo cajoled out of a naïve flat mate, showing the pretty girl in short skirt and revealing top, clearly the worse for drink, cavorting at a recent party that convinced the tabloid editors of the merits of allocating a full page to the story.

"Barman at a pub in Cheshire thinks he may have seen the girl on the night she was murdered."

"How far is it from where the body was found?" asked Mike.

"Quite a distance, thirty miles, maybe forty," replied Whelan.

Godfrey supplied directions and they agreed to meet there and question the lad together. Driving over Mike reflected that Godfrey was being more than fair in his handling of the case; the murder had occurred on his patch, he could have shut up shop and kept Mike at arm's length. Mat was twenty-three, the son of the local vicar, and shared the flat with his mate, Luke. Leaving university with a pass degree in political studies the job market appeared totally underwhelmed by his academic achievements and after eighteen months of fruitless searching he had been unable to secure a decent job and now had several part time professions to earn the beer money, one of which was as barman.

"You think you saw the girl a week last Thursday?" asked Godfrey.

"I'm not sure. I only saw her very briefly, when she first came in. After that the chap she was with always came to the bar so I didn't see her again. It was more the drink thing that struck me; she was drinking raspberry flavoured Hooch. I remember because we rarely sell any but she drank about half a dozen bottles of the stuff and then he ordered a couple more to take out as they were leaving."

Mike and Whelan looked at one another.

"They took drinks out with them?" asked Godfrey, perched forward now on the edge of the armchair that had seen better days.

"That's right. That was the other reason I remembered. It happens occasionally, but it's pretty rare. It's much cheaper to buy from the off licence, the pub charges an arm and a leg."

"What time did they leave?"

"Not late, about 10.15 I would say."

"How can you be sure it was the Thursday night? It's easy to confuse one night with another isn't it? asked Mike.

"I only work at the George on Tuesdays and Thursdays. It was definitely the Thursday."

Mike and Godfrey looked at one another, it all fitted. If they left the pub at 10.15 then driving to the murder spot in time to kill her at 11.30 was not a problem. It was the take out drink that had confused them. They had both assumed, because the pathologist's report had stated quite categorically that she had taken her last drink not more than fifteen minutes before she died, that they were looking for an establishment not far from where the body was discovered.

"But you can't be absolutely certain it was her." It was Mike this time.

"No. She was definitely a young girl with blonde hair, nice figure, dressed in dark clothes, but I can't be definite it's the girl in the photos."

"What about the man? Would you recognize him if you saw him again?"

"I'm sure of it."

Mike asked him to describe the man; it fitted Craig to a tee.

As the two detectives left the flat Mike called the Super.

"No doubt about it, the murder has to take priority. Pity to ruin the drugs operation but if you think you can nail him on the Linda Walker murder then bring him in."

"Number 4. That's him. Definitely," said Mat, looking through the plate glass window at the line up of young men standing facing him. In the interview room the two detectives sat opposite Craig, a uniformed officer standing by the door. He was beaten and he knew it. He put on an act of bravado for a couple of minutes but the weight of evidence against him was overwhelming. He broke down, face hidden behind his hands, sobbing.

"OK, I was there that night, I admit it."

Mike read him his rights and officially cautioned him. Although distraught, Craig was still sufficiently in control to request that his solicitor be present. They had to wait half an hour for the solicitor to arrive and another half hour while he and Craig were in conference. The two men whiled away the time in the canteen, swapping stories, convinced it was only a matter of time before they wrapped the case up.

"My client would like to make a statement."

The tapes were running in the interview room, the four men present had identified themselves to the machine and now the stage was all Craig's.

"On the night in question I picked up Linda Walker from her flat at about 8.30. We drove to the George where we stayed until approximately 10.15. On leaving we drove down one of the lanes near the pub, I'm not sure exactly which one, and Linda, who had drunk a considerable amount of alcohol in the pub, said she felt sick. I stopped the car and she got out. I wasn't having her being sick inside the car. We had a row about it, Linda was drunk and her language became extremely abusive. I tried to calm her but she was totally out of control, shouting and swearing at the top of her voice. I eventually lost my temper with her and drove away leaving her by the side of the road. I know it was dreadful behaviour but at the time I wasn't thinking straight. I wanted to frighten her, to quieten her down. I drove a couple of miles down the road and realized it had gone too far. I turned around and went back to get her but she'd gone, couldn't find her anywhere, and after twenty minutes or so I presumed somebody else must have given her a lift so I drove home. The next day, when the body was found, I was scared; I knew it would look bad for me leaving her like that in the middle of nowhere. I panicked, made up the story about being in all night."

"So you're saying that when you last saw Linda Walker she was alive," said Godfrey.

"Definitely, yes. I didn't have anything to do with her death," Craig replied.

"You realize you could be in serious trouble for failing to tell us this in the first place. Valuable time has been wasted because of your actions."

"My client realizes that he made a mistake. However, as he has already explained to you, he was extremely frightened and acted in panic," the solicitor cut in.

Jesus he was good, thought Mike. The act was convincing: the contrite look; the quivering voice; the lost little boy who made an innocent mistake.

"You're gay aren't you, Craig?" asked Mike.

The solicitor and Craig conferred, heads together, whispering.

"Yes, I am, although I don't see the relevance of the question."

"I was just wondering what you were doing out with Linda that night. It obviously wasn't a date."

"We're friends, Chief Inspector, or is it beyond the comprehension of the average male that a man and a woman can enjoy an evening out together without there being any sexual motive?"

Stupid question, thought Mike, he'd given Craig the upper hand, the moral high ground.

"What about the car?" Mike asked.

"The car, Chief Inspector?"

"On the night of the murder your own car was outside your flat all night. Which car did you use that evening?"

"One of the pool cars from work. My car was playing up, something wrong with the timing, kept on cutting out. I took a taxi over to the depot, picked up one of the pool cars and took it back later that night."

"Which taxi company did you use?"

"I can't remember. I walked to the main road and hailed a passing taxi, I didn't really take much notice of which company it was from."

"What about the bottles of Hooch you purchased from the pub?"

"Linda took them with her when she got out of the car. I remember she was clutching them even while threatening to throw up."

"Did you see her being sick?"

A fractional pause. "I'm not sure. No, I don't think I actually saw what happened. I must have driven off before."

Two hours later they had to release Craig from custody. His story was undoubtedly a load of baloney but the Director of Public Prosecutions, the government legal body responsible for determining which cases came to court, didn't give them a prayer without further corroborative evidence.

Chapter 32

The night vision goggles protruded from the man's face, the two small black lenses like the bulging eyes of a creature from a science fiction movie, as he picked his way carefully across the rough terrain in the pitch black of a moonless night. Jean Paul followed in his footsteps, keeping two steps behind him as instructed; the photographer followed Jean Paul with the other red beret bringing up the rear. They all wore camouflage jackets and trousers, faces blackened with charcoal, haversacks containing the equipment slung over their shoulders. The two paras were distinguishable by their choice of footwear and headgear; they both wore standard issue canvas army boots with the thick rubber soles and dark blue woollen hat pulled down over the hair. Jean Paul had been able to muster a pair of brown leather hiking boots but had opted to dispense with the headgear, while the photographer sported black Adidas trainers and a rather natty black fedora, an outfit that had done little to impress the already sceptical paras when they'd rendezvoused at the meeting point two hours previously. Joint ventures between the police and the armed forces were extremely rare – a certain friction existed between the two and such situations were normally confined to terrorist hostage situations – but Jean Paul argued that they would probably do themselves serious injury attempting the climb in the dark without the specialist knowledge and training of the elite parachute regiment, and the commissioner had reluctantly agreed to his request.

The pace they set was frightening, no allowance made for the civvies in their midst, and the canvas webbing of the rucksack was already causing Jean Paul considerable discomfort, cutting into the shoulder, chafing the skin with each step, the base of the hill still half a mile away. He could hear the laboured breath and occasional curse of the photographer behind him as Charles struggled to keep up. He decided to call a halt – a ten minute rest would do no harm – and it was time to take control. He addressed the paras in hushed tones as he laid the rucksack on the ground.

"Listen, I know you guys are super fit and you think all us civilians are wimps but the object of the exercise is to get me and Charles in place and in a fit state to do our job, so let's cut out the macho crap and take things at a reasonable pace. Comprendez?"

He saw the gleam of the white teeth against the charcoaled faces. The paras had enjoyed the joke.

"OK, boss. We were quite impressed by how well you were doing actually."

He could see there was no malice in the men. They lived in a world where the physical challenge was everything, each obstacle to be taken by storm, no weakness ever shown, especially to your mates, and found it difficult to adjust to the different requirements of this civilian exercise. He went over and spoke with Charles.

"Everything OK?"

"I think those buggers are out to kill me," the photographer wheezed, sitting on a small rock outcrop, massaging the soles of his feet through the trainers. He was a freelance who occasionally undertook work for the police in between the numerous wedding assignments and very occasional fashion shoots that came his way, a man more at home in the afternoon sunshine of the village churchyard than climbing a mountain in the pitch black.

"It's alright, I've told them to take the heat off. I think they just wanted to show us civilians what big balls they all have in the army. We've plenty of time so if you need a rest let me know."

They started to climb the hill. It was steep but walkable in most places, the men scrabbling forward with their hands on the ground in front of them on the steeper sections. It took them a further hour and a half to reach the summit, where the sheer wall of limestone fell away in front of them, formed when the rock had been hewn from the quarry. The four men made their way round the lip of the quarry to the far side where the sun would be behind them and the three sheds, caravan and loading area clearly visible when dawn broke in a couple of hours' time. The paras took them directly to the spot, having identified it during the reconnoitre the previous week. It was perfect, the ground was relatively flat at this point with not too many sharp rock outcrops breaking the grass cover, and a couple of small bushes perched right on the rim afforded a degree of cover.

Settling down in the small clearing they started to unload the equipment. Charles carefully removed the bodies of the two Nikon F100s from their cases, handling them with loving care, attaching the bayonet-fit five hundred millimetre telephotos that Jean Paul had been carrying, screwing each one to a small tripod no more than eight inches high, adjusting the feet until he was satisfied with the position. The paras were removing and assembling the listening dish and tape recorder from their own packs. Battery power was the biggest problem, they were restricted to two six-volt heavy duty batteries – even the paras couldn't hump more than one each – which would give him thirty minutes maximum. Satisfied that the equipment was ready one of the paras produced a flask and they shared a cup of thick, sweet coffee. After a minor argument, Jean Paul overrode the paras and Charles was permitted to disappear behind a rock some ten yards back from the rim for a quick smoke, having been warned of the consequences should he allow the red tip to become visible, the smell of the Gauloise drifting up the hill in the still morning air.

One of the paras carefully removed the sniper's rifle from its canvas cover and fitted the telescopic lens, checking the alignment with the marks on the barrel. He spoke quietly to Jean Paul before making his way further down the lip. The rules of engagement were simple: if he judged the driver's life to be in danger he should take whatever action he deemed necessary to save him.

Jean Paul reached the team at the depot on his mobile.

"Everything alright at your end?"

"All present and correct. We have the truck under surveillance, the compartment is definitely empty and we've wiped it down. Any prints will be new ones."

"Good. Time to wait and see what happens."

As the sun rose behind them the base of the quarry became visible approximately five hundred feet below. They were positioned three quarters of the way up the left-hand rim of the quarry as it was viewed from the road, the rear of the quarry and the three sheds being to their left and the caravan almost opposite and on the far side from where they lay. Charles adjusted the cameras slightly, fine tuning the positions of the tripods. Jacques and George arrived in the Toyota just after 7.00. Charles took a few snaps for the record, the oversized motor wind making a dull whirring sound as it spooled the film through the ratchets. The father appeared from the caravan, scratching his unshaven chin, shouting greetings to the boys.

At 7.15 the team at the depot called back to report that the truck was on its way. Although the volume was at its lowest setting Jean Paul's heart missed a beat as the muffled sound of the ring emanated from within his parka, shrill in the early morning stillness, Jean Paul convinced that it must be clearly audible to the men in the quarry below. He looked across at the remaining para who gave him the thumbs up. No worries.

At 8.05 the Daf rolled through the gate at the far end of the track and Charles picked up the Sony video camera from where it lay on the ground sheet, tracking the truck as it made its way slowly along the unmade road. Jean Paul turned on the tape and Charles abandoned the Sony, switching

to the left-hand Nikon as Frank brought the truck to a halt outside the
middle shed and climbed down from the cab. Jean Paul heard the greetings through the headphones as clearly as if he had been standing next
to them: the offer of breakfast; Frank and the old man walking across to
the caravan; Pierre calling as he appeared from the left-hand shed and
walking over to join them. Charles switched to the right-hand Nikon as
the three of them made their way over to the caravan that stood square
on to the quarry entrance, its front window facing the four men on the
rim. The table was positioned in front of the caravan and as the men sat
down the lorry was hidden from their view. Charles reeled off a few more
shots of Pierre and Frank sitting at the table, Eric had disappeared inside
to prepare the breakfast.

Charles switched back to the left-hand Nikon, reeling off shot after
shot as Jacques appeared from the shed shortly after the men settled
at the table, pushing the small oxyacetylene torch in front of him. He
quickly set to work removing the plate and then vanished once more
into the shed returning almost immediately with a plastic sports bag
slung over his shoulder. Crouching once more under the trailer, he
began loading the packages. They couldn't capture the whole thing, the
angle was wrong to see the actual compartment, but they could see the
hand reaching into the bag lying on the floor and emerging with the
polythene-wrapped packages before reaching up under the trailer and
returning empty for the next one. It was enough. He finally welded the
plate back on and wheeled the torch back into the shed. Less than fifteen
minutes had elapsed since the truck arrived when Jacques strolled across
the quarry, joining the others at the table, helping himself to coffee and
a large hunk of bread.

They watched the truck trundle back down the track, Charles tacking
a few final shots, before packing up the equipment and heading back
down the hill, the other para joining them halfway down the slope. This
time they didn't circle the hill but headed straight down and on through
the Mediterranean scrubland to the east, the nearest road on this side of

the quarry being over six miles away. The paras led them straight to the rendezvous point, the four wheel drive hidden beyond the remnants of what had once been a shepherd's hut. They climbed on board and began the bone-jarring journey back to the road, following the deeply rutted goat track, Charles clutching the bag containing the precious Nikons to his lap.

The police car was waiting on the road at the previously arranged location. Jean Paul stopped for a moment to look at the two paras now they were in daylight, hats removed and some of the charcoal wiped away. He guessed that they were barely out of their teens. He also understood something of what he had read about fighting men in action, about the sense of camaraderie that develops in such situations, the close bonds of friendship that quickly form. He barely knew these men, had worked with them for less than a day, yet already he knew he would instinctively trust them with his life, would be happy to call them friends. Jean Paul was feeling like death after the long and arduous night, the tension of the surveillance and the drive that had left him feeling as if every bone in his body had been smashed to pieces, but the two young men were standing by the roadside, broad grins on their faces, ready for the next adventure, the night's work no more arduous than a Sunday afternoon stroll.

"Next time you're in Marseilles look me up boys, I'll buy you a beer. I might even be able to get the charges dropped next time you destroy one of our bars." They were still laughing as the police car pulled away.

Jean Paul phoned Mike to let him know that stage one was proceeding as planned and to confirm that the driver apparently had no knowledge of the contraband stored beneath his trailer. The Super had taken some persuading before he finally agreed to allow the operation to go ahead without the driver's knowledge.

"We already have one driver missing, presumed dead. I'm not prepared to take the risk of that happening a second time."

"But they have no reason to harm Frank. Besides we'll have him under surveillance at all times, any sign of danger and we'll pull him out. We can't be absolutely sure that the drivers aren't involved. If they are then the whole operation gets blown the minute we confide in Frank."

The Super had acquiesced. Mike hadn't been strictly honest. He was sure that the drivers weren't involved but felt that if they told Frank he wouldn't be able to keep up the act, would give himself away. That was if he agreed to go through with it in the first place. The alternative was to put in their own man, but that too held dangers; the change in routine might spook the smugglers, make them change their plans.

The truck was never out of sight as it travelled along the motorway that cut a swathe through the French countryside. Thirty miles north of Lyon he was pulled over by a motorcycle cop and told to pull into the service station one kilometre ahead. Adjacent to the services was a small police station, a modern low level glass and concrete affair, the gendarme waving him into the parking area and ushering him through to the far end of the building. Frank was perturbed at first but the officer in charge assured him it was routine, a random check, nothing to worry about, just checking the truck and paperwork were in order, which put Frank's mind at rest. They brought him coffee and biscuits as he sat waiting, the gendarme on the other side of the desk continuing with his paperwork, ignoring Frank, occasionally looking up and smiling apologetically. Fifteen minutes later the officer in charge appeared, assured him everything was in order, led him back to the truck, apologised for delaying his journey, thanked him profusely for being so understanding and bade him a safe journey home. Frank had never been sure about the French but, well, they certainly seemed a very pleasant bunch.

Every pack was carefully opened, a minute sample taken from each, the evidence bag meticulously labelled, the pack resealed and placed back in the compartment. Within minutes the samples were in the back of the police car, siren screeching as it sped off down the motorway, en route to the laboratories at Lyon.

Chapter 33

Mike leant on the metal railings watching the propellers churn the water into a white froth as the captain gently brought the ferry to a halt against the dock wall. Within seconds the giant bow doors began to swing open and passengers scurried across the gangplanks that now connected each of the three side exits to the dockside, shopping trolleys in tow, the early risers heading for the giant supermarkets to stock up on cheap groceries and booze. Mike scanned the car park opposite from his position on the upper deck, trying to pick out the truck from among the serried rows of traffic waiting to embark, the first eight rows to the right being ordered lines of cars, vans, and the odd motorcycle, the three on the left reserved for trucks. The bright red livery wasn't hard to find and he spotted it halfway down the first row of trucks, could see Frank through the windscreen reading the paper, polystyrene cup of coffee in hand, totally oblivious to the drama that was unfolding around him. He was still watching, taking in the controlled chaos as the trucks and cars were unloaded from the ferry, when Jean Paul appeared at his shoulder. They exchanged greetings.

"Are your people still on him?" asked Mike.

"What is the expression? Like a limpet." It had been agreed that the French team would be responsible for the truck until it disembarked at Dover, where Mike's team would take over.

"Four of our people are positioned in the hold, they will stay with the truck throughout the crossing."

"Good, we'll nail the bastards this time. Any results from the tests?" asked Mike.

"Confirmed what we thought. Cocaine. The lab came back to us ten minutes ago."

"What about the suppliers at your end, any joy?"

"No. I don't think we will be able to track back any further. It would take weeks of observation and even then we'd have to get lucky. This whole operation's going to blow as soon as you move in at your end. We are happy with the Martine family, taking them out of circulation for ten years will suffice."

The trucks began loading as they were talking and they watched as the red Daf cab and trailer passed between the bow doors below them and into the hold.

"Come on then," said Mike. "I'll buy you a proper English breakfast."

Mike's team picked up the truck as it left the ferry, the operation coordinated by Daniels, the watchers tracking the truck through the flat Kent country-side as it headed into London, following it around the south circular, seeing it pulling off the Old Kent Road, make its way down Baltimore Street and turn in between the giant doors of the old warehouse. The cars stayed on the main road, the static watchers taking over. The two detectives hidden in the rear of the old Transit van that had arrived in the early morning and now sat apparently abandoned, the driver engaged in business elsewhere, snapped off a few shots as Frank and Mick wandered up the street, exchanging small talk, heading for the transport café round the corner. They took half a dozen more as the two men returned from breakfast half an hour later. Following the truck back to Bolton was straightforward, the driver wasn't looking for a tail, didn't realize that he was in a box, protected front and rear at all times.

Craig followed the schedule. Mid-morning he left the depot, drove a few miles, made a brief call from a phone box, returned to the factory. Half an hour later and he was on his way. Mike left the truck making its way slowly through the traffic of North London, its secret guardians watching over it, and headed on up the M1. He found Blake and her partner in the rear upstairs room of the terraced cottage in Northamptonshire, the coffee dregs in the cups and plates empty apart from a few crumbs, testimony to the generous hospitality of the old man he had met downstairs. A tripod stood by the window, a camera with telephoto lens mounted upon it. A pair of binoculars rested on the bedside table.

"I see you two are being well looked after," said Mike.

"That's Fred, Sir. He's an absolute darling. Proposed to me twice this morning already," replied Blake.

The other detective, also a female, stood by the camera, grinning.

"I hope you two haven't been using your female charms to take unfair advantage of him."

She gave him a look of mock outrage. "As if we would do anything like that, Sir."

They settled down to wait, the idle banter continuing, listening to Craig's progress on the radio.

He arrived at 2.10. The detective clicking away with the camera as he followed the routine they had witnessed on their last visit, the motorcyclist departing into the distance, the microphone concealed in the hedge picking up nothing other than the roar of the motorbike's engine and the quiet clunk of the car's boot as it closed. They used five cars on the motorway, just to be on the safe side, with a further two already in place at the airport. The engineer monitoring the rank of twelve payphones at Stafford services picked up the call at 2.20 and played the short message back to Mike.

"That must be the meet, 4.00 at the airport," he said to Daniels who had now joined him, satisfied that the watchers were all in position.

"Sounds like it."

"It's all starting to make sense. The stuff comes over in the truck and is offloaded at the tile warehouse while the driver's taking breakfast – that way the truck's clean when it arrives back in the depot. Craig then picks up the merchandise in Northamptonshire and passes it on to his contacts in Manchester. We'll pull him as soon as he meets his contact at the airport."

"Charlie six to Charlie seven, he's just passed us, should be with you in a couple of minutes." Charlie six was parked on the ninth floor of the car park, Charlie seven on the top floor. Apart from the Renault van the only other car on the top floor was an Audi 80 parked some distance away. The Saab appeared up the ramp, swung round the car park and parked close to the lift doors, facing the van parked twenty yards away. The man driving the Saab sat and stared at the blacked-out rear windows of the van for four or five minutes without moving a muscle. The two detectives in the rear of the van stood stock still, aware that the slightest move would cause the suspension to shift, the movement of the van's body revealing their presence to the man in the Saab. They were sure that he could see them through the one-way mirrors, the intensity of his stare penetrating the mirrored glass. Neither man spoke.

The crackle of the radio broke the spell, sounding like a thunderclap as it echoed in against the metal of the van's body shell.

"Charlie six to Charlie seven. What the hell's happening?"

One of the detectives grabbed the radio, whispering an urgent reply.

"Keep it down for God's sake. He's sitting in the car looking straight at us. I think he's sussed us."

There was something about the van with the blacked-out windows that didn't seem quite right to Craig but surveying the empty car park he was aware that if the drugs boys were on to him his escape routes from the rooftop were virtually non-existent. He made a decision, climbed out of the Saab, walked to the rear and lifted the boot.

"Hang on, he's on the move. He's doing something in the boot. Can't see what, the boot's facing away from us." It was the man on the radio again. "Here we go, he's heading for the lifts, carrying a briefcase. He's entered the left-hand lift. He's on the way down."

Mike deployed twelve detectives in the airport; eight were assigned to static positions covering the route Craig took on his previous visit, the other four were floaters. He waited in the car at the far end of the departures drop zone, listening to the radio traffic, directing operations, fearful that Craig might spot him if he entered the airport. Craig followed his usual route, discrete whispers into lapel microphones confirming that he'd entered the concourse, was heading for the bookshop, scanning the shelves, checking his watch. Now he doubled back, took the lift, headed for arrivals. As Craig entered the passageway leading to the gents' toilets Mike was listening to the details of his progress on the radio.

He shouted into the transmitter, "Somebody get in behind him, follow him in there."

The man in the blue denims, red polo shirt and black leather jacket leaning nonchalantly against the railings, apparently waiting for some homeward-bound relation, immediately turned and headed for the corridor, entering not six feet behind Craig. Hearing the footsteps behind him Craig pushed through the inner door, gave a single, almost imperceptible shake of the head, walked past the man in the black leather jacket and took the right-hand urinal, placing the briefcase on the floor beside him. The man picked up the holdall, swung it over his shoulder, and brushed past the detective, almost bumping into him as the two of them tried to push through the door from opposite directions at the same time. He didn't look back, he didn't run. Walking purposefully across the arrivals hall he queued at the car park pay machine, took the lift to the fourth floor, and drove off towards the centre of Manchester in the black BMW.

The detective had a problem. The three urinals faced him, Craig occupying the one on the right, briefcase at his side. To the right were four empty stalls and to the left the wash basins and hand driers. He realized in that split second that he didn't want to go, that if he went and stood next to Craig at the urinal there would be an embarrassing and suspicious lack of action. Entering the first stall he closed the door behind him, dropped his trousers, and went through the motions, although not in the literal sense. He heard the water in the basin, heard the hand drier operate and then the door slam shut on its spring as Craig left. Yanking his trousers back up he quickly did up the fastenings and followed Craig back out into the arrivals hall.

Upon emerging from the passageway Craig strolled to the seating area in the middle of the hall, about fifteen feet from the entrance to the toilet, and studied one of the monitors hanging from the roof beams that display the latest information on the inward-bound flights. He was now almost certain somebody was tailing him and, keeping his line of vision broadly fixed on the monitors, he concentrated for all he was worth on the peripheral vision in his left eye, catching the man as he appeared at the corridor's entrance thirty seconds later, aware of him standing at the exit to the corridor looking around a little too frantically until he saw Craig standing five yards away studying the monitor, noted how he sauntered off to his right, out of Craig's field of vision. The man was following him, he was sure of it now. He tried to stay calm. He could feel his heart pounding in his chest but he knew this was not the moment to panic. Nobody had pounced on him; no handcuffs were being placed on his wrists. He needed to buy time, to take stock of the situation.

Benjie watched the drama unfold from his position in the coffee bar. He watched as the man followed Craig into the toilets, guessed that there might not have been time to make the exchange. Interesting, he thought. Let's see how the back-up plans work.

Apparently satisfied with the flight arrivals information Craig turned, strolled over to the far side of the hall and bought an Evening News from the newspaper vendor. Tucking the folded paper under his arm he walked to the coffee bar at the rear of the hall, bought a cappuccino and seated himself at one of the small round tables, his back to the wall, the whole of the hall visible before him. Opening the paper he began reading, feeling the eyes upon him, resisting the temptation to try to spot the watchers among the crowd.

Benjie was seated two tables away. Shit, he thought. Is Tommy going to join him at the fucking table? Time to make a hasty exit. Draining the last of the coffee from the cup he stood up and walked as casually as possible down into the main arrivals hall, strolling over to the far side and finding a convenient pillar to lean on and partially conceal himself behind while still keeping an eye on Craig.

"What's he doing now?" queried Mike.

"Drinking a coffee and reading the paper, Sir," came the reply.

"Can you see the briefcase?"

"Yes, Sir. It's on the floor beside him."

"Whatever you do, don't let that briefcase out of your sight."

Mike switched to the general frequency. "Attention all teams, the suspect is sitting in the coffee bar in the arrivals hall. We're pretty sure he has the drugs with him in the briefcase but we don't know what his next move is going to be so we'll have to play it by ear. Whatever happens we must not lose contact with the drugs. Use your discretion. If you feel that there is any danger of losing the drugs then move in and arrest the suspect. Over."

What the bloody hell is he up to, thought Mike; at this moment in time he'd give a million dollars to know the answer to that one.

Craig's mind was racing. He was carrying ten kilos of coke in the bag and he had to presume it was the police that were on to him. When had they first picked him up? What did they know? Why hadn't they arrested him? Too many unanswered questions clogged his brain. Think, for God's sake. Why haven't the police arrested you? Because they are waiting for the contact. That had to be it. It gave him a chance, not a great chance, but a chance. He made a call on the mobile, speaking quietly but quickly for five minutes, checked his watch once again, and settled down with the paper and coffee.

Chapter 34

It was Mike again. "Anything happening?" It had been thirty minutes, Mike's nerves were frayed, he wanted to get this over with.

"Still there, Sir, reading the paper."

Benjie was also becoming agitated. He would have to move soon if he was to be back in the flat in time to take the call from Tommy. He decided to give it another fifteen minutes and then split.

Five minutes later. "He's on the move, Sir."

Thank God for that, thought Mike. Come on Craig son, make your move, let's see what you're made of.

Craig retraced his steps through the corridor and took the lift back up to the main concourse, two of the watchers slipping in discretely behind him as he made his way through the corridor that led back to the large departures hall. Timing was going to be all-important and he wasn't sure of the exact splits, would have to play it by ear. There would be no chance of a practice run now.

Benjie spotted them immediately. He'd been hanging around long enough to know who was who in the hall, those arriving recently and those that had been present throughout the drama. Were they Craig's minders or something more sinister? He decided to join the procession, tailing the tailers.

Turning right at the top of the lift Craig headed back towards the car park lift but instead of passing through the large glass automatic doors he took the short escalator situated to the right of them, the overhead sign indicating that this was the Skylink route to terminal two and the railway station. The Skylink is a modern contraption, a glass and steel oval about ten feet high by fifteen feet across with a flat floor supported on concrete stilts which lift the entire structure twenty feet above the surrounding countryside, allowing foot passengers to traverse the mile and a half from the older terminal one to the recently opened terminal two. Along the floor of the Skylink are moving walkways, each about one hundred yards long, a handrail on either side, each section separated by ten feet of the standard grey tiled flooring. In-keeping with the British road system the left-hand walkways move towards terminal two while the right hand moves in the opposite direction. By stepping on and off the walkways the foot passenger can transfer between the two terminals in a relatively short time and with comparatively little effort.

Craig jumped on the first walkway. He guessed that they were following him but didn't look back. It was important that they thought he was still oblivious to their presence.

"He's doing what?" enquired Mike.

"He's taken the Skylink, Sir, the pedestrian route to terminal two," one of the watchers whispered into the lapel microphone watching the man in front of him, unaware of the man fifteen feet to his rear.

Benjie saw the contact and in that instant he knew it was the drugs squad who were on to Craig. The set-up was too sophisticated to be anything else.

"Right, well don't let him out of your sight. I'll organize a welcoming committee," Mike told the watcher.

He moved four of the watchers from terminal one to terminal two. They sped round the internal road system, left the car in the short term departures drop zone outside the first floor entrance and positioned themselves at strategic positions on the first floor, within viewing distance of the walkway entrance. Craig continued along the Skylink, past the entrance to the Radisson Hotel where the concierge, dressed in smart green uniform with brass buttons waited to greet the guests, and continued on towards terminal two, checking his watch at regular intervals. He emerged from the Skylink and out into the large departures hall, the long line of check-in desks to his left, with four and a half minutes to go.

The terminal is built on two floors, the upper floor containing the check-in desks for departures while the lower floor is reserved for arrivals, with the short term car park situated adjacent to the front of the terminal building. The road system for terminal two is a simple affair, the main point of entry and departure, a dual carriageway with two lanes on either side, is reached from the short dual carriageway that provides access to the airport from the M56. A roundabout is situated at either end of the road that passes across the front of the terminal on the far side of the car park, fifty yards from the terminal building. Two spurs lead off from the main road just prior to the car park and pass between the airport building itself and the car park, the first spur giving access to the lower level for cars arriving to pick up passengers, while the second spur leads up a ramp to the first floor level for cars wishing to drop passengers off. It was here, in the departures drop zone, that the detectives had left their car. The main road carries on beyond the car park for another hundred yards where it terminates at the second roundabout. The two spurs rejoin the road at this point and the return journey is made by proscribing a three hundred and sixty degree turn around the roundabout and returning along the opposite side of the dual carriageway.

Craig strolled halfway down the length of the departures hall, working his way between the throngs of people with their trolleys of luggage queuing at the check-in desks, before stopping to examine the electronic notice boards displaying flight information. He was too early; he needed to stall for time. The watchers held position behind him and Benjie waited behind them, trying to blend in with the crowd.

"He's looking at the departures boards, Sir. Still has the briefcase with him."

Mike was becoming increasingly worried, something didn't feel right. "Keep close, don't let him out of your sight."

"Right, Sir," the voice came back over the radio.

At that moment Craig turned and went straight for the lift heading for the ground floor.

"He's off again, Sir, going to the lower floor."

All the detectives were now behind him, two staying on the upper floor, four descending the escalator some ten yards behind him. Benjie stayed on the upper floor, the glass-fronted building affording a panoramic view of the action as it unfurled. Craig stepped off the end of the escalator, walked twenty yards across the arrivals hall and turned left and out through the automatic glass doors. He may have looked calm on the exterior but sweat was pouring from him, he could feel his shirt soaked beneath the fleece jacket. He was still counting the seconds in his head as he walked across the lower spur road and into the ground floor of the car park. The watchers were uncertain what to do. They had him in sight, could clearly see him walking into the car park. Was this still a covert operation? If they followed him across the road they would expose themselves, there was nowhere to hide, nothing to cover their movements. The delay was fatal. As he strode the fifty yards across the ground floor of the car park the mobile phone he was holding in his left hand rang three times and then stopped. He quickened his pace, left the car park through the entrance on the far side where cars were queuing at the automatic barrier, stepped over the kerb of the raised concrete pavement that separated the two carriageways and jumped into the passenger seat of the blue Mondeo waiting on the far side. One of the detectives, now at the entrance to the car park, was just in time to note the number of the Mondeo as it sped off towards the motorway.

"He's done what?" Mike could feel the blood rising in his face.

"He's got away, Sir. Car picked him up." He gave Mike the details. Mike put out an all-points.

Benjie turned casually and wandered back towards the Skylink, the detectives far too busy in their own world to notice the tall black man as he made his way back to terminal one.

The Mondeo took less than thirty seconds to reach the roundabout. By the time Mike received the radio message it was speeding along the main airport access road, taking the left-hand lane signposted M56 Chester where the road splits two hundred yards further on. As Mike issued the all-points the car was on the M56 but dropped straight off again, taking the A538 at Junction 6. They were held up at the bottom of the slip road, the lights on red, the driver agitated, gunning the engine, cursing the lights. Craig looked across and put a hand to the back of his head, kneading the muscles at the base of the neck.

"Relax. We're OK now. Just take it easy."

The car swung right towards Wilmslow, turning right a mile and a half further on, just prior to the tunnel that carried the runway over the road. The headlights split the darkness as they made their way down the country lane, the road twisting and turning as it dropped steeply down into the Bollin valley, leaving the traffic far behind. Not half a mile from the busy main road and motorway system and yet they could have been in a different world. The car pulled into a short track leading to a field at the bottom of the hill. Craig knew the area from his youth when he had spent many a summer's day swimming in the waters of the babbling river that gave the valley its name. Motioning to his accomplice he left the car and walked the short distance to the stone bridge over the river.

Crossing the bridge he forced his way through the makeshift fencing on the far side, slithered down the grass bank, found the more level ground by the river side, walked a short distance downstream to separate himself from any passing motorist and stopped when he found a suitable spot. Taking the Swiss army penknife from his pocket he slashed open each of the plastic bags and scattered the contents into the waters at his feet. Forty thousand quid down the drain. Still, he had already made well over half a million and it was better to take the loss than risk the alternative. There should be some happy fish in the Bollin tonight, he thought, as he made his way back to the car. His accomplice had completed the task of switching the number plates by the time he returned and they resumed their journey through the unlit countryside.

At about the same time that Craig was disposing of the evidence a blissfully unaware Frank Jones pulled into the yard, disconnected the trailer, and parked the cab up. He was glad to be back. With any luck he'd get home in time to see the kids before they went to bed, plan the next day's adventures, give them the presents he'd purchased in Marseilles. Two minutes after he left the yard the technicians descended on the trailer, confirmed that the compartment was now empty, and lifted the fingerprints from the cold metal.

"Shit, shit, SHIT!" Mike was fuming. The team was slumped in chairs around the ops room, adrenalin drained, the thrill of the chase over, aware that they'd blown it. Mike knew it was down to him. He hadn't done his homework properly, should have spotted the potential escape route. Time was against him. With Craig on the loose he couldn't afford to hang around, a couple of phone calls and the rats would be diving for cover. He spoke to Daniels, sitting next to him, nursing a mug of coffee.

"Keep the surveillance on Craig's car. I don't suppose it will do us much good but we might as well stick with it. And find out who he called from the airport. Are the watchers still at his flat?"

Daniels nodded.

"Good. The rest of the watchers can call it a day. I want a debrief here tomorrow at 8.00. In the meantime I have some calls to make." With that he left the room and wandered down the corridor to his own office.

The Super was at home. He'd asked to be kept abreast of developments, was aware of the fiasco at the airport.

"Sounds like we don't have much choice," said the Super. "At least we'll have something to show."

Mike rang Jean Paul. Fifteen minutes later Jean Paul, accompanied by two fellow detectives and ten burly gendarmes, entered the small back street bar, dragging the Martine family from the table where they were enjoying a quiet evening drink and out into the waiting police cars. The patrons looked on, shrugged, but did nothing. It was not a bar the police normally entered but the show of numbers was sufficient to convince the locals that on this particular occasion discretion may well be the better part of valour.

In the East End of London the drugs squad raided three homes that night while their compatriots, search warrant in hand, jemmied the lock and entered the old warehouse on Baltimore Road.

Chapter 35

He slept fitfully, more of a whisky induced coma than a real kip, his head throbbed and somebody was trying to knock a hole in his temple with the sharp end of a pickaxe. The clock was showing 9.30, panic took hold. He'd made them all come in, foisted the 8.00 meeting upon them, punishment for his cock-up, and he'd overslept. He walked through to the lounge to be greeted by the rank smell of old tobacco, grimaced as he noted the ashtray full of butts, an empty bottle of Grouse and packet of Marlborough on the coffee table, the remnants of an evening spent licking his wounds. Forrest lay on the sofa, nose wrinkled, doleful eyes giving him a disapproving look. He showered, dressed, swallowed a couple of paracetamol, bundled Forrest into the car and headed for the station.

The place was deserted apart from Daniels.

"I overslept, what happened?" He wasn't one for hiding the truth; he'd take it on the chin.

"Not to worry, Guv, I told them you'd gone to London, sort out that end. We ran through the debrief and then I sent them home. Not a lot we can do until Craig turns up."

The guy was a diamond. "Still no sign of him?"

"Not a dicky bird."

"Anything come out of the debrief?"

"Looks like it was the gents' toilet. That's when he changed his pattern, right after he left the gents. And a man left seconds after Craig entered. I think that was where the exchange was planned. Our man followed him in, spooked him. Somehow he cottoned on that we were on to him and that's when the routine changed. He called his friend from the coffee bar and arranged the escape plan."

It all fitted, thought Mike. "What about the phone call at the airport?"

"Didn't happen according to Vodafone," replied Daniels.

Mike pondered this new bit of information.

"He's using a different phone, one of the other carriers. Have you checked them out?"

"Been on to them this morning. He's not registered with any of them."

The penny dropped. "It will be one of the pay-as-you-go phones."

"Probably," replied Daniels despondently, both men aware of the implications. The pay-as-you-go mobiles could be picked up at any supermarket, required only minimal information which could easily be falsified and were paid for by buying phone cards which held credits from any number of retail outlets. With no billing to worry about the mobile phone companies had little interest in who owned the phone or where they lived.

There was nothing further they could do. He sent Daniels home, still feeling guilty about the missed meeting, and after catching up on the paperwork he headed off himself after giving Helen a ring and arranging a date for the evening.

Helen heard his tale of woe, sensed the anger and frustration bubbling beneath the surface. She did her best to cheer him up but her efforts had little effect. On the Saturday night he drank too much wine, became loud and aggressive in the restaurant, caused a scene with a waiter, had to be calmed down. Helen apologizing, paying the bill, retreating out of the door with him. It was a side of him she hadn't seen before and she didn't like it. She would have sent him on his way but he was in no fit state to drive; she relented and allowed him to sleep on the sofa. In the morning he was all apologies explaining that the pressure of the case was getting to him, and they effected a reconciliation.

Over lunch in the local pub, he on tonic water, paying the penance, Helen introduced him to the young man that joined them.

"This is Doug, he's doing his PhD. Something to do with digital communications isn't it, Dougie?

"Potential effects of wireless technology on demand patterns for copper wire technology," he replied with mock seriousness. "That way I get sponsorship from both camps. The mobile boys want to know how much they can charge for their third generation services and BT is worried sick about the revenue implications for their traditional services. Cunning, eh?"

Mike perked up. "So you're a bit of an expert on mobile phone systems."

"Absolutely, anything you need to know about mobile phones, I'm your man." He said it in a playful way, a broad grin creasing his boyish features.

It was worth a try, thought Mike. "Supposing I wanted to know the details of a phone call from a mobile phone and I knew the location and time of the call, would that be possible?"

"No, not unless one of the government bodies was listening in and recorded the content. Once the call has disappeared from the stratosphere it's lost forever," replied Dougie.

"Not the content. What about the number of the phone that called and who it was calling?"

"You could get that from the sector information. Be a bit like trying to find a needle in a haystack though."

"What's the sector information?" asked Mike.

"The phone companies divide their area into sectors. A transmitter serves each sector. The monitoring equipment used by the mobile phone companies knows which call emanates from which transmitter. That's how they gauge demand patterns. They also record the number of the phone making the call and which number was called for their billing systems."

"How big would a sector be?" Mike was becoming animated.

"Varies. In a rural area it could cover a huge area, in an urban area it would be more localized."

"And what about the pay-as-you-go phones? They don't need the billing information for those, do they?"

"No, but it's still recorded. The systems are generic, they work the same across the board regardless of the type of phone being used," replied Dougie.

Helen noticed with relief that Mike seemed to be back to his old self.

"Let me get you a drink, Dougie. What are you having?"

"Very kind of you. Mine's a pint of bitter, please."

"Sure you won't have something more exotic? How about a nice drop of single malt?"

"Well, if you insist."

Mike returned with the drinks, a spritzer for Helen, a large Glenmorangie for Dougie and a pint of Fosters for himself. He decided he'd done enough penance for one day. Arriving back from the pub Helen announced that she was feeling a bit woozy after the lunchtime drink and why didn't they have a lie down for half an hour until her head cleared. The way she saw it she'd also done more than enough penance for one weekend.

Craig surfaced on the Sunday, arriving by taxi at the airport where he retrieved his car and returned to the flat. The taxi driver had picked up his fare in Piccadilly Gardens in the centre of Manchester and had no knowledge as to how he had arrived there.

Mike was in the Super's office first thing Monday morning.

"There are five major networks, the chances are it's one of those. We need their cooperation and we need it quickly. Can you pull some strings, Sir, use your influence?" Pander to his vanity, that should do the trick.

"And you think it will take us to Craig's accomplice?"

"It's the only lead we've got. It's either this or the bastard gets away scot-free. We can't pin the murder charge on him because we can't place him at the scene and we can't nail him with the drugs' charges because there's no proof he actually handled any of the contraband."

"Indeed," replied the Super. "Leave it with me, I'll see what I can do."

Ten minutes later he had the first contact number. He explained to the vice president of operations what was required. Five minutes after that the vice president was back to him with a name.

"She's the best we've got. If she can't get the information out of the database then nobody can. I'll transfer you now."

Laura listened as Mike explained his requirements.

"And the call was made from the airport between 6.15 and 6.25 on Friday?"

"Correct."

"And you want calls made from pay-as-you-go phones separated out?"

"That's right."

"Shouldn't be too difficult."

"When do you think you'll have something for me, Laura?"

"About an hour, hour and a half max. What's your email address?"

He told her.

"I'll drop the results into an Excel spreadsheet and email them over. OK?"

"That would be brilliant."

The first email reached them at 10.30. There were eight hundred and twenty calls on the list.

"Concentrate on two areas. Number one, we think the call was probably from a pay-as-you-go so make that a priority. Number two, it only took forty-five minutes for the driver to reach the airport so the call must have been to someone local. It might be another pay-as-you-go phone but we'll have to take that risk. Concentrate on local numbers and mobiles registered locally."

The ops room was a hive of activity as they attempted to determine the validity of all the calls featured on the lists. They rang the calling phone first and were able to discount a large number; the giggling schoolgirl, concerned housewife and enthusiastic vicar unlikely candidates as murderers and international drug traffickers. They similarly discounted the call girls who answered with exotic names and the offer of even more unusual services, the girls quickly terminating the call when they realized who they were speaking to. Several hung up immediately when they heard the unrecognized voice on the other end of the line and many never answered at all. For these they traced the recipient of the call. Again they were able to discount the majority from the information received.

"That would have been my son arriving back from Greece calling to cadge a lift. He's reading physics at Edinburgh, went back on Sunday. Oh no, you won't get him on the phone; he's left it behind. Found it in his bedroom this morning. Absolute scatterbrain. Never knows whether he's coming or going."

By Wednesday they had a list of seven suspect addresses and nearly two dozen unaccounted-for mobiles. Mike decided to concentrate on the addresses. They drew a blank at the first four on the list; the fifth was an address in Rusholme. Nobody answered the door of the shabby mid-terrace and there was little sign of occupation. The electoral register had drawn a blank, nobody was registered as living at the address and nobody was paying poll tax. They tried the neighbours. The young lady who answered the door on the left was dressed in a brightly coloured sari, black hair pulled back, the red spot on the forehead, gold bracelets on the wrists. She looked extremely worried when she realized the men were policemen and started to talk and gesticulate excitedly, but as her only language was Urdu and neither Mike nor Daniels possessed the slightest knowledge of the language communication between the three of them was, well, nigh impossible. She was becoming increasingly agitated and the two detectives, despite what they hoped looked like repeated assurances that they meant her no harm, were beginning to wonder how they were ever going to extricate themselves from the situation. The noise brought the next door but one neighbour to his door, a middle-aged Indian gentleman dressed in a smart suit with a white turtleneck shirt underneath.

"What is going on here, please?" He spoke perfect English but with an unmistakable Indian accent.

Mike explained who they were. He spoke to the woman in Urdu, calming her down, allaying her fears.

"Please forgive my niece, she has only been in the country a short while, does not yet speak the language. She was frightened by your presence, thought that she had done something wrong, that you were going to arrest her and send her back to India."

"Please assure her that she has nothing to fear, we only wish to ask her some questions," replied Mike.

The man spoke to the woman again; she smiled, nodded at the policemen.

"Ask her if she knows who owns the house next door."

"There is no need, Chief Inspector. I own the house. I own all the houses in this street," the Indian gentleman replied with some pride.

"And who is living there at the moment, Sir?"

He noted the slight change in the facial features as the man thought for a moment before replying. "Nobody, Chief Inspector. Nobody has lived in the house for six months. I have not been able to find a suitable tenant."

"Listen, Mr Er..?"

"Mr Bangani, Sir, at your service."

"Listen, Mr Bangani. This is a serious matter we are investigating. I have no interest whatsoever in whether or not you are paying the correct amount of poll tax, that is a matter between you and the local authority. But if I find that you have lied to me then I shall make sure that the health and safety inspectors and the poll tax people and the VAT man and the income tax man and anybody else I can think of descend upon you like a swarm of bees. Do we understand each other?"

"I think so, Chief Inspector."

"I will ask you again, who lives at number 12?"

"A young man. He has been there for the last four months."

"And when did you last see him?"

He spoke to the woman again. "I have not seen him for several weeks, he keeps himself to himself. But my niece heard someone in the property last night."

"What name did he give?"

"Tony. Tony Osborne."

The detectives looked at each other. So this was Craig Osborne's secret lair.

"Do you have a spare key?" The man nodded. "I'm sure you would like to invite us in for a look around."

He went into the lounge, sending Daniels to check out the upstairs. The furniture was Spartan. An old TV in the corner, a couple of armchairs that had seen better days.

"Guv, up here." It was Daniels.

The body lay on the floor in the bedroom, no obvious signs as to the cause of death. He estimated the man to be in his early twenties, about five ten, lightly built. He was wearing blue jeans and a grey sweatshirt.

They waited while Dr Seymour and the scene-of-crime people did their work. When they had finished Mike asked Mr Bangani for a special favour. Mr Bangani knew that it was always worthwhile staying on the right side of those in positions of power. Besides, he wasn't a squeamish man.

"Yes, that is the man that rented the flat, Tony Osborne."

"Don't you mean Craig, Craig Osborne?"

"No, Chief Inspector. The name he gave me was Tony Osborne."

They found the brazier at the bottom of the garden, the contents reduced to a heap of grey ash. The trainers were in the bottom of the wardrobe. Mike was fairly certain they'd get a match with the cast they'd lifted at the golf club. There was no sign of the car in the immediate vicinity.

"Where was it Craig took the taxi from?" he asked Daniels.

"Piccadilly Gardens."

"Put a team down there. The car won't be far away. That's how Craig got there."

Chapter 36

They found the car the next day in a small car park down a side street not far from Piccadilly Gardens. The Dunlop radials matched the tyre print found at the golf club.

Somerset House came back to Daniels late morning.

"Changed his name by deed poll four years ago. Sorry, Guv, should have checked it."

"Don't worry about it, it wasn't down to you." It was me who cocked-up on this enquiry, not you, thought Mike.

The background check on Tony Osborne showed very little.

"Only interesting one is a credit card transaction back in January. Turns out he was in London buying ladies underwear," said Daniels.

"Confirms what we thought but it still doesn't put us any closer to nailing Craig."

The Super collared him just as he was returning from lunch.

"This Tony Osborne chap, formerly Tony Mellor. You say he committed the first four murders. The Cheshire Slasher case."

"That's right," replied Mike.

"Can you prove it, now that he's dead?"

"The evidence is all circumstantial but, yes I'd say we can put together a pretty strong case."

"And the London gang, the case against them is rock solid?" asked the Super.

"The DPP has had a look at it, they don't see any problem."

"I spoke to Commissioner Delon this morning. He's delighted with the result. Apparently the case made headlines in the French nationals."

"Which just leaves our friend Craig."

"Perhaps you'll get him for killing the boyfriend. Forensic turned anything up yet?"

"Not yet, and I very much doubt whether they will. Whatever else Craig may be he's certainly careful. He guessed we'd trace Tony through the phone call sooner or later, that's why he finished him off. Make sure there was no trail back to Craig."

"We'll get him, Judd. Perhaps not this time but we'll get him. You mark my words." Superintendent Anderson returned to the paperwork on his desk.

Mike made a call to Mr Chalmers of Chalmers Lomas in the afternoon.

"In such circumstances he wouldn't be due a penny," Chalmers confirmed.

He rang Superintendent Hargreaves.

A special meeting of the renamed George Lister Trust met that evening. Mrs Elaine Smedley tendered her resignation with immediate effect and left the meeting head bowed, unable to meet the eye of the remaining four committee members. The trust passed a motion calling for a board meeting of Lister Haulage the following morning as it was entitled to do, being the majority shareholder. The only item on the agenda was a motion calling for the immediate dismissal of Toby Mathews on the grounds of behaviour incompatible with his position as managing director of the company.

The call from the pathology lab came through the following day.

"Something turned up that may be of interest to you, perhaps you could pay us a visit when you have a minute," said Dr Seymour.

Mike and Daniels were in his office half an hour later; if Craig had left any clues they wanted to know about it.

"You've completed the post mortem on Tony Osborne?" asked Mike as he once more found himself seated in the cheap plastic covered chair.

"Oh that. Yes. Straightforward really," said Seymour dismissively. "Time of death between 6.00 and 7.00 Tuesday morning. Cause of death, strangulation. Someone wrung his neck. Homosexual activity within last eight hours, evidence of anal penetration. That's about it."

"Is that what you called us over to tell us?" asked Mike somewhat brusquely. The two men had built up a grudging admiration for one another over the last couple of months but Mike was on a short fuse, still smouldering over Craig's apparent escape.

"No, I thought this might interest you." He wafted a piece of paper in the air. "Came in the post this morning. Remember you asked me to perform a second autopsy on Linda Walker?"

Mike nodded.

"Well I took the usual samples of body fluids and sent them off for analysis in the normal way. This is the result of the DNA test on the saliva sample I forwarded. I don't know why the lab take so long, it must be three weeks since I sent them in."

I don't know why you take so long to get to the point, thought Mike, but he kept his counsel.

"However, most interesting result. DNA testing is still in its infancy, obviously, and all sorts of interesting facts are coming to light that would otherwise have remained hidden. The level of analysis we are now seeing was just not feasible even a few short years ago. This is a classic example. What the implications are I'm not sure, but there, you have it."

He placed the paper on the desk with a final flourish, having finished his speech. Mike didn't know whether to laugh or cry. He tried to stay calm.

"There we have what, Dr Seymour? What is it that the tests show?" asked Mike.

"Gracious, didn't I say? Two sets of saliva, Chief Inspector. Miss Walker's saliva, as we'd expect. But someone else's saliva as well. There were two sets of saliva in her mouth. There's only one circumstance I can think of where that might happen. I believe the modern euphemism is 'swapping spit', Chief Inspector. In my day we used to call it French kissing."

"And if we can match the second DNA sample we'll know who was kissing Linda immediately prior to her death," suggested Mike.

"Ah well, we might have a slight problem there," said Seymour. "That's the thing with DNA you see. As I explained, a lot of the concepts have never been tested before. Now common sense would suggest that the foreign saliva would only remain in the mouth for a relatively short period of time after the kissing ceased. But proving it, that's quite a different kettle of fish."

They talked for a few minutes more, the plan finalized, before Mike and Daniels headed back to the station. Craig was brought in for questioning in the afternoon. They asked him about his relationship with Tony Osborne, when he had last seen him and what he knew about his death. As Mike expected Craig was well prepared for the questions and was unable to throw any light upon the unfortunate death of his friend. There was nothing out of the ordinary about a constable delivering three mugs of tea during the interview. Craig took no note of the fact that his mug was red while the other two were blue and gratefully drank the tea, seeing nothing strange when the constable returned to collect the tray and three empty mugs fifteen minutes later.

Under extreme pressure from the Super the lab returned the tests within twenty-four hours. The match with the saliva found in Linda Walker's mouth was confirmed.

The Super's elbows rested on the desk, his hands covered his face.

"I hope you aren't serious about this, Judd. If this ever reaches the grapevine I'll be the laughing stock of every seminar from John O'Groats to Land's End. I'll never be able to attend another conference as long as I live."

Mike stood his ground, facing the Super across the desk.

"It's the only way, Sir. Without the evidence we'll never get a conviction."

"And what happens if it doesn't work?" asked the Super.

"Then we will have failed and Craig walks free. But that's a risk I'm willing to take."

"And how much did you say it's going to cost?"

"Ten thousand pounds, Sir." Mike cringed as he said it.

"Where am I supposed to find ten thousand pounds from? The budget's already stretched to the limit, the surveillance operation has seen to that. I've had to stop all overtime as it is."

"I'm sure you'll find it somewhere, Sir."

The Super groaned. It was against his better judgment but the man was like a terrier with a rat once he got a sniff of something.

"Arrange it then, I'll have to find the money from somewhere. But strictly confidential, understood? I don't want word of this getting around the other divisions."

"Absolutely. And you'll have a word with the lab, Sir?"

"The lab?"

"Yes, Sir. The samples, as we discussed."

"Quite so, the samples." The Super was a defeated man. He tried to remember back to the interviews. What was the word that had cropped up? Tenacious, that was the word. Tenacious indeed.

It was a completely different Dr Seymour Mike saw that morning as they stood in the middle of the large hall. He was like a kid in a candy shop, rushing from here to there, white lab coat billowing behind him, organizing the test stations, making sure everything was in place. It was Seymour who had explained to Mike what needed to be done.

"Empirical data, that's what's required. Human body you see, can't apply mathematical formula, it doesn't work like that. No, the only way to test the theory is to put it into practice and then measure the results.

Do that enough times and you have a sample. Then you feed it into the computer. Work out the correlation coefficient. See if the results are statistically significant. It's all a bit technical so I won't bore you with the details. But you will have seen it in court enough times with expert witnesses. Ninety-nine point nine percent positive that such and such must have happened. The court will accept that. That's what they're doing. Using statistical sampling to prove that in all probability the event occurred."

The response to the advert placed on the college notice boards had been overwhelming and Mike judged that the incentive of a ten pound payment had probably been a waste of the Super's precious budget. The volunteers were divided into groups of one hundred and scheduled to arrive over the next two days with strict instructions as to behaviour prior to the tests. As they entered the hall the girls were shepherded to the left and boys to the right and each allocated a number from one to fifty, the position indicated by a sticky-back label attached to the clothing. A strident young female immediately confronted Seymour.

"This is typical reactionary bourgeoisie stereotyping. I'm a lesbian. I refuse to kiss a man."

Seymour scratched his head, bewildered for second, then turned on the girl.

"Right. Is there another lesbian here that you can kiss?" he asked almost shouting. Mike was in the wings, tears streaming down his cheeks. It was pure Fawlty Towers. The Super was right; if this ever got out he'd never live it down. A mousy, shy girl among the group put her hand up.

"Good, come here. Now what number are you?" he asked, addressing the girl who had originally caused the problem.

"Number twelve."

Seymour marched over to the boys on the other side of the hall.

"Where's number twelve?"

A gangly lad stepped forward.

"Right, give me your number." He took the sticky-back label and walked over to the mousy haired girl.

"I'll take your number, you have this one and go and stand over with the boys."

The fiasco carried on for another ten minutes as Seymour realized he was now left with two lads with the same number and couldn't find any homosexual volunteers from among the lads to even up the situation. He eventually sent the two unfortunates away, ten pounds in hand, but complaining bitterly about the lost opportunity.

When all was ready Seymour, who was now standing on the raised stage at the end of the hall, looked at his watch.

"Right couple number one step forward, technicians take the swabs please."

The lab-coated technicians took a swab from each participant to ensure that the saliva was pure prior to the tests.

"On my mark begin. And don't forget we need the tongue in there. Ready, steady, go!"

The couple was going at one another hammer and tongs, the other students shouting ribald comments from the rear of the hall.

"Keep the noise down at the back, this is a scientific experiment not a football match. Step forward couple number two. Swabs please. And ready, steady, go!" shouted Seymour from the stage.

More like Come Dancing, thought Mike, trying to stifle his laughter.

At the end of five minutes the couples were stopped by the technicians assigned to them, some stopping on command, others having to be prised apart. The technicians took a swab from the mouth of each participant as they parted, carefully placing the swab in a plastic evidence bag and labelling it. Five minutes later another swab and so on until they had nine swabs in all for each couple. Mike had decided if the saliva was still present after thirty minutes then he wouldn't have a case.

At the end of the day all the swabs were bundled up and sent off to the DNA lab. The news that they were to receive four and a half thousand samples had not been well received but the Super had used all his influence to have the matter given priority.

It was over a fortnight later when the final results came through.

"Two percent spoiled, that's acceptable. No foreign saliva showing in eighty-nine percent of samples after five minutes, ninety-eight percent of samples after ten minutes, ninety-nine point seven in fifteen minutes and none at all after twenty minutes. I should say we have a result," said Seymour.

"So you're willing to stand up in court and testify that Craig Osborne must have been kissing Linda Walker within twenty minutes of her death."

"Quite so, without a doubt."

Mike stood up and held out his hand. "Thank you very much, Doctor. Your help has been invaluable in solving this case."

Seymour took his hand. "My pleasure young man, I can't remember when I last enjoyed myself so much."

Craig was in his office when they entered. Mike let Daniels do the honours; he felt he'd earned it.

"Craig Osborne, I am arresting you for the murder of Linda Walker."

Daniels read him his rights.